CHASE HER

CHASE HER

BOOK THREE, COME FOR ME SERIES

KELLY FINLEY

Chase Her

Kelly Finley

© 2022 Kelly Finley Publishing, LLC

Visit the author's website at www.kellyfinley.com

ISBN: 978-1-7374516-6-2 (eBook)

ISBN: 978-1-7374516-7-9 (paperback)

All rights reserved.

No part of this publication may be reproduced, distributed, or transmitted in any form or by any means, stored in or introduced into a retrieval system, or transmitted, in any form including photocopying, recording, or other electronic or mechanical methods, without the prior written permission of the above author of this book.

This is a work of fiction. Names, characters, places, brands, media, and incidents are either the product of the author's imagination or have been used fictitiously. Any resemblance to actual persons, living or dead, events, or locales is entirely coincidental.

The author acknowledges the trademarked status and trademark owners of various products referenced in this work of fiction, which have been used without permission. The publication/use of these trademarks is not authorized, associated with, or sponsored by the trademark owners.

Line Edited by Kat Wyeth (Kat's Literary Services)

Proofreading by Meredith Sweet (Kat's Literary Services) & Deborah Richmond

Cover by Caroline Johnson

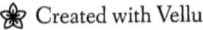 Created with Vellum

ALSO BY KELLY FINLEY

Come for Me

Protect Her, Prequel Novelette

Pierce Her, Book One

Hunt Her, Book Two

Chase Her, Book Three

All for You

After Him, Book One

With Him, Book Two

FOR YOU, MY READER

Want Bonus Scenes and a free copy of
PROTECT HER,
the Come for Me Prequel Novelette?
Get my monthly news tease for giveaways, special gifts and more.
I share it all!
Join at KellyFinley.com and they'll be coming your way.

To Ru,
Keep loving and fighting till the very end

CHASE HER PLAYLIST

Creature by BONES UK
Climb by ADONA
Say It [*SG Lewis Remix*] by Flume, Tove Lo
My Honest Face by Inhaler
Two Weeks by FKA twigs
It Was a Sin by The Revivalists
breathin by Ariana Grande
Kiss It Better by Rihanna
Not Going Down by ADONA
Sextape by Deftones
One Space Left [*Ty Unwin Remix*] by Lost Colours
What's Up Danger by Blackway & Black Caviar
Legend by The Score
Be Your Love by Bishop Briggs

Listen to the CHASE HER playlist on Spotify

PROLOGUE
ANONYMOUS

THERE ARE three types of people.

The first type are those that never try. Too paralyzed by what others think, they can't think for themselves. They do nothing.

Then there are those who try but quit. They don't have the faith, the fortitude to finish. They fail themselves.

Few are like me, the third type—those that never give up.

You can beat us, ruin us, and take everything away, but until we draw our last breath... we fight back.

It's an elite group.

She was in it.

CHAPTER ONE

DANIEL

Creature by BONES UK

OCTOBER. **Now...**

"Hey, y'all. This is Charlie Ravenel... talkin' into a damn device. Smile, 'cuz now it's your turn."

Guilt edged with grief burdened my exhale instead.
"I miss my wife."
I wished I was ringing just to say hello, or "Babe, I'm running late," or to plan a sexy date.
I prayed actually.
No, I just needed to hear her voice—that honey accent dripping those smart-arse words. I hated my life without it or her touch by my side.
My fingertip ended the call, longing to trail down her neck instead, savoring every luscious inch of her soft flesh until her moan filled my ears.

A year before, I joked with her in bed, "Great love comes at a great cost." That was for the stubble rash I was giving her. Because I couldn't get enough of her lips. Or of the journey down to between her thighs, her body twisting with wet gratitude while my tongue devoured her, sipping her taste while my whiskers tickled her most tender flesh.

Those foolish words held grave foreshadow.

Any price I'd pay now for our love. But there was an ultimate one not even my bloody "Daniel Pierce" celebrity or millions could afford.

The ache for her. It tortured me with half-breaths heaved into my bruised ribs, my lungs burning with sorrow. Memories sliced my mind, marring other thoughts. Every beat of my battered heart bled for her, leaving drops of red anguish behind.

How long can you barely survive live like this?

A giggle chittered the air. A tiny finger pierced the space between my lips.

Shoving my phone in my pocket, "Cheeky little monkey," I said, gazing at peach cheeks under aqua eyes and dark curls matching mine.

I knew better than to play at night. Caroline was the funniest baby yet worst sleeper. But not Duke. No, my son slept like a champ—once on his back, he was out, fastest in the land.

Caroline though? Every minute she smiled her way through. She had to be tricked to sleep, only waking hours later.

Just like her mum. Just like Charlie.

Resting her head on my shoulder, I bounced with her. My calves were sore from this nightly dance with my restless daughter, but I didn't care. We shared these lonely hours, both needing her, missing her.

I gazed down at Duke in the cot, at how my son already had my cleft chin, but the breath from his little body sighed from a nose that was Charlie's. He had her hair and stubborn streak too.

Our beautiful twins appeared nothing alike but were bound by blood and a tragic beginning.

"Placental abruption."

The doctor's face had been kind delivering the cruel words, explaining that the fraternal twins had their own placentas, but my son's was in peril from the fall.

"We need to make the call now, Mr. Pierce." The doctor had patted my hands covered in dried blood. Whose blood? I didn't know. "They are thirty weeks along. The survival rate is high."

"Survival rate." Another brutal term confronting me that night.

If they did it then, it would be their birthday... sharing it with the same one someone wanted their mother dead.

Every year they'd stand with smiles over their birthday cake while the bloody memory would smoke through my mind along with the candles they blew out.

"You can be there if you like." The doctor kept prodding me. "You can hold her hand."

Oh, God. Her hand will be limp in yours. I feared, *would it be warm or cold... with blood everywhere?*

I could endure so much, but blood was my weakness, especially my wife's.

But for her, I could take it. The paramedics had to drag me away from Charlie when they rushed her behind swinging doors. All I wanted was to live by her side. Never would I abandon her, not even now.

"Do it" was all I could utter.

The doctor stood at my decision. "I'll send someone out to help you get scrubbed up."

The memory of washing the blood from my hands into pink streams down the white porcelain sink still lingered. I remembered crying, letting go of Charlie's cold limp hand to hold Duke first, then Caroline.

Swaddled in white blankets, they nestled in the crooks of my arms, their new home, before they were whisked away to the NICU.

Those same arms cradled my ten-month-old daughter now. Hers hung slack against my chest. Finally, she fell asleep.

I kissed her hair and laid her next to her brother. Another thing they shared—they slept better in the same cot. They had to eat and play together, too, until Caroline would bite Duke when he tried taking something from her. Then I'd have to rescue my son's offense from my daughter's fury.

Yep, that had Charlie Ravenel written all over it.

I stood over the cot, over my whole world.

Alone.

It wasn't supposed to be this way, I shook my head, furious. She was supposed to be here with me.

Fuck you, Charlie. Fuck you to hell and back.

The thought mocked me. I didn't mean it. Anger forced the taunt... and fear.

The baby monitor camera blinked on. Taking out my phone, I opened the monitor app. They appeared on the screen with me standing over them, almost unrecognizable to myself.

After ten months on Daufuskie Island, my dark curls fell in long waves lightened to auburn by the South Carolina sun. Flip-flops, cargo shorts, and T-shirts were my daily uniform, usually with a cloth nappy over my shoulder and pockets full of teething toys I couldn't live without.

The only thing that looked the same? My physique. I'd never let that go. The home gym kept me sane. Often, it was my only break for the day.

The door to the nursery closed gently behind me. Sand-colored carpet silenced my heavy steps down the hall to our bedroom. The sight of our four-poster bed neatly made with indigo throw cushions Charlie had trained me to "properly place"—smacked me with a cruel irony.

It lay perfect... and empty.

Go to hell.

Walking past our bed, out the French doors, I stood on the covered second level deck for my nightly ritual—a cigar to puff away the day.

Inky waves rolled under stars twinkling above. The quarter moon in the sky was my only company. Pop had told me this was the Hunter's Moon.

Huffing at that irony, I lit my cigar with practiced puffs over my S.T. Dupont gold lighter, a wedding present from my dad.

I huffed again—*our wedding*.

The Hunter's Moon beamed a cruel spotlight over the sacred sand where we had the ceremony. Next month, November, it marked our one-year anniversary and Charlie's birthday.

Fuck's sake, Pierce, irony is a wicked bitch, not to be rivaled.

Puffing on tobacco smoke, I inhaled regrets; a pile so high of what I should've done that I couldn't see the summit. Standing in a wealth of privilege and power, none of it protected me from pain.

Pain I'd caused. Pain that spread like napalm through my every muscle.

You deserve it, Pierce.

Yet, you dare imagine. To stop time at any moment of your lips on hers, her body under yours, the tight wrap of her around you, your heart and life.

Moments like this, agony was all I could breathe.

I wanted to give up. To walk into that ocean and not look back.

Never would I. With all that had happened, all I did, in the least... I owed her this.

Taking out my phone, 12:55am glowed back. I checked the camera. The twins were fine. I pressed Charlie/Wife again on the top of my FAVOURITES list.

A cynical cloud of smoke rolled over my lips as it rolled to her voicemail again.

"Hey, y'all. This is Charlie Ravenel... talkin' into a damn device. Smile, 'cuz now it's your turn."

"I love you." Another angry puff. "And I'm so sorry." That one choked, forcing my pause, reeling my pain.

"But you've got me so bloody afraid, it's hell. You didn't ring tonight, like you always do, and I can't take it. Not again." I punched the cigar toward the floor. "I can't fucking take this fear for you anymore, Charlie. Goddammit, it's too much."

How long could I rant, I didn't know. But I needed something. Some connection. Some assurance. Please, God, I loved her.

And what I did the night before? The shame crushed me. Nothing left but shards of disgrace remembering...

How I'd gutted her. How I left her gasping through

tears from her marine eyes, streaming over her freckled cheeks, pooling into the corners of her supple lips.

And now, the sick of it churned, rotting my soul.

Was that it? Her last memory of me? Knifing the heart she gave to me, trusting me to the bitter end? She shouldn't have.

"Babe, please. I know I hurt you, that you're mad at me, but please... just let me know you're alive, that you're okay." I hated himself. "Or I swear, I'll leave the twins with Fran, take the boat into Savannah, and come for you myself. I'll kick the fucking door down, and all the tourists walking by, they can hashtag Daniel Pierce and post the spectacle. I don't bloody well care."

If I thought *my* celebrity life was the risky one, I was a fool. Hers was lethal. And all I found myself doing for months was chasing after her in a pathetic attempt to keep her safe.

And now, irony's red lips smirked at me, doling out the punishment I deserved.

Because above all... I was her greatest risk, her gross harm.

No one could hurt her more than I could.

And I did.

"Please, Charlie, come back to me."

Ending the call, I threw my head back, cursing the Hunter's Moon.

Take me. Not her. Not again.

CHAPTER TWO

CHARLIE

Climb by ADONA

FEBRUARY. **Eight months before...**

"Eighty-seven."

Fuck the doctor. Telling me to take it easy was like telling the sun to cool off. Not happening. Cesarean or not, my body would deliver one hundred decline sit-ups... or else.

"Eighty-eight."

The words strained from my lips. My feet were hooked under padded foot holders—a fulcrum against the force trying to keep me down.

Hell no. It didn't work. I was so stubborn; gravity could kiss my ass.

"Eighty-nine."

I winced. A scar rubbed tender against my leggings. Rolling my eyes with the descent. *Another damn scar.* Another moment created by a bullet.

I stopped there. A tear fell at the bottom. Not for me, it fell for Rob. He took the bullet meant for me. It exploded through his ribs, collapsing his lung.

You're a lucky bitch, doing sit-ups in your home gym while Rob struggles, still barely able to take a full breath.

Recognize that taste, Charlie Girl? It's guilt—your favorite meal.

"Ninety."

But Rob did as we're trained. He was on guard, protecting me.

He heard it too, "Ravenel! Ravenel!" turning his head while I aimed my eyes toward the sound, at a man's arm rising from behind *The Druid* banner-draped stanchion with a black gun in his hand, targeting me.

Suddenly, the ceiling of the white tent filled my vision as Rob threw his massive body over mine. A percussive blast split the air at the same time my pregnant body hit the red carpet with Rob's heft draped over me like a tragic weighted blanket.

Gasping at the searing pain in my pregnant belly, I couldn't breathe. The weight of Rob. The ache at my core. There was no air, only Daniel shouting my name. I tried finding him with my eyes, but only saw black, the moment disappearing.

"Ninety-one."

Flexing my abs, I surged up, a flamethrower blazing over my torso, protesting.

Fuck you. You owe me this.

The next thing I remembered? The smell of sterile air. A tube tickling under my nose. Something warm squeezing my hand—Daniel's. A voice—Daniel's. It pulled my lifeless body out of my unconscious ocean.

"Babe? Come on. Wake up for me." His warm hand caressed my cheek. "You're okay. The twins are okay."

The twins!

With a quick inhale my eyes flew open.

I tried to speak, but my jaw was a thick rubber band that wouldn't stretch.

My eyes worked instead. The fluorescent light was brutal, but the sight I focused upon, beautiful—Daniel, his aqua eyes full of relief.

He rubbed my hair. "It's all right, babe. They did an emergency Cesarean. There was a placental abruption from the fall or Rob's weight, we don't know. But it was Duke. We had to get him out. Caroline too. They're in the NICU and doing well."

My jaw finally opened. My tongue was sandpaper in my mouth. I couldn't ask, "What about Rob?" But Daniel read my terrified brow.

"Rob is out of surgery. He has a collapsed lung, some shattered ribs, but he'll be okay."

He held a white Styrofoam cup with a bendy straw up to my mouth, always knowing what I needed.

With one weak suck, cool water blessed my mouth. I had to ask the next question.

"Ninety-two."

Fuck the burning, I didn't care. This memory gave me the fury, fighting through it, remembering how I asked...

"Who?"

That was the first question I seethed.

Who tried to kill my children? Me? Who's on guard outside the NICU? Outside of my hospital room? Guarding our Daufuskie home? Our hotel room there in Manhattan? The questions fired through my mind but all I could whisper was, "Who?"

Daniel couldn't answer then, and over two months later, we didn't know much more. We have a name now—a who—but we may never know why.

The man turned the gun on himself, his next bullet ending all answers. He had no ID on him. It took the detectives a couple of days to trace the gun to Colorado Springs, to find it was legally purchased months before at a Bass Pro Shop.

Who tried to kill me?

"Ninety-three."

Brad Jenkins. White male. Twenty-two. Lived in Colorado Springs and worked at a Best Buy. His colleagues said he was a quiet young man.

The FBI scrubbed his PC, finding only searches for "Daniel Pierce", "Captain Charlotte Roberts", and "Charlie Ravenel". But FBI Agent Beverly Cooper told me she was suspicious.

"It's like he set it up." Agent Cooper had flown to New York, visiting me, standing beside my hospital bed.

I always liked her. She was sharp as hell. Agent Cooper helped me catch Mason Hunt, the actor who stalked me and Daniel. The one who got his the demented fans of his *White Flag,* white-supremacist film to do his bloody bidding.

"I can't prove it yet," Agent Cooper had said, "but I've got a twitch."

I knew that twitch. *Trust it. Worship it. Build a damn religion around it.*

Agent Cooper had explained, "The computer was a floor model at Best Buy before Jenkins bought it, so they wiped the drive clean for him. That was May first, and for months all he searched were your names. No *White Flag* activity. No shopping. No porn even. Nothing else for months? It doesn't make sense."

While Cooper sipped her coffee, it made sense to me.

"Ninety-four."

My thighs shook now with my forced exertion, the sit-ups torture but my mind held firm, remembering...

May first?

That was when a picture of my scarred body passed out in Daniel's celebrity arms in the Madrid gym blew up social media. One #danielpierce with my face, and the pin had dropped on me.

And the shooter had been hunting for me ever since... for over seven months.

"Who was he working for?" I had asked. "How did he get money for two trips to New York?"

That much they knew and told me.

Brad Jenkins made two trips to New York City. One during Daniel's *Swipe Right* movie premiere in July. The final one for his deadly return to *The Druid* premiere then, in December.

Those two trips were his only footprint outside of his mundane pattern of life.

"We don't know," Cooper had replied. "Other than your names, travel for the trips was all he searched. He used a credit card and only charged travel to it. There's a couple thousand in his bank account, not enough to be paid for a hit. From what we can tell, he was a loner, only had a few friends in a gaming club."

The agent pursed her lips continuing, "That's just it though. The odd thing. For an avid gamer, there's nothing on his PC. No damn games. He's got to have a PC out there with more on it. I haven't found it yet, but I will."

"Mason Hunt is a gamer," I had told the agent.

Well, Mason was before his ass went to jail the month before for inciting the attack on Daniel in Wilmington, North Carolina, near the film studio where Daniel was filming.

Those attacks?

Mason had conspired to have them committed on his behalf, for his revenge. After that? We'd hoped his torment was over.

Maybe not.

"Mason could've connected to the shooter through the gaming," I said. "Hell, he used Instagram to encourage the man who attacked Daniel."

"I'm on it." The agent had assured me.

"Ninety-five."

My heart hammered now at the reality.

Mason Hunt could've recruited the shooter. Mason was a smart, sadistic motherfucker, always three steps behind me. Never would I underestimate him, even when he was sitting in jail.

But that attempt on me didn't feel like Mason's doing. His *White Flag* hits targeted Daniel first... he wanted me to suffer before he came after me next.

So why change tactics now?

And what about the past seven years? Is it your PTSD? Or a premonition? Have you been right this whole time—that someone is coming for you?

Either way, it didn't matter. Fear was ripped from my body along with my twins. All I had left was clarity. No haunting instinct. Just the certainty.

Get the fuck up and get even stronger, ready to fight again. End this... once and for all.

"Ninety-six."

I nursed that certainty. Hell, it was all I could do. The

trauma from the shooting, the surgery, the travel home to Daufuskie, it robbed me of my milk. I didn't have the birth I wanted, didn't get to nurse the twins. All I got was a "bikini line" scar—a sexist, insulting description of what my body had endured.

The Cesarean left me with that scar—that makes four now—and little strength to stand, barely able to walk with my babies in my arms.

Just like seven years before when I was shot in Afghanistan.

Fist bump, Irony. You never let me down.

Today, February twenty-second, was the anniversary of that day in Afghanistan. Also, one year ago today, I accepted the job protecting Kierra Williams.

And look at my life since—three hundred and sixty-five days full of the greatest love and terror I'd ever known.

"Ninety-seven."

I'd do it all again. A wildfire torched through my molecules—*let it*—I'd fucking fight for every ounce of my strength back... and then some.

It's on. You have more to protect now.

"Ninety-eight."

My muscles shook. My head pounded upside down, but my stubborn will wouldn't relent.

Get.

The.

Fuck.

Up.

"Ninety-nine."

I spit the number out. So why the tears too?

Because it humbled me.

I survived... again. Rob made it. I had my beautiful daughter and son. I had Daniel, a love beyond words. Here in our island home, we were safe, secluded away from a world descending into concern over a virus.

Bow your head and be thankful.

A few weeks later, as soon as we were allowed to travel, Daniel booked a private charter to take us home. We spent the next month in bed, the little ones lying bundled between us. I couldn't stop marveling at them. They were tiny perfection, growing stronger every day.

And Daniel took such care of me. He picked a flower for me everyday. Our bathroom mirror had cute daily notes he'd write in red dry erase markers. Every night, he'd hold me while I read Aesop's fables to the twins; featuring my famous mouse voices, of course.

Once I was cleared by Dr. Patterson to resume exercise, I was obsessed, demanding my body back.

Because I knew, I always did, that I'd need every weapon—even my own flesh—to protect this precious life we shared now.

"One hundred."

I slid down the bench, collapsing into a pile on the rubber-mat floor. Tears fell with every emotion down my cheeks. Stomach convulsing, my earbuds fell out and I could hear myself crying.

"Babe?" From the floor, Daniel's shoes appeared in my line of sight. "Are you okay?" He knelt beside me, cupping his hand over my cheek.

"Yes," I lied.

CHAPTER THREE

DANIEL

FEBRUARY. ***Eight months before...***

I scooped her into my arms from the gym floor. "I'd ask you what's wrong"—I wrapped my hand over her sweaty belly—"but I know."

With every week of her possessed workouts, the swell had disappeared to her strong abs showing back through. But I knew—this wasn't about weight or vanity. Not my wife. She had none.

This was about the shooter.

For two months, I'd watched her. How, if she wasn't smiling at the twins, she was lost in thought. What was she plotting? It concerned me.

She wrapped her arms around my neck. "I'll be okay."

I didn't believe her. "I know what's driving you, but you've got to pace yourself. If you don't, you'll tear something, and then we're fucked. The last place we want to be now is in hospital, not with this virus out there."

The baby monitor I set on the bench cried out. I

glanced at it. Caroline stirred. Of course, she was awake... again.

"I'll get her." She pecked my cheek. "You get your workout in."

"Fran's got them." I grabbed her hand gently. "Stay with me, just for a minute."

I stood up with her, watching the monitor while I nestled her against my chest. Fran appeared on the screen in front of the cot, softly shushing Caroline back to sleep.

Thank God for that sweet woman. Fran gave us the breaks we needed. Charlie had protested at hiring a nanny, but I searched anyway now she's glad I did.

I called Fran for a phone interview from the hospital. She was perfect, from London, ending a job in Nashville with celebrity musicians whose teens no longer needed her. She had the experience and fifty-two years of wisdom.

Once I explained to Fran the situation, fully disclosing the risk, she didn't hesitate. She met us at the dock in Bluffton for the trip out to Daufuskie Island and hadn't left since.

"See." I nodded toward the monitor. "She's got them."

Charlie's body relaxed against mine—and a tension stirred within.

She'd welcomed my hugs and kisses, but that was all. I tried a few times after the six weeks we were told to wait. Fuck, I was desperate for her. But each time, Charlie gently removed my hand from between her thighs. Now, I didn't even try, digging deep for patience instead. It was hard.

My cock didn't get the patient message, tenting my thin black gym shorts with a stiffy.

"I feel you, Sex God," she murmured.

My hand pressed down to the small of her bare back. "I feel you too, Sex Goddess." Her workout clothes always turned me on. Hell, she could wear a Hessian sack and make me horny as hell.

"I'm not ready yet."

"Your patient husband knows that, but his lonely cock doesn't."

"Should I leave you here for a workout and to rub one off?"

"Only if you watch me... and you do the same."

"You little shit." She pulled back with a sly smile. "You tryin' to tempt me?"

"I've got to. I know you're not ready, babe, but I'm going to break my dick off wanking without you." I meant it. It had been months, a lonely hell.

She sighed, eyes half-rolling. "I'm not trying to starve you. I know we can now, but I don't feel like myself." Pulling her body away. "I don't know how 'mom', 'wife' and 'Charlie' come together now. It's fucking weird. It's like I'm out of my body and need to get back in it, but I don't recognize it. And now... I've got this."

Her gesture only turned me on more. Staring down at the pussy I missed, knowing its hidden beauty, I didn't give a damn about a Cesarean scar, even though I hadn't seen it yet.

"Good God, babe, you're even more beautiful to me now." I smoothed over her hourglass waist. "All I do is admire you and want you but you've been hiding from me for months."

I lifted her chin. "Let me at least hold you, in the shower, in our bed, with nothing on." I kissed her lips, aware of how my new beard tickled them, dusting over their sexy slope, confessing, "I miss us."

We needed this. It was our connection, our love. The instant we met, the urge for the other was so powerful it overwhelmed us. The greatest desire thrilled my flesh from the moment I touched Charlie.

And I'd almost lost her.

I needed to cherish every inch of her, lavishing her with tender touches before fucking her so hard. I had no choice; I had to show her how much I loved her and would until my dying day.

"Even if we tried that, just being naked," she said. "I won't be able to relax. I don't think I'll have an orgasm again in this house, not with the twins and Fran down the hall."

"Fran's not uptight. Have you heard her talk? She's an old-school feminist. I assure you when her wife can travel here from London, we will hear them down the hall."

"Okay, fine. But what about the twins? Between Caroline, who never sleeps, and Duke, who demands my attention when he's awake, I don't get a second to relax unless I'm in the gym." Her hand caressed my bicep. "It's not fair between men and women. Your cock is a hot light switch, but my vag is a cold oven, it's gotta warm up, and it can't with all this baby stuff going on."

That amused me. And challenged me. "Give me a chance, babe." My lips climbed up her neck while I murmured, "You always switch my cock on, and you know I can melt you into the wettest heat you've ever dripped."

I took gentle bites before she snapped her neck closed. "Fuck, your beard tickles."

"Oh, yeah?"

Nuzzling into her, I made her squeal, squirming from my snatching embrace—a futile effort. I wouldn't let her go.

"Quit it." Her eyes twinkled. "Or I'll tie you down and shave that thing off."

I ceased the tickle, but not my smile. Fuck's sake, I loved

her like this. Laughing. Playful. Warming up to me, I could tell, her nipples pebbled under her sports bra.

My dirty mind devised a plan; my hard cock signed off on it. "I'm getting us an afternoon, alone, in the house for a few hours. We'll just shower and cuddle, I promise."

"How do you propose to do that?"

"Those two cherubs have grandparents on this island ten minutes away. Pop and Evelyn would jump at the chance to have them for a few hours. And Fran could visit with them or take the time to herself."

"I feel like shitty parents sending our babies away for an afternoon so we can fuck."

"Yes! Are we finally going to fuck?" That was all I heard. Not the "shitty parent" part, because that, I didn't buy.

"I'm serious, Daniel. How does that look? We send our kids away so we can have an afternoon of sex?"

"Since when does my fit wife give two shits for what people think?" I took her hand. "I'm serious, Charlie. We've been through enough. If we don't stay connected and strong as a couple, we are no good to them as Mum and Dad."

"Quit trying to make that stick, Pierce." She tongued her teeth, smiling. "I'm not gonna be 'Mum' and you're not gonna be 'Dad.' More like 'Mama' and 'Daddy' in these parts."

"You're off your trolley. Fran and I will see to it that they have proper English accents."

I teased her, relishing how it pissed her off, adoring when she fired back...

"Bless your heart, Pierce, and count heads. You're outnumbered." She wiggled against my cock begging for her. "I've got you beat."

Yes, she does, Pierce. Grinding on you. That's your wife.

"So, it's a plan then, Mrs. Pierce?" I seized her firm bum,

pulling her harder against my raging hard-on, wanting to take her now.

"That's not my name."

Deploying the grin I knew caused millions of thirsty posts, "It is when I'm fucking you," it wet her pussy too.

That naughty truth flashed across her eyes. The last time we made love, months before, I made her moan that name while rousing her with slow thrusts from behind.

"All right, Mr. Ravenel. Give my body a few more weeks to heal before you come at me with all this hard hotness. Then we'll see if you get lucky."

Breaking from my embrace, she delivered a swat to my arse before swishing out of the room. Minutes later, she appeared on the monitor with Duke, kissing his forehead before lying him down to change his nappy.

I watched the spectacle, a smile taking my heart. *Gawd blimey, I love her.*

CHAPTER FOUR

CHARLIE

MARCH. **_Seven months before…_**

I hovered the coffee pot over Pop's cup. "Need a refill?"

"No thank you."

"You're gonna need the jolt." I nudged him. "These two will keep you up all afternoon."

He nudged me back, his grin sparkling. I loved Pop's smell—Old Spice cologne. It was nothing but safety to me… like my dad had been.

"I've got this." Pop tickled Duke's belly. He lay in his car seat on the kitchen island, cooing back up at him. "Ain't I, Duke Beauregard Pierce?"

"Y'all sure you don't want the whole night?" Evelyn swayed with Caroline in her arms. "This grandmother does this for a living. We'll be fine, you know."

Evelyn was an obstetric nurse with more knowledge in her pinky than I'd have in a lifetime about infant care. Still, "I'll miss them too much," I sighed. "Let's do this in baby steps."

"For now"—Daniel's heavy arms wrapped me from behind—"we'll just enjoy the afternoon."

Pop winked. "Y'all are gonna give me another grandbaby soon."

"Oh, *hell* no." I twisted from Daniel's embrace. "Two is enough."

Daniel groaned, "Way to kill the romance for a bloke," making Pop cackle.

"Text me when to bring them back," Evelyn said, setting Caroline down in her car seat. "Until then, I'm spoilin' 'em rotten." Suddenly, the baby grabbed her long locks.

"Watch out," I warned. "Her hand grabs everything she aims for."

"Wonder who she gets that from?" Pop put the spotlight on my lethal skills.

"Speaking of," Daniel chimed in, "I want to go to a range and learn how to shoot Charlie's .380."

"What?" That snapped my head around.

"I want to learn how to shoot it," Daniel answered. "And the rifle hanging on the office wall, if it still works."

"Oh, it fires," Pop said. "That was Charlie's dad's rifle and the first one she shot. She won twelve competitions with it."

My hands flew up. "Whoa, you two, before you start going all *Die Hard* on me." I turned to Daniel. "Since when do you want to use a gun? You gave me such hell about it months ago."

"You bloody well know why." All beauty faded from his dead serious stare back.

"I don't know how I feel about this." My glare matched his. "Yes, I own guns, but I fucking hate them. And we've had enough of them lately, don't you think?"

Pop and Evelyn quieted at the tension filling the room.

"Respectfully, Charlie, you can't stop me." Daniel towered over me. "Just like I can't stop you when you've got your stubborn mind set."

"Why don't you leave the firearms to me, and you keep doing the ass-kicking, okay?"

"We need more than that now and you know it. We're still not safe." His cleft chin cocked, challenging me. "Why can you use one, but not me? That's not how our marriage works. Fifty-fifty, remember?"

Fran appeared in the kitchen, lifting her nose to the tension burning the air. She didn't say a word.

"Daniel, beating the shit out of a man is one thing. But shooting him? Killing him? That's another."

What Daniel did to the man who attacked us in the airport, and then again in Wilmington, it jolted my mind. How Daniel almost killed him. I saw it—the murder in his aqua eyes protecting me and the twins.

He would've if I hadn't stopped him.

"You don't want that on your soul," I said, "taking someone's life, even if it's justified. Trust me."

I almost said more. That he only knew props and stunts, not real war, and death like I'd known. But I tightened my lips, keeping the smart-ass comment from flying out.

But he squinted, saw it in my eyes anyway and smirked.

"I'm not a sheltered, celebrity arsehole, Charlie. Remember? *I* took down the threat to us in Wilmington. *I* rolled Rob's bloody body off yours in New York. If that man hadn't shot himself, I would've if I'd had a gun... with no regrets. I just need the training."

I winced.

No, I didn't remember. I'd passed out. But Daniel had the memory haunting him. I knew how that felt.

No memory served me, but online videos did. The press

was there, capturing the nightmare for millions to see. We couldn't escape the story until this virus took over the news, and we were ironically, thankfully, forgotten.

I'd insisted that Daniel show me the video while I sat in the hospital bed, wanting to glean more intel.

The reel played on Daniel's phone, skyrocketing my pulse while I watched...

How Daniel stands to my right on the red carpet after giving me a kiss. He turns, following his publicist, letting go of my hand while I turn back to stand with Rob and Elaine, his assistant.

A mic picks it up—"Ravenel! Ravenel!"

Rob turns his back to the sound, making his body wide in front of mine. A gun shot explodes the levels on the mic while Rob falls over me.

Screams erupt as Daniel turns back in an instant, shouting my name. A second shot explodes. More screams. The cameraperson has nerves of steel keeping the lens on the bloody spectacle.

How Daniel looks into the crowd before security swarms us. Then all you see between the legs of the guards is Daniel kneeling over my pink dress splattered in dark blood and Rob's mammoth legs splayed across the matching carpet.

What do you think? Teach Daniel to use your gun?

Do it. My old friend, that instinct, whispered in my ear. *You're not a one-woman army. Or Corps. You're gonna need him.*

I nodded at its wisdom, "Okay," raising my hands in surrender. "But good damn luck finding an open range in this virus mess. They're closing everything down."

"We can go before we fly to Madrid," he said. "*If* we fly to Madrid. While we wait, you can teach me."

"I'll call Bill." Pop spoke with the tension gone. "He owns the Bluffton club where Charlie's dad taught her to shoot."

I blurted, "This is fucking weird."

"Charlie!" Evelyn chided my foul language in front my children.

"Sorry."

Though that would be a daily occurrence and probably the third word my kids said. It amused me, the idea of little voices saying "fuck". They'd probably drop the f-bomb at the best time... like at dinner with their grandparents.

"I want to see where you learned to shoot." Daniel neared me for a conciliatory kiss. "I'll get as good as you."

"Everything's a competition with you, isn't it?" I met his eyes. "Try, if you think your male ego can handle the ass-whoopin'."

His lips curled into a panty-wetting grin. "Oh, an arse-whooping is on, Ravenel." The gleam in his eyes? It was already fucking me.

"Well, that's sorted," Fran spoke up while Pop grabbed Duke's seat and Evelyn picked up Caroline's.

I walked them to the haint blue front doors. Saying goodbye to my two little bundles welled tears in my eyes.

Fran patted my arm. "You're doing what's best for them, love. Mum needs to be happy too." She nodded to Daniel standing behind me. "And you're the lucky lass among millions who gets that delicious morsel all to yourself. Enjoy him."

The front doors closed gently behind them. I watched them leave through the beveled window.

Daniel pressed into me, steaming over my ear, "Hey, lucky lass. Ready for me to make you *very* happy now?"

CHAPTER FIVE

DANIEL

Say It [SG Lewis Remix] by Flume, Tove Lo

MARCH. **Seven months before...**

I handed her a glass filled with a sentimental cocktail—rum and Coke. Curling up behind her on the outdoor sofa of our bedroom deck, I pulled a blanket over our legs.

"Do you know what today is, Mrs. Pierce?"

"I don't even know what day of the month it is."

"March twenty-second. A year ago today, we had our first date. The picnic. Remember?"

She turned to me, shocked. "You remember the date?"

"Really?" Like she didn't know my obsession with numbers and dates. "We met on March second, and it took me a torturous twenty days to get this far from your lips." I held the same spot, an inch away from her sweet kiss.

"When was the first time we made love?"

"Depends. What do you consider that to be?"

"When you were inside of me."

I grinned. "My fingers, tongue, or cock?"

"I may not remember the date, but I remember that day—it was the same one."

"Then sixteen more times that week, and one, no, probably two at the rate we were going, became Caroline and Duke."

I kissed her to that truth. God, the craving for her, tightening my every muscle, ready to unleash on her.

She hovered her lips over mine. "So, what was the date, Mr. Ravenel?"

Not that we changed our names when we married, but if I teased her with "Mrs. Pierce" of course she threw it back. Fuck's sake, I loved that about her too.

"May fourth."

"Well, may the fourth be with you, Sex God."

She took my mouth, teasing her tongue over the seam of my lips, and hell yes, grabbing a fist full of my hair, demanding more.

I pulled back, taking the drink from her hand, setting it down on the table along with mine. "Get up here, Mrs. Pierce." I lifted her to straddle me.

Swinging her leg clad in yoga pants over my thighs, "I can't believe it's only been a year," she touched her forehead to mine. "So much has happened."

"Do you ever regret it? All that it's put you through?"

That was my secret guilt. One of them. It cursed my soul from the moment my horrified vision filled with her pregnant body splayed bloody on the red carpet.

She never wanted to be there. I'd assumed it was her paranoia, her PTSD tormenting her, telling her someone was chasing her. That she just wasn't used to the stalking paparazzi and fans.

I was wrong. And I ran every morning, to the abandoned hotel on the island and back, telling myself that it was my fault. And fearing... we were still at risk.

"Is that what you think?" She sat up. "That I regret us?"

"I ruined your life, Charlie. You don't have your privacy or your career. Bloody hell, you don't even have your safety anymore. I can feel it. We're still being chased."

I respected her too much to bullshit. She was safe until I carried her, passed out, into my celebrity world.

"Daniel, you didn't ruin my life. You gave me a new one. And no one gets great love without putting it all on the line." Tracing her fingertip down my nose, "And FYI, I'm not giving up my career, I'll keep protecting us, so I have no regrets," she tickled next over my lips. "But if I could do March twenty-second over again, I'd change one thing."

"Oh, yeah?"

"I would've fucked you that night instead of making us wait so long."

I neared her lips, "That was the hottest part, and you know it," hovering over them like we did a year ago. "Are you going to make me wait for May fourth again to fuck you?"

Shyness flickered in her eyes. "Maybe."

I recognized it. Like the first time she was afraid to show me her bullet scars. The irony we were here a year later in the same dance. *Dance. Yes.*

"Will my wife at least dance with me?"

"Always." She climbed off, offering her hand to me.

I took it to stand. "You really take this equal feminist stuff seriously, don't you?"

"You deserve to be romanced too." She trailed her other hand down my chest. "Besides, the equal stuff is what makes it so erotic, doesn't it?"

"Fuck yes." I yanked my shirt off, tossing it on the balcony floor. "Your turn. Fifty-fifty."

"Damn, Daniel." She stood, wide-eyed. "Holy hell, what have you been hiding under sweatshirts for three months?"

I smiled, my flesh tingling under her gaze. I'd been going heavy in our home gym, needing to thrust my frustration into something, so the weights took it.

"What have you been hiding, Charlie?"

I lifted her sweatshirt, thankful she didn't stop me and thrilled to see she wasn't wearing a bra. Her shirt landed on the deck next too.

"Fuck's sake, babe." The sight squeezed my cock. How goosebumps rose the flesh of her pert breasts. How they were still small but fuller now, curving up, nipples hard and tempting my tongue. "Fuck, I need to touch you again."

"Let's go inside first. It's cold out here." She grabbed my hand. "Besides, someone owes me some romance and a dance."

I flipped the switch on for the gas logs in our bedroom fireplace. It started in an instant, warming the room. From my phone on the nightstand, I knew the song to play.

"Say It"—it was *my* song, the one she introduced me to on our Seychelles holiday. The one that looped while she fucked me so maddeningly slow, drenching me, claiming my body, and altering my life forever.

I put it on loop again before crossing the room. "Remember this?"

She put her arms around my neck. "I remember knowing that night, that I'd spend the rest of my life with you, though I was scared as hell to admit it."

I grabbed her small waist, her nipples tickling my torso, making me crazed. "Are you still scared?"

"Not when we do this."

Her kiss reached for mine. I gave back, again and again, taking her top lip until she moaned. Our mouths, our breath, wet twirls and twists curled across my every nerve. Not one time throughout the song did my mouth leave hers making my heart scream for more.

"Can I take these off?" My fingertips tickled under the band of her leggings.

"You first."

Agreement hit me hard and fast. My shorts fell to the floor with no boxer briefs underneath. I'd been going commando for days. To say there was a never-ending mountain of laundry for us now put it mildly.

Pushing her leggings down, she was naked underneath too, kicking them across the floor before she quickly wrapped her arms back around my neck.

I knew why—the new scar—she didn't want me to see it.

Lacing a hand through her hair, I pulled her body into mine. She was my return to church, worshipping her neck with kisses and gentle bites. "I've missed you so much." A sigh escaped her lips while my hand teased over her delicious ass crevice, urging her harder against my desperate, heavy cock. "Goddamn, I want you so bad." She moaned even more, grinding back.

Dropping to my knees, she flinched away, but I said, "Shhhh," grabbing her trembling hips, pressing my lips to her flesh. The neat, dark-pink curved line greeted me. I kissed it, from one end to the other, and back again, cherishing her with my praise. "I love every inch of you, Charlie. Everything you did for us, what your body gave to us."

She finally exhaled, relaxing into my kiss, her hands in my hair, letting my worship continue. Her musk lured me to open her again, but when I glanced up there were tears down her cheeks. "Let me try, babe," I soothed, determined to take all the time she needed.

Silently, she nodded yes.

Standing up, I turned her around. We stood in front of a large floor-mirror propped beside our closet door. "See how beautiful you are?" I felt every word, taking her hands in mine and guiding one pair down between her thighs, while our other pair cupped her breast, palms and fingers thrilling swirls over her nipple.

She gasped, "Oh God, they're so sensitive now," arching into me.

"Really?" Oh, the delight when I rolled my fingertips around her budding nipple, guiding hers to the same. "This, Charlie?" Lingering, barely brushing over, her nipple rose even more to our touch. "This is more sensitive now?"

She answered with a deep groan. Lifting her hand to hold onto my neck, I slowly trailed my fingertips down her arm, lightly across her tender armpit, slowly tickling to the very tip of her nipple before gently twisting the nub with thumb and finger.

That made her gasp again, grinding back on my cock, both her hands reaching up, clasping around my neck like I had her tied up. "Fuck, Daniel. Don't stop."

Shuddering, she almost closed her eyes but I demanded, "Watch us," while I dedicated my hands to her pleasure.

She obeyed; our gaze enthralled with our reflection, her breath rising, her ribs bowing, pushing her breasts into my grasp, begging for my kneading touch.

My deft fingers explored this new storm of sensation for her, with gentle circles, with twists and pulls teasing over her nipples, it had her panting for me after minutes. Watching, groaning with my growing intensity, she trembled.

God, I couldn't believe it, marveling at the sight, recognizing her writhe. She was getting there, crawling back into her fit-ass body that I wanted to fuck so bad.

"Spread your legs, Charlie." I knew how to help her find who she was now... with no shame.

Purring the words over her ear, it was the only time she craved my control, "Spread them wide and show me how naughty you are. How you come so hard for me." She did; her open stance urging me on, my lips taking her ear, commanding, "Show me how fucking wet that pussy gets," delivering one final brutal pinch to both her nipples.

She screamed, "Oh, shit!" Her legs buckled. I grabbed her waist, keeping her standing while we witnessed her lust drip to the floor, trickling down her thighs. "Fuck, Daniel."

Good God, this woman. I set her against our bed. "Don't move." Falling to my knees, I wanted her back. I put her leg over my shoulder before licking the tangy trail up her inner thigh. My fingers spread her open for more. Taking in the vision of her wet, pink feast—I was ravenous.

I glanced up at her, "Watch me eat your sweet pussy and remember who you really are," before I devoted my mouth to her folds.

The return of her taste forced my moan, feeling her hands gripping my hair, pushing my tongue in to fuck her more. Fuck me, I looked up. She *was* watching me, not shy, only hungry.

Her grasp controlled me, rolling her pussy hard over my face, back and forth before boldly saying, "Make me fucking come in your mouth, Daniel."

Fuck yes, Pierce, she's back. So fucking naughty... and all yours...

My lust turned to sweet lechery to obey. I didn't need breath, my lips sucking her clit before my tongue licked down to fuck her cunt. "Yes, Daniel. Like that." It didn't take her long. Not with my tongue flicking, pummeling, hammering her flesh with every thrill I knew she craved. "You love it, don't you? Eating my pussy because it's your favorite meal."

My groan answered. Holding back the urge to bite, my mouth played her like a fucking maestro, all the way to her soaking crescendo. The one that shook her thighs while she groaned deep, her pussy pouring into my mouth with what I thirsted for, baptizing my tongue, blessing my lips and chin and dripping down my neck. I slurped her last drops until her body stopped shaking.

I rose while she fell back on the bed with a satisfied smile. "I don't know what I love more. Your beard tickling my pussy, or when your smooth chin presses hard against it, but Jesus, I'll take you either way."

No smile found my wet face. I was in pain, aching and throbbing for her. "What do you want me to do to you?" But I'd always ask, loving the sound of the dirty request from her mouth.

Lifting her head, she opened her eyes, recognizing my desperation. Her finger curled. "I want that big, thick cock of yours to fuck what belongs to you, Daniel Pierce."

Crawling over her, across the mattress, I controlled the urge to flip her over and fuck her from behind so bloody hard, like the savage animal I felt inside. The desire taunted me before I flipped to my back, surrendering instead.

She leaned over for a kiss, exploring her flavor in my mouth. Then her lips teased down to my pleading, hard cock, taking me with the best glucking sucks that forced my hips off the bed, blinding me with desire.

Grabbing a fistful of her hair, "Yes, suck my fucking cock, Charlie," the starved monster in me wanted to bang her throat until her lips drooled down my shaft and my cum spilled creamy over them. "Goddamn, babe. You're so fucking good." The memory of her like that on her knees before me so many times in the past, it made me strain not to come. I almost did, "Charlie, no," pulling her off instead.

The moment let me catch my breath and control, watching her crawl on top of me.

"Let me do this." She held my eager tip at her soaked entrance. "I need to be careful. Slow. Okay?"

"I can go slow with my wife." My hands revered her hips and our history. "It's the sexiest thing I've ever known."

She smiled down, her hair falling in a golden curtain around my gaze. I stared up at the vision. How her beauty was the sky to my world, everywhere and my home. The descent of her tight, soaked pussy down my cock offered me the most breathtaking experience—fucking and making love at the same time.

Once I was inside her, I held on, taken by her careful tempo until her gradual rolls became an unhurried, glistening glide up and down my length, her strangling piston driving me crazy with lust.

It had been so long. The need to fuck her harder, like a goddamn animal, it threatened but I couldn't forget all she'd been through. "Are you okay?"

"Yes." Her palms braced against my chest, breath strong, her thighs flexing, riding me faster. "God, you feel so good." Her eyelids were heavy, her mouth lax with desire. "I'm so sensitive now. I can feel every inch of you."

It was in her marine eyes. How she found it—the shameless merger of mom, wife, and woman who started fucking the hell out of me with more power than I'd ever felt from her before. The sight. The sensation. I reveled in it for as long as I could last.

The pad of my thumb started pressing, playing hard

against her clit. "That's it. Fuck every hard inch of me." My hips thrust into her ride, forceful and hard. "I'm yours. Take it."

Lips trembling, her fingernails dug into my pecs, her eyes possessed with lust, her stunning face softening to let go, waiting for my command. "Show me, babe." I rattled my thumb over her clit, coaxing her fall. "Come on. Show me how much; you love fucking my thick cock, don't you?"

She bucked with an orgasm so strong her eyes rolled back while little rivers of her pleasure streamed down my shaft, wetting with smacks over my lap. Her ride still searching hard for it, I could tell she needed more. So did I.

The perky tips of her breasts beckoned my mouth. "Again, Charlie. Come on, fuck me as hard as you can." I grabbed a fistful of her mane, pulling her down to my lips, growling, "Do it. Make us come like there's no tomorrow."

With a merciless suck to her nipple, yank of her hair, and bruising grip over her hip, I made her cry out, "Oh fuck, Daniel," shaking in my hands.

Grunting, my lips held onto her nipple while I quaked with my fierce release—need, love and lust for her barreling through, taking my breath and words away. No other senses had me but the one pulsing into her.

I held onto her, my world, panting, breathing in a truth we survived. "I love you, Daniel," she sighed my favorite sound. Feeling her tears on my chest; mine threatened.

"I love you too. More than life itself."

This tragic truth we knew—tomorrow was never guaranteed. Just this now... our perfect moment together.

CHAPTER SIX

DANIEL

OCTOBER. **Now...**

It was a sin. How I demanded that she change, knowing she couldn't.

The Hunter's Moon rose higher in the sky. It disappeared behind the roof over my head, leaving me to black waves taunting with the ugly truth.

How she never consented to this. How I had picked up her unconscious body and carried her into my celebrity hell without her permission.

After that viral spectacle, there was no going back.

From that moment, she struggled, but at least she tried, suffering its brutal spotlight with grace because she loved me, promising she'd never leave me. She confronted her fear and stood by my side, in the path of another bullet.

And still... she came back to me, even stronger this time.

Yet, when she asked me to do the same, to join her world—not this one of her enchanting island home—no, the one of her own lethal destiny. I shouted, "No!"

I fought back, firing furious words at her, making her sob. Her pain didn't stop me. I turned my back on her and walked away... leaving her alone.

All I did was lie to her. Then hurt her. Then try to change her. Then... I left her.

And all I could do now was try like hell to get her back. If she could ever forgive me.

Again.

I gave one more desperate glance to my phone.

2:39am

It's crazy, cosmic torture; how minutes last longer when they're filled with agony.

A prayer closed my eyes, begging to have her back. I couldn't open them again. The truth before me, of a world without her, I couldn't face it.

My vision swam in the darkness, the void with her gone. A storm raged in my heart, mocked by the sound of gentle ocean waves lapping the shore.

CHAPTER SEVEN

DANIEL

APRIL. ***Six months before...***

Duke cried out from the cot. I picked him up. "Come here, mate."

It was my turn at the four a.m. feeding. Me, Charlie and Fran—we took turns so all got rest, and if we were lucky, the babies would go back down for another four hours.

Sitting down with Duke in the rocker, my son reached his chubby hand up, gripping the bottle. I watched him with an adoring smile. "You're hungry, aren't you, little man."

"Love" was such a simple utterance. It couldn't contain all that overwhelmed me gazing down at my son. He had started off in peril, so tiny, but his ferocious hunger made him grow fast, catching up to his sister one day soon.

It was a quiet moment liberating me from my colossal ego, exchanging it for the most vulnerable creature in my arms. My beautiful son. My cherished daughter. Daniel Pierce didn't exist anymore, only them and their mother, the only ones who mattered.

It jolted me. My phone in shorts' pocket buzzed against my thigh. Must be a London call. No one else would ring this early.

Wedging the bottle under my chin, I freed a hand to answer it. It was Elaine, my assistant, starting her workday right on time.

"Hello," I answered quietly, resting the phone in the crook of my shoulder so I could hold the bottle again.

"Hiya," she said. "Didn't know if I would get you at this hour, but we have urgent issues, and I need to update you."

"What is it?"

"The studio just announced an official halt to all productions for months because of the virus. Everything is locked down across Europe. Lorraine and the production team have scheduled a video chat with the cast this week. I'm putting it on your calendar."

"This is bloody for real, isn't it?"

"Yes, love, it's frightening. I've sorted your flights. Canceled everything. Just stay safe with your family and I'll keep you posted."

"Likewise. Maybe get out of London, yeah? The fewer the people you're around, the better."

"I will. I'm locking up your townhouse and the office. Then I'm off to my mother's in Bampton tomorrow. I can work remotely from there. And you?"

"We're fine. We're already isolated and prepared for this."

"Charlie and the babies all right?"

"Yeah. She's back up and running. Literally." I squeezed Duke. "And they're getting big. I'll text you some new photos."

"Please do. And also, Gareth's office phoned twice yesterday. They're desperately trying to reach you."

My solicitor? Why was he calling? "Thanks. I'll ring him next." Why did my stomach just cramp?

"All right, love. Send my best to all. I'll phone once I'm settled in. Cheers."

"Cheers," I muttered, ending the call, and setting the phone down.

Duke drained the bottle. Slinging a cloth nappy over my shoulder, I rested him there, getting a good burp before I laid him back to sleep. I did the same with Caroline, distracted the whole time with why Gareth's office was trying to reach me.

Once finished, I treaded downstairs. Chances for sleep were nil. Anxiety had me wide awake.

Fearful steps took me onto the deck to place the call while I waited for the coffee to brew. I checked my phone. Usually, I left it on the nightstand, silenced because of the twins. Three missed calls glowed back, all from Gareth. *Fuck.* Tapping the screen, seconds later, Gareth's London office picked up and quickly patched me through.

Gareth answered, "Daniel, glad to get your call in these crazy times, yeah?"

"Indeed. You all right? Mary and the kids?" I suffered through small talk; it was only polite.

"We're fine." Thankfully, Gareth jumped to the punch, clearing his throat before continuing, "I'm afraid we have some difficult business again. The business we dealt with years back? It seems things have changed."

I closed my eyes. The ground cracked open beneath my feet and hell appeared below. My soul was terrified of "the business".

Nikki Sampson.

"What's changed?" The question iced over my lips.

That's what I felt for that woman. Frozen fear. Bitter anger. Raw pain.

"She wants you to meet him again. Seems eleven years and the threat of a global pandemic has made her re-evaluate the situation." Gareth huffed, "That's how her attorney put it."

"Meet him again?" *No, it's too late. Yes, it's what you've always wanted.* "Why? Where? How does she propose to do that? Now?" Frantic questions shivered up my spine.

"They still live in Florida with her family. I don't know how or when, but her attorney reached out to broker the terms." Gareth advised, "But I have to tell you, Daniel, we must be careful. She has been one of the most erratic parties I've ever dealt with. I never trusted her, even with everything signed and sealed."

I snatched at my hair in a vain attempt to yank myself from the doom I fell into.

I knew too well how unstable Nikki Sampson was. That's why her deranged plan never worked. Why I had to walk away eleven years ago. And why toxic guilt plagued me ever since.

But now? Who did I fear more? Nikki Sampson, or my wife, Charlie Ravenel.

Because if I told Charlie about "the business", it would destroy her. Our marriage. Our family. Our love. Done.

Nothing sat in my stomach, but still I gagged on the truth, the one that left me no choice. I had to tell Charlie. Because if I didn't, I'd lose my chance to finally do the right thing.

And the fear of losing this last chance? It clenched my heart, especially now...

I had two sons in this world, and I wouldn't abandon either of them. Never again.

CHAPTER EIGHT

DANIEL

My Honest Face by Inhaler

APRIL. **Six months before...**

"You okay?" Charlie patted my hand shaking on the breakfast table. We sat, drinking coffee while the twins were still asleep. "You've been awful quiet this morning."

I wanted to dive into the blue-green water of her eyes and never emerge. Instead, I closed mine in shame. "We need to get Fran to tend to the twins today."

"Why? Did you make us some sexy plans again?"

I wished. I could kiss that goodbye too. "I need to talk with you about something, and we'll need the privacy."

She raised her chin. Calm. Calculated. *Please stay that way.* "You're scaring the shit out of me, but okay, let's talk."

Rising for my sentence from the marital jury, I stood up. "I'll tell Fran we're going for a walk."

Charlie's gaze was glued to the horizon whenI returned to the breakfast room. It featured an octagon of windows overlooking our backyard and ocean. It was my favorite part of our home, a home I was about to wreck.

"Fran's got them in the nursery." I offered my hand to her. "She'll sort their lunch."

"We'll need that much time?" She offered her soft palm but hard tone, one that sounded ready for an ambush.

I didn't answer. I just cherished her hand in mine while we walked across the long grassy yard, kicking our flip-flops off by the wooden boardwalk before stepping into the sand between the dunes.

The morning beach awaited us on the other side. The tide was out, so were the beachgoers. It was just us and one awful secret.

Lie was more accurate—a lie of omission.

She raked her fingers through her long blonde hair getting whipped by the warming April breeze. "All right, Daniel. What is it?"

I held her other hand in mine, praying she wouldn't snatch it away once she knew.

"This is hard, Charlie. And it's going to hurt. And I'm so bloody sorry." I looked up, facing her. "Just let me explain what happened and then you can unleash on me, okay?"

"Okay." Her face stood at attention.

I peered down at the sand, at our bare feet and our big toes almost touching. The words jumped from my mouth without a parachute, plunging to their death.

"Eleven years ago, I made a massive mistake. I was filming in L.A. Partying like mad. Out of control, really. One night at a club, two women were all over me, insisting I go back to their hotel room. I did. I was pissed drunk and had sex with both of them."

I glanced back up to her eyes. Her stoic stare wavered, making me ill because the threesome wasn't the offense.

"A few days later, my solicitor phoned. Nikki, one of the women I was with, she got a lawyer. She claimed that I raped her, and that she was going to press charges and go public."

Her hand twitched back from my grasp, but I held it tight while she snarled, "Did you? Did you rape her?"

"No. I'd never hurt a woman. You know that. Yes, I was drunk. We all were drinking—"

"That means you didn't have her consent, Daniel." She ripped her hand from my grasp. "If she was that drunk, it was rape."

"Charlie, I swear, she wasn't that drunk. She did consent. Unbeknownst to her or me, her friend recorded the entire thing, proving it."

"What?" Disgust twisted her face. "Some woman videoed you? In a threesome with her? And the other woman in it claims it was rape? What the fuck, Daniel?"

"It was a trap. The other woman, Jodi, she hid the camera. So when Nikki claimed later that it wasn't consensual, the video proved otherwise. It showed she was coherent, initiating the sex over and over for hours. Later, my solicitor got them to sign statements swearing to that. We got the only copy of the tape, paid Jodi and Nikki off and they signed NDAs."

"So, one woman claimed you raped her, and another secretly taped it, proving your innocence?" She widened the gulf between us. "That's too fucking convenient."

"No, it was my fucked-up young life. Jodi was a wardrobe assistant on the film with me. She confessed that she planned it. That she wanted to blackmail me. And it worked. Nikki was her friend. They were at the club that night and Jodi convinced her to do the threesome, never telling her about the camera, knowing it would only make it more damning for me. That's what she confessed to before I paid her off."

"Why would Nikki claim you raped her?" Charlie's eyes narrowed. "Women don't lie about that."

"Because the next morning, Nikki acted like we were a couple, making plans for us, wanting to go to the Oscars with me and such, but I got out of there. It felt wrong. I didn't want to see either of them again. But the next day, Jodi confronted me on set, showing me the video, demanding money. The day after, Nikki devised a plan for her own revenge, claiming it was rape, not knowing about the tape. But once we showed it to her, that backfired, and my name was cleared."

"So... this is what you've been hiding for a year?" Goddamn, her tone was glacial—slow and freezing her heart before my eyes. "You had a threesome, got blackmailed, accused of rape, but a sex tape proved your innocence and money bought their silence, saving your precious career?" Judgement seethed from her eyes. "And now what? The tape has leaked?"

"No." My lips quivered, terrified of the destruction from my next words. I held onto the sight—the way Charlie looked before I broke her. Before I destroyed our marriage. The words choked my throat, tearing me open too as I spit them out. "I got Nikki pregnant. Nine months later, she had my son."

Shock hit Charlie's face like a bullet. Eyes wide, her lips started trembling.

"Charlie, please. I tried doing right by them. I tried after he was born to be with her, to be with my son. It didn't last a month. Nikki was so unstable. She knew I didn't love her, that I never would. So she used our son as a pawn, and it got so ugly. I couldn't raise my child in that environment. But I couldn't get custody either. Not with the tape and false accusation. Not if I wanted to keep it all quiet."

Wind pushed the tears falling down her face back to wet her hair. No words came from her shaking face.

This is what a shattered heart looks like, Pierce. Don't you dare look away.

"I'm so sorry I didn't tell you. It's been my greatest crime. How I gave up on my son, giving Nikki full custody. I agreed to a massive payout, signed the papers, walked away, and grieved it for years. Then I met you and you saw my pain; you healed me and you didn't even know how. But now he's eleven, and Nikki claims things have changed, that she wants me to meet him again."

Hair lashed her face, but she stood frozen, her jaw clenched, pink cheeks smeared with betrayal.

I'd seen her like this before, the last time I hurt her, when I fought like hell to win her back.

This time? I wouldn't be so lucky.

"Charlie, please understand. I don't know what to do. He's an innocent boy who is my son, who deserves to know his father. And I must do right by him this time. But the idea of letting Nikki back into my life scares the hell out of me. I don't trust her."

She stepped farther away from me.

"Why, Daniel?" The searching in her eyes, all the pain I could see in them, it sliced across my heart. "When you said you wanted a family with me, that you wanted to be a father, you were lying to my face." The trembling in her lips wouldn't stop. "I told you all my secrets, all my pain, and you told me *nothing*. Not when you said you loved me, not when you married me, not when you held our children in your arms." Oh God, the hurt. It was pouring down her face. "Not one fucking word of truth came from your mouth."

"I was afraid I'd lose you. You *are* my first family, Charlie, my first love. I never had a chance with them. They felt like a painful secret buried in my past, and I couldn't bring them back to life if I wanted to, so I just left them there."

Fuck, I didn't know how to describe it. "I should have told you; I know. But when we first met, I couldn't. You had to know me first. To know that I could never hurt a woman. And so many times since, I came close to telling you. But I couldn't hurt you and steal your joy, what we finally had together. But I was determined to tell you after the premiere, before the twins were born, but..."

We knew what happened next.

"You have another son. Another woman you tried to have a family with. And you lied to me, your wife about it." The light in her eyes shifted. Never had I seen such agony on her face. Rage threatened too. "Tell me now, Daniel. Everything. How many other kids do you have?"

"Charlie, don't."

"I deserve the truth. I've counted three so far. Could there be more?"

"Okay, fine. Yes, there could be more, but I don't know about them. I wasn't always careful."

"You weren't always *careful*?" She shook her head. "So then how many women?"

"Don't ask me that."

"I know you counted them. You count everything, and now I want to know."

"No, you don't. I've only loved you. And we aren't fucking prudes. We're married adults who love each other now, so let's carry on."

"We'll carry on when you answer my damn question. Respect me as your wife and don't lie to me anymore."

I cursed the sky and every egotistical, horny twitch in my pants I had until this moment. Clenching my jaw, I confessed, "Sixty-one."

"Sixty-one women." She smirked, but I saw it in her eyes—that hurt her, deeply. "All of legal age?"

"Yes. Except for my first, Gemma. We were both teens. I told you about her."

Next question. "Any men?"

"One drunk night in Rome. I was twenty-two. One man. Hand jobs. Then he signed an NDA. That's it."

"How many other threesomes? Or more?"

"Charlie, stop."

"Finish breaking my heart, Daniel." She wasn't backing down from this. "No more secrets."

"Two other threesomes. Me and two women I met at a bar while I was filming in Vancouver. I got them to sign NDAs too." I raised my chin, no more to hide. "I was twenty-five. No more after the bloody one with Nikki."

"Did you like it?"

"The man? Not really. The threesomes? Yes, a bit exhausting, but yes." Fuck it, nothing but candor now. This was pushing me to my breaking point. "Why? You want to do one?" It just blurted out.

"You fucking wish."

That was daft, Pierce. "No, I don't." I reached for her hand. She jerked it away again. "I only want you, Charlie. You know that."

"No. I don't know that. One year in with you, and it's not safe. Truth bullets are firing. How could you do this to us?"

"You do know me, Charlie. You know our love."

"Lies kill love."

"Can you still love me?"

"I can do whatever I want." She was fighting it; fury and pain storming her eyes. "But I swear, one more fucking lie from you and it's over. And I promise, you won't survive how I end things."

Was she giving me a chance? "That's it, Charlie. I swear. No more secrets. No more lies."

"Are we going to see a tweet one day, or a post, or get a call that you really did rape someone?"

"Never. I'm not that kind of man."

"That's what those other men said too. Seems they had a real fucked up, criminal idea of what consent is. So help me God, if that ever happens, I won't defend you. You're on your own."

"Charlie, I had some wild times, yes. But I swear, I've tortured myself, asking the same question. I recall no time when consent was ever in doubt. Hell, there were times when they came on to me, and I didn't consent. But I swear, it was done to me, never did I do it to someone else."

She paused, like a fresh wound opened, bleeding on the sand between us. "Is that why you ask me so much? For my consent? Is that why you got so upset the first time you tried kissing me without asking? Why you were so sweet and willing to go slow with me?" The anguish in her eyes; my world was crumbling before my face. "It wasn't because you cared for me, was it? It was because you felt guilty about Nikki. About the false accusation."

"God, no, Charlie. What happened with Nikki was hell. And then all the 'me too' stuff, I grew up even more. My sister schooled me. How power exploits. How silence isn't consent. How I could always be very sure it's what a woman wanted."

I stepped toward her. "How I was who *you* wanted." This ruin couldn't happen. Never. Our sex? Our love? I'd defend it with my last breath. "I cherished going slow because I was falling in love with you. I was so honoured to be with you, that you let me be your first after so long. Your wanting me is the most beautiful sound to my ears, Charlie. It's my soul's symphony. That's why I ask. Why I need to hear you. It's always about love with us."

She shook her head and looked out at the waves, tears streaming down her face. "God, I want to trust you." She didn't look back at me. "But I don't know how." Her eyes closed; agony dropped her strong shoulders. "I've buried a husband once. But I've never been betrayed by one. I've never known this death before."

That punched my heart. My knees wanted to fall to the sand, my soul begging for forgiveness. But that felt wrong. Manipulative. I had to stand and face what I did.

She turned and started walking away. "I need to think."

"Are you coming back?"

Her glare curved around. "It's a five-mile island in a global pandemic, Daniel. How far can I go?"

"What about the twins?"

"Don't you dare use our children as pawns for your fuck up." Hypocrisy slammed me in the face. "You can go back inside, be a man, and at least take care of two of your three children for a day."

Her shoulders lifted, turned, and she walked away.

CHAPTER NINE

DANIEL

APRIL. ***Six months before...***

While I washed the dishes after the twins' lunch, I watched out the window, up to the dunes, hoping to see her appear on the horizon. She didn't.

The baby monitor sat on the kitchen counter, the display illuminating two bundles sleeping in their cot. Shame drowned me. Closing my eyes I begged, *please forgive me.*

Afternoon turned to night. The house quieted after the twins went down. I'd busied myself all day with their care, thankful for every moment. But without her, I ached.

You've lost her, Pierce. She'll come home, but not back to you.

No tears I shed in bed that night. I didn't deserve them, not for myself. When my eyes opened to the dawn, the bed was empty beside me. Leaning over, I checked my phone.

No calls. No texts.

Next, I checked the baby monitor. Fran had covered the

four a.m. feeding. The twins were on their backs, fast asleep.

I knew where Charlie went—the last place I'd ever want her to go. With a pathetic wave to Fran in the kitchen, I darted off in the golf cart, afraid to find her there.

Rain sprinkled through the trees onto the narrow sandy road. Our electric cart quietly hummed toward its destination while anger crept through every muscle in my body, nearing the house.

Charlie's boat bobbed at the dock—its usual spot now. A Jet Ski rested on its floating ramp too. An old, tan Bronco was parked outside.

Yes, Silas was home.

Like a little brother to her? Like hell.

Silas let his love for Charlie be known many times. Fuck's sake, every day, I stared at the massive blooming row of calla lilies Silas planted in the backyard for Charlie, professing it.

With ten steps up the weathered planks, I found the screened-in porch unlocked. The spring creaked when I pulled it open. With one look to my right, my heart dropped.

I could see into Silas's bedroom. There were no blinds. My eyes fell on Charlie lying there, curled on her side, her back to the window. She was on Silas's bed, in his T-shirt, in her panties, holding his sleeping hand.

Charlie seeking Silas after I'd hurt her—it torched my lying heart. Her sleeping with him, touching his skin, lying vulnerable beside him in his bed, it lit a match to my soul.

The punishment was fair. My jealousy didn't care.

The back door was unlocked too. By the time I turned the brass knob, swinging it open and slamming it back before quick steps found me at the threshold of Silas's bedroom, the man was sitting up.

"Hey, dude" was all Silas said while he sat beside my half-naked wife stirring on his bed.

Was it Silas's fear of me or his fierce protection of Charlie that made him confess? I didn't care.

"Dude, she was crying," Silas said, "shouting out in her sleep. I came in here, held her hand and talked to her until she got quiet. I don't think she ever woke up from whatever nightmare she was having."

"You don't owe him an explanation."

The sentence came from a voice that seared my heart. Charlie sat up, twisting her long hair into a bun, her eyes puffy from crying.

"I would never cheat on you, Daniel. Wish I could say the same for you."

More pain punched my chest, all deserved. "Charlie, I—"

"I came here for my boat." She interrupted me. "I went out all day. It's like I couldn't find a place on the water. I couldn't find a place in my head or in my heart to forgive you. All I found, for hours, was a drenching rain and a hurt so bad I couldn't breathe."

Silas ripped a tissue from the box beside his bed, offering one to her swollen eyes crying again. "Thank you." She took Silas's offer with a broken smile before looking back at me.

My feet wobbled at the agony wrenched across her face.

"I didn't want my family to see me like this," she said, "or our children, so Silas said I could stay, and he gave me a dry shirt. I don't know what I dreamt last night, but it was about you and lies and pain." The sound of a squelched sob strained her voice. "I don't deserve this. You did the one thing I've feared the most. You took my family and my husband from me." The sob escaped. "Again."

"Charlie, please." This time I fell to my knees. Not out of manipulation. A remorse, a sorrow so strong it dropped me there, hard on the sandy, wooden floors. "Please come home with me. Give me a chance. Give our family a chance. I swear I will rip my bloody heart out to make this right with you. I'm so sorry."

More sobs heaved her shoulders with her face buried in her hands. She disappeared into a grief I didn't know if she'd come back from. I didn't move. Neither did Silas. We held silent while her pain washed over the entire room. After minutes, it ebbed, her tears stopped, and her eyes lifted to mine.

"Get up, Daniel." No emotion in her voice, it was only resignation. Were we over?

She crossed her legs on Silas's bed. The comfort she found there made me sick. "I will come home to our children today," she said. "Just give me time, give me space, give me whatever the hell I need right now."

I rose from my knees, unnerved by her body touching Silas's gray sheets. Disgusted because it should be my body beside hers, not Silas's naked, ripped torso next to my wife with nothing but allure in his eyes for her. I couldn't stop the surge, the words over my lips. "I'll do whatever you want, Charlie, just get out of his bed. Now."

The implication shot her eyebrows up, like the thought just occurred to her, but she'd relish it now, needing this jolt out of her grief.

"Why? Does the sight of me beside another man make you feel sick? Make you feel betrayed? Like your whole world is destroyed before you?"

"Yes." I seethed.

I had no right to be possessive. It didn't stop me. Silas's silence, his lack of protest at the suggestion of an affair with Charlie, it dug deep into my gut.

"Good." She surged up on her knees, the flash of her slinky, white lace panties only raging me more. "Then swim in it till you're drowning in pain like me." Why? Because Silas eyed them too.

"Is that what you want, Charlie? To fuck Silas to get back at me?" The young man didn't flinch at my questions. "Or better yet, what about the three of us? Like the one I had. A threesome with him and me? Will you forgive me then?" Desperation poured from my mouth. "I mean it. I'll do anything to get you back."

She jumped up off the bed, feet landing like a pouncing cat on the floor.

"Goddamn, motherfuckers," she said, yanking Silas's T-shirt off, revealing her white lace bralette underneath. The sight widened my eyes and made Silas grin. "Is that all y'all fucking think about?" Bending over, giving us a helluva seductive show of Charlie on a rampage, she snatched her dried shorts from the chair next to the bed. "You fucking men think fucking fixes everything."

But she didn't put them on. They swayed from her fist while she stood before us in one of the most alluring displays of her I'd ever seen.

Hurricane Charlie. Category Five. Sexy, pissed as hell, and ready to destroy any man's world.

"Sure," she said. "Let's all fuck now. I'll rock both your worlds to wet rubble. Is that what you want? You actually think that will fix your lie?" Her chin snapped toward Silas. "You in, Silas? Want to fuck me with my husband?"

"Hell yes." The words sang from his smiling mouth with no shame in them.

"What?" Charlie's head jerked back. "We're just friends."

"Yes, we are." Silas combed his fingers through his long blond strands. "But I care for you, Charlie Girl. I always have. I've fantasized about you since my first wet dream and every day since. And I'd do anything for you, and I'd never hurt you."

That back hand was for me. It worked.

"Charlie, he cares for you, but I love you. I'd go through hell and back for you. I already have. This is more than fantasies. This is our family, our life together, one we fought like hell to have. Don't you see that?"

"Yes, I see." Her small feet stepped into her jean shorts, pulling them up, covering what we desired. "I see two men who have lost their damn minds—my sweet friend who wants to fuck me, and my lying husband who doesn't mind."

"The bloody hell I don't mind, Charlie. I do." I watched as she swiped her sweatshirt from the chair. "I never want to share you. But I mean it. I'll do whatever it takes to get you back."

"An eye-for-an-eye only leaves two dumbass half-blind people who didn't think shit through." She snarled. "How dare you insult me! This isn't about sex. It isn't about threesomes. Go fuck glory holes in the wall for all I care. This is about love and family. It's about *my husband* lying to my face for over a year, not believing in my love for him."

She thundered toward me; her conviction trapping the breath in my lungs.

"A year ago, I believed in you, in us. I told you what I did. How I murdered a man to save those girls. I didn't hide from my truth, no matter how damning it was. You could have told me then about the son you left behind, and every day since. But you didn't. Your silence only damned our love too."

She slid her feet into her flip-flops by Silas's bed. "I tell you what. If you think sex will fix this, you two have at it. Suck some cocks. Fuck some asses. Have at each other all you want because I'm not available for dicks anymore."

She pushed past me, storming out the back door and letting the screened one slam behind her.

"Dude, I know you love her," Silas said, "more than me. But I'd beat the ever-livin' shit out of you for hurtin' her if I could. Lucky for you, you got fifty pounds of muscle on me and I ain't stupid enough to try."

"You win anyway, Silas. She came to you."

"I don't want to win her, dude. She had nowhere else to go. And she loves you. I ain't ever seen a couple so in love as you two. But you got a fucked-up idea of honesty." He sat back on his bed, completely right.

I couldn't hate him or a word out of his candid mouth. "I was afraid I'd lose her. And then... I was afraid I'd hurt her."

"Yeah? Well, how'd that work out for you? For her?"

My sight fell to the floor; all I saw was ruin. "I destroyed our life, our family, our marriage."

"Look, I know her too, longer than you have. For every ounce of badass and beautiful in Charlie Girl, she has the biggest heart and a ton of forgiveness. You just need to stay on your knees till you earn it."

I turned on my heels to try. I was halfway down the stairs of Silas's deck, surprised that Charlie didn't take our cart since I left the key in it.

"Does the threesome offer still stand?" Silas had followed, shouting out from behind the screened door with nothing but amusement in his voice. Like he wanted me to feel better. Like he knew it would be okay. Someday.

I hoped he was right. Calling out over my shoulder, "I'll do anything for her." Even that.

"Me too. Y'all just lemme know."

But sex was the last thing on my mind. Charlie wasn't walking on the sandy road home. I saw no trace of her, not even when I got there. But something deep inside told me while I spun the platinum wedding band on my finger...

We will survive this.

CHAPTER TEN

DANIEL

APRIL. **_Six months before…_**

Caroline kicked in her infant rocker while Duke reached, fascinated by the toy hanging over his. The sandwich in my hand was half gone, so was my hope.

Beep-beep. The door to the garage opened. Seconds later, she appeared in the doorway of the kitchen looking like a platoon no man would want to fight.

"I don't want to argue with you," she said, "but I want answers. And I better not smell a whiff of another lie from you."

"Okay." I set the sandwich down on the plate. "Go ahead."

"What's his name?"

"Keats Flynn Sampson."

"After your favorite poet and twin brother who died?" The register of her voice echoed my pain.

"Yes, just to lure me in and torment me, I suppose."

"Do you have pictures of him?"

"Yes. One. I had a private investigator take it. I used to keep it in my wash bag, but I hid it in some boots, afraid you'd find it when we traveled and figure it out. And I've seen a few online. Since Nikki got famous on that reality show, paps snapped her with him outside a grocery store a couple of years back."

"Does he look like you?"

"Yes. He has my hair, my chin, my nose."

"When's his birthday?"

"He turned eleven this April fifteenth."

She didn't move from the doorway. "What's the arrangement with Nikki?"

"I gave her one million pounds up front, one million in a trust for him when he turns eighteen, and two hundred and fifty thousand a year for them until he does. She signed an NDA for complete silence."

"Does he know about you?"

"I have no idea what she's told him. That's the part I fear. I don't trust her."

"Well, trust her or not, it's the right thing to do. That boy has a right to know his father. And you've got a responsibility to have a relationship with him as much as she will allow."

"I agree. It's all I ever wanted."

She crossed the room, nearing me and the twins. "Can we sue for visitation rights for you?"

"What?" Shock pushed me back from the table. "You'd be willing to do that?"

"Yes. If she won't amicably agree to it." Her hands reached, unsnapping Caroline from the seat, lifting her up to kiss her cheek. "This isn't about us fighting adults. It's about an innocent child. He's the brother to my kids, the son to my husband, and a sweet boy who deserves better than bullshit NDAs and pathetic egos."

Her hand caressed over Duke's peach fuzz. "Help me with him," she said. I stood up and unsnapped Duke, lifting him up to rest in her other arm.

"I'm not afraid of Nikki Sampson or the truth," she said. "I don't care if the threesome or false accusation gets out. You'll have to face it because I'm done being afraid of anything. And I'm done with the lies too. So, let's fix this and do the right thing now."

My lungs filled with hope, overwhelmed by her. "So you forgive me?"

"Go ahead and hold your breath 'til you're blue in the face on that one."

Nuzzling her nose into Duke's hair, she inhaled his smell and stood quiet for a moment before looking back at me. Like holding our children in her arms changed something in her.

"I'm a fighter, Daniel. That means I fight for my family too. But give me time. I don't know what's on the other side of this because I'm so angry with you. And we'll have to figure out how to do this with this virus out there. But yes, I support whatever we need to do for"—she swallowed hard, eyes piercing me—"for your other son."

"Can I hug you?" Not knowing what else to say, it's all I felt.

"Once," she answered, not smiling. "Can I knee you in the balls when you do?"

"Yes." Believing she would, I embraced my world, humbly burying my nose in her vanilla strands. "Thank you. Not for the forgiveness I must earn. But for supporting Keats. Every time I hold Duke or Caroline, I grieve for him, what he's missed."

"I bet." Her body held stiff in my arms.

This wasn't going to be instant. I would live hard over this for a long time. "Should I sleep in the guest room?"

"No." She pulled away from me, our babies content in her arms. "You need to lay right next to me so I can contemplate putting a pillow over your damn face in your sleep." Her feet turned and aimed toward the laundry room.

"If I do all the washing, will you not kill me?"

"That's a start," she said over her shoulder.

CHAPTER ELEVEN

CHARLIE

MAY. ***Five months before...***

They split the skin over my knuckles. Punching with no wraps on my hands, the leather mitts made for boxing drills returned the punishment with each blow I delivered, ripping my bare flesh. I loved it, needed it.

"Go again." Scarlett wore the mitts, turning them toward the ground.

I liked Scarlett. A lot. When HGR Security sent a list of potential guards for our house, I hand-picked her. Impressed with her MMA rank, I liked Scarlett even more on her first day.

"It's about time I work for a woman," Scarlett had said with a firm handshake. "I promise; I'll do everything I can to keep your family safe."

Standing in our home gym with her now, I ran the combo again. My brutal right uppercut forced Scarlett to brace for it. Then I punched another rapid-fire uppercut into the mitt before switching to my left jab, my left hook bombing next.

"Full speed," Scarlett commanded.

My right foot struck high above my hip, kicking the mitt before I spun around, landing a final hammer backfist from my right.

"Good." Scarlett tapped the mitts together before she resumed fighting stance. "Again."

This was my favorite combo. The blood dripping from my fingers delighted me too. My black hand wraps lay like militant ribbons on the gym floor. I didn't want their protection. Not today. Not this past month.

If I wasn't seeking the solace of holding my babies, I was fighting. Running daily drills with Scarlett was the only other contact I had with human flesh.

Because I wasn't touching Daniel. Or hugging him. Or really talking to him. Hell, some days, I could barely look at him.

The first week, I woke up wanting to hurt something like I did. Someone had tried to kill me. And I knew... a threat was still out there. This wasn't done.

And now my husband had lied to me.

Daniel's betrayal knocked me against the ropes, but after a month, I was back with a vengeance. My bare feet shuffling on the rubber floor. Sweat sliding down my furious flesh. It formed drops beside the boxing gloves I wouldn't wear either.

I didn't feel pain. Not the searing hot needles shocking through my torn flesh. No. I only felt release. The drug for a fight found me seeking the one thing I could safely annihilate with no consequence.

Those poor punching mitts? They didn't stand a chance.

And Scarlett holding them? She disappeared from my vision sometimes, drilling this pugilistic dance such that neither of us thought about it. We just sparred, understanding the other with few words exchanged.

Stopping for a swig of water, I glanced at the baby monitor on the bench.

Daniel was reading to the twins. Propped up on his elbow on the floor, he gave the best show, adding his own dramatic twist to *Winnie the Pooh*.

Caroline sat up, rapt against him. His voice and animated faces were the most dazzling spectacle for her. Duke lay down beside him, content to play with Daniel's beard.

It was adorable sights like this that turned down the burn in my heart. I knew it would be this way. That my solar flare of fury would eventually diminish to merely a bonfire, then to a hearth of scorching logs, to maybe a burning candle dripping hot wax over his beautiful, lying flesh.

Maybe. Maybe not.

Because the questions, the images, they kept pounding my mind.

Scarlett raised the mitts to her forehead height, slightly angled inward, signaling to me to run the punches.

I put down the water bottle before my bare knuckles took to the mitts again. The memory returned with the hits —how the second I met Daniel in Madrid at the gun club, my instinct warned that he was hiding something.

And I'd known it for over a year. But this? The quadruple assault of what Daniel did?

Punch. He had a threesome.

Punch. He was accused of rape.

Punch. He has another son.

Punch. He abandoned him.

Was there enough fight in my heart to defeat this? With each strike of my bleeding fists, I knew... Daniel wasn't a rapist... but he was a liar.

Truth was, I remembered the few times he almost told me, but *I* stopped him.

Maybe I didn't want to know.

Scarlett darted left. My footwork followed, the targets not evading my violence.

Maybe I already knew. At least that Daniel had been in a threesome? Yes. That dish on the delicious Daniel Pierce menu I suspected a few had ordered over the years.

He mentioned hours of it. Ones I could imagine of all the pussy eating, fucking, and cock sucking he desired. The vision of it? How his face must have reflected lewd delight with the orgasm he shot into Nikki. And another woman? How many times?

Was I jealous?

Scarlett shuffled again, turning her mitts perpendicular at her eye height. Like she could read my mind. Like she knew what my body needed right then.

A flurry of my hooks mauled the mitts, fists forcing the truth out.

Yes. I was jealous—not a familiar emotion. But what bothered me more? That he had such wanton adventures? Or that I had none?

That I never had the chance.

The reason why?

That's where the pain came from. Blood caked into the web of my fisted fingers; fresh drops trailing down my hands; that wasn't what hurt. So. Fucking. Much.

What pain gripped my neck so tight? A hard swallow I forced down, fighting the next thought?

When I was twenty-seven, I was a Marine, in a war and shot three times. I tried to protect two girls, to free them from their abuser.

Sex was so far from my mind. It was only there, in rushed moments with Kai, my first husband. We tried to keep the war outside the bedroom door at bay long enough for us to have some pleasure, some peace before we were thrust back into a violent reality. A reality Kai died for, and one I almost did too.

Scarlett lunged, mitts down, asking for my most brutal punch—the right uppercut.

Contracting my core, pivoting on the ball of my right foot, turning my right hip with glute flexed, I dipped my right shoulder, my bicep bracing for every muscle in my body exploding up through my right fist into the mitt and...

Boom! My uppercut knocked Scarlett back two steps, feet faltering.

Scarlett re-set while my mind wouldn't stop either. Reasoning...

When Daniel was twenty-seven, he was a millionaire—an A-list celebrity hunk of hot man flesh with millions craving him, everyone loving him.

Apparently, sex was always on his mind. Days worshipped on sets. Nights of sin in hotel beds. Luxury and lust surrounding him. What did he ever sacrifice? Did he even suffer over his first son?

That's what hurts so much. He ran from his consequence, his child, while you stood up for two girls, willing to die for them.

Fuck, that was a seductive logic—a judgment, a resentment that could kill my heart if I let it.

I dropped my fists. "I'm done." My lungs heaved from the fight, fighting that last thought with everything.

It wasn't fair. None of this was.

"Sympathy for the Devil" by The Rolling Stones crooned with melodic angst. That ring tone on my phone made me grin.

I high-fived Scarlett, "Thanks. I gotta get this," before I answered the call. "Your timing is spooky."

"That means it's spot on." Anders laughed back. "From Copenhagen to the Carolinas, I'm a fucking genius. What's going on?"

I chatted with Anders while I nodded "thanks" again to Scarlett, watching her sanitize and hang up the mitts before she quietly left the room.

Updates about life during lockdown took minutes of our chat. Anders, his wife Maja, and their kids were like family to me. We met on the set of *Fated,* my first job with HGR, and then we worked together again on *The Druid* with Daniel. We were bonded for life, texting pictures of the kids, calling to catch up.

When I got to the lie, the betrayal that Daniel exposed last month, it silenced Anders's usual loud mouth.

He finally spoke. "Can you forgive him?"

"My head and heart are battling that out."

"Ha! That's a fight you'll win. You'll forgive him long before he forgives himself."

I considered the bleeding cuts on my knuckles, the crimson smears down my hands. "What makes you so sure?"

"Because I know you. Your karma and all that wise shite you say. What's that saying you don't shut up about? 'Holding onto anger is like drinking poison and expecting the other person to die.' You used to say that about Afghanistan, about your PTSD. What's different now? Staying angry at him will only hurt you and the kids."

I glanced back at the monitor. Daniel was absent from the screen. Duke was sleeping in the crib. Caroline was playing with her toes beside him, completely happy to never rest again. I smiled. *Such your daughter*.

"I feel like I don't know him anymore," I confessed. "When someone lies to you like this, trust is gone. Nothing is certain, just crazy-making questions that leave you walking a tight-rope, waiting for the next fall."

"You *do* know him." A clatter hit my ear. "Hang on," Anders murmured before shouting at Erikson to keep it down. "Just a minute." I could hear him moving through the house, the buzz of kids in the background growing dim.

"I can't wait to get our kids together," I said. "I want to curl up and read the entire Aesop's fables to them."

It made me smile. I imagined our kids together one day soon. And I could imagine Anders now, scurrying to hide from his so he could drop more truth bombs on me.

A door closing clicked before he said, "Now, I can speak freely and school your stubborn arse."

I stood in front of the floor-to-ceiling mirrors, not seeing my reflection, only imagining Anders's long red beard smiling with his crude candor.

"You do know him, Charlie. Daniel is me. Like me now and more in love with his wife and kids than his own damn life. And living with a long list of mistakes from a selfish prat of a past. I fucked up too you know."

"Not like this."

"Yes, almost exactly like this."

That shocked me. "What do you mean?" I always teased Anders about being a devil. Never did I suspect his teddy-bear heart actually acted upon it. "You have a secret son somewhere?"

"Or a daughter. No one has told me otherwise but fuck

all do I know. I just know how much I fucked around. Just like Daniel. That's our entitled life, kiddo. We're celebrity cunts through and through. We all go through a phase of being arrogant arseholes until life kicks our inflated egos down a notch or two."

"But you didn't lie to Maja about it."

"Worse. I told her."

That skipped a beat in my heart. Worse? Poor Maja. "What did you do?"

"The first year we were dating, I spent four months filming in Atlanta without her, and one night, I fucked up."

I didn't need to hear more. But Anders needed to confess it. "I was staying at the St. Regis. Three months there and having a lonely pity party. My pathetic ego needed a boost, so I stayed up late one night by the pool. Too many drinks in and then too easily swayed into going upstairs with another couple."

That dropped my jaw. And kept breaking my heart for Maja, how that must have devastated her.

Anders kept going. "I could've kept the secret. Maja never had to find out. But when I came home and saw her trusting brown eyes and tiny belly swelling with Erikson, I told her all. And we fought like hell to survive it."

Reconciling what Anders did against Daniel's crime—not the same, but not entirely different—I didn't know what to say.

"Maja forgave me faster than I thought she would. That's her big heart, like yours. Both you two, you're strong women. That's what it takes to suffer us, our egos and lifestyle, until we get our shite together."

A shuffle over my shoulder lifted my eyes, focusing on the reflection. Daniel stood in the doorway, his stare on my shredded knuckles.

"Thanks for telling me." I talked to Anders with my gaze on the man who hurt me the most.

"I told you because whatever punishment you give him; it'll pale to how he'll punish himself. Trust me. I was there. That man has loved you from the second he laid his eyes on you. Women over the world fall at his feet, but he's on his knees for you. This will only make you stronger"—his roar made me chuckle—"if that's even fucking possible."

"I love you." I missed him, so much. "You fuckin' devil." Now I knew… that was a bit true of him; of everyone, I was learning.

"Love you too, you stubborn fuck."

The call ended. Daniel closed the distance between us. "How's Anders?"

"A sweet devil as usual."

His chin nodded to my fists. "Need some ice?"

"No," I said. He reached out, his gentle hand landing on my bare, sweaty shoulder. I flinched, pulling away. "Daniel, don't."

That wounded him. I could tell. The pain in his eyes, in the reflection. Fuck. I couldn't stand that either. The anger? The separation? Both hurt like hell.

The energy to keep fighting this; it fell to the floor along with the last drops of blood from my fists.

I turned around, facing him, reaching for his rejected hand. "I'm fighting for us, I promise. I don't do hate. I don't do drama. I'm trying to heal. But it doesn't—"

"I understand. I'm sorry I rushed you." The aqua in his eyes was so deep, pools of love for me with no bottom. He stepped back, giving me space. "I promise. It won't happen again."

This ache between us? This distance? It hurt worse than the lie.

More than most, I didn't take love for granted. I'd lost too much, buried too many, suffered years of the longest, lonely nights and dragging days of isolation.

I knew, if you get the gift of love, it wouldn't be perfect, but it should be cherished. Because it can be taken, in one phone call, in one bad decision—it burned behind my eyes —in one night by a bullet at a movie premiere.

Then the days you spent in petty fights, or weeks you iced the other out, you'd be a fool. You'd be selfish not to fight like hell for love.

Because that's what love takes—a humbling fight to keep it.

"Please let it happen again." I reached for his hand, holding it, the gesture with him so sacred to me, it rushed tears over my lashes, seeing them pool in his eyes too. "Don't stop fighting for us either, Daniel. Don't ever stop reaching for me. I promise, one day, I'll come back to you."

Fuck this. One month without him and I needed something. Wrapping my arms around him, hanging onto his back, I buried my face in his chest.

He squeezed me back, his words hushed, "I'll wait forever for you, Charlie," and he didn't let go.

A fight for love? That, I could probably win.

CHAPTER TWELVE

CHARLIE

JUNE. **_Four months before..._**

"Sup fucker." I beamed at Rob, taking the first duffle bag from his hand. It was obvious he'd lost a lot of strength. "You better just be bringing this damn luggage with you, and not that nasty virus."

"Shut up, boo, and take my bags." A dazzling grin lifted his face. "They're half full of the sex toys you and Daniel had me buy anyway."

Joaquin jumped down in the boat first. We offered our hands, helping Rob step over the side while Quincy spotted him from behind. There was no easy way to do this. Rob was still too big for us to lift and lower onto the boat.

The landing winced Rob's face. And hurt me too. *He almost died for you. Dammit. Don't cry.* My face twisted, holding it back.

His right arm hooked around me while his left hung slack. "Don't, boo. It's not a good look on you." The bullet hit through that side, obviously hurting him to move it. I knew that ache too.

"I love you so much, mi primo," I said, mindful not to grab his back where he was still healing.

His kiss landed on the top of my head. "Love you too, mi prima."

I broke from his embrace, wiping tears away before reaching for Joaquin. "Hola, hermoso." I kissed his handsome cheeks.

He returned them. "Hola, bella."

"Don't forget this, Charlie Girl," Quincy called out from the dock, handing me a box full of toilet paper, baby wipes and diapers. "They're a hot commodity 'round here. Use em' wisely."

"Well, that's what wash rags and boiling water are for," I replied. I couldn't believe the scarcity of products, but that was the least of my worries. "We'll make do with what we got."

Quincy started laughing, lighting a Newport. "Got that right." He echoed our Southern mentality. "See ya next weekend for a refill." I slapped his hand in gratitude and turned to untie the boat.

"Get me home," Rob called out, slowly lowering himself onto the bench in the bow.

"Home is Brooklyn." I turned the engine over, always pausing with praise at its deep roar.

"Not in this virus shit it's not." Rob spoke loud enough for us to hear. "We've been quarantined in my apartment for months. Joaquin was going to swim back to Madrid if I didn't get us out of there."

"We had to get you stronger, mi amor," Joaquin said.

I put the throttle down, going slow. I didn't want to

jostle Rob. Besides, we had lots to catch up on. It wasn't two minutes into our trip before I updated them on Daniel's lie.

"I'm surprised he doesn't have more offspring," Rob said. "That hot ass man must've had all kinds of pussy thrown at him over the years. That's what you married, boo. Better accept it."

"Sixty-one pussies to be exact." We were going so slow we could easily talk over the engine.

"Only sixty-one?" Rob looked shocked. "I would've scored into the hundreds if I looked like that."

"Well, you tried." Joaquin gave him a kiss and pat on the knee.

"I stopped at four with you, and now I'm ruined forever"—Rob rested his head on Joaquin's shoulder—"in love and all that shit."

"It's not the number that bothers me so much," I said. "Hell, if I hadn't been married so young and in the Marines, maybe I would've fucked my way into the twenties myself."

I steered the boat right, then gently took the quick left, glancing over. Rob winced again at the turn. It made me do the same at his pain.

"It's the lie, y'all," I said. "He should've told me a long time ago."

"I get that, Captain." Rob held my eyes when I looked his way at that official title for me. "But we all got a painful past that can be hard to share."

He raised his eyebrow. We knew. The Marines. Afghanistan. Paksima and Esin, the two girls. How I killed a man to protect them. How I planned it. And how I was forced to tell Daniel my secret. It wasn't really my choice.

"Bella, he loves you more than I've ever seen a man love a woman," Joaquin added. "The terror in his eyes that night at the hospital after the shooting. What he felt for you, for the twins? It took three men to drag him away from you. He fought them all, yelling 'no'. He wouldn't leave your side. There is no question. He deserves a chance."

I closed my eyes for a quick second. The water before us opened wide and so did my heart. I could only imagine what Daniel suffered that night and the months that followed. And what Joaquin had endured too, worried for Rob.

"How long you gonna keep him in the doghouse?" Rob asked.

"He's not in the doghouse."

"Yeah, but you're not fucking him right now, that I can tell." Rob knew my sexless past all too well, must've smelled it on me.

"We'll see," I said. "Guess I gotta put my big girl panties on for this. We're meeting his son and the mom in a couple months. She wants to drive up here from Florida and come out to visit."

"Oh! I want front row seats for that show!" Rob's favorite pastime—teasing me. "I'm gonna pop some corn and pour a glass of Prosecco for that shit—Nikki Sampson meets Charlie Ravenel. Damn, bitch." Rob's face lit up like fucking Broadway lights. "DRAMA!" He sang out.

Joaquin laughed, imagining the spectacle too.

"There's no fucking drama." I shook my head. Damn, I'd missed them. "Y'all know me. I won't make an ass of myself over any man. Besides, there's a little boy caught in this mess, and I'll protect him from it."

"Speaking of"—Joaquin dipped his hand in the water when I turned again—"what's your current security protocol with HGR?"

Leave it to Joaquin to focus on the job.

"There's a detail of two on the house," I answered. "Scarlett covers day. Curtis covers night."

"They're out of the Atlanta office?" Joaquin asked.

"Yep, they know the terrain. Curtis worked *Death March* for years outside Atlanta. Scarlett's kinda new but has great instincts. HGR recruited her off the MMA circuit."

Joaquin nodded, agreeing with the plan. "Any updates from the FBI?"

"Nope," I answered. "It's like this virus has stopped the world. Who knows for how long though?"

"Not long enough." Joaquin's face was stone. "You know better, bella. We can't rule out any threats. The cold trail that shooter left is more suspicious than if he had left a mountain of guilty evidence."

"Tell me about it." That worry kept me awake every night. "Talk about the calm before the storm."

Was someone still out there, wanting us dead? Were we really free from the threat, or would it wash up on our shores again one day? Though I refused to live afraid anymore, a premonition remained.

That's why I took no chances.

We had security around the clock, my gun hidden under the nightstand, and a secluded location the press and fans didn't know about. All tactical advantages I planned to keep.

But Rob and Joaquin's days covering me and Daniel were over. They came back to Daufuskie to get away from the crowds, to enjoy their condo down the road from our house.

"Wait! Wait!" Rob lowered his sunglasses, gawking over the bow low in the water minutes later. "Eye candy—ten o'clock."

I rolled my eyes. Silas stood on his dock, waiting for us. Even with a mask on his face, I had to admit, all else glistened hot with his perpetual tan body that knew no shirt. And his blond hair fell even longer without anyone visiting the island to give us haircuts.

I felt it—my cheeks flushing while heat surged between my thighs remembering Silas's shameless okay to a threesome with me and Daniel. Yes, I knew Silas wanted me, but that idea was next level. Never could I. I only loved Daniel, no matter how pissed I was.

Throwing the throttle in reverse, I slowed our approach. I was actually thankful Silas was here for me, yet again. We needed his help getting Rob and all their bags out of the boat.

After a lot of effort and a few jokes, we pulled away from his house, puttering down the familiar lane in my golf cart... toward Bloody Point Beach.

The historic name for my home always haunted me. It came from the blood spilled on the beach during a battle between the indigenous tribe and English colonizers. Then with the evil slavery and cruel segregation that had plagued this area for centuries, it was a brutal yet fitting description.

Even to this day, something about the name—Bloody Point Beach—it taunted me like a prophecy.

"Take us to our godbabies!" Rob shouted out making me turn for my house instead of toward their condo.

Ten minutes later, after both gave Daniel back-slapping hugs, Rob held Caroline while Joaquin held Duke.

Rob kicked his feet up on the upholstered ottoman. "Oh, I'm in heaven with my babies"— kissing Caroline's forehead —"and I'm moving back in."

"I think they have enough on their hands, mi amor."

Joaquin tickled his fingertip across Duke's cheek, making him smile.

"Yeah, besides," Rob said, "you'd keep us awake again with your loud-ass sex." He winked at a sheepish Daniel. "Eventually."

Daniel shook his head, eyes down to the floor in shame, saying nothing.

"She can't stay mad forever, man," Rob said to him. "She loves that D too much. Remember? And I brought an entire sex store in one of those duffle bags for you two, so have at it with some kinky makeup fucks."

Daniel looked up at me with a hopeful smile.

"All right, fucker." I got up to warm some bottles. "Feed your godbabies and then get your asses home. You've had a long trip and need to rest."

One hour later, they left, and Daniel stood in the nursery, watching me bounce Caroline to sleep in my arms. Duke was already out.

"I guess everyone will know, yeah?" Daniel asked. "They'll all know how I lied to you."

"Some will. We told my family. Yours already knew. And the relief in your mother's voice that I finally did and didn't leave you made me want to hug her from across the ocean. You burdened your family for too long keeping that secret." I lay Caroline down to sleep. "But most won't care."

Caressing my hand over Caroline's curls, then over Duke's fuzz, I said, "Besides, this is about Keats. Focus on him."

"I'd like to focus on how to earn my wife's forgiveness too."

I had to give him that. He wasn't running from it. He swam in the deep end of remorse until his fingertips became lonely raisins. I took his hand, "Come with me."

"Are we playing with the bag of toys Rob brought?" If he wasn't apologizing lately, he joked, trying anything to stay connected.

"No." I led him down the hall to our bedroom. "We're not fucking."

We kicked off our flip-flops and climbed onto the bed. I glanced at his bare feet. Was it possible for a man to have sexy feet? Put money on "hell yes" because Daniel Pierce had a beautiful pair. Every part of him seduced me, making it hard to stay celibate.

I needed something more with him than the hugs I allowed this past month. But first, I had to know. "Are you sure you didn't hurt Nikki or any other woman?" We faced each other, heads on pillows.

"I'm sure. I watched that video three times. So did my solicitor. So did an independent expert he hired, a woman. None of us could see how it was anything but consensual." He paused; his forehead crinkled with concern. "Do you want to watch it? I can get it for you if it helps you to believe me."

"I couldn't stand to watch it."

"I can't either. I just had to be sure."

"Tell me what's on it. Just the basics. I need facts, not my imagination anymore."

"You sure?"

"Yes. Tell me now, just once and no more."

He sighed. "We're not in the hotel room minutes before Nikki kneels, going down on me. Jodi was kissing me, helping get my pants down. I had a drunk dick. It took a while to work. Eventually, I had to lie down. Nikki climbed on top of me. Jodi was into her, sucking her tits, making it a good show for the camera and me so I finally came. They played for a long time with each other until I got hard again.

It was Jodi's turn. I was on top of her. Nikki sat on her face, and she was all over me too with her tits in mine. An hour later, I fell asleep, but Nikki started rubbing me off. She woke me up and climbed on top of me again, asking Jodi to stand in front of her. She ate her out while she fucked me. That was enough to make me come again and that was it. I slept and woke up to Nikki making plans for our life together, and I left as soon as I could."

The picture he painted across my mind? It sounded consensual. Three times or more over. And not as bad as I'd imagined. "Did you know Nikki before this?"

"I met her twice at clubs in passing."

"So, this wasn't about favors or coercion?"

"God, no. I'd never do that."

"I have to ask. I have to be sure."

"Okay." He reached for my hand. I let him. "I get it. Ask me anything."

"Are you sorry you did it?"

"How can I be?" He paused. "I didn't hurt her, and I have a beautiful son from it. My only regret is the last time I held him, that I ever let him go—it felt like when my twin brother died. I couldn't fucking breathe when she took him from my arms that last time. It's like I died too. That's why I must see him again. I won't make the same mistake."

"Okay." I rolled over. "I believe you."

He pulled the blanket at the foot of the bed over us before nestling behind me, wrapping his arm over me, and reaching for my hand. "I'd say 'sorry' again for hurting you, but it feels pathetic now."

"It is, so quit saying it for a while."

He lay quiet for a time before whispering in my ear, "I don't deserve you, Charlie Ravenel." It sounded pained, regret strangling his throat.

I turned over, offering him a kiss—our first in so long. A deep one with pain morphing into passion, changing our breath, melting my ice, my heart heating to him again. It made my body rise to him, a moan lulling from his throat at my desire, at my return to him.

But not yet.

"You do deserve me, Daniel Pierce." My lips dusted over his. "I'll always love you." I turned back, settling into his embrace. "And I almost forgive you."

CHAPTER THIRTEEN

DANIEL

OCTOBER. ***Now…***

"Wake up, dear."

A voice sounding like my mum pried my heavy eyelids open. Briny ocean air hit my senses before my gaze found focus.

Fran stood before me, her face twisting with concern.

I shook the sleep off my brain. "What time is it?"

My back muscles boycotted any movement. My legs weren't breaking the picket line either. I'd fallen asleep in the hard deck chair and my body was on strike.

"It's just before six, dear." She sat down next to me. "Has she phoned?"

"Where are the twins?" I reached for the phone in my back pocket, noticing my burnt-out cigar on the floor of the deck. Sleep must've finally taken me while I waited for Charlie's call.

Bloody lucky you didn't burn the deck down, Pierce.

"They're still asleep. I just checked," Fran answered. "Did she ring last night?"

The worry in her voice sickened me. I knew before checking. We slept so lightly with the babies, her ringtone, "Adore You", would've woken me.

I checked my almost dead phone anyway, and bloody hell... the screen mocked me. Empty.

My heart dropped two stories below to the ground under us. "No, she didn't." Wanting to slam the phone down, I rested it on my thigh instead.

Fran reached for my hand. "I'm worried, dear. She wouldn't do this, go this long without reaching out for her family. Something's wrong."

The hammer of my heart coursed terror through my veins. Fran was right. Charlie would've phoned. No matter what I did or how much I hurt her, she'd never abandon our children.

Something. No. Everything must be terribly wrong.

CHAPTER FOURTEEN

CHARLIE

Two Weeks by FKA twigs

JULY. **Three months before...**

"Don't do that Hollywood bullshit and walk with your gun pointed out in front of you." I positioned my arms down at a forty-five-degree angle, showing Daniel the safe way to hold the pistol. "You hold it at the ready, finger off the trigger. If you walk around with your gun out in front, it can get knocked from your hands or you could fire before you think."

Pop stood behind us at the indoor shooting range, cleaning his 9mm while I showed Daniel how to handle my .22 pistol.

"Do a quick peek around every corner before you enter a room," I said. "We have too many people in the home not to always be sure."

"Yes ma'am," Daniel replied, taking the empty gun I handed him.

"Okay. Now, tap 'n' rack it like I showed you."

He picked up the full magazine of bullets, tapping it into the bottom of the pistol before pulling back a quick rack of the slide.

"Good. Now one is ready in the chamber." The focus in his aqua eyes behind protective lenses impressed me. "I always leave one in there. That's another stupid thing they do for show—you don't have to rack the gun every time, wasting the round. It's in there; ready to fire."

"What about your other guns? Will you teach me those too?"

"Learn to use this .22 first. You've got fifteen chances in that magazine to hit your mark. The .380 gives me six stronger ones, but I only need one," I said, "because I don't miss."

Pop chuckled over my shoulder. It was true.

"Okay, GI Jane." Daniel kept charming me with that look in his eyes, like he wanted to fire his cock instead. "Any other orders?"

His flirting made me grin, but I refocused. "Travel these lanes and practice like I showed you. Use the front site, aligning the shot with the rear one. Empty the magazine, reload with the one in your pocket and do it again."

Taking several steps back, I pulled my earmuffs on and stood with Pop. We were the only ones here. Bill, Pop's old Navy buddy, opened the gun range just for us.

Bill was loyal, filling Daniel's ears with tales of how my dad taught me to shoot here. How he bet with other members on my shots until Bill stopped him. The wagers weren't fair. I never missed, especially with my dad breathing down my neck.

Wonder if somehow my dad knew it all along? That this lethal skill would save my life. At least once so far.

Shots exploded, jumping me out of the memory.

Daniel traveled the lanes, aiming at the silhouettes, going for center mass like I taught him. He did as instructed, holding the pistol down at the ready before lifting his arms and taking the shot.

When he was done, we brought the targets forward. Not half-bad for his first time with a real gun.

Bill joined us in the room, slapping Daniel on the back. "Y'all are gonna get that bastard if he comes for you again."

"No need." Daniel started loading the empty magazine with bullets. "He's dead."

"Yeah, but this ain't done." I leaned against the wall. The men looked at me, surprised by my prediction.

"Wasn't he just a crazy *White Flag* fan?" Bill asked.

"We may never know." Daniel clicked the full magazine back in. "I think Mason Hunt got that man to take the shot at Charlie. Mason wanted revenge against her. And now they just moved the prat to house arrest. His lawyer played the famous actor and COVID cards to get him out of prison."

"Imagine that," I sneered, "pretty, rich, White boy gets away with it. No fucking surprise."

"Got that right." Pop shared my sentiment. "They would've thrown my Black ass behind bars, but that White son-of-a-bitch is sittin' at home like the whole damn world is right now. That ain't justice."

"Nope. It's the usual corrupt racist bullshit," Bill said, looking over at me. "You think he'll try again? Get someone else to make an attempt on you two?"

"Don't know," I said. "But I ain't takin' any chances, and I ain't runnin' scared either." I nodded at Daniel. "Run it again, hot stuff."

Once Daniel finished, getting better each time, Bill

waved me over. He tapped my rifle case. "Why don't you take this beauty outside for ol' times' sake."

We loaded up our cases and walked down the hallway toward the side door to the outdoor range.

Daniel walked in front of me. Damn, his spectacular ass in those jeans. He wore a tight, white T-shirt too, using every weapon he had to lure me back.

Good God, his body could seduce a saint.

And this felt good. We were together again, laughing over the babies, holding each other at night. And sharing moments like this, as a team, as a couple.

But he had respected the last divide between us; he didn't make any moves on me.

Today though, he neared, smelling like a buffet of sex, arms wide, holding the heavy metal door open for me. "Ladies first." He grinned, knowing I hated that phrase, winding me up with eyes on my tits.

"Careful who you tease, Pierce." The energy crackled between us as I brushed against him to step outside. "I'm the one with lethal aim."

And oh, the touch of him. *Quit starving me, bitch.* My pussy stomped its foot while my libido agreed.

Steel targets stood in the field from twenty to eight hundred yards out. Bill grinned at Pop. "Whatcha wanna wager? I got a Benjamin that says she hits the eight hundred."

"Thought we ain't allowed to bet on her anymore," Pop said. "Besides, I ain't bettin' against my girl."

"I'll take that wager," Daniel called out. "One hundred says she misses."

Putting the muffs over my ears, I grinned at his taunt then tuned it out. I was trained for this. My mind could shift focus in a nanosecond. Dropping five shells into my vest pocket, I fixated on the targets, pulling the protective lenses resting on my head down over my eyes.

The close targets are too easy. Start at the three and go down the line to eight hundred yards.

Wrapping my hands around the familiar wood of the rifle, Daniel's comment about Mason and revenge ricocheted through my mind. *Where's the evil coming from now?* My instinct whispered. *This is your mission.*

I exhaled, loading the bolt action rifle. At twelve, this was the first gun I fired. Now? The weapon was another bone in my arm, adding over two more deadly feet to my wrath.

My mind traveled with the bullet, with every farther target I hit. I couldn't hear the *tink* of the far metal targets, but my scope confirmed it.

Then came eight hundred yards.

Through the scope, I checked the range flags for the wind, making adjustments. With an inhale, I focused the crosshairs. A shiver poured down my shoulders, radiating through my thighs, tingling to my fingertip over the warm trigger. *Exhale.* Like an omen was in my sight. *Pull.*

The shot traveled an inch left of the target. *Fuck, you missed.* Staring at the missed target, I sucked my teeth. *Next time, you better not.* I yanked the muffs off and turned to my audience.

"Damn." Bill slapped a hundred-dollar bill into Daniel's outstretched palm. "You're gonna need that, son. Better buy roses betting against your wife like that."

"Oh, I'm not betting against her," Daniel said. "I'm seducing her."

It worked.

Bill and Pop disappeared to the front parking lot to puff

cigars while we stayed inside, setting our gun cases on the bench outside the restrooms.

When Daniel turned to enter the Men's Room, I snatched him by his leather belt, pulling him into the Women's Room with me before slamming him hard against the wall. "I got a hundred that says I'm gonna get exactly what I'm aiming for, Pierce."

I needed this control, to let my body take over, to take back what I wanted—him, our love, our sex, our fucks, right now.

My lips grabbed for his, one hand snatching his curls, yanking his mouth to mine while my other hand kneaded his cock. Fuck, I was hungry for him. Our mouths collided in a hellfire of reunion, tongues and lips igniting a blaze, his erection surging in my grasp.

He ripped his lips away, "You're on, Ravenel," taking me like a rabid dog, fast and fierce, charging me back against the countertop.

Answering my aggression with his, he took my lips and then my neck with gentle bites until he released my moan. His impatient palms cupped my breasts, fingertips teasing my nipples under my T-shirt and bralette before he ripped both off of me, freeing my flesh for his taunting tongue. Trapping me there, he bent down and sucked my nipple, hard. It sent shivers through me, the urgency building. His muscles tensed under my clutch when he growled, taking the other next. I let him indulge, getting them dripping wet, until I was a slave to lust, my patience gone.

I pushed him back, my mouth watering at his cock surging past the waistband of his jeans.

"This is just the beginning of payback," I said, kicking off my cowboy boots before unzipping my jeans. The denim in my grasp fell to my ankles before I pulled a foot free.

Lifting my body to sit atop the counter, I spread my thighs wide open for him before pulling my black lace panties to the side. "Come fuck your wife, Daniel Pierce." I slipped two fingers inside and pumped them for his gaze. "Now."

"Yes, ma'am." He looked like a crazed animal watching my juicy show while he freed himself of his jeans and boxer briefs.

"Wait." God how I missed this sight. It kept my fingers smacking through my lust. "Take your shirt off. I want you naked and hard in front of me." His eyes didn't leave my pussy spread open for him while he quickly obeyed, his chest huffing like a mad dog on a chain. "Stand there and let me relish what belongs to me."

I played with my clit while my eyes devoured the commanding sight of him nude, every carved muscle on his massive frame tensing to pounce, his wide eyes and cock aimed at me. Fucking hell, he was bestial art.

"How bad do you want me, Daniel?"

He took his length into his choking grasp. With a few twisting jerks, "I want you this bad, Charlie," his fingertip swiped the early drops off his fat tip and offered it to his tongue. Eyes on me, with a shameless lick, he tasted himself.

His erotic submission shuddered down my spine to my pussy. The jolt. The heat of it. "Do that again for me." The first wave of my lust threatened to splash to the floor.

The practiced twists over his cock delivered the cream again. "Like this." He was loving it too. "I want to drink every drop of our fucks." The tip of his index finger lifted another bead to his mouth. He took it, grinning; eyes never leaving mine.

The tension, the delight, it coiled tight, ready to snap

my body. "Give me the rest, Daniel, as hard as you fucking can."

With three rapid steps, he was on me, his clutch jerking me to the edge with rough hands grabbing my hips, holding me suspended there.

"Is this what you're starving for?" Pressing my two glistening fingers to his lips, I offered them for his suck. "That's it." He answered with a moan, his gaze still devouring me. "Taste what you've been craving."

Once he cleaned my fingers, my grasp reached next, guiding his crown into my greedy sex. My other hand snatched the waves at the nape of his neck, pulling his mouth to mine. "Who do you want, Daniel?"

"You, Charlie." His words answered as his thick cock delivered the first brutal thrust, releasing a satisfied snarl from his throat. "You." And another one, lifting me off the counter. "I want to fuck my wife." And another. "I want to fuck your pussy so fucking hard."

We were magnetic. Bodies belonging together, aching when apart. The friction, the tension, the force pulling me to him, there was no resisting it. His gravity secured me to his world, wrapping me around him.

His soft, full lips parted; grunting "so good" with each delicious, savage pound into me. "Fuck, you feel so good," pressing his forehead to mine, his eyes glimmered, possessed, desperate with need.

There was no space between the hard countertop and his hard ramming cock, my every nerve screaming out, responding immediately to his return, my walls drenching him from base to tip. Good God, I was home again.

"Say it again, Daniel." His body, his voice, he was going to make me come so hard, so fast. "Say what you want."

I wanted this. The ache only he could satisfy. It healed

me more, more than pushing him away. His touch. His love. It faded the bruises of betrayal. He was the only remedy to my pain.

He bent his knees, curving his shoulders, abs straining, rasping his lips over hers. "I want to love you." Another thrust of his hips. "I want to fuck you." And another. "Always." I grabbed his back, steadying myself and my quaking thighs. His response to me, so sure, so hard, hitting that exquisite spot deep inside. "Jesus, Charlie. Only you, so fucking much."

I gripped his slick, massive base, not able to wrap around but squeezing it tight, feeling it jerk in my grasp. "Whose cock is this, Daniel?"

The hinge of his jaw clenched. He groaned, looking down at my possession. "Yours."

Wrapping my legs around him tight, I scratched at the hard flexing flesh of his ass. Sixty other women? One other man? No, he was mine now. No one could take him away. With the strength in my quads I lifted up, "That's right," and slammed my pussy back down his shaft, "Motherfucker, you're mine."

"Oh, fuck!" He huffed at my power, lifting me up again. "Yes." Slamming me back down again. "Yes, I am." And again. "Just like this."

I squeezed tighter, my hips circling with my syrupy ache over his mass, "You want to share me, Daniel?" My fingers pulled tight through his waves.

He snarled, "Never," his grip making sweet bruises on my hips.

"You'll let another man fuck me?" I rolled my hips, grinding over him, sparking my clit to burst.

He grabbed my hair. "I'll fucking kill him."

"Then make me yours again." The violent shakes in my

body, in my thighs, it was too late, I always was. "Make me fucking come for you."

That wasn't a demand. He had me there, biting his shoulder, muffling my cry into his flesh, moaning at the spasm while I came, the pleasure flooding me. The reunion with his body shook mine, sweating, clinging to my world, dripping down his thighs and to the floor.

"Oh fuck!" He stumbled back, holding up the weight of our climax as it crashed over us, his cock buried deep and pulsing inside me. "Yes, babe. Yes." He went rigid, locking up for a second before he stepped us back toward the countertop. Setting me down, he buried me under kisses before nuzzling his face against mine. "Charlie, I swear. I'll never hurt you again."

"Don't bet against us again." I cradled his jaw, lifting his gaze to mine. "No matter what, Daniel, believe in us."

"I know, babe. I do." He kissed my lips, sealing the promise. Pulling back, he held my cheeks. "From the moment I met you, it humbled me how incredible you are. I wanted to be worth you and that's made me a better man. I'm just so sorry it took me this bloody long to do it."

"And it took me this long to find you, so don't make me lose you again." I caressed his ass, feeling the welts I left on his flesh. "We'll never be perfect, but we'll always be together."

He nodded, lips reaching for mine like he wasn't ready to let me go, our kiss as much of a reunion as our fuck. God, how I could stay here forever, joined with him, but time returned. "We better get dressed before someone knocks on that door."

"This isn't done." His body left mine. "I owe you more than this. I want to make up for everything." Reaching down for his jeans and briefs, he put them back on, tucking in his cock that hadn't limped yet. "And I know how."

I hopped off the counter, intrigued. Getting myself decent again, "What do you have in mind?" My pussy still tingled, craving five more rounds with him.

"I've shared my secret. Now, you have all my life." His hands took my cheeks again, swearing it to my eyes, "It's time I share all my body too."

What he meant by that kept my cheeks flushed, curious as we made our way out of the restroom, down the hall, through the building to the front door.

"Y'all settle the score in there?" Pop wore a knowing grin as we walked across the parking lot, out of breath, disheveled hair, and clothes... and holding hands.

I answered with a satisfied smile, "He'll never bet against me again."

CHAPTER FIFTEEN

CHARLIE

JULY. ***Three months before…***

Bits of banana speckled my face. Caroline giggled from her highchair, blowing a food-filled raspberry at me. I sat next to her, turning away, hiding my laugh and trying not to encourage her.

"You taught her this, didn't you?"

"I don't know what you're talking about." Daniel wore a guilty grin feeding Duke. "Besides, you like bananas."

"Uh-huh. Then why are you getting out of the line of fire?"

He was starting to unstrap Duke from his chair, ending his lunch. That made Duke cry out, protesting.

"Quieres más?" I asked Duke, putting my fingers to my mouth, using the "more" hand sign. Duke slapped his hand against his lips, answering me. "He's still hungry," I informed Daniel.

"How many languages are we going to use in this house?"

"As many as we can."

"You're certainly teaching me all the naughty Spanish words." His smile grew, giving more banana slices to Duke who smashed them in his tiny grasp.

The front doorbell chimed.

I jumped up, "I'll get it," darting to answer it. Through the beveled glass, I recognized Silas.

The sight of him made me kinda nervous... and turned on. Ignoring it, I opened the door. "Hey, what's up?"

He spoke through his mask. "This just came off the ferry from a courier for you."

The rectangular box in his hand stopped my heart. Jeremy, my boss, sends those special delivery from the HGR London office. The last one contained the stalking note to Kierra, the one that started this beautiful, terrifying journey I'd been on since.

"Thanks." Reluctantly, I took it. "Wanna come in for lunch?"

Tugging his hand through his long strands; he always did that around me. His hazel eyes told me he was smiling at me too, even though his lips were hidden. "Nah, better keep y'all safe," he said. "I've been off this island too much lately."

Could he be any sweeter? "Okay. Maybe come by this afternoon. We're going out on the beach. Rob and Joaquin are coming too. You can sit downwind from us for a few beers."

"Sounds good," he said before turning to leave.

I closed the front door, dread filling every cell of my body.

Daniel met my "oh shit" gaze when I walked into the kitchen. "What is it?"

"Not good." I ripped the perforated ribbon. "It's from Jeremy."

Daniel stood up, joining me. We read the note taped to the top of a document envelope inside.

Ring me before you open this.
J

"Can you hand me a pair of gloves from under the sink, please?" I asked Daniel while I tapped my phone screen.

A few seconds later, Jeremy was on the other end. "Mother Ravenel, how's life over there?"

"We're hanging in there," I said. "How 'bout y'all?"

"We're fine. We were away in Highmoor for four months. We're back in London now."

"Glad y'all are okay. I just got your delivery though. You and your damn boxes. I'm afraid to open it." I put the phone on speaker so Daniel could hear too.

"Sorry, but I had to get this to you," Jeremy replied. "Somehow it got lost in our mailroom and it's been sitting under packages for months because of isolation. I just found it now that I'm back in the office, sorting through the pile."

We listened while I snapped on the gloves Daniel handed me, his furrowed brow holding enough worry for us both.

Jeremy continued, "It came addressed to you care of HGR. The mailing label is dated December seventeenth, last year. The day after the premiere and shooting. I didn't open it. I wanted to get it to you immediately. I have a feeling about it. I'm sure you do too."

A feeling? Hell, a Mack truck just ran over my body, hit reverse, and did it again, squealing the tires for extra effect.

"I need to open this outside with a mask on." I turned to Daniel. "We need Fran to watch the twins."

He ran upstairs to fetch her while I spoke to Jeremy. "Hold tight, boss." Grabbing a mask off the counter, I took the box outside, setting it down. I ran back inside for my phone and a knife, just in time for Fran and Daniel to join me.

Fran sat with the twins while we went outside, standing over the box like it was an alligator about to pull us under in a death spiral.

Daniel held my phone while I took the box a few feet away. Slowly, I sliced the cardboard open at its seam instead of the clear tape used to seal it. If there were prints on the tape, I wouldn't cut through them.

You know what this is. My instinct stood beside me. *It's here.*

Reaching into the envelope, I pulled out a stack of white copy papers bound with a black binder clip. The top page showed the picture of me passed out in Daniel's arms last spring. The word "TARGET" was scrawled over the image in red marker.

I flipped to the next page—another picture—Daniel and Mason in Menorca where we filmed episodes for season two of *The Druid*. It was the two of them drinking at a rooftop bar. A fan had posted the image on Instagram, dropping a pin on our location.

"That was a year ago." Daniel watched over my shoulder. "The first day we shot there."

My instinct whispered, *"Psst, that was also two days before you felt someone in the darkness, watching you outside your hotel."*

"What is it?" Jeremy's voice called out from the phone speaker.

"It's a bunch of photos printed from social media of me and Daniel. The word 'target' is written on each one," I said, thumbing through the stack.

It documented our entire past year. Every single shot a person could get of us in public, all except for anything from here on Daufuskie.

Told you. Instinct patted my shoulder. *All this time, you knew it.*

But when I got to the last photo, shock punched me, making me gasp while Daniel exclaimed, "Bloody hell!"

It was last December, taken from the underground parking garage of the hotel where we'd stayed in Manhattan. In the photo, Daniel's holding my hand, walking with me from our car to the hotel's door, my pregnant belly obvious under my fitted dress.

That moment was twenty-four hours before someone tried to kill me, hitting Rob instead. The big red X marked over my expectant belly made my stomach lurch.

He was right there... and you didn't sense him. You let your guard down, Charlie Girl, and he got that close.

"What is it?" The uncharacteristic fear in Jeremy's voice only made me sicker.

Daniel described the image to him while I put the stack back in the envelope, studying the address label before returning the envelope into the box.

Snapping the latex gloves off, I took off the mask. "I'm calling Agent Cooper to have someone pick this up for analysis."

Jeremy added, "Maybe Jenkins printed that last one from his hotel's printer in New York? Maybe he had someone at the hotel send it the day after, yeah? The FBI could go back and find something."

"I don't think so, boss," I said. Apparently, Jeremy didn't

read the mailing slip too closely before rushing the package to me. "It wasn't mailed from New York. It was mailed from Richmond, Virginia... the day after the shooting."

Both men fell silent while I spoke aloud the new terror. "The shooter wasn't a lone wolf."

CHAPTER SIXTEEN

CHARLIE

JULY. ***Three months before...***

This wouldn't ruin my day. It's not like I didn't know all along that the shooter didn't act alone. This evidence only validated my instinct, like a twisted present wrapped in a bloody bow.

Why send photos though? What was someone trying to say? Was it a triumph, a trail, or a trick?

I left a voicemail for Agent Cooper who called back minutes later. Rubbing sunscreen in while we spoke, we shared suspicions, hoping to glean answers from the package.

Cooper said she'd send an agent to meet me at the Hilton Head dock tomorrow to retrieve the evidence.

I dropped my phone on the bed once that business was settled.

Fuck you, asshole. I'm still alive. And as long as I am, like hell if I ain't gonna enjoy it.

Focusing on my family, with each act defying fear, I was getting better at leaving worry behind.

But when I joined everyone outside reclining under a beach tent with the twins, they were talking about the package. The nearest family was a quarter mile away. No one could overhear our conversation.

"Let's just drop it, y'all"—my beach bag dropped next to Daniel for emphasis—"and focus on what we can control."

Daniel sat in his chair, caressing his hand up my calf to comfort me, but I needed more.

I nodded at Joaquin. "Up for a grapple?" That'd settle me down. Scarlett was off today, so no boxing. Joaquin smiled, nodding yes. We liked keeping these skills fresh too.

Rob started laughing. "Lucky for you, mi prima, that I'm still recovering, or you'd really have a match on your hands."

"I can take you both on." I smiled at Rob reclining in his chair. "You're big, but I'm fast, remember?" He almost looked like his old self. The tan helped too.

"Why won't you grapple with me?" Daniel asked.

"Because it turns you on, and we end up fucking." I gave him a kiss, "and I can't even *pretend* to hurt you," before I joined Joaquin on the sand outside the tent.

Joaquin wasn't easy on me. His pseudo hits were hard, tagging me twice on the mouth, once drawing blood. I grinned with bloody teeth, responding in kind, taking him down to the sand and clinching his throat tight between my bare, crossed legs. He tapped out. We started again.

The next time, I went for the same move, and he stood up with my legs wrapped around his neck. I hung upside down while he walked forward, over me, forcing me to flop onto my stomach. He grabbed my leg back in a painful hold, making me tap out.

"Don't do the same move twice, bella," Joaquin chided

me. "You know better. Your body is small, but strong and limber—use it."

We went through more moves. I coiled my legs from one hold into another, forcing him to roll over to where I was on top of Joaquin, my arms going for his throat in a mock choke. He tapped out.

Then he trapped my hands behind my back, mimicking handcuffs. But I was able to tuck my body into a ball, slipping my hands under my legs to up in front and snapping them free.

For an hour we grappled while Rob and the twins napped, Fran read, and Daniel watched. Finally, we stopped, covered in sand with scratches, bruises, and grins.

Daniel joined us in the waves to cool off. "Give me a go." He wrapped his arms around me. "A rematch at Paddleball."

I agreed after we guzzled down cold beers. Joaquin laid at Rob's feet, cheering me on. The first few points were mine, but Daniel came back, tying the game, then scoring five more.

"I tired her out for you," Joaquin shouted out.

"Hopefully not too much," Daniel replied.

I didn't need to see his eyes smoldering behind sunglasses to know what those words meant.

Joaquin put his head down, joining the group in the shade and slumber, while I came back, taking the score to 18-18.

I twirled the paddle in my hands. "You're going down, Pierce."

"No." He returned my serve. "Loser goes down." 18-19 now, and he enjoyed the lead.

A rare occasion of wanting to lose filled my naughty mind. He looked so hot in his black swim trunks, his dark hair falling in long waves lightening in the sun. A deep tan stretched over his defined muscles while his groomed chest hair and happy trail glistened with sweat I wanted to follow down to its destination.

I had two addictions—fighting assholes who torment others and fucking my hot husband to forget about them.

One fix I had to have today.

Turning around, I bent over for the little ball. My white, string bikini bottoms responded in kind, one side wedging into my ass. Glancing over my shoulder, I smiled.

He stood there, licking his bottom lip. "Nice moon."

I turned back, tugging my bottoms into place. Tossing him the ball, he snatched it from the air. I bent forward, twirling my paddle, giving him a good look at my cleavage. I played both games until he easily won one, 18-20.

Throwing his paddle down with a huge grin, "You're mine, Ravenel," he jolted toward me. Dropping mine, I stifled a squeal, turning to run, but he plucked me up in his arms, racing us into the waves like he did after our wedding.

He waded us in chest-deep. "How shall I celebrate our first anniversary?" The memory was on his mind too.

"I like spoiling you too." I wrapped my arms around his neck. "Why don't you take the odd years and I'll take the even ones?"

"Good. That makes the first go mine." His embrace cradled me under the lazy tide. "I'm thinking a picnic with paella, fried chicken, Tito's, and dancing."

"Sounds familiar."

"Exactly. I fell in love with you that night. I never want to stop celebrating it." The water reflecting in his eyes made them electric blue. "What will you do for your turn?"

"Do you want something sweet or sexy?"

"With you, it's always both."

"Come on. What's romantic to you?"

"Standing beside you, washing the dishes." He dipped me back in the water.

"Be serious." I laughed.

"I am serious." He lifted my lips back up to his, the intensity in his eyes deep. "It's the simple things we share that warm my heart. I lived grand and hated it. This is romance to me, a day playing on the beach with you."

"Speaking of"—I fired up a series of salty kisses—"I gotta pay my debt. This loser needs to go down on you."

His lips brushed over mine. "You're a water girl, but no one can hold their breath that long." Snaking his fingers under my bikini bottoms in the surf, his middle finger teased in practiced circles.

It inspired me. "Let's go inside and get some snacks."

Three adults and two babies slept content under the tent. Grabbing our towels up, Daniel held his hand out for mine, leading me behind the dunes on the path toward the boardwalk in our backyard.

From there, between the sand dunes topped with patches of tall, golden beachgrass, you couldn't see back to the beach and had only a partial view of our house.

I yanked his hand. "Right here."

"We'll get caught, babe."

"No, we won't." Dropping my towel to the sand, I knelt on top of it. "If they see we're gone, they know we'll be right back."

His cock rose, not disagreeing, tenting his wet swim trunks. This distraction, this drug mixed with our love, he was my favorite escape, even if only for an hour.

Untying the white string on his trunks, I pulled the Velcro open, tugging them down and leaving them dripping over his hulking quads.

I gazed up at him. Sunglasses rested atop his tousled waves while his towel hung around his neck, his gaze darkened with lust, awaiting the coming show.

I teased, "I see you like the idea of us getting caught, don't you, Daniel?" My tongue delivered a long lick up his shaft while I swam in his eyes.

"Yes, I do," he answered, saltwater mixing with his flavor, offering two tastes I craved. "I'd love for someone to catch my beautiful wife sucking my hard cock."

The quasi-public display turned me on too. Pulling the fabric aside, I exposed my wet breasts before I did the same with my bikini bottoms, continuing what his hand started in the ocean.

The kiss of a breeze across my public nudity with him full in my mouth while giving him this salacious show—it made me moan. One hand twisted firmly over his wet cock while my other played with my slick pussy.

"Fuck, Charlie." Daniel bent his knees, giving me more, grasping my head in his hands and slowly thrusting into my mouth. "You look so fucking sexy like this. It makes you feel dirty, doesn't it?"

My pussy confessed, hungry for more. Closing my eyes, hollowing my cheeks, I relaxed my throat and took him all the way, hearing him groan, "Yes, babe," at my glucking descent to his base and back up.

With each plunge of my mouth, his filthy praise encouraged me more. "I've got a naughty wife, don't I? That's it, taking all of me. You love it, don't you, fingering your pussy with your dirty mouth sucking my cock?" It drove me harder, starved for him and wanting even more; never getting enough of him. "Yes, I can hear it; how it's making you dripping wet with my dick fucking your throat."

He was getting close. I could taste it. Switching hands, I

grazed my fingers slick with my lust across the sensitive raphe line of his balls to where I could massage the tender spot behind them.

"Fuck, babe." He hissed, his thighs shaking. "You're going to make me come doing that."

I took his fist from My hair and put it to his cock. "Then come on me, Daniel." I kept massaging the spot he enjoyed while my other hand took my pussy to the edge. "Show me how dirty you like to make me."

Offering him my gaze, he jerked his cock off to my eager tongue while he gasped, "Goddamn." The sight of his surrender, spurting his taste over my tongue, it took me too. He moaned, watching his cum drip from my chin while I shook with my own splashing over my fingers.

I couldn't speak at the heat, at the spasm racking my body. He knelt beside me on the towel, replacing my hand with his. His strong fingers started pounding my pussy with a fast-jerking grasp. "My naughty wife only comes for me. Don't you?"

His force made me cry out. "Yes, Daniel." Burying my head against his shoulder, my arousal poured again, all over his expert hand.

I trembled there while he softly pulled out. "See, babe," he whispered in my ear, "the loser going down is a massive win."

His joke made me laugh into his salty shoulder. I wiped my chin on the towel hanging over it.

"I wanted a photo of that first." His grin wouldn't stop.

"Next time."

He stood up, offering me his hand before pulling his suit up from his thighs. "You missed a spot." Wiping his fingertip over my exposed nipple, he took the drop of his cum to my mouth. I sucked it clean while he informed me, "And FYI.

Whatever you did to me with your magic hand must be on the menu in the future."

"Only if I lose again." I covered myself while he kissed me, tucking his cock into his suit before tying it closed.

Then we both turned toward our house... and froze.

Silas stood right there, at the end of the wooden boardwalk. He'd watched our X-rated tryst.

"Hey, Silas," I said. Fuck it. My yard, my husband.

"Hey, y'all." He shifted on his bare feet, not nervous, only aroused, the tall tent in his board shorts declaring it. "Sorry to interrupt." The smile on his face said he wasn't sorry at all.

"We're going inside for some snacks." I grabbed Daniel's hand. "Meet us on the beach, and we'll bring an extra chair for ya."

"Sounds good." Silas raked his hand through his hair as we neared. The walkway was only wide enough for two people, so he backed a safe six feet away. But his gaze didn't back down, joking with his eyes on my cleavage. "You missed another spot."

I gasped and glanced down. Nothing was there.

Daniel tossed his chin up, laughing. "Hope you enjoyed the show, mate." He tugged my hand, gently pulling me away from Silas.

"I did." Silas said, "I'll be enjoying it for many years to come," making us laugh and stop giving a damn.

He turned toward the dunes while we turned toward the house.

"We really did get caught." Daniel grinned as we rinsed off under the pool shower. "Seems he liked it too."

"Hugely," I said, not feeling the appropriate level of embarrassment. We climbed the deck stairs, entering the house. "I know you love that he caught us."

"It satisfies me in many ways, Mrs. Pierce." He pinched my ass as we walked into the kitchen. "Enough to want more."

"You can't be for real and ready again?" I questioned before turning around, eying his package. I was half wrong.

Fuck this man, jealousy and public displays really did turn him on. Good. They did me too.

He walked me up against the wall before plunging his hand into my bikini bottoms. "Whose is it, Charlie?" He played with my pussy still singing from minutes before.

"Keep making it yours, Daniel." Opening my thighs to him, issuing a challenge, I pushed his head below.

Winner went down that time.

CHAPTER SEVENTEEN

CHARLIE

AUGUST. ***Two months before...***

Minutes clicked down while I stood with Daniel behind the console of our boat. He steered it toward Hilton Head, on our way to meet his son and Nikki Sampson.

I didn't know what to expect. A sweet little boy? Yes. A mature woman who had moved on from her unhealthy obsession with Daniel? I hoped. Still, I had to know...

"So, what did she do that was so unstable?"

"I don't know where to start."

"Shit. There's that much?"

"After my name was cleared, she followed me around LA. One night, she followed me into a restaurant's washroom and told me she was pregnant.

"I never doubted Keats was mine. Before she was due, I suggested she move in with me, got us a nanny and our families came round. They all could tell we were a bad match. Still, I tried. She had an easy birth. Keats was the only good part."

"Did she get better after he was born?"

"No, she got worse. We never had sex after that awful first night. I couldn't be with her; I didn't trust her. But she'd try. I'd be gentle turning her down, but she'd beg and cry, falling to the floor in a state. One night after I refused her, she locked herself in a room with Keats, screaming at me through the door. That made him cry. I wanted to break it down to get to my son, but that would only make matters worse. It made me so bloody sick."

"So, what finally ended it?"

"I found her the next morning in the kitchen, crying. I tried comforting her, but she started throwing things at me. I just protected Keats. I grabbed him up and locked us in my bedroom and let her trash my place until her parents arrived. We checked her into hospital. She got better on medication. Counseling worked too, but she was advised that the best thing for her was to get away from me."

"Is that why you gave him up?"

"He deserved a healthy mum, and she wasn't that around me. She was fine when I wasn't there." The words twisted his mouth, confessing, "And I feared if I stayed, she'd get erratic, exposing Keats to a scandal he didn't deserve. And to be honest, I feared the publicity too."

"Well, maybe motherhood and eleven years has changed her."

I sure hoped so. Drama sloshed over the brim in our lives. We didn't need another drop of it.

Keats, Nikki, and her mom were meeting us at the Harbour Town Yacht Club. That was the arrangement. Daniel had insisted one of her parents be present. Thankfully, Evelyn agreed to join us so it would feel balanced.

The plan was to get them, go back to Daufuskie and visit for a few hours at the Freeport Marina. A little playground was there, some picnic tables too. On a Tuesday morning, hardly anyone would be around.

Daniel told me he wasn't comfortable hosting Nikki in our home yet. We had to test the waters first.

He throttled back to neutral. "God, I'm so nervous. She's told him I'm his father. But what if he's mad at me for not being there all this time?"

"Children come around." Evelyn stood up on his other side, offering him a hug. "He may not open up at first but give him time. He'll warm to you."

"He's gonna love the rugby ball you got him." I rubbed his back. It was sweaty with nerves. "And they've been quarantined with her elderly parents for months. I'm sure he's going to love playing outside with you."

He leaned over for a kiss before throttling back down, nudging the vessel into the harbor.

I saw them in the distance. Nikki wore a floral sundress; her long black hair fell over one shoulder while she stood next to a boy. He had dark, loose curls like Daniel. Beside them stood an elderly woman. Age hunched her over, but her pink outfit screamed with life.

The greetings were awkward, all while the boy wouldn't take his eyes off Daniel.

We loaded onto the boat to escape recognition, though I wasn't as worried these days. Daniel barely looked like himself with his longer hair and short beard, hiding his famous face under a baseball hat.

The engine roar was too loud for us to chat much on the trip back. Nikki put Keats in a life jacket and kept him sitting between her and her mom. Me and Evelyn sat across from them while Daniel stood at the helm, glancing over at Keats, offering him kind smiles.

The silence let us study each other.

Nikki kept peeking my way.

I clocked it from behind my Aviators. How Nikki's red manicured fingertips nervously played with the strap on Keats's life jacket. How her sandaled foot bounced nervously on the white fiberglass.

Nikki offered me shy grins like she was intimidated by me. That softened my guard.

Give her a chance, Charlie Girl. Don't be one of those mean women who hates on other women when they haven't done a damn thing to hurt you.

Once we settled at the playground, Evelyn opened the picnic basket she had packed. Nikki's mom was full of pleasant small talk. She put us at ease too. Score one for grandmothers and their wise ways.

"How come you don't visit me?" Keats asked Daniel after he gave him the rugby ball, explaining how it was from his home in England.

"Because he used to live on the other side of the ocean, sweetie," Nikki answered him, "and work kept him very busy."

"But I'm here now"—Daniel squatted down beside him—"in the States, with you, and here anytime you need me, or just want to play."

I could see Daniel taking in every freckle and curl on his son's facade. The boy's face was a mirror of his, but Keats's narrow shoulders tensed up to his ears, obvious that he wanted to play, instead of standing around adults dripping with tension.

"Why don't you teach him how to throw that ball backward while we set out lunch?" I suggested.

Daniel beckoned Keats to the grassy field while Nikki turned around, sitting down at the picnic table with us.

"Lemonade?" I offered her a cup.

"Yes, please." She took it.

Evelyn struck up a conversation about the island's history. That led to a chat about families. Nikki's congratulations to me for the wedding and twins sounded sincere.

"I haven't told Keats about his half-brother and sister yet," Nikki said. "I wanted to talk it over with you and Daniel, to see if you're comfortable with it. I don't want to break his heart if this doesn't work out."

Okay, this woman has some healthy boundaries. That's progress.

"Why don't you and Daniel tell him? You can do it today if you like." I wanted to trust her, to make this work for everyone. "Then we can schedule a time when he can meet them."

It didn't take long for Keats to warm to Daniel, so much so that I dreaded the goodbye. But Nikki kept checking the time on her phone, explaining they had a long drive home and had to get back to the harbor by four o'clock.

We loaded onto the boat on schedule. I was captain this time and traveled slowly so Daniel could ride at the front bow with Keats, pointing out the dolphins, explaining how he goes flounder gigging using night vision googles. Keats asked if he could come with him. Daniel smiled and rubbed his back, making promises for a future with his son.

It choked me up. The worry was gone from Daniel's brow. All I saw was love in his eyes. The same love he showed holding Caroline and Duke.

I slowed the boat into the slip we rented at the marina. A group of guys stood farther down the dock by a yacht.

Daniel helped Keats, Nikki, and her mom step onto the dock as I finished tying up the bow.

Then my periphery clocked it. How a man turned from

the edge of the group and aimed our way. He approached quickly, calling out, "Hey, man. You're Daniel Pierce!"

My glance snapped up from the boat cleat, heart rate soaring, eyes scanning his hands. *The pockets of his shorts? No gun. Just a phone.* I leaped onto the dock, blocking his path.

"Sir, let's respect social distancing." I held up my hands. "We have elderly folks and a child here. No one wants to risk their health."

The guy stopped and stared me down. He wasn't a threat. But there was an intent in his eyes I tracked glaring back at him wearing a faded "Joe's Crab Shack, Jacksonville, FL" T-shirt straining over his potbelly.

I'd take him down in two moves. The only thing that unnerved me was the phone in his hand.

"Hey, no worries." He lifted it high, snapping shots over my head. "Just wanted a picture. I love *Zeus* and *The Druid*."

I spun around. Daniel was standing with his arm on Keats's shoulder. Nikki smiled beside him with sunglasses resting on her head. Daniel turned his face away from the lens, but Nikki didn't.

"All right, sir." I turned back, wanting to snatch the phone from his hand, but feared the larger spectacle. "That's enough. You're upsetting the boy."

The guy shrugged and turned away. I watched him. How he didn't speak to the men standing by the yacht. How he sped up the ramp, disappearing between the condo buildings at the harbor.

I whipped around. Daniel caught my stern look. We needed to get out of here. Now.

"All right, little man." Daniel squatted beside Keats. "We're going to visit soon, yeah?"

"Promise?" He wrapped his spaghetti arms around Daniel's neck.

"I promise." Daniel squeezed him tight, the look on his face didn't want to let him go.

I stared down Nikki who wore the most satisfied grin. Not one of love to see her son with his father. It was full of glee. I knew why. Nikki had paid that guy to snap that picture.

Once they said their goodbyes to Daniel who jumped back into the boat, I offered hugs too. I saved Nikki's for last, whispering in her ear, "Someone tried to kill us. You post that photo, and Keats will be at risk too."

I pulled back from the embrace, aiming my eyes at Nikki's. They were dark brown and full of shock. The poor woman had no idea who she was fucking with.

"I don't know him." Nikki's tone mocked with surprise.

Tell that to your lying face, my eyes answered back. But I wouldn't make a scene in front of the boy. Instead, I jumped back into the boat. "Y'all have a safe trip home."

The minute they were far enough away, I turned to Daniel. "That dumb bitch."

"Charlie!" Evelyn chided me for the slur.

"I know. I'm sorry. I don't like hating on a woman, but she set that up." I rushed to untie the bow. "That guy was waiting for us. Four o'clock. Right on time. Because no way he spotted Daniel from that far. You can hardly tell it's him. And the guy's an amateur, covered in Florida apparel like he's Nikki's neighbor."

"Babe, that happens to me all the time," Daniel said. "It's possible he just recognized me."

"No, she set it up. The woman had her sunglasses on for the ride back, then they're on her head so you can identify her face when she's standing on the dock?" My mouth and mind worked a mile a minute. "And when he took the picture, she smiled back so you'd be damn sure it was her in the shot. So, you can clearly see it's Nikki Sampson standing next to Daniel Pierce with a little boy that looks like you spit him from your mouth."

"Fuck." Daniel shook his head. "You're right."

"Exactly." I untied the stern whip fast. "If that photo gets dropped, pinning our location... *we... are... fucked.*"

"That bitch," he muttered.

"Okay, you two, stop with the language," Evelyn warned. "I don't care what she did. Don't speak with such hate."

Evelyn was right. I knew better. *Don't lose your temper. Think.*

"When we get back to the island and have a signal, call her," I said while Daniel turned the engine on, and I pulled the fenders into the boat. "Talk some sense into her. Tell her we're still at risk. Surely she wouldn't risk Keats's safety and her own."

Daniel nodded before racing back across the sound.

But it was too late.

By the time we were back and had a strong signal, there it was on a random fan account. The photo from the dock with #danielpierce. The screen populated with reposts, growing by the minutes to thousands witnessing it all.

Fear dropped adrenaline so fast through my muscles that it weakened my thighs. Why? Because the location was pinned too—Harbour Town, Hilton Head Island, SC.

You could scope our home, Daufuskie Island, right across the water.

CHAPTER EIGHTEEN

CHARLIE

AUGUST. ***Two months before...***

The next day was the aftermath of the hurricane. I surveyed the damage, mourning what we lost.

Our secret location? Our safety? A digital storm washed it away.

"Why would she do something so foolish?" Evelyn asked. "Risking her son and herself?"

The Watsons, the closest I had to family, came over to commiserate... more like to strategize given how we were raised.

Life on a small island prepares you for disaster, living every day to its fullest knowing one day, destruction will arrive.

So, we did. We sat by the pool, enjoying a beautiful day after the storm.

"Well, she's earned a degree in dumbass by posting that photo." I lounged back with my son asleep in my arms. "Daniel called his publicist. Seems there's talk of Nikki being cast for a new series, so she's desperate for publicity to seem relevant."

"Well, she's got it now." Evelyn bounced Caroline on her knee beside me. "The Zeus love child story is all over the place online."

I rolled my eyes. We fucking fell for Nikki's trick, but it brought Keats back into Daniel's life. That's what mattered.

Daniel's publicist issued a statement last night, spinning the photo as a love child story—nothing about a threesome gone wrong. The press ate it up for a news cycle. How Daniel Pierce had secretly fathered a child while filming the first Zeus movie but wanted to protect his son from the media.

Though we'd never trust Nikki, it wouldn't keep Daniel from his promise—he was back in his son's life for good.

"Y'all are gonna need a plan," Pop said, drinking a beer beside Daniel on the pool steps. Though retired from the military, he'd never stop strategizing. "Best get ready for whatever comes this way."

That quieted us, settling into the new reality. One that clenched every muscle in Daniel's jaw. I'd watched that anger twist over him since Nikki exposed us.

"Sometimes this island feels like a safe haven." Evelyn broke the silence. "And sometimes it feels cursed like trouble is destined to find this place."

"Well, we certainly found it a few times." My tone tried lifting the mood. "Hell, I went looking for trouble. Remember? Me, Quincy, and Silas went sneaking into the ol' Melrose Inn after it shut down and looked all haunted."

"Talk about cursed," Evelyn said. "You kids talked like you'd find treasure in there: jewelry, money, or such."

"Y'all had no business in there." Pop sucked his teeth. "We kept tellin' y'all to stay out, that it was dangerous. That old, abandoned hotel ain't caused nothin' but trouble since the day it opened."

"I run past it every morning." Daniel finally spoke. He'd been quiet all day. "They could shoot a horror film there. I'm surprised no one has."

"No one would be stupid enough to go in that place," I said. "It's been years since we stepped in there last."

"Best leave that place and the past behind. Focus on the here and now." Pop wouldn't relent. "What's your plan?"

I shrugged. "If someone wants to find us, they'll know where to look. Hell, it's what I'd do—find Harbour Town on a map and find the smart places to hide near it. This is one of them. We have security and people here who'll protect us. This is as good as it gets."

Yes, a few tourists may drive by our house and gawk, but we always had a guard outside while warning signs, cameras and motion sensors were aimed toward the beach if someone trespassed that way.

Scarlett was training a guard dog for us too. Daniel loved the idea of a family pet, but I reminded him that the German Sheppard was for protection first. But Daniel had already named him "Captain", a romantic joke about my rank.

If tourists were the worst to expect, that we'd be the other celebrity home on the island to watch, then I was grateful. We were lucky to be quarantined here, even though everyone was losing their damn minds with the limited routine.

"Ready for a break?" Daniel's voice and wet kiss shook me from my thoughts. He had climbed out of the pool and was reaching to take Duke from my arms.

"Sure." The sight of him dripping with muscles and

pool water while lifting our son into his arms—it lifted my cheeks into a smile.

My phone chimed next to me on the patio table. I glanced down. So did Daniel. A name glowed on the screen.

Lorraine Morris

Exchanging a bewildered glance, the same question troubled us...

Why would Daniel's boss, the showrunner for *The Druid*, be calling me?

CHAPTER NINETEEN

DANIEL

OCTOBER. *Now...*

Fran reached for my hand. "I'm worried, dear. She wouldn't do this, go this long without reaching out for her family. Something's wrong."

The hammer of my heart coursed terror through my veins. Fran was right. Charlie would've phoned. No matter what I did or how much I hurt her, she'd never abandon our children.

Something. No. Everything must be terribly wrong.

But it would be another fight, another betrayal if I did the one thing Charlie told me not to.

How much would I hurt her this time?

We had a plan, a way to stay safe since Nikki exposed our location.

"Trust me." Charlie had told me two days after Nikki's trick, her hands meticulously cleaning her grandfather's rifle in our home office. "Give me twenty-four hours before you raise any flags. With the kind of threats that can come for us now, I'll need the time."

The smell of gun grease had filled the air while I glanced from her, back to the monitors for the security cameras around our dark property, an ominous fear filling me too.

"What do you expect me to do? Nothing?"

"No. You get our babies, take the .22 on the bookshelf, and keep our family safe. That's the most important," she said. "I'll take care of the rest."

"Don't phone the police right away or the FBI?" Moths flitted in front of the cameras surveilling our backyard. Something about that night, about that conversation had disturbed me. "Just what are you proposing?"

"I'm not proposing anything aloud, not admitting to a thing." A white cloth in her hand wiped the barrel of her rifle. The pause she gave made our eyes meet. "There's an ocean around us full of safe secrets."

I knew what she meant then, and I was sure now.

The coral light of the October dawn filled the horizon, filling me with sure knowledge of what my wife was capable of. If she was protecting someone she loved? Indeed, it dropped to the ocean floor of my fear.

"Use your instinct," she had said. "I trust you. If you think I need help, that I'm in danger, call for it. But if you can buy me time, do it. That's all I'm asking."

5:56am

My phone informed me now.

Does she need you, Pierce? I conjured breaths shared with her, moments we couldn't be more connected. *Is she okay?*

A flutter, a sudden palpitation punched my heart, constricting my throat in pain.

No.

I forced my legs and mind to work. I stood up, answering Fran, "She didn't ring last night. And hasn't this morning. She always said to give her time, but not like this."

Glancing down, I had a 9 percent charge left on my phone and I used it on one desperate call.

After four rings, Rob finally picked up. "Hey, man. What's up?" His voice cracked with sleep on the other end, sounding like he already knew... we were in trouble.

CHAPTER TWENTY

CHARLIE

SEPTEMBER. ***One month before...***

The trip to the Bull River Marina in Savannah by boat was less than an hour. I took the time, thinking through Lorraine's initial request.

It wasn't news that Lorraine was in Savannah, Georgia. It's her hometown, and she was in pre-production on a new series there. The woman had four.

Her biggest show—*The Druid*—would resume production at the end of November in Madrid with Daniel. Two more shows were back to filming in LA, and this one was starting—the pilot season of *The Tour*.

Lorraine quarantined in her Savannah home for weeks after leaving LA. The small cast and relatively small crew did the same. Everyone followed strict safety protocols. Thankful to be back at work, back to being paid, no one took risks.

When Lorraine called me, she said she needed help for

the star of her new show—a young woman. That was all she said she could share over the phone.

"Can you meet with her?" Lorraine had asked. "Her name is Riley Chase, and I just want you two to chat. You were so strong protecting Kierra and resolved that situation on *The Druid* so well. I thought of no one else but you. And only you. No one else can know."

That was Lorraine's dire request.

And Lorraine Morris was not a woman you reject over the phone. But Daniel made me promise that was it—a nice visit, a polite chat, and a gentle decline, whatever the ask.

I pulled my boat into the slip and tied it up.

Minutes later, two figures appeared at the top of the ramp. Even with a mask on, I recognized Lorraine. Her signature braids fell around glowing, brown skin, along with the red cat eyeglasses she always wore.

I jumped onto the dock and waved.

Holy shit, the young woman walking beside Lorraine was stunning, owning the floating platform like a runway model.

Her long hair cascaded to her elbows in a trendy white shade with six inches dyed ombre blood-red to the ends. Damn, she looked fierce, earning extra points for her black, Doc Marten boots covered in hand-drawn Sharpie art upon closer inspection.

I liked her instantly.

"Ms. Ravenel." Lorraine dropped her overnight bag. "Our tests are clear, so can I shake your hand?"

"Oh, hell no. Come here." I offered her a hug instead. "And you better call me 'Charlie'."

Lorraine took off her mask, keeping her arm around me in a side hug while she made the introduction. "Charlie

Ravenel, a.k.a. Captain Charlotte Roberts, meet Riley Chase—my muse, my talent, my hero."

"Nice to meet you, Riley." I extended my hand. "Please just call me 'Charlie' too, 'Roberts' or 'Ravenel', I don't care."

Riley took it in a firm shake. "Hi, Ms. Ravenel, so nice to meet you." She pulled her mask off revealing her ethereal face with cute freckles across the bridge of her dainty nose and smiling petal pink lips. But that funky nose ring gave her an admirable edge.

"Lorraine has raved about you," Riley said. "Of course, I've seen the stuff online too. I'm honored you're meeting with us this weekend."

"Meeting? No." I joked, bending down to grab both their bags before tossing them into the center of my boat. "This is a friendly weekend getaway; time to spend with new people instead of the same old faces for the past six months."

I jumped back in, helping Lorraine down while Riley silently pounced like a snow leopard, needing no help.

When we pulled into Silas's dock, he stopped tinkering with the boat engine in his backyard and sauntered over.

"What are y'all filmin' here?" Silas asked, keeping a safe distance.

"It's a pilot for another series for SHOWZ," Lorraine explained with a thrilled smile. "It's about a family that runs a ghost-tour company in Savannah. Riley plays our mystic lead, the daughter of the owners, and the one who discovers she can see and talk to the ghosts."

"That's bomb." Was that praise in Silas's eyes for the show or Riley? Either way was fine with me, enjoying any relief from his adoration.

We jumped on my golf cart, waving goodbye to him. Thirty seconds into the drive and Lorraine marveled at the island's beauty. "Oh my, I could do a whole show here."

"Don't you dare," I warned with a smile. "That would ruin this place with too many people." I glanced over my shoulder. "Where you from, Riley?"

"Yes, ma'am," she answered, "Fayetteville, Georgia, just outside of Atlanta."

I laughed. "Oh, I'm a sucker for a good 'sir' or 'ma'am', but please don't use them for me or Daniel. It makes him think he's a fucking knight, and it makes me feel over sixty."

Riley answered back with a "yes, ma'am" making us laugh at how she did it again, just like me, on Southern instinct.

"Riley's a sweetheart of the industry," Lorraine added. "She's twenty-four now but started off as a child extra on films in Atlanta and the rest is history. One of the youngest ever nominated for a Golden Globe with two superhero films in the pipeline. And she signed on to this series, because she's a fellow Georgia girl, and God likes me."

Riley touched Lorraine's shoulder. "And it's a great show, and an amazing role, thank you very much." Lorraine reached up, cupping Riley's hand in return.

I admired that about Lorraine, how supportive she was of all her cast members, particularly the women.

And when Lorraine set her sights on Daniel minutes later, the star of her other cherished show, she about fell off the golf cart.

He stood proud at the bottom of our front steps with Caroline in one arm, Duke in the other, and Captain, their new dog sitting at his knee.

"Oh my Lord, Daniel Pierce," Lorraine cried out. "If you weren't the sexiest man alive before, you've raised the bar now. Standing there like a smokin' hot, lumberjack with your two beautiful babies in your arms."

Riley politely greeted Daniel with a handshake once I took Duke from him. "Nice to meet you, sir."

"Riley, what did I tell you about that?" I said. "You and Lorraine are going to explode this man's ego. It's already swelling with all the thirsty Daniel Pierce posts."

Daniel cocked his eyebrow. "You say that of the man with applesauce on his shirt, a teething ring in his pocket, and mushy peas smeared on his shorts." He flashed his white-hot smile. "I abandoned my ego the day I fell in love with you, Charlie Ravenel."

Outnumbered by women all afternoon, Daniel loved it.

Later, he and Lorraine sat by the pool, talking about the direction of *The Druid* for season three. So, I asked Riley if she wanted to join me for a stroll with the twins.

"I really want to thank you, Charlie, for inviting us out here." Riley pushed the stroller along because she asked to, saying she couldn't wait to be a mom one day too.

"Any friend of Lorraine's is a friend of mine."

"Well... that's what I'm hoping." Riley's pace slowed. "Lorraine told me how you helped Kierra Williams. About what Mason Hunt did and how you protected her. That's why she suggested that I meet with you."

I glanced over. Stress marred Riley's pretty face. "What's going on?"

Riley's grip tightened into white knuckles squeezing the stroller's handle.

"Someone is blackmailing me. It started with cryptic comments on my Instagram a few weeks ago. I didn't catch them because there are thousands I don't see. But they got so odd that my publicist brought them to my attention. So, I checked my Instagram message requests, which I never do, and there they were, dozens of messages from an account threatening me."

Hear those words, Charlie Girl? "Threatening me." *A young woman said them. Now feel that? It's the needle filling your vein with your favorite drug—PROTECT HER.*

"Do you know who it is?" I asked.

"No. It's a fake account with only one picture posted of the fountain in Forsyth Park in Savannah, just down the street from the house I'm renting. The account is only following me and all my fan accounts."

"What are they threatening you with?"

Riley got quiet. My heart broke when tears spilled down Riley's cheeks, flushing her alabaster skin with red fear.

"They're threatening to supposedly out me." Riley stopped and turned to me. "And I need your help."

I reached for her hand. "Riley, so many actors are out nowadays. It's something to be proud of. Why would someone think they could blackmail you for being gay?"

"That's not it. Everyone knows I'm a lesbian." Riley's hand shook, tucking her hair behind her ear. "But only five people know I'm trans. I started my gender confirmation at five years old. As far back as me or my mom can remember, I knew I was a girl. And my mom listened to me and wanted me to be happy and healthy, and to be me. So, we worked with doctors over the years and moved from Atlanta to Fayetteville so I could live as myself when I was seven and I never looked back."

The tears kept falling. Riley wiped them away with the back of her hand. It touched me. I did the same stubborn gesture.

"And now, someone is messaging me, saying they know my supposed secret and if I don't pay them a million dollars by September thirtieth, they're going to tell everyone." Anguish poured down Riley's face. "And it's bullshit, Charlie. It's not that I'm ashamed. It's the opposite. I'm a woman and I don't have to reveal it, explain it, justify it, or have it questioned by others. To have someone try and say otherwise and violate my privacy and terrorize my life, it scares me."

She started sobbing, swaying like she wanted to crumble to the ground and give up.

But I pulled her into an embrace. "It's okay, Riley." Though Riley was inches taller, holding her was like holding my own daughter, firing my protective instinct like a supernova in my heart. Whispering into Riley's silky strands smelling like gardenias, I swore, "Don't worry. I won't let anyone hurt you."

Those words to a girl? To a woman?

They were my mantra—making one promise, breaking another, and sealing my fate.

My instinct stood off to the side, watching. *Be careful.* Something loomed large about my vow. *This job feels bigger than you.* Like jumping into raging dark ocean waves at night. *You may never make it back to shore.*

CHAPTER TWENTY-ONE

CHARLIE

SEPTEMBER. **_One month before..._**

For the rest of the night, Riley sat by the pool, her shoulders shaking with laughter. She seemed relieved, knowing she wasn't alone, that me and Lorraine would help her.

But who'd help me tell Daniel?

I didn't mention it to him that night or the next day. We enjoyed our visitors, cooing over the babies, splashing in the pool when Rob and Joaquin came by. All the while, I strategized how I'd ease into a convincing conversation with Daniel.

You're blowing sunshine up your ass, Charlie Girl. This ain't gonna be an "oh, by the way," kinda chat with your husband.

This is gonna be a high flyover, open the doors, listen to the whistle of the bomb falling through the night sky, exploding into orange flames in your life kinda talk.

And we already had enough shell-shock this past year,

and even more this summer with Nikki, Keats, and Daniel's big lie.

That was the irony though. It didn't faze me. Bombs kept dropping in my life, and I didn't flinch anymore.

And my heart was decided. No way would I'd let some asshole threaten Riley.

That's the thing about blackmail. If they think they have something on you, they'll be back for more. Even if Riley paid them off, they'd torment her forever.

I understood why she couldn't go to the authorities. We couldn't trust they'd keep Riley's life protected. The story would leak, no doubt.

My mind schemed ten steps ahead.

The post was a few weeks ago with the fountain in Savannah—a warning they were close to Riley, probably working on the show.

My plan for now?

Filming started in a week. I'd go into Savannah before and meet with the producer in charge of set security. I'd do an audit of the apartment Riley rented. Then I'd talk with Riley and comb through the entire cast and crew list—no one was above my suspicion.

I'd have to get a COVID test Monday so I could go to set two days later. In that time, I'd call for backup from HGR in Atlanta.

All my backup had to know was we were personal detail for Riley Chase, that she had incoming threats. They didn't need to know more. I'd handle the rest.

We made it through the entire weekend until Sunday brunch, two hours before their departure. And then...

Boom!

"I'm so thankful you're gonna help me," Riley said,

reaching for my hand on the kitchen table, squeezing it in gratitude.

"You're welcome," I replied before slowly turning my chin, knowing what awaited my glance.

Daniel glared at me from across the table, his handsome face tensed with silent rage. It twisted across his mouth before he lifted a coffee cup to his lips, breaking his glare to look out the windows, taking a long sip.

Thank God the man was a talented actor. He played it off the rest of their visit, was all smiles with Lorraine and Riley. I called Silas to have him take them back to Savannah in my boat, knowing I'd have to face Daniel the minute they left.

"I'll see you Wednesday after my test clears." I gave Riley a hug before she hopped onto the golf cart.

Lorraine sat on the front seat next to Silas, reaching for my hand. "Thank you," she said.

We stood on our cobblestone driveway, waving them goodbye. "May I please speak with you inside?" Daniel sounded like the headmaster of an English boarding school, not my irate husband.

Scarlett sat in her chair in the alcove of our garage, guarding the house while chewing a red Twizzler with Captain by her feet. I clocked Scarlett's knowing glance; that woman was perceptive as hell.

Yep, there'll be no shitshow for Scarlett to witness. No sparring with her either. The only fight? The next one with your husband.

I followed Daniel inside. Fran had the twins playing in the living room. He marched upstairs to our bedroom, storming past our bed and out onto the deck, his anger palpable.

Closing the doors behind me, I pushed down the dread and turned to face his fury.

"Do you have a death wish, Charlie?"

He wasn't speaking in hyperbole.

"Daniel, Riley needs my help. It's a scary situation for her; that's why Lorraine trusts me and not someone else."

"I get it. Riley is a lovely young woman, and I see Caroline in the eyes of every girl and want to protect them too. But no. Not this time. This is fucking dangerous. Call HGR and find someone else to help her. Joaquin or someone."

"It's not that simple. She needs a woman protecting her, and this is a tricky case. It involves blackmail, and not just any officer can handle that."

"That's bloody bullshit and you know it!" He stepped toward me, punching his fist toward the floor. "*You* want to be the one to save her. *You* want to be the one to protect her. I know you. You fucking *crave* the hunt for any man threatening a woman. It's a drug to you."

"Okay, yeah. It's my calling and I'm going back to work, just like you." I stood up to his hulking chest. "We're off to Madrid in two months for your work, so why can't I do mine while we wait?"

"Oh, I don't know"—his fingers snatched through his waves—"maybe because someone tried *killing* you ten months ago, and we still don't know if the risk is gone. The only thing that's kept us safe since is this fucking quarantine."

"News flash, Daniel. The risk isn't gone. It's still out there. And I ain't sittin' around and twiddlin' my damn thumbs waiting till it strikes again."

I threw my hand out, gesturing to the horizon. "Now that Nikki exposed our location, it can chase us anywhere.

Here. Savannah. Madrid. London. It doesn't matter, so let's live our lives like you said we would."

Lowering my voice, I soothed, "You're the one who promised we'd be a normal family as much as we could. You'll go back to work, and so will I."

"That was before you got shot at! Again!" He towered over me. "News flash, Charlie. We're not fucking normal. We're fucking stalked. To a deadly degree. Over ninety million people follow us. And now you want to go cavorting about Savannah, Georgia like we don't have to be careful? Like you just want to dance in front of another bullet, asking for one to hit you again?"

"Don't you dare, Daniel!" My nostrils flared. "This is my job, not a game or a dance. It's what I do. Remember how you met me? Before I was pulled into the riptide of your celebrity life? I've lost pieces of me along the way, but I'm not giving away this one. I'm going to protect her."

"I know you want to help her, Charlie, her, and every woman or girl. But you're also a mom and a wife now. Where's your responsibility to us?"

I shook my head at that outdated notion, teeth clenched. "You know I love you and our family. More than anything. But I'm no different than a husband or a dad who risks his life for his job. What do you think the military and police do when they're actually doing their job right, protecting people? They have families who love and fear for them too, but someone has to do it."

"It's not the same, Charlie. Our children need their mother."

"And they need their father too. Are you any less important in their lives, Daniel? No. Trust me. I miss both my parents, equally. That's how it is in our world—equal."

Now my fist punched the air with my stubborn truth.

"I have equal rights and I fucking fought for them. I don't want anyone's goddamn special treatment because I'm a woman or a mom. That's a dangerous logic that leads people into believing they can make all my decisions, and I won't allow it. Never. Over my dead body. Literally."

"No." Veins popped in his neck at the image I uttered into existence. "Nothing will be over your dead body. I've already knelt over it once, thinking you and the twins were taken from me. Don't you bloody dare put us through that again!"

I winced at my choice of words but wouldn't take them back.

I meant it. There were things worth dying for. My freedom to make that choice? One of them. I hated the pain in his eyes, the brutal conundrum we were in, but I'd live no other way.

"Daniel," I said, "we love each other. So, if one of us asks the other to stop doing what we're passionate about, we won't recognize the person it would reduce us to. I don't ask you to abandon your career, and it puts us at risk too. So, let's support each other." I reached out to hug him. "You know I'll be careful."

He jerked away from me. "No. What I know is that you won't stop until you're dead, no matter what I say, so what's the bloody use in me caring anymore?"

Storming past me into the house, he slammed the door behind him.

CHAPTER TWENTY-TWO

CHARLIE

SEPTEMBER. ***One month before...***

Standing in the doorway of our home gym hours later, I watched Daniel bench press his fury into the steel bar and plates above his head.

"You sure are hot when you're pissed off."

He stared at the ceiling, exhaling anger with each exertion. "It's not bloody funny." Another rep up and he spewed the words, "It's only bloody, isn't it?"

Oh, that's a good one. He's fuming for sure.

I walked up to his muscles sprawled over the bench. His shirt was thrown to the floor. His black gym shorts could barely contain his mass and rage. Fuck, how many reps did he have in him?

"Are you going to be a beautiful dick all day, or are we going to talk about this?"

The bar banged down into the rack over his head. "I'm not being a dick by worrying about your safety, not after all we've been through." He wouldn't look at me.

"I know," I said, "and I love you for that, and I don't want you to stop. But I also need for you to believe in me. I'm your wife and a mom. But I'm also a professional. I'm fucking good at what I do, and I love it. We made our vows, remember? I'm asking you, please, live up to yours now."

The huff of his ribs slowed. He was trying to calm down. It was a slow burn.

"I forgave you about Keats," I said, "about your lie because I accept you. I'm not trying to change you. Can't you do the same for me?"

"Charlie"—he talked to the ceiling—"you know I love you and want to support you. And I know I owe you. But bloody hell, babe, this is pushing it too far."

Yeah, going back to work was perfectly normal for many new moms at some point. But going back to work ten months after someone tried to kill me was flipping my middle finger at whatever the fuck "too far" was.

Still, we knew, breathing in the silence—there was no changing my mind.

Finally, he put his eyes on me. I stood there with my hand on my hip, patiently waiting for him to come around.

"Fuck's sake." His tone changed to total shock. "What are you wearing?"

Given our obscene amount of dirty laundry, I had to reach to the back of my dresser drawer for the last, old workout clothes I had—red athletic dolphin shorts and a white "Carolina" tank top.

They were from my college days. They still fit me, except for my full, post-baby boobs straining under the thin tank. And you could forget a sports bra. They were all sweaty on the laundry room floor.

"This was all that was clean. I wore this in college for track team." My mouth explained, but my libido was distracted by that sudden gleam in his eyes. "Why? You like it?"

His head didn't move from resting on the bench, but his smile surged. "Oh"—his eyebrows danced—"I *fancy* them." The rise in his shorts surged too with his answer. "You look like a naughty footballer with a fit body demanding sin."

Damn, every time he said "naughty" with that accent my pussy jumped to a standing ovation. And he knew it.

Fran tended to the twins upstairs as usual during our afternoon workout. But today, we needed to work out more than the muscles between us.

Inspiration hit me, twirling my long ponytail. "Can we take a halftime break on our fight, Coach Pierce?" This would bring him around.

"Coach Pierce?" His grin and hard-on grew at the role assigned.

That's how we'd settle this. Okay, maybe I was wrong back at Silas's place about men—fucking can solve a few things.

"Teach me how to be a naughty player for you, Coach Pierce." My fingertips circled the thin cotton straining over my pebbled nipples. "Is this right? Is this how I do it?"

"Bloody hell, woman, you drive me fucking mad. Mad angry to mad horny." His fist started stroking his cock straining under nylon shorts. "Dear God, I'm going to run hard drills on you."

"You're not supposed to fuck with your players, Coach Pierce." I lifted my tank top, resting it above my breasts, tempting him even more. "But you make me so wet, I can't help myself." This was too fun, and melting away our anger... and really turning me on.

"You're not supposed to play with yourself in front of me either." He smirked. "But you'll do as I say. Right now."

I grinned at his coaching methods, arousal already pooling between my thighs. Slowly sliding my hand into my shorts, yep, a slick of it awaited my fingers.

He watched me, commanding, "Show me that sweet pussy, Charlie. Pull your shorts down and give me fifty of those."

Pushing them down to hug my thighs, I confessed, "This is what I do thinking about you." My hands played, one toying with my nipple, the other with my clit. "What do I make you do, Coach Pierce?" I teased with my most lurid tone. "After practice? In your car? I tempt you, don't I? You sit there, jerking off, wanting to fuck me like you do right now."

Lifting his hips up, he pushed his shorts down until they featured his glorious cock seized into his pumping grasp.

"Yes, I do. I watch your pert tits on the pitch and want to suck them. I see the outline of your pussy in those shorts and want to eat it raw. I watch your ass bend over, and I want to fuck it all night long. To make you so dirty for me." His gaze didn't leave my teasing hands. "Give me thirty more."

I obeyed, loving it when he took charge like this, biting my lip at his early drops tempting my tongue. Sliding slick, closer to my edge, our fight was gone, only this tension building now, my body clenching for him. "Watch me come for you, Coach Pierce." I was right there, my dam threatening to burst.

"No." His bark stopped me. "Obey me and come sit on my face." I pushed my shorts down, but when I tried stepping out of them, he barked "No!" again. Damn, he was getting off on controlling me. "Leave them around your ankle because you're too horny for me to care."

Fuck, how could a pair of gym shorts wrapped around

my ankle turn him on so much? Don't know. Don't care. It did.

Swinging my leg over the bench, I centered my pussy over his waiting whiskers, bracing myself on the Olympic bar in front of me. His hands reached up, spreading me open, my flesh pulled taut for his full, wide lick, cunt to clit, his beard tickling through my folds.

"Show me how naughty you get for me." He demanded, "And ride this pussy over my face."

And oh, hell yes, his tongue started fucking me with his nose pressed against my clit. His fury turned into famine, devouring what he could command of me.

Our spectacle in the wall of mirrors beside us shook my thighs. "Like this, Coach Pierce?" I stroked over his face in tempo with his hand stroking his cock. His moans vibrated through me, his fingers sneaking under and banging me from behind.

That was all I needed, minutes watching this pleasure, and I quaked over him, struggling to keep the strength in my legs while I groaned, releasing wet streams through his beard in a slur of curses. He gave me four full, beautiful slurps before kissing my pussy with a glistening smile.

His turn now. He gripped my waist firmly. I thought he wanted a hard ride, but he sat up instead.

"You'll do as I say and watch me fuck you." Standing up, he forced me to rise with him. Stepping over the bench and turning me around, he slapped my hands against the mirror before slapping my ass. "Bend over so I can fuck the bloody hell out of you."

Hell yes, please, and thank you. I liked angry Daniel, dominating my sex since he couldn't control me otherwise. I obeyed, arching my back. Maybe we should fight more?

He squatted behind me, snapping the shorts still wrapped around my ankle. "Spread your legs wider and show me how your pussy drips for me."

The vulnerable stance took my body. Bent over and open only for him, his gaze took me in. His warm breath steamed up the back of my thighs before his tongue trailed from my clit to cunt, up to my ass—every part of me I'd let him claim.

This was how much I loved him. Furious or tender, I trusted him, submitting only to him, only like this. "Please fuck me." I looked over my shoulder. "Punish me and fuck me hard."

We'd never done it like this before but our life was reaching the boiling point—scorching our passion even hotter for each other too.

"Careful what you beg for, Charlie." His fingers spread the desire from between my lips to over my ass, and oh fuck, they slammed inside, claiming both my aching holes. "Tempt me and I can break you." They started pounding. "And you'll fucking love it as I do."

Yes, I did. I'd never seen him like this either. And I knew why.

Control was all he knew; everyone did what he said... but not me. I challenged him, pushing him to this dark, new edge with me.

"You love me like this, don't you?" He stood up to his favorite question, the force of his hand, his words, overwhelming me. "You're all mine to fuck, aren't you?" His fingers crescendoed in a ferocious jerk between my cheeks. "Only I can control you, can't I?" A scream left my body with another wave over his palm, dripping a puddle to the floor.

That was his answer.

His cock took my pussy next, stretching for his mass while his fingers kept pummeling my ass, circling, then plunging back hard inside. I found no breath, only love, only lust. My hands splayed as wide as my thighs, pressing against the cool glass, watching his hot image in the mirror.

"Fuck me so hard, Daniel." I wanted his rage, his forgiveness, his release, his love—all of him.

"No." He smacked my ass again. "I'll fuck you how I want."

He was in charge, his cock and fingers thrusting slow. And slower than that. And oh God, even slower still.

"You're *mine*, Charlie." Changing to circles inside, he dizzied me. "Any. Fucking. Way. I. Want." Taunting me, grinding with an expert touch, he urged into my ache. My eyes rolled back. "*No.*" More of his raunchy demands. "Watch how only I can fuck you."

The reflection made me obey, watching...

How sweat glistened his perfect body. Restraint shredded his every muscle. Greed possessed his gorgeous eyes while his full lips parted in awe. His shorts were around one of his ankles too, while his other hand slowly traced down my spine before seizing my waist. His stare lifted, holding mine in the reflection.

"That's it, babe." He found a torturous rhythm and wouldn't relent. Relishing the control he had of my pleasure, pulling me higher, and higher, dangling me over my favorite edge. "Take my fingers in your tiny ass and my cock in that tight pussy. Nice and slow."

Submitting to his lewd demands, I whimpered in bliss. No control. Only need. The pressure of him sliding so slowly inside ignited a beautiful fire across my nerves. It trembled in my ankles, quaking my knees, twitching my thighs, making my muscles faint.

"Good God, Daniel, you feel so good." I reveled in every stalling, hard, penetrating inch of him, dripping like honey down my walls, he was so fucking sweet.

And the sight of him in the mirror? Of his mesmerizing eyes? "You're going to come so hard for me, aren't you?" His deep voice and plunge, his cock, his fingers, they wouldn't stop. Moving inside me, his aqua stare was glazed with lust, controlling me at any pace, in any way. "Show me how you're mine." Yes, he was in control, marking every part of me as his. Almost, almost, stopping there, all the way pressing in, stretching my pain into pleasure. "Do it, Charlie. Come for me."

It burst through my body with no sound, pleasure so powerful, leaving me open and vulnerable with him, safe as I detonated in a flood of devotion to him. "Daniel" was all I could huff through the onslaught, the craving tears surrendering to him, to his reflection.

He knew the rest. Yes, he loved me too.

His lips kissed between my shoulder blades, leaving them there, warm and tender against my skin while he grabbed my hips. His thrusts quickened into brutal grunts with his beautiful pounding so hard my feet left the ground until his body seized behind me with his loud, painful gasp of release, and another, and another before he whispered, "Charlie, *please*," against my flesh, "I love you."

He rested his cheek on my back. Everything about us softened in the minutes we stood there catching our breath together.

Slowly, I stood up, pressing my back to his chest, reaching around for his kiss, feeling our love trickle down my thighs. "I promise I'll be safe, Daniel. That I'll come home to you."

He nodded, wrapping his arms around me, taking my kiss and oath.

"Love, honor, cherish, respect and support"—that was our vow, and he'd honor his.

CHAPTER TWENTY-THREE

DANIEL

SEPTEMBER. ***One month before...***

Curiosity found me searching for her. With Caroline sitting on my forearm, I found Charlie in our bathroom. My squirming daughter was just like my wife, the one squirming to go to work.

"Wow," I said," this brings back memories."

My comment made Charlie grin while the sight clenched my heart. The black tactical pants and white athletic T-shirt she wore were basic garb for a job I knew could be anything but. The only thing diluting their ominous function was her long blonde ponytail swishing behind a black baseball hat.

She turned to me. "From the set of *The Druid* where we fell in love, to our home now, married and with kids. Yeah... it's weird for me too."

She stretched her lips up for my kiss, landing them on Caroline's cheek next. Caroline tried grabbing her hat, but she pulled away with a smile just in time.

"Yes, well," I said, "tell that grin on your face that this is serious business and not for jolly fun."

"Don't worry. It's both." She sat down on the edge of our soaking tub. Shoving her foot into her tactical boot, she laced it with practiced hands, looking up at me. "What are you doing today? Other than daddy duty?"

"I'll keep writing while they sleep and maybe distract myself with porn until you get home tonight." Maybe I was joking.

"Save that for me." She nodded toward the bulge in my shorts before taking a small knife off the bathroom counter and sliding it into a hidden compartment in her boot.

"I didn't know you kept that in there."

"I'm loaded with surprises." She repeated the same ritual with her other boot. "There's a razor blade in the hidden pocket of this one."

"Razor blade? What for?" Caroline yanked at my beard. I pulled away from her painful grab. "No," I admonished her cute face with a stern look.

"The razor blade is for whatever comes my way: rope, tape, someone's throat." She winked before slapping her kneecaps and standing up. "I have bobby pins in my hair and hidden in my back pockets to pick the lock of handcuffs. And I always carry two stainless steel pens in my vest. They're good for taking down notes and taking out eyes."

"Jesus, Charlie." Her covert arsenal made me sick... and impressed. "I would laugh, but I know you're serious."

She slid a black leather belt with a gun holster into her pants. "Damn right, I'm serious."

"You weren't wearing that when I fell in love with you." Guns strapped to my wife's body skyrocketed my fear.

"I didn't need to on *The Druid*. I knew it was Mason and

that I could beat his ass. He couldn't carry a firearm in Spain, so it wasn't an issue. But they are here."

"I don't need reminding," I said right as Caroline yanked at my beard again. I set her down on the bathroom floor with another firm "no" to teach her to stop and she started crying.

Charlie tickled her hands through my whiskers. "As much as I love this, you might as well shave it off. She won't stop pulling at it, and you'll have to when you start filming anyway."

"Either way, she needs to learn to listen to us." I caressed her right cheek and scar, talking over our daughter fussing at our feet. "I need for at least one woman in my life to obey me."

"Well, don't look at this one"—she pecked my lips before marching out of the bathroom, aiming toward our closet —"unless it's your turn at our sexcapades."

"Speaking of... when will you be home?"

I picked up a crying Caroline, who quieted, resting her head on my chest.

"I'm not staying late. I'll tour the set, check Riley's trailer, and meet with a producer. If I have time, I'll check Riley's apartment too. If not, I'll do that tomorrow. My backup is meeting us there at eleven."

We followed her path, watching Charlie reach behind rarely worn winter coats. Hidden behind them was a gun safe.

Buttons beeped as she entered the code. The door popped open. Grabbing her .380 out, it was always loaded and went straight into the holster at her back. At night, it hid under her nightstand.

Her tactical vest yanked off the hanger with the snap of her hand. It slid over her like a second skin. Reaching into the safe, she grabbed extra bullets, securing them in her vest before turning around, seeing us standing there.

It was like watching all beautiful hell about to break loose.

When she walked out of the closet toward me, I sighed, "You look like a fit SWAT team sniper. I don't know whether to be turned on or terrified."

"The only thing hot about me will be the sweat down my back, especially since I have to wear these." She picked up the KN95 mask and face shield all had to wear on set, packing them into her rucksack along with her phone and extra flash charger.

"Do you think you'll be recognized behind that mask?" I plopped down on the bed, patting Caroline's back. "It hides your famous scar."

"I hope so. I want people to recognize me."

"Since when?"

"If my face is going to be so damn recognizable now as Daniel Pierce's wife, a.k.a. Captain Charlotte Roberts, then I might as well use it to my advantage. If the threat to Riley is on set, they'll go on high alert when they see me protecting her."

"Do you think that'll make them stop?"

"Doubt it," she said, "but it's worth a shot."

That phrase screeched my mind to a stop. Oh, the fucking irony... and the fear.

But it didn't stop Charlie. She kept going, zipping up her gear with determined hands. I beckoned her over with my free one. That stopped her.

She neared, offering the one comfort I could have—her touch. "Thank you for supporting me," she said.

"Does it matter?"

"Your love means everything to me. I feel even braver now, able to help more people because of you."

That was bittersweet news. Brushing my lips over her wedding band and ring, I said, "Text me when you leave Savannah and I'll meet you at the dock."

"Won't you be busy watching porn in the office?"

"I prefer our naughty videos and photos to porn. But lately, if I have free time, I'm writing."

"I can't wait to read your next screenplay. It's shaping up into a great series. Watch. One day, you and Lorraine will produce it."

"Flattery will get you everywhere, Mrs. Pierce." I stood up, giving her a one-armed hug.

She kissed Caroline's cheek resting on my chest before putting her lips to mine.

If I could secure Charlie to this moment forever, I would. But no. Next, she'd go find Duke with Fran, offering our son a goodbye kiss before she left for work.

I loved the thought but hated the fact—there was no stopping my wife.

"Okay, Sex God," she said. "See ya 'round six."

Letting go of my hand, she turned away, grabbing her rucksack. I listened for her steps down the stairs and heard her give goodbyes to Duke and Fran. Then the garage door beeped before the rumble of her Jeep minutes later hit my ear.

I tried reasoning it away, the foreboding terror squeezing my ribs. Was it my scar, my PTSD after everything I'd witnessed, everything I'd almost lost? Or was it something more?

Sunlight danced on the placid blue ocean outside. The spectacle would relax anyone. Not me. All I stared at was our wrecking storm on the horizon.

CHAPTER TWENTY-FOUR

CHARLIE

SEPTEMBER. ***One month before...***

Lorraine had a production assistant pick me up at the marina. The P.A. was prompt, quickly driving me to the location being used for the show.

Savannah didn't have a major film studio like Madrid or London. Here, they had converted an empty retail building, adjacent empty parcels, and a couple dozen trailers into a make-shift studio. They would use the buildings for interior shots while much would be filmed on location around the historic city.

This show, *The Tour,* was a true ode to Lorraine's hometown. Savannah, Georgia, would be featured like a principal cast member.

The good news was the city sat on the horizon from my island's shores. I knew every historic garden and enchanting block.

The bad news? The old city hid dark alleys, haunted cobblestone streets, and historic buildings surrounded by water on one side and highways on the other, providing easy access to it all.

Melissa, a producer on the show, met me at the Testing Station by the gate to the fence they installed around the production. They had security in place, keeping the property secure. Melissa informed me that the rest of the principal cast didn't have personal protection on set.

"Is there a threat against Riley we should know about?" Melissa asked.

"Nothing of great concern." I was thankful a mask covered my lying face. And thankful Riley wasn't on set today, per my instructions.

Walking around, noting the grips setting up their rigs while set dec finished dressing the interior sets, it struck me as odd. All worked behind masks and face shields. You could barely tell people apart or read their expressions.

Fuck, this wasn't going to be easy if I couldn't watch people's faces.

You sure you wanna do this? The blackmailing son-of-a-bitch could be standing right next to you, and you may not even sense it.

Suddenly, this job felt different.

But I kept going, the protocol the same. I combed Riley's trailer for cameras or other surveillance. It was clean. Nothing felt off.

I sat down on the little sofa to make a video call.

"You already miss me, don't you?" Daniel's rich voice filled the hollow silence of the trailer.

Taking the mask and shield off my face, "Yes," I confessed.

"As much as the twins?"

"Sure do. Same amount."

I loved the way Daniel's eyes glowed on-screen. Me and

ninety million fans apparently. But the way he smiled back at me, that was for me alone.

He laughed, making me grin even bigger. "That's a bloody lie," he said before turning the screen. "Look at what this cheeky monkey's doing."

The phone in my hand showed our daughter pulling up to stand using the sofa as her accomplice while our son crawled by, taking careful notes for his first attempt.

Watching them grabbed my throat. "Please don't let them do something without me there."

The screen moved back to his face. "It's all right, babe. We love you." He held it up high so I could see him and our babies behind him. "And I'll miss a few things too. But we'll video for each other, okay?"

God, if I could leap through the screen and jump his bones, I would. He knew just what to say. I *did* already miss him. "How's it going?"

"Fine," I said. "It's a much smaller production which is a plus. It feels good being back on set, even if everyone is wearing masks. It's a relief and surreal. You'll see when you go back in a couple of months."

"I can imagine," he said over a loud cry.

He turned his head. The screen caught Caroline sprawled over the top of Duke and Duke's protest. She must've fallen back. Nothing new. They were always all over each other.

"Gotta go, babe," he said. "Love you. See you at six."

"Love you all. Bye." They disappeared.

With a big inhale, I moved on instinct. *Get up and do your job.*

For the next two hours I wandered around the lot, cataloging everyone by their shoes or jewelry they wore. I started matching eyes and introductions to names I saw on the crew sheets. No one seemed suspicious but then again, how could they? They hid behind masks and shields. *Damn.*

I found Melissa and asked if a P.A. could give me a ride to Riley's house. The car stopped in front of a three-story pastel pink townhome with black shutters matching the iron stair railing leading up to the second-level black front door.

I liked what I saw climbing the stairs, taking my mask off, and putting my baseball cap back on.

The ground-level windows had ornate iron bars over them. The second-floor windows had the same over the lower panel. No one could break in through these. The large front door was an old, heavy wooden one—same goes—it was secure.

One ring and one minute later, Riley opened the front door. She offered a hug. "My goodness, I almost didn't recognize you through the peephole with that hat on."

"Glad you're in the habit of checking it."

Riley gave me a tour. It was the usual in these historic homes. The kitchen, parlor and living room were on the second floor. A guest bedroom, library, and laundry room were on the ground floor with a back door out to an enclosed courtyard. The top floor had two more grand bedrooms with a bathroom for each.

"Which one are you using?" Both bedrooms looked so tidy. Riley was a woman after my heart—organized and neat.

Riley pointed to the one at the top of the staircase landing. "That one. Why?"

"I know that one has the fancier ensuite bathroom." I pointed to the other. "But this one has a balcony for escape. It's safer for you."

I led Riley into the front bedroom and out onto a black

iron balcony perched above the street with two pedestrians walking below.

"But it's three stories up," Riley said.

"Yeah, but you can escape and climb down from here. There's an iron balcony and railing below it and a lamp post beside it. Even if you fall down a bit on the way, that sidewalk will be much kinder to you than anything that comes up those stairs after you. Okay?"

Riley nodded her head in quick agreement.

"I know it's scary to have to think this way, but a few changes can make all the difference."

"I understand." Riley smiled, tucking her gorgeous, ghostly hair behind her ear. "What else should I do?"

I outlined our plan. Wade, my backup from HGR Atlanta, would meet us tomorrow. I liked him from our first phone conversation. He didn't mansplain or minimize the situation—score one hundred points for him.

Wade would sleep in the ground-level bedroom, covering Riley most nights. I'd be there for most days. Occasionally, we'd have to switch, giving each other breaks.

Thankfully, due to health restrictions, this show wasn't filming at a break-neck pace. There'd be some night shoots, but no weekends.

It felt odd to me, giving a shit about days off. But for the first time in seven years, I had a family to go home to.

I checked my phone. We had two hours before my ride back to the marina. My laptop in the parlor came on with that satisfying *whoom,* and I started digging. "Let's look through all the cast and crew."

We sat on the green velvet sofa, staring at the list on the screen. Riley shook her head. "I have no idea how anyone on this show would know."

"Who does?" I respected the hell out of Riley's privacy. But this? This I had to ask.

Riley held out her hand, counting with her fingers through the short list.

One, her thumb. "My mom, of course. My dad was out of the picture before I turned one, and never heard from again. If you think this blackmailing asshole has to fear you, you haven't met my mom yet."

Hell yes, another badass mom. I liked her already.

Riley's index finger and two. "My doctors. No way they'd do this. It's not in them to hurt their patients." My instinct nodded in full agreement.

Her middle finger and three. "One mean kindergarten teacher in Atlanta who said I had to use the boys' bathroom or the teachers' lounge on the other side of the school instead of the girls' bathroom with my friends. I refused and had so many accidents that year."

Sudden tears threatened me with the image. One of a sweet little girl in kindergarten, probably getting laughed at because she wet her pants. What evil adult would do that to a child? "I'm so sorry, Riley," I said.

"Well, she passed away, so that's that."

Ring finger and number four. "Ashley Lynn, my sorta ex-girlfriend." Then her pinkie. "Lorraine. I broke down in tears a few weeks ago while I was having dinner with her and told her everything," Riley said, "and you."

I didn't earn a place on the one hand Riley counted with, but that was it—six possibilities and none made the hinge of my jaw tingle with a threat. Yet.

"Could that kindergarten teacher have told someone?" I asked. "Was she married? Or did she gossip to other teachers at the school?"

"I have no idea. It was supposed to be a privacy issue. Like my mom only told her, but I can't be sure to be honest."

Riley tucked her hair behind her right ear. Not that it fell. It was a nervous habit of hers I clocked.

"What about Ashley Lynn?" I asked. "Are y'all on good terms?"

Ex-anything? I trusted swimming with a starving alligator more than I trusted an ex.

Riley's smile warmed her coffee-colored eyes.

"Yes. We still love each other. We've been together for four years. She acts too. We met on *Death March* in Atlanta, but she was written off after season one and travels a lot for auditions. I say 'sorta ex' because we're long distance and give each other space. It's hard staying together with our careers."

"Tell me about it." I propped my boots up on the tufted ottoman. "Between the Marines and this job, I know how hard it is."

"Are you and the twins going with Mr. Pierce to Madrid in November?"

I knew why worry curved across Riley's brow. This show wasn't scheduled to wrap until late January.

"Yes. That's my promise to Daniel. We stick together. But don't worry. We'll wrap this shit up long before that."

"How?" Riley wrung her hands adorned in funky rings.

I dropped my boots to the floor, propping my elbows on my knees, running it through.

"It's someone on set. I don't have proof yet, but I know it. And I have a few games to get a stalker to come out and play."

I looked at Riley. "In the meantime, our HGR Atlanta office is following the digital footprint on those messages. Today, you'll reply to the most recent one with, 'I'll need more time.' Let's get that dumbass to stick their foot in the sand, and we got their location. Make sense?"

"Yeah." Worry wouldn't leave Riley's face. "But how would someone on set possibly know from the six that do?"

"There's always going to be more than one footprint in the sand leaving a trail, right?" I winked at her. "When we find who the other foot belongs to, we got 'em both."

CHAPTER TWENTY-FIVE

CHARLIE

SEPTEMBER. ***One month before...***

Daniel stood on Silas's dock with his hands shoved into his pockets. The sight of him waiting for me revved my heart. I tied up the boat quickly, leaping onto the dock beside his imposing form.

"Hey stranger. I've missed this face." I cupped my hand under his freshly shaven and famous, cleft chin. "Did you walk over?"

"Yes. I needed some time to myself." His bare bowed lips neared mine. "And I missed you."

Damn, his kiss. It was like we'd been apart for months instead of a day. I savored his pillowy, warm lips, his expert tongue toying over the seam of my lips, teasing its way in.

One positive of being married to a talented, eye-candy actor—the man could kiss. He had to do it so many times on screen. Pair practice with his real passion, and he made my knees go weak. I reached for his long waves, at least he didn't cut those. With his beard gone, I moaned at the return of his smooth, sexy face.

"You better take me home now, or we're going to give Silas another show." I nodded toward his house thirty feet away. He was home. His Jet Ski and Bronco were there.

Daniel held my hand, walking back toward the Jeep. "So is it solved? Can I have you back home and safe with me again?" He jumped into the open passenger seat while I fished in my backpack for the keys.

"No. But I promise we're off to Madrid by November no matter what."

"It felt odd today, scary almost. I haven't left your side a single day since the premiere. I've been spoiled with ten months of you."

"It was weird for me too." I hopped into the driver's seat, loving that about him. How he was man enough to say what he felt. "And I confess... I missed you too." It made me grin. "I guess I'm really fucking in love with you."

He laughed back at the obvious. "So, what is she being blackmailed about?"

"I can't say. Not that I want to keep things from you. It's just"—I turned the engine on—"it's private for Riley."

"Okay. I get it." He placed his hand on my thigh, his support as much of an aphrodisiac as his touch. "As much as it scares the fuck out of me, I'm proud of you, you know—helping her and all."

Sweet mother of God had he ever looked so fucking gorgeous to me? Yes, thousands of times. "Thank you." I tried refocusing, starting down the sandy lane, and counting my blessings. "Did you have a productive day? Did you get to watch our porn?"

His laugh deepened, heating my core. "No. You told me

to save it for you." He squeezed my upper thigh, his fingers oh so close to... *yes, now*.

I shifted down and turned, leaving the one-lane path.

"What are you doing?"

Gunning the engine, I steered over the sandy embankment, pulling the Jeep into a small clearing under the tree canopy. Turning the car off, I reached over, searching between his sculpted thighs. "I want to withdraw my savings right now."

Today, being away from him, the deep feeling of unease about this job; it had me desperate to touch him, to grab on to the one thing that made me feel safe—our love.

His hips thrust toward my grasp. "Anyone driving by can see us."

"I know."

"This is why"—he gave me a devilish grin—"my beautiful, naughty wife is better than any porn."

"Yes, I am. Now take your shorts off," I said while freeing my feet from boots and socks. My hat was already off from the windy ride over. Quickly, I undid my pants next, sliding them along with my panties down to the floorboard and kicking them off.

And oh hell, and when I looked back at him, he sat there with his shirt off, shorts and boxer briefs around his ankles with his hard cock screaming at me like a loud maître d' telling me exactly where to sit.

Fuck yes. I pulled my shirt and sports bra off too. *God, you love him. And you need him. Now.*

We sat naked, vulnerable in the evening air, open to each other, the smoky dusk light, and any little bugs that wanted a bite. I took mine first.

My head went down between his legs, teasing his fat crown with licks before plunging my mouth down his shaft, his groan filling the air along with the crickets chirping.

"Fuck yes, babe, suck my fucking cock." I heard his hand lower the seat next while his other gently pulled my ponytail elastic out. It freed my hair, falling in a blanket across his thighs. He laced his fingers through my strands, "Fuck you feel so bloody good," thrusting to the back of my throat.

I wanted this so much, so eager for his pleasure and taste, it ignited my libido as much as his. With all he proved to me, his love and devotion, there wasn't an inch of him I didn't want inside of me. Every husband would get their cock sucked off and fucked like mad if they loved their wives this way.

He enjoyed my gratitude until his gentle grasp pulled my hair up. "I want all of you," he said. "Stand up."

Now, that command I'd obey.

He helped me, placing one of my feet between his legs on the passenger seat and swinging the other over his shoulder. Thank you, Jeep, for the roll bars that met my grasp while I rolled my pussy over his outstretched tongue.

What sweet saint delivered to me a partner who got off on eating pussy? Could I build a shrine to her? Yes. And every woman alive would make a pilgrimage to it—daily.

The feeling of his smooth mouth and hard chin buried between my lips took me back to the first time he lavished me, opening my body and heart to him forever. And where we were today? Everything we shared. Every blessing we had. And everything we almost lost. His tongue and moaning throat received me again after just one... no, five decadent minutes until his huge hands held my quaking hips still for his reward, making me cry grateful tears down my cheeks.

God, I loved him so much. It overwhelmed me, so

exposed, so naked to him and always feeling so secure; his touch my refuge.

My weak thighs fell upon him, taking his lips with my kiss, I tasted my lust on his tongue while I wrapped around his. His legs stretched underneath me, passive to me except for his greedy hands gripping my hips hard. I sealed him inside of me, always, with a slow roll in a divine circle over his every inch.

"Fuck, I cherish you." Two of his fingers pressed into my mouth. I sucked them before he rolled them over my clit. "So much," he said, moving in a circle opposite my grind, "so fucking much."

"Oh God, Daniel." I cried with joy, lost in him. He was everywhere inside me—body, heart, and soul—there was no end to us.

"Promise me." His fingers pressed harder, his hips lifting, matching mine. "You'll never leave me."

A groan lulled up his throat when that command made me flex every muscle below my waist, taking him even harder. "I promise," I said just as the putter of a golf cart nearing filled the air.

It broke my intensity, almost making me giggle.

But it only drove him harder, knowing we'd get caught. His tongue was on my nipple before his whole mouth took me with a hard suck. Oh, fuck yes, if we were going to be seen he was going to make it a helluva show.

The sound of the cart approached. The engines under the space shuttle of my clit roared for a take-off. His tongue shamelessly played with my nipples, leaving them dripping wet with all his mouth could offer while he switched to his stronger, slick thumb circling, rousing over my clit.

I watched over his shoulder. How the faint lights of the cart approached, two voices filling the evening air. But nothing could stop us, so overwhelmed and on the edge, we didn't care.

It only possessed him more, his hands tight in my hair, pulling my gaze to stare at him. "I want the whole world to watch me fuck you while you only look at me and come so fucking hard on my cock." He growled, and his hips started jackhammering, smacking his cock into me, relentlessly against my clit. "Now, Charlie. Show them how I make you come so hard."

Yes, sir. Right there and then. The cart passed by while my every nerve roared in screams of soaking silence staring into his eyes, my cum pouring over his lap.

Daniel's hips bucked harder under me; he wasn't so quiet. "Fuck yes, Charlie!" he cried out like he wanted them to look, to know who we were, not caring about our X-rated celebrity spectacle.

If the people on the cart would stop talking and turn their eyes, they'd see us in an open Jeep, my naked body fucking his, my wet nipple back in his sucking mouth with a groan grinding up his throat, making him come at the risk.

But they kept going and so did I. Needing more of him always, I started a hard rock back and forth on his shaft. His hot show of a finish gave me one more victory lap, making me throw my head back, convulsing with another rush over us.

"Charlie." The bass of his voice woke me from the explosion of light I disappeared into. "Come here." He caressed my cheek, his lips dusted over mine. "Promise me I won't lose you again." Our kiss, over and over, it made me cry again.

"I promise, Daniel." I knew what he was really asking—everyone we'd loved, lost and buried—he feared I'd join them. "I'll always come home to you. I swear."

CHAPTER TWENTY-SIX

DANIEL

OCTOBER. ***Now...***

Glancing down, I had a 9 percent charge left on my phone and I used it on one desperate call.

After four rings, Rob finally picked up. "Hey, man. What's up?" His voice cracked with sleep on the other end, sounding like he already knew... we were in trouble.

"Sorry to wake you, mate, but I'm worried about Charlie. She's been MIA since last night with Riley in Savannah. She hasn't phoned. Shit isn't right. I can feel it."

I heard Rob blow the sleep off his brain with a big exhale before he agreed. "Yeah, that's not like her. Lemme call HGR Atlanta. We'll be at your door in fifteen." I could hear him waking up Joaquin before ending the call.

Fifteen minutes before they got there? Before I'd have more answers?

That was too long.

I tried one more pathetic time ringing her.

The call went straight to voicemail this time. Her phone had no charge.

That's not my wife. She kept a charging cord and portable charger in her rucksack. Nothing would keep her from a connection to her family.

"Hey, y'all. This is Charlie Ravenel... talkin' into a damn device. Smile, 'cuz now it's your turn."

I ended the call, panic cracking through my bones.

Oh, please, God. No. No. No. Not again.

The memory of *The Druid* premiere knocked me back into the deck chair.

How blood was all over my hands, the smell of it hitting my nostrils. How I rolled Rob's body off Charlie before pressing my stained palms to her belly, our babies. How the horrific sight bloomed before me—her dark blood seeping through the fabric between her thighs, scorching terror through me. How Rob lay alive but struggling for his breath while Charlie lay pale, looking lifeless at my knees.

Once was enough to fear your wife was gone from this world.

The wife I thanked the heavens for every day. The wife whose smile was my compass. Whose body was my anchor. Whose love was the water keeping me alive. I couldn't live without her.

A sob wanted to escape my soul. I choked it down, burying my eyes in the palm of my hands.

I remembered how later that night of the shooting, standing at the window of the NICU, looking at our tiny newborns, how I'd added it all up.

For thirty-three minutes that night—from the time the

report said the man had fired the shot, to the time on the scanner I noted in the back of the ambulance when the EMT said she'd make it—I'd believed my wife was dying. Right in front of me. Just like my twin brother did when we were ten.

I relived those thirty-three minutes almost every day, tasting a minute of their hell each time.

No, Pierce. It should be you. You deserve this. Not her.

Sitting back up, I gasped for air, opening my wet eyes to the clear October morning and the fifteen minutes now until I'd find out yet again.

Fran's hand was on my shoulder, but nothing could comfort me while the same question ate my soul with ravenous bites.

Is my wife dead?
Is my wife dead?
Is my wife...

CHAPTER TWENTY-SEVEN

CHARLIE

SEPTEMBER. ***One month before...***

It was the first day of filming and though there was excitement in the air, it didn't feel like a usual day on set.

The makeup artist and hair stylist wore paper gowns along with latex gloves, plastic shields, and masks over their faces while they prepped Riley for the first scene of the day. Filming a show during a pandemic made for odd moments for sure.

It was a nice break, sitting in Riley's trailer with her for lunch, able to take the protective gear off and feel human again.

Sitting across from Riley, I caught her considering the scar on my right cheek over our shrimp n' grits and iced tea. It made me smile. "You can ask me anything, Riley."

"Is that really a bullet graze on your cheek, or did the press make that up?"

I didn't mind her questions. Riley had been so honest with her story, I shared mine too. The bullets. The scars.

The girls in Afghanistan. My plan to free them from their abuser. The brother who almost fired on me next before Jax took his bullet instead, losing his foot.

It was a hell of a story just before the P.A. knocked on the door for us to return to set. It left Riley with more questions as we rode toward the marina at the end of the day.

Wade, my backup from HGR, drove us. He'd take me to my boat, then Riley home, covering that night, then pick me up the next morning.

This was day two of our new routine.

"You did all that for those little girls?" Riley asked, sitting beside me in the back of the SUV.

"Yeah, I think I'd do about anything to protect girls and women like you," I said. "Daniel thinks I'm obsessed, but it's my calling."

"I can't bear the thought of you getting hurt protecting me. I'll quit the show before I let it get to that."

"Don't ever quit, Riley. Not for me. Not for anyone." I spoke from my soul; a foreboding hitting me. "Fight until your last breath."

"You don't think it'll get that bad, do you?"

"I'm not gonna lie"—I nodded to Wade turning his ear toward our conversation—"we don't know what we're dealing with yet."

I liked Wade the instant I shook his gigantic hand. He towered over me with a shiny bald head, gorgeous ebony skin, and a comforting smile. We hit it off with a slew of Army versus Marine jokes since we served in different branches. But he fell in line on this job, taking my lead without hesitation.

"Tell her about the report from HGR that came in today," Wade suggested.

He parked the car and watched in the rear-view mirror

as I turned to Riley. "We got the footprint on the messages. He's here. In Savannah. On set or within a quarter mile from it."

I hated frightening Riley, but it was her safety, her right to know.

Riley raised her eyebrow. "He?"

"You're right. We can't assume it's a man, but it usually is. Either way, it's someone on set."

"Well," Riley said, "whoever it is replied that they want the money by the end of this month."

"Don't fret over that bullshit deadline. He wants the money. He'll wait if he thinks he's gonna get it."

"I can get a million together if we're gonna pay it." The anguish on Riley's face broke my heart. "Anything to make this stop."

"Hell to the No," I said. "You're not paying a damn red cent to that motherfucker."

Wade chimed in, "You just let us protect you, Riley. This isn't about money. It's about keeping you safe."

I'd told Wade about the blackmail threats but didn't tell him why, liking him even more because he didn't ask, respecting Riley's privacy.

I squeezed Riley's hand, smiling to assure her. "I'll figure out soon who the asshole is, don't worry."

But while I walked down the ramp toward my boat... my smile faded, thinking it through.

When I found out who it was—when not if—that wouldn't be the hard part.

It was the next.

If we couldn't press charges, using law enforcement, what could I do to protect Riley? What would make this person leave Riley alone, and never bother her again?

I could think of only one guarantee of silence. It was one I never wanted to have to do again.

THE SECOND DAY of filming on set, my ass twitched. That actor kept looking at me with eyes that were more than curious.

Lucas Denton was Riley's co-star on the show, playing Riley's father and playing my nerves.

I stood behind Riley's cast chair while Riley reviewed her lines for the next scene. Each time we sat together in the green room on set, Lucas kept glancing my way.

Damn, take a picture. I rolled my eyes behind my face shield. *And shove it up your ass.*

The P.A. called them to set for their next scene. Taking his mask off for the camera, Lucas was in his early forties and oozing with more sex appeal than a European soccer team.

Leave it to Lorraine—I grinned—she liked casting masculine eye-candy for her shows, Daniel being the sweetest score.

"I have to ask." Lucas beamed at me. "You look familiar, but I can't place your face, especially hiding behind a mask."

Here's your chance. Tell him and most of the crew since his mic pack is hot now for most on set to overhear.

"Nice to meet you, Mr. Denton. I'm Charlie Ravenel."

"But how do I know you, Ms. Ravenel?" The grin he wore tried to seduce for more than my name.

You don't know me. It didn't work. *Just because my face, scars, and torment have been blasted over screens this past year doesn't mean you know a damn thing about me.*

I felt a small measure of what Daniel must all the time—

people assuming they know your soul because they recognize your face.

Riley stood up. Her mic pack was up for all to hear too. "She's also Captain Charlotte Roberts, a Marine veteran, here working for HGR Security as my detail, and married to Daniel Pierce."

There, he heard all he needed. Everyone did. Add it up.

Lucas's face shocked in recognition. "Wow! You're the woman from *The Druid* premiere, from the shooting last year."

Get used to this. That story is another thing now that will chase you till your last breath.

"Yes, my detail thankfully did his job that night protecting me," I said, "and I'm here to do the same for Riley."

"Glad you're here for her." Lucas raised his eyebrow, admiring Riley. "She's a beautiful, young woman, and surely needs it."

Was that a genuine compliment or a creepy admission? I wasn't sure. Even though the man played Riley's father on the show, that wouldn't keep him from being a sick fuck.

I didn't take my eyes off him all day, all while I sensed others staring me down now that they knew it was me—Captain Charlotte Roberts.

Yes, the same one someone tried to kill last year. Yes, the one who took down Mason Hunt. Yes, the one married to Daniel Pierce, mother to their twins. And hell fucking yes, the woman working Riley's detail despite it all.

Good, make them squirm, and watch for the sweat from the guilty one.

BY THAT FRIDAY, Lucas Denton was still in my scope. That man spewed more flirting lines than the ones on the script. I knew his type—flirt with all and see who bites.

But he didn't feel like a stalker, just a player extraordinaire.

I joked with Riley about it over lunch, betting fifty that he'd hook up with someone by next week.

"Romance on set is cliché for a reason." I slurped shrimp bisque. "Hell, I've got a marriage and two kids to show for it."

"Tell me about it." Riley slurped back. "Makes me miss Ashley Lynn."

"Are you two exclusive or are you free to date?"

Riley ripped off a piece of French baguette, dunking it into her bisque with a sigh. "I don't know anymore." The wet bread slipped over her crimson lips before she explained, "I thought we were still together, but the last few times I talked to her... she seemed distant or something."

"Why don't you just ask her and not bullshit around? You deserve the truth." Those words rang powerfully from my mouth given Daniel's damning secret revealed.

"I know. I just don't think I'm prepared for her answer."

"Why is it up to her alone? What do you want?"

"I still love her. She's my first and only." Riley went for another chunk of bread like she was feeding her frustration at the same time. "I just miss her, you know."

"Oh, I do. I missed my first husband when we were stationed apart. I got used to it, but my heart still hurt. And then after he was killed in action, it redefined missing someone for me, so much so that nowadays... I'm missing Daniel just after a long day on set."

"I have to be honest." Riley's face cast a big smile. "If I were into men, I'd miss Daniel Pierce too."

That made me laugh. I was all too familiar with the effect my husband had on everyone around him, regardless of who they were attracted to.

A knock on the trailer door sounded, ending our lunch and fun.

I scooped through the cast and crew gathered for the next setup. I had no time to waste. If instinct served me, I needed it to pony up now, through all the damn masks and shields.

I had to find my target.

The first Assistant Camera guy adjusting focus on Riley? Something about him rang my chime. I looked back at my mark, back at Riley with the slate in front of her face, then over to Riley's image on the monitor.

She was stunning.

Riley's character, Bonavie Tucker, is named after the haunted Bonaventure Cemetery and fashioned to look at home in it too. With silky, ghostly hair, lips, and fingertips matching her signature crushed velvet dress in crimson red, Bonavie reigns over the hallowed ground in tall black lace-up boots for every tour.

In this scene, Bonavie meets the handsome, live descendent of the ghost of the Union soldier who haunts her and The Marshall House. The striking young man doesn't know his own history. He doesn't know he looks exactly like his ghostly ancestor.

But Bonavie does. She's troubled by the ghost and her sexy, new customer who wants a tour... and her.

I was troubled by the heart-stopping actor playing both the ghost and his descendant.

Redix Dean.

Anyone with an appetite for man flesh would crave

him. Cast for a guest appearance in a few episodes, I sensed it—Redix posed no threat to Riley.

He was a friend of Lorraine's, a local kid who escaped the Lowcountry years before to find Hollywood mega success. His return to a production shot here was a favor to Lorraine, firing up his fanbase and firing up even more threats I had to protect Riley from. His fans surrounded every location, screaming for him.

That's what troubled me.

Redix Dean on set had too many fans with too many phones posting jealous threats toward Riley, adding to the real one I scoped for.

Still, I liked him.

Redix reintroduced himself, reminding me that we went to Hilton Head High School together, not that I'd forgotten.

"You still livin' on Daufuskie?" He started up easy small talk.

"Yep, when I'm back in the States." I felt the magnitude of his eclipsing appearance. How his beauty was so enchanting it almost hurt your eyes to look at him. "You still the King of Coligny Beach?"

His heavenly face deadened. "That's a curse now."

That comment wasn't cryptic to me. I knew—the price Redix paid for his allure was high. The risk of being wanted by all wasn't romantic; it was risky.

We chatted a bit more about fishing until it was time again, time for me to scope for the real target.

The assistant director called for action. Riley and Redix were two minutes into the romantic scene when "cut" rang out. The boom mic operator was throwing shadows over the set. They had to start over.

I watched them re-set, watching the boom operator too.

At first, I felt bad for the guy. His boss, the Sound Mixer, wasn't happy with him. But my calculating stare didn't leave him, letting that reaction pass, and the real one drift in.

Even with his face covered by a shield and mask, a red flare fired across my mind, signaling trouble.

The boom operator.

His hover over the cast was right for the job, but wrong for me—the certainty charged through my veins. Watching him near Riley, a sudden electrical storm sparked down my body.

It's him.

What was his name? I mentally scrolled through the crew list I kept on my laptop. Scott. That's it.

Scott Harris.

First call I'd make after we wrapped would be to HGR, to pull everything they could find on him.

This wasn't worth mentioning to Riley yet. It would only unnerve her, making it difficult for her to work.

But I had my work cut out for me. Eyes aimed dead at him, I had my target now.

CHAPTER TWENTY-EIGHT

DANIEL

It Was A Sin by The Revivalists

OCTOBER. ***Now...***

"Wade's on his way to Riley's place," Rob said, standing stoic in the kitchen, updating me while all I could do was pace the room like a caged animal. "He hasn't heard from Riley or Charlie either, but he's ten minutes out."

Rob had called HGR Atlanta for Wade's number, and thankfully, Wade answered his phone to an unknown caller and saved us all.

I tapped my phone charging on the counter.

6:16 am

"I think we should just phone the police now," I said.

"They'd only be minutes behind Wade," Joaquin replied. "Let him get there first. He's not bound by rules of engagement like the officers. He's allowed into Riley's home, has the keys, and is our best, rapid defense right now. If we don't hear from Wade in fifteen minutes, we call the police."

I closed my eyes. Fear gurgled to my throat. And regret. And guilt. I felt sick.

What I said. What I did. I should've talked to her. I should've held her. I should've run after her.

Instead, I'd left it there—yelling at Charlie that our marriage was over—and letting her walk out the door alone, believing it.

Those will be the last words you said to her, Pierce.

I didn't realize I spoke aloud, "I'll never see her again," but I did. I didn't feel it either. It just appeared when I opened my eyes—my tear dropping to my phone.

Suddenly, Rob's arms wrapped around me, pulling me into a hug. That broke me. One gulp and one sob escaped. It let me breathe, and all I inhaled back in was pain.

Memories flashed. A cowgirl hat. A red skirt. A mouse voice. Blue water and pearls. A dance in the Manhattan night. A pregnancy test. A wedded plunge in the ocean. Two white blankets swaddled between us. Her contagious smile. Her blonde head on my chest. Her small hand in mine.

I pulled back from Rob's embrace struggling for air, shaking my head "no" but words failed me. Only memories taunted my mind.

Then I saw it. How Rob had tears in his eyes.

I glanced at Joaquin. They welled up in his too.

Fran was in the nursery. I could hear her on the baby monitor, sniffing back her sobs.

Oh God, they all believe it too, Pierce.

Charlie is gone.

CHAPTER TWENTY-NINE

DANIEL

SEPTEMBER. ***One month before...***

Sunday mornings in bed were my church. I scooped up Caroline and Duke and brought them into our bed for morning play. The beauty of Charlie's face smiling at our children was the masterpiece of my life.

She was teaching them to wave. Duke had the hang of it while Caroline kept crawling over her instead.

"I think she's missed you," I said. "I told you my days as her favorite were numbered."

"I missed them too." She held Caroline over her before blowing raspberries on her belly, making her squeal with laughter. That made Duke jealous, crawling over her too.

I propped up on my elbow, enchanted by the show.

"Guess I'll return to the flavor of the month once you're on mum duty in Madrid, and I get to be the one missed all the time."

"I'll miss you too, you know. We'll wait by the door for you every night."

That made me laugh, imagining how she would. "Now that will be a glorious picture."

"Cheesssseee." She laughed back with me just as Duke smashed his hand over her talking mouth, making us laugh even harder.

I was about to rescue Duke off her when my phone sounded with a tone I knew to fear. My publicist. On a Sunday morning, I already knew... this wouldn't be good.

I rolled over, answering my phone with dread. "What's up, mate?"

"Hate to do this man, but I have to ask. A photo just dropped from some account in Madrid, claims to be of you and Charlie having sex on a car on the set of *The Druid* last year."

"What?" I shot straight up.

"Yep. It's a pretty racy shot. It's blowing up today. Check the text I sent you both and tell me if it's legit."

Feet thudding to the floor, I walked around the bed to Charlie's phone on the nightstand. She watched my approach, her eyes questioning what was going on.

I opened the text message on her phone while talking on mine. When I saw the image... I didn't know whether to laugh or punch a wall.

"That's not her." I huffed. "One hundred percent not."

I held it up so Charlie could see what I was talking about.

It was a photo of the back of a nude woman with long blonde hair, sitting on the hood of a car with a man that looked like me between her thighs and with his lips about to kiss hers. It was taken from far enough to look like a voyeur fuck shot, but close enough to look like me and Charlie. Like someone did a deepfake of our faces.

The photo was posted to a random Instagram account

with fifteen hashtag versions of our names, sparking a pool of gasoline that ignited a blaze of thousands of reposts and climbing.

Charlie looked at it, shaking her head. "Tell him," she mouthed.

"Look, mate," I explained to my publicist, "we never fucked on the job. And that definitely isn't Charlie. She has an exit wound scar on her back above her right hip and that woman doesn't. I want the balls and bank account of whoever posted that shot. Now."

"On it," my publicist confirmed. "Sorry to disturb your day. I'll call when I know more."

"Thanks," I muttered, ending the call.

"You know exactly who's behind this," Charlie said.

"Yes, I do."

I looked at the image again and had to give it to him. Mason Hunt was clever. House arrest couldn't stop him. The photo was staged but steamy, the tech impressive, easily passing for me and Charlie by face alone.

"We can issue a statement," I said, "but it's salacious so people want to believe it's us and repost it."

"Makes me want to post a picture of my body and prove that it's not."

"No, Charlie. It's no one's right to see your body, to see all your scars."

"Daniel, I'm not ashamed of them. Everyone sees the one on my cheek and the one through my shoulder. I don't care if the whole world knows about the other one, the worst one."

"I'm not saying you should be ashamed of them. I'm saying if Mason Hunt hadn't dropped that photo claiming it was you, you wouldn't be proposing to expose your body to the world, would you?"

If I could wrap my hands around Mason's neck, I'd squeeze until Mason's spine collapsed in my bloody fists.

"Maybe not, but still"—Charlie sat up—"I'm sick of this. No more secrets, shame, or fear. Let's be free of it all."

"And what? Go on national telly or do some interview and show the world your scars? God, babe, your body isn't public domain for fucking hearts and comments because you're married to me. Or for any reason for that matter."

"No, but it *is* my body and my life. And Mason Hunt isn't threatening it anymore. He has no power over me."

"Well, someone does. Whoever tried killing you wasn't working alone. That fact still holds great power over us now."

"I know. That's why we won't play into his hands. No national media or interviews." The smile on her lips rose devious… and cute. "But I'll figure out a way to get him back one day."

That stopped me dead with a smile. "God help any man when you get that look on your face." I plopped on the bed across from her, refusing like her to let this spoil our day. "I'm glad that look isn't aimed at me anymore."

She leaned all the way over, offering me a soft kiss, confirming that was true.

"Besides," she said, "whoever thinks I'm stupid enough to fuck my colleague on the job can kiss my ass. But I don't care who knows that I fuck the husband I love by the side of the road."

The list of things I loved about Charlie was miles long, but this trait was at the top. How she wasn't intimidated. Not by any man. Not by any post. Risk? She respected it. Rumors? She didn't give a rat's arse.

And she looked so bloody cute leaning back in her USMC T-shirt, reminding me of our roadside adventure.

Deepfake photos didn't stand a chance against her. Nothing did.

"Shall we have an encore in the Jeep then?" I asked. "Hire a photographer to get all our good angles?" I was joking but that sent a twitch to my cock. "Or how about the dunes again? I'm firming up for that one as we speak."

That made a devilish grin appear on her angel face again. "I'm sure I could get Silas to take those photos for free."

"You're lucky I'm a confident man because you sound half serious."

"I am *not*." Her tone shocked up. "And this sexy conversation needs to stop right now with our children in our bed."

"Why?" That made me laugh, feeling my cheeks hurt from the smile, from the vision staring back at me. Of my stunning wife across the bed, her blonde mane tousled around our son climbing over her shoulder and our daughter resting across her lap. *This* was the shot I cared about. "No more shame, you said. That's how we'll have fun and have two more babies real soon."

A pillow flew from her hand, bopping me in my laughing face. "Get off this bed right now with that confident alpha sperm. I'm getting pregnant as we speak."

"I fucking wish!" I jumped up and grabbed Duke. Bollocks if a photo could take this away from us. Our family. Our love. It was too strong.

"Come with me, mate." I started walking out of the bedroom with our son on my arm. "It's time we men had a wee chat about alpha women."

Charlie's laughter trailed behind us as I walked downstairs to start our coffee.

Our long day playing on the beach together was perfect

until another ping lit up my phone. The sight on the screen brassed me off.

NIKKI SAMPSON
Call me ASAP

Against my better judgment, I went back inside the house and phoned her back, worried something was wrong with Keats.

Nikki answered after the first ring. I started off polite with a "Hi, there. Everything all right?"

"All right?" Her shrill tone screamed, "No, it isn't all right, Daniel Pierce!"

Oh, for fuck's sake, bloody hell, bugger off, goddammit and every other curse I could think instead of banging my head against a wall.

What now?

"I can't believe you, Daniel Pierce."

Nikki's voice was fingernails down a chalkboard. I'd heard its jagged scrape many times years before signaling that a tirade was coming. I met it with silence. Anything else would only light her fuse more.

"You and that slutty wife of yours. This filthy picture of you two is all over the place, and your son is embarrassed," she said. "Devastated!" she yelled. "This is beyond inappropriate. Neither one of you are fit to be parents to your children or to our son. What makes you think I'd ever let either one of you near him again?"

I called upon every molecule of restraint I had not to unleash on this woman. Wanting to verbally annihilate her, I knew better. It wasn't worth it.

"Nikki," I seethed, "the picture is fake. It's not us. We would never be so unprofessional. And—"

"That's what they all say. 'Wasn't me.' It sure looks like you two. She's low-class, country trash, and I already know how you like to fuck around. You did it with me and many other women. You're an egotistical man-whore. The whole world thinks you're an amazing husband, father, a hot hero, and all that bullshit. But they don't know the cocky, selfish, arrogant, cruel man that you really are."

Oh, this bitch.

I hated thinking that way about a woman and the mother of my son. But really. She got off on yelling at people, punching them with nasty words, most of which weren't true.

Yes, I'd fooled around and fucked Nikki. And she was the last woman I fucked so casually because she was such a nightmare that I swore never to do it again. No random, unprotected fuck was worth the hell she put me through. After her, I vetted my choices, protecting myself with condoms and advanced NDAs.

And now, I knew better. I wouldn't justify her insults with my own. The fact would speak for itself.

"Nikki, Charlie was shot three times during her military service for *your* country. She has exit wound scars through her right shoulder and her lower right back where she took bullets trying to save two girls from violence. That photo is *not* her. Do you need more proof?"

Stone silence.

"I thought so," I said. "I *will* see my son in two weeks' time as we planned, and you will never threaten me otherwise, or speak ill of my wife again. She possesses more honour, more integrity, and more class in her thumb than you and I have combined in our entire, selfish lives. Do I make myself clear?"

Again, stone silence.

"Right, then." I gave a long, audible exhale, gaining my composure. "Nikki, I will not have a volatile relationship with you. You are the mother to one of my children, and I would like to respect that, to keep this civil for his sake. Do you think we can do that?"

"Yes, Daniel. We can," she answered quietly. "I didn't know that about Charlie." I could hear how bad the bite of crow she was eating tasted in her mouth. "I was just worried about my son."

I rolled my eyes at her self-righteousness.

"I'm sure you were. I worry for our son too. Perhaps it's best he stays offline given our careers. We can't control the lies posted about us, so our son is best served if we get each other's backs instead of putting knives in them."

Wanting to lecture her on why she thought it was a good idea to let an eleven-year-old online, I shut my mouth at her white flag and left it at that.

Bloody hell, parenthood makes you eat your ego in sweet and sour bites.

I said, "I'd like to speak with Keats tonight after we get the twins down. Charlie can be on the call if you don't mind. We can help explain things to him. He's old enough to understand about war, bullies, lies, and scars."

I didn't plan the irony of that last statement but gave myself points on the board for it anyway.

"Okay," she said calmly. "I'll have him call you tonight."

"That would be nice." I put my sword down. "Thank you."

Once I ended that call, I headed straight for the bar cart in the living room and a shot of Jack.

What was it with our life? I felt like I was playing a daily game of Whac-A-Mole with tragedies and drama.

CHAPTER THIRTY

CHARLIE

SEPTEMBER. **_One month before..._**

It was ninety degrees outside with enough humidity to swamp a desert. All weather I was used to but without having to wear a mask and face shield. I was breathing in a steam sauna of my cinnamon gum breath.

We were on exterior shots. Production was pushing hard to get through as many pages as they could because rain was coming that week.

Filming near Oglethorpe Square, the woman who owned the coffee shop nearby brought us iced coffees, keeping us cool and caffeinated. After Riley scored her first free cup from the shop and posted about it on Instagram, we had a constant supply. I made a mental note—circle back to the shop for more.

And we would. Oglethorpe was known for haunts from victims of Yellow Fever centuries before. The show was shooting an entire episode here.

When I got to set that morning, the damn photo was the

first thing Riley and Wade asked me about, knowing it was fake, but still wanting to dish on how pissed I was. Everyone on the crew did.

"I mean, no disrespect, Charlie"—the makeup artist working on Riley had joked about it with perfect Southern sass—"but if I were married to Daniel Pierce, I'd say yes to wherever he wanted to have sex too."

I didn't take offense, laughing. "Well, I'm not saying we only stick to the bedroom, but I'm smart enough not to screw at work."

But once I got there, to work, all jokes were off. I focused on Scott Harris, the boom operator who flashed guilty like a casino's neon sign.

The HGR Atlanta office had pulled his records. I read them. There wasn't much.

Scott Harris was twenty-eight and from Macon, Georgia. He had one DUI two years before, that's it. His employment history revealed he had a short stint bartending for a few months, nothing else.

That raised more flags than the front of the United Nations building to me.

How does one survive to twenty-eight with no employment? I knew how—income from an unlawful source.

I watched Scott like a hawk. Three times he dipped the boom mic into the shot. It can happen. But three times? In one day? Too amateur. I thought the Director was going to blow a gasket, but the Sound Mixer came over and smoothed out the situation.

This felt wrong. Like the sensation that itched through my veins for months. Hell, for years. Like a bomb ticked down here at work while another one burned a short fuse outside my home too.

Something was about to explode.

Finding a couple of minutes away from prying ears, I called Wade. "Can you come in early? Come watch this guy with me and let me know what you think."

Wade had enough experience to know when something wasn't right on set either. I wouldn't raise alarms until I was sure.

"I think the man is using." Wade side-whispered to me hours later. "I saw it with my sister before she got clean. I mean, we're all sweating out here and exhausted, but watch, he's nodding out and any second, he's gonna drop that boom pole. And notice how he's wearing long sleeves? It's eighty-six degrees. He's covering track marks."

That's all I needed confirmed.

Money for drugs motivates people to do desperate things to get it. I knew now *why* Scott wanted the money. The real question was *how* he knew to blackmail Riley to get it.

I asked Wade to wait with Riley in the car when we wrapped that evening. Waiting patiently for most to clear the set, I took my chance.

"Hey, Mike." I offered a fresh cup of iced coffee to the Sound Mixer. "Been a long, hot day, huh?"

He smiled for the cool drink before answering, "Yeah. Thanks. I'll be glad for fall to roll around, that's for damn sure." He gave a quick cheers, taking a big sip, then looking at me with pause. "I've seen your interviews and such. Thank you for your service."

Not a freckle of guilt on this man. He's a good guy. So why would he hire such an obvious bad one?

"Thanks. All in a good day's work." I nodded back to the set. "Speaking of—your boom operator—he sure is making it hard on your team. Is he an apprentice or something?"

Mike's face flashed with skepticism at my question, obviously wanting to hedge the truth.

All right, Charlie Girl. Academy Award time...

I smiled, quickly joking with a wink, "I thought he might drop the boom pole on Riley's head. I didn't know I'd have to guard my girl from falling mics too."

That made him chuckle. "Yeah. Sorry 'bout that."

He set the coffee down on his cart and returned to wrapping up the mic packs, explaining, "He's my nephew. My sister begged me to give him a chance. He shadowed me on *Death March* some, so I hired him for this show. I thought he knew the ropes by now, but to tell you the truth, he's about at the end of his with me. One more fuck up and I'll have to cut him loose."

Tink. You hit the target.

"Oh, you worked on *Death March*?" *Keep sounding innocent. That was Riley's show. Get the intel.* "Seems lots of crew here were on it." *Not really... but build the familiarity.*

"Yeah. My team ran Second Unit for a few seasons."

"Well, a big production like that would teach anyone how to run sound in the Georgia heat." *Okay, that's enough. Don't push your luck.* "And you gotta do for family, right?"

"Humph. Yeah."

"Well, have a good one. And the next cup I bring ya will be a little stronger next time." I raised it and walked away... with a smile.

Son of a bitch. That's it.

Mike and his sound crew ran Second Unit on *Death March*. They focused mainly on filming crowd scenes and exterior shots.

Their work didn't involve the principal cast Riley was in. That's why Riley didn't recognize their names and faces. Their paths never crossed.

My path now found me lost in thought, walking over the brick sidewalk, aiming for the waiting SUV at the curb.

I'd ask Riley about any encounters she may have had with the Second Unit team. Doubtful to probably not, but I had to tick all boxes.

And even if their paths had crossed at a distance on set, it didn't explain how Scott Harris would have any knowledge of Riley's history.

There was only one remote connection I could make and my stomach soured considering it.

CHAPTER THIRTY-ONE

DANIEL

OCTOBER. *Two weeks before...*

We settled into a routine that Charlie enjoyed, and I secretly hated.

She gleefully fed the twins early each morning while I watched over my cup of coffee. Then she was out the door and gone until the evening.

I didn't like her out on the water so late, but she had dismissed my concerns, saying, "The water is like my sidewalk. I know its every crack, landmark, and smell."

Days I spent between missing Charlie, being jealous of her, and being bored. Then I'd feel like a prat. I loved this time at home. This crazy virus with all its suffering had moments of grace—time with family was one of them.

It gave me months with our babies before work consumed my life again. Had it been a normal year, I'd be gone for over ten hours a day on set and missing so much.

But that day something happened that troubled me more.

I was preparing lunch. Caroline fussing for her food rushed me into accidentally knocking a ceramic dinner plate to the floor. It broke with a loud crash, startling Caroline to cry... but Duke sat quietly.

I observed my son, clapping my hands loudly. Caroline only cried more, but Duke sucked his fingers, waiting for his food. I sat down in front of their highchairs. Once they were content and eating, I snapped my fingers beside Caroline's ear. She turned to the sound. I did the same to Duke. Nothing. His beautiful sea-glass eyes just kept looking at me while he chewed, happy.

That day, I did more little tests and my heart broke.

Duke couldn't hear me. He responded to the hand signs Charlie taught the babies, but he didn't flinch at a sound.

The truth crushed me as I put the twins to sleep that evening. By the time Charlie entered through the garage door that night, concern oozed from my pores. But Riley walked in behind Charlie, and I had to keep a stoic face.

Now... I was fucking pissed too.

"Hey, babe," Charlie said, completely unaware. "Wade is off this weekend, so Riley is spending it with us."

Riley stood in the kitchen with an overnight bag and a shy smile. "I don't want to intrude upon your family time, Mr. Pierce. I'm happy to babysit a bit or hide in a guest room with my pages for next week to give you privacy."

Riley's polite words disarmed me immediately. She was just like Charlie with her manners.

Don't be cheesed off, Pierce. Riley doesn't know what's going on. Bloody hell, Charlie doesn't either.

"You're welcome anytime, Riley, like family," I said with a genuine smile before pressing the dishwasher on. "And please, call me 'Daniel'."

I reached for a glass from the cabinet and walked to the

fridge for a bottle of Guinness. It was Friday night and Dad needed a beer... or four.

Charlie came up to me for our usual greeting and kiss, pausing at my tense muscles. "You okay?"

"Why don't you help Riley get settled in upstairs, and then we can chat out back," I suggested.

Minutes later, Charlie came out to join me with a sundress on and a beer in her hand.

"I'm sorry. I should've told you I was bringing Riley home with me, but it just happened. Wade worked the last two weekends. He has this one off. But when I was leaving with Riley from set today, she started getting nervous about a random officer staying at her house. She didn't ask. I offered. I hated seeing her so afraid."

She plopped down in the Adirondack chair next to me and reached out her hand. I held it back. I couldn't be mad at her. My wife's big, damn protective heart was not our problem right now.

"It's okay." I took a gulp of beer, sitting quietly for a moment until I couldn't anymore. "I don't mean to come at you with this after a long week, but I have to tell you something." Never would another lie or omission occur in our marriage, I swore. "I think Duke has a hearing problem, that maybe he's deaf."

My eyes locked on hers. Tears started falling over Charlie's dark lashes. She didn't seem shocked. It's like she already knew.

"It's my fault," she said.

"It's no one's fault."

"Yes, it *is* my fault. He was born premature, and I read it could be one of the risks."

"Our babies being born at thirty weeks is not your fault,

Charlie. If anyone is at fault, it's me. You didn't want to be at that premiere in the first place."

"Yes, I did. I was having a great week, and I was proud to support you. I always will be. But I should've listened to my instinct, maybe have met you inside and not on the carpet. I knew something was going to happen, and I let it."

"We can't do this," I said. "We can't sit here and second guess the past. We're blessed to be alive, to have the money to get him all the help he needs. It's not the end of the world."

"Then why do I feel like a shitty mother right now?" She wiped away tears with the back of her hand.

"Because you're tired. And you feel responsible for your children, for Riley, and anyone who needs you... and that's a lot."

"You're dealing with a lot too, Daniel. I see it. It's a lot trying to support me working, even with Fran's help. And I'm so thankful for you."

Her gratitude lifted three stones off of my heart.

Fuck's sake, Pierce. This is what so many mums must feel all the time.

It's amazing how a little thanks can change the weather in my heart to sunny so quickly.

"I have an idea," I said in my chipper accent.

She shook her head, surprised at my quick change in tone. "Okay. What?"

"Let's call Jax and Ara tonight and see if they can come over tomorrow. I need another dad in my life, and you need another mum."

Jax was more than a fellow dad. He was Charlie's best Marine buddy who was also shot on that fateful day with her. And his wife, Ara, was one of her closest friends. They were a few miles away, quarantined in Beaufort with their one-year-old son. Their company would be the perfect medicine.

A smile warmed her face along with her next move. She stood up and sat down on my lap, nuzzling into my embrace. "Daniel Balthazar Pierce, I love you so much."

I played with the platinum wedding band on her finger that matched mine, the one under my gran's ring I proposed to her with, twirling both back and forth.

"Just keep coming home to me, Charlotte Sophia Ravenel... Pierce." I added that last name before I kissed her lips and she didn't protest, returning my kiss and much more.

CHAPTER THIRTY-TWO

CHARLIE

OCTOBER. ***Two weeks before…***

Something wouldn't let me sleep that night. It wasn't the truth about Duke.

I kept waking, sensing someone standing over me, watching me.

It pissed me off because exhaustion weighed through my every muscle after a long week, but then that anger only fueled my insomnia more.

Fuck this.

Quietly, I got out of bed and slipped on a pair of jeans, flip-flops, and a T-shirt. Downstairs in the home office, I found one of Daniel's cigars. Grabbing his gold lighter, I stepped outside to sit on our back deck.

The black night was giving way to the navy blue of dawn arriving. Puffing away in the dark shadows of the deck, I couldn't take my eyes off the dunes. The horizon kept calling my name. Once there was enough light to see, I made my way across the grassy yard to the sand singing out for me.

Bending over, I rolled up the hem of my jeans before kicking off my flip-flops and stepping off the boardwalk into the powdery sand. A quick smile took my face as I passed the spot where I was on my knees for Daniel months before. But that happy memory swiftly faded to the instinct rolling in around me while the tide rolled out.

I walked through the dunes and out onto the beach. It was empty but for the pale-yellow light to my left. As far as the eye could see, no one was on the beach.

But I sensed it.

You're not alone.

Low waves lapped before me. They greeted me with the familiar calm of a beautiful coming day. The birds weren't out yet for their morning dives into the depths for their meal, and the dolphins were absent too.

The only sound? Water and wind. The only smell? Salt and sea. The only sight? A familiar, placid nothing.

There's no one here.

But the taste? Wrong.

The feeling? Something.

It quickened my heart rate.

Yes, there is.

My mind rebelled.

Look over your shoulder.

My chin snapped around, turning to the dunes between the beach and our house. Golden beach grass topping the dunes bent left in the often-eastward breeze. Driftwood and the large shell of a dead horseshoe crab adorned the sand. The usual.

No. Look.

I walked back toward the dunes and the unmarked winding path through them to our home.

There. It whispered in my ear. *On your left.*

Fresh footprints were in the sand. Not flat from flip-flops. Not curved treads from running shoes. They were large, deep, rigid indentations—a man's combat boots. Their path came from the western point, over the dunes, stopping in front of our house before doubling back upon themselves.

Fuck!

With a sudden glance, I saw nothing but didn't trust what the dunes could hide. Ducking low through the shadowed piles, my head was on a swivel, back and forth in case a threat jumped out from behind the low mountains of sand. I cleared them.

Go! Go! Go! Go!

My bare feet landed on the wooden boardwalk with a fast sprint, across the soft, grassy backyard, up onto the sharp concrete pool deck, they jumped onto the wooden deck steps.

Shit!

I'd left the backdoor unlocked. Entering the breakfast room, I turned around and secured it behind me before peering out of the windows...

No one is there. But did he get in here?

Scanning the kitchen, I grabbed a knife from the wooden block before checking the other side of the huge kitchen island. *Clear.*

I snuck left down the hallway into the office, knife in one hand, the other reaching behind the leather-bound first edition copy of *Frankenstein* on the bookshelf display.

Got it.

My .22. Safety off. One in the chamber. My steps took me back to the windows in the office facing the backyard.

No one is out there. Don't trust it.

Through the house now. I held my gun down at the ready with a peek around every corner. First level? *Clear.*

Captain rested on the entry rug, guarding the front door. Curtis stood on night guard by the front driveway outside.

No time to tell him. Clear the house first. All doors locked now.

With a snap of my fingers, Captain was up. I pointed him up the stairs and followed behind with my pistol.

The nursery was first. Tiny bodies were safe and sleeping. *Clear.* I locked it behind me.

Fran's bedroom. Door locked. All quiet. Riley's guest bedroom? Same. *Clear.*

Back down the hall, soft carpet masked the sound of my steps.

The library. *Be careful. What's hiding on the other side of the leather sofa in the center of the room?* Walking around, I sliced the pie, angling my aim with my back to the bookshelves. Turning, slowly. Checking. *Clear.*

Back to the hallway. To our bedroom. The door was cracked open, peeking around it, Daniel lay in the bed.

Snapping my fingers, Captain entered the room before me. The metal ring clanking on his collar woke Daniel up. I stood at the foot of our bed with my pistol aimed at the floor.

He opened his eyes, bare chest sitting up. "What is it?" he asked.

I signaled "quiet" while aiming right, toward our bathroom. Captain stood guard by him.

Kicking the door open wide, it made Captain bark while I scanned the bathroom. *Clear.*

The last room? Our walk-in closet. I flipped the light

on. *What's behind your long skirts? Booted feet hiding? No. Clear.*

Final check. The second-story deck off our bedroom. I unlocked the doors and stepped outside, scanning the horizon of dunes and ocean beyond, finger off the trigger but ready to pull...

Nothing. He's gone, Charlie Girl.

But he was here...

CHAPTER THIRTY-THREE

CHARLIE

OCTOBER. ***Two weeks before...***

"Could've been a curious tourist trying to take pictures," Curtis, our nighttime security said while we stood on the edge of the dunes that morning, staring down at the footprints in the sand.

Scarlett, my sparring partner, and our daytime guard added, "Last rain we had was Thursday afternoon, and y'all haven't been out on the beach since, so these could only be a day old up to last night." She bent down, pointing to the tread marks. "It's an unusual pattern too—long ridge rows with narrow treads on the edges."

I appreciated how observant Scarlett was, noting the pattern too.

"I checked the security footage," Daniel said. "All the camera recorded was you walking out and then running back into the yard. Nothing before or after. Maybe the 'Under Surveillance' and 'Guard Dog' signs scared him off, stopping him here."

I heard the sound of chewing tobacco spit before Jax said, "Well, shit, let's follow 'em and see where they go."

Jax and Ara had arrived early that morning while I waited for daylight and backup before pursuing the path of the footprints. Fran, Riley, and Ara stayed with the babies in the house while we ventured out to investigate.

I soothed my thumb across the hard ridges on the handle of my .22. Curtis and Scarlett had theirs secured in their holsters, with the straps unsnapped. Jax led the way. I fell in behind him with Daniel behind me, our guards behind him. Slowly, we walked the path beside the prints, dune over dune.

Jax waved off black, biting flies from his face in the rising morning heat. The familiar curve of his broad shoulders and his cleanly shaven neck walking in front of me flashed the memory—the recall foreboding.

So many times I'd walked in formation behind Jax, staring at this vision.

The last time we did this... we wore flak jackets while walking through the bazaar in Marjah. Then bullets flew and we fell that day.

Over seven and half years later, I swore...

No fucking way you're going down again.

Having Jax around, even for a day validated me. The trauma. The PTSD. The paranoia. He never judged me. He had it too. Everything he understood about me except this—why I exposed myself to even more.

But he also knew how much I loved Daniel. Why our love and family were worth this risk.

The footprints disappeared into the carpet of pine needles on the other side of the empty lots west of our house. Our search party walked through the woods, past our nearest neighbor's house on the left, steps headed toward the road in front of our homes.

I spotted it—a small, freshly broken pine branch, snapped in half. It was too thick to break at the weight of the small deer on the island but thin enough for the weight of an adult man to break it.

We all followed the path in silence, all the way to the road finding no other trace of anyone.

Jax spat on the small road. "Damn. Y'all really gotta love each other and your jobs to put up with shit like this." Only tobacco left his mouth, no bullshit. His amber eyes fired straight at me and Daniel. "You ever think about quittin' the jobs? May be the only thing that'll keep y'all safe."

"Nope," I said. "I don't quit, and I ain't hidin' from it anymore."

"We're not going to stand around for it either." Daniel's tone was equally rigid.

"Y'all both ain't wrong," Jax said. "I guess some fights are never over." He spat at the dirt again for emphasis. "Guess they'll always come around for ya. I mean, hell, look."

We all did.

On our one side, there stood a handful of large, waterfront homes leading out to the point. On our other, five miles stretched to the other end of the island. Yes, it was a small one with a diminishing crowd in the off-season, but it was big enough to hide a person... or two.

"Let's switch the cameras on the west side of the house to motion-sensored ones," I said to Scarlett. "We need this entire angle covered too."

"How could they get past the sensors facing east?" Daniel asked. "You have to come up the road from that direction for the house."

Pointing to the abandoned golf course on the other side

of the road from our home, I said, "Yeah, but you could come up through there." Then I pointed to my left. "Or west, from the water over there."

"Yeah, but a tourist wouldn't do that," Daniel said. "There are alligators in the ponds on the course, and that's swift, open water meters away to the west."

"Exactly." I focused on his aqua eyes with my eyebrow raised. "*Not* a tourist."

We laid out by the pool the rest of the day. We all tried swimming and sweating our anxiety away. I sat in the shade of the deck with Caroline on my lap while Riley played with Duke. I had to tell her now about Scott Harris, the boom operator with a drug problem.

It could've been someone after Riley last night, not me and Daniel. I filled Riley in on my suspicion, making Riley's face drop with fear. "So, you think Scott could've followed us here, to your house last night?"

"There's no telling who's coming for who, or why they were here," I said. "We can't rule anything out."

Damn right, you can't. My instinct lounged beside me. *You could be chased by anything. The threat against Riley. The threat from Mason. The threat from the premiere. Or something more. Something that's always haunted you.*

"Now, we're past the deadline," Riley said. "It's October and I haven't paid the bribe. I have no idea how long this asshole will wait me out." Riley gave a long pause before asking, "Can you teach me how to shoot a gun?"

The question didn't surprise me. I knew better than to let Riley's angelic face and warm heart fool me. There was a lot of fight in her too.

"Look at me, Riley." She did and I gestured to the scar across my right cheek. "I fucking hate guns. But you're a grown woman. I can't stop you from using one, but I strongly advise against it. It's far more likely to be used against you if you aren't trained to fight too."

"Then can you teach me to fight, instead?"

I caressed Caroline's growing curls. "I can show you a few moves. They'll be far more helpful, okay? Leave the guns to me."

I heard myself say those words like they didn't belong to me. Like they belonged to an oracle instead.

CHAPTER THIRTY-FOUR

CHARLIE

Kiss It Better by Rihanna

OCTOBER. **Two weeks before...**

Agitation flopped me like a fish in bed. On my right side with a huff, I stared at the moon through the windows. No sleep. Flipping to my left, I looked across the bedroom with another huff. Only frustration now. I tried closing my eyes...

There ain't no pill you can take or face you can punch that will give you rest tonight.

I gave up and opened them again.

Daniel was staring back at me. "Me too, babe. I'd pay a thousand pounds to watch the back of my eyelids for the next five hours." He rolled to his back, offering my favorite spot to rest. My soft cheek nestled against his hard chest. "Do you have a copy of the *Financial Times*? My dad used to read that to me at night, knocked me right out."

"My mom used to play with my hair."

"Like this?" His fingertips tickled across my cheek, brushing back through my strands.

"Hmm." His touch was soothing... but not enough. "I keep thinking about those footprints."

"Me too." He caressed more strokes through my hair. "Are you afraid?"

"No. I haven't felt fear since the shooting like my fear was the only thing killed that day." Drawing my hand across his chest, this spot always comforted me. "The only thing I feel when I think about all this is anger."

"I feel numb."

That lifted my chin, my gaze considering his face in the moonlight. "Do you feel that about everything?"

That worried me. When we met, Daniel said he was numb, that our love brought him back to life. Now he was back to numb? Was his life that bad again?

"Sometimes." He squeezed my arm, holding me tighter. "It worries me. Like that's what it takes to survive this—to be numb—and I don't want to be, but I feel it creeping back in."

"Are you unhappy with me? Is it my work?"

"No, but I'm jealous. And I'm a prat to say it, but I'm restless too. You know I love you, the twins, our home, our life... but I'm going bloody insane around here. Like I'm just sitting here, waiting for something to happen, and when it does... it's shit like those footprints."

Lifting my body up to straddle him, I cupped his square jaw in my curled hands.

"You're not a prat or insane. It's understandable. It's a normal reaction for unusual times. Next month, it'll change. You'll be back at work and anything but bored."

"I know I'll go from numb to knackered, wishing for more time like this. That I need to be patient." He held my waist. "What about you? I don't want you angry all the time." With a slight nudge, his hips lifted, and I could feel his hardening cock. "You're too beautiful when you're happy"—another firm thrust up—"and I *like* making you happy."

His seduction was involuntary, our bodies couldn't help it. Attraction pulled us together every time. "Are you suggesting an alternate plan?" I asked. "A sure cure for insomnia?"

His hands skated up my ribs, thumbs nearing my breasts tensing for him under his old rugby shirt. "I know one thing we're never numb to." His fingertips started swirling over the nipples calling for him. "One thing that makes us forget everything."

The urge hit me too. My hips started rolling over him, firing my body up, and my memory. "I have a question."

"I have a *hard* answer."

Yes, he did. It was granite under me now. "You mentioned months back at the range about owing me more, about me having all of you. Then, you didn't bring it up again. Why?"

"I was afraid you wouldn't be into it."

"Into what?"

"Of you having all of me."

"What do you mean by that?"

He sat up, hands gripping my hips, gaze meeting mine in the moonlight.

"I meant that you've shared everything with me. Your secrets. Your body. I wanted to do the same with you. I finally told you my secret and you gave me your forgiveness. So, I wanted to give you my body too. The one part no one has ever had, just like I did with you."

I knew what he meant, the last barrier between us. It raced my heart, flushing between my thighs, mind dizzying, not quite sure what to do with the rush of lust. "Is that still what you want?"

"It is with you," he said. "There is no part of my body, my heart, my life, future, or past, Charlie, that I won't share with you now. I'm man enough to give you everything. We're equal, right? Why is it okay for me to do it to you, but you can't do it to me?"

"But I don't want a revenge fuck. Like you owe me something. Like it's a punishment for lying. I would never do that to you."

"It's not." His grasp lifted the hem of my shirt overhead and tossing it to the floor. "I want to watch you do it to me. Let me see what it feels like. I'm not into men. I'm into you, only you. And with what all that your Tantric books say about it, the pleasure it gives men too, with the way you touch me with your fingers now and that spot you hit, I see stars. It feels so fucking good because I trust you, because it's you, and I want to feel you even more. If it's your beautiful face and fit body, it'll turn me on so fucking much."

The marble of his cock pressed into my panties, confirming his wishes. "But how?" I asked. Yes, fingers I'd taken him with. What he suggested was much more.

"The duffel bag Rob brought." His chin nodded toward our closet. "Check it. I asked him to get one for us, something we can both use."

"You asked Rob to get us a strap-on?" Just saying the word made me shy... and horny. As fuck.

"Yes. He wasn't kidding about buying out the store for us." The tip of his tongue circled my nipple, raising my desire even more to do this. "There are lots of toys in there, but I want you to use that one with lots of lube on me tonight."

"Daniel, I don't want to hurt you."

"Does it hurt when I fuck your fit ass?"

The suck of his lips over my nipple and that question took me to visions I never imagined with him, my body soaking to them.

"Not when you take your time," I sighed, arching for his mouth. "Not when you play with me while you do it. It's fucking incredible."

His mouth skated over my cleavage. "I trust you with every part of me." Before he indulged my other nipple, he said, "If I don't like it, I'll tell you."

Many minutes later, he more than liked it. After taking our time, after his chin dripped with my cum, getting me so wanton to do it, his hefty, oiled cock filled my hands.

He wouldn't let go of my breasts, palming their curve while he moaned at my slow thrust. I gripped his length with slick pumps making his hard body writhe, swearing my name, eyes locked to mine.

The sight of me fucking him was so erotic it made me come. My smooth plunge, his granite pleasure, my tight pump, it was all under my control, shuddering through me twice with deep moans while I gave him this, while we shared this.

"Are you still numb, Daniel?" I put more power into my pumps. "Do you feel me?" All the way inside him. "Do you feel us now?"

"Fuck yes. So much." His strong hips met my tempo, his massive thighs spreading wider to receive me while his stunning aqua eyes were riveted to mine. "I feel everything with you, Charlie."

He wouldn't let me have all control. Pulling me down, taking my kiss, skating his tongue across the seam of my lips before teasing my top one, he offered his bottom one next to my gentle suck.

Mounting my body over his, urging into his curve, we couldn't be more bound together, pledged to the other's pleasure. His tongue probed my mouth while I probed him, gasps escaping his throat through our kiss. I wouldn't stop. I wanted this for him, from him, he was so fucking hot like this—his body, his might, his ego, all so strong, enough to take me and the indulgence.

I pulled away from his kiss. "I want to watch you come like this." We both did, looking down at my hands stroking him off, at my hips and dildo thrusting into him.

"Don't stop." The breath shallowed in his lungs, bowing his ribs, building, climbing up, his body sweating for more. "Fuck, babe. I can take it. Fuck my ass harder. It feels so good."

I treasured the map of his every response, moving faster, harder, witnessing everything I was doing to him.

"Let me see it," I said, marveling at his hulking thighs, his concrete abs, his massive pecs, his steel jaw—they were shaking. "Show me how good I feel." His fists grabbed our bed sheets like a lifeline, gripping as tight as I was pumping his cock. "Show me how much you like me fucking your ass." I was entering him, watching it quake him apart, crumbling him into pieces as he did to me, before forming anew to the shape of the other, only around each other. "Come on. Let your beautiful cock come for me, Daniel. Come while I fuck you."

He wouldn't close his eyes, they were promised to mine, vulnerable with his powerful hips convulsing, his cock swelling in my grasp. While his soft lips trembled, his deep voice cried out, "Oh God, Charlie."

Breath rattled through his lungs, his ribs heaving as I got my wish. Ropes of his cum traveled across his quivering abs, glossing over my tight fist, drops glazing into the deep groove of his Adonis belt. The look in his eyes—shock, relief, love, devotion—it bonded our trembling bodies. The sight of his pleasure hit me so fast, that it made me come again, making him swear to my gaze down at him, "You have all of me now. Forever."

Our connection didn't stop. In the shower, we washed the stress away with soap and long kisses, our bodies entwined, slippery in the steam and water, but not letting go of the other.

Something changed between us, for good. I could sense it. That we'd never go back to numb half-lives, to half-truths again, to anything hidden. Everything we shared; the totality of us complete.

We had each other, always.

No threat could take that away.

Right?

CHAPTER THIRTY-FIVE

DANIEL

OCTOBER. **Now...**

Silence rang in my ears with a high-pitched squeal of her absence, of the ten minutes I had to wait before my world was destroyed.

I'd hear the call come from downstairs, of Wade calling back Rob with the finality of it. I couldn't bear to have any other vision at that moment. When the news wrecked me, I wanted to be staring at her face, thankful for the short time we had shared.

I went upstairs and sat on our bed, my eyes on our framed wedding photos sitting on the nightstand, my mind on that day—our wedding.

"You know," she had said smiling in my arms as we swayed on the dance floor under the twinkling lights of the wedding tent in our backyard. "Seven years from now, everything you love about me is going to annoy the hell out of you."

"Seven years from *now*?" I spun her around. "What about seven minutes ago, Mrs. Pierce?"

"Seven minutes ago? What did I do? We've only been married an hour."

And it had been the best of my life so far. "You wouldn't let me smash the wedding cake in your face. You know, like they do in all those funniest videos."

"You should know this about your wife of sixty minutes." Her fingertip tickled over my lips, I loved hearing that—"your wife"—from hers. "If I want cake smashed in my mouth, I'll ram my face into one. I didn't marry a practical joker. I married a grown-ass, sexy, strong man who'd rather make love to me than make me the butt of a joke."

"Then you should know this about your husband." Those new words along with her dazzling eyes gazing back up at me? I smiled from depths I'd never known. "He secretly loves that you're always right, especially about that sexy, strong part."

"So, you admit it?"

"That I'm sexy and strong?" Winding her up would be my pastime for life. "Fuck yes."

"What about me being right? Always?"

"Yes. You're right that I always want to make love to you. Or fuck you. Depending upon the mood."

Her hands rested on my chest, laughing chatter filled the air around us, but my gaze wouldn't leave hers. "What else am I always right about?" She wouldn't let me off the hook. I was thankful for it.

"I'll confess this—you're always right for me." My nose nuzzled against hers. "Consider it my wedding and birthday gift to you, all wrapped up on the same day."

It wasn't. Her birthday surprise—a first edition Virginia Wolfe—it was waiting, wrapped for her on our bed.

Her dancing had stopped. Tears rose in the ocean of her eyes. *"You* are, Daniel." One fell down her cheek. "*You* are the greatest gift to me. I thought I'd be alone forever. I never thought I'd be loved again."

My palms cradled her jaw, the dance floor and everyone disappearing, all except for my world in my hands.

"You are so very loved, Charlotte Ravenel. And I swear to you—I'm right about this—I will love you well beyond seven years; I will love every bloody annoying thing you do. I'll love you until my last dawn and then an eternity more."

The distant song of salsa music hit the air. Rob's phone.

My mind hated this, not wanting to return to the present moment, wanting to stay forever in memories of her.

"Hello?"

I listened to the painful gravel, the low rumble of Rob's voice answering his phone downstairs while the wedding photo stared back at me, taunting me...

"You were a fool to take her and tomorrow for granted."

CHAPTER THIRTY-SIX

CHARLIE

OCTOBER. ***One week before...***

That Monday on set, I returned the stalk. I stood behind Scott, watching his every move, twitch, and exhale. We were filming interior shots, but he sweat at the heat I burned into the back of his neck with my glare.

I didn't say a fucking word to him, and he heard me loud and clear, couldn't even return my stare.

Instead, he fidgeted with the boom pole between setups. He tried chatting casually with the guy running first assistant camera. But there was nothing relaxed about him or their conversation.

That's why I didn't like the camera guy either. That's who Scott scored from, both acted tweaked out by the end of the day.

Misery and addiction love company. It's tragic how easily they find each other.

I studied their boots. They were like every deep-treaded pair most men on set wore for standing long hours. No way to confirm if it was Scott's footprints in the sand. Not unless I could get a good look at the bottoms, and I sure kept trying to.

I asked Riley during lunch if she knew the camera guy. She didn't. I double-checked with HGR and confirmed he came from a different show that wrapped in Atlanta last year. The camera guy wasn't in on the blackmail, just the drugs.

"I can tell it's him," Riley said of Scott while she pushed her salad around with her fork, apparently having little appetite from the stress of this. "Now that you told me, I can see it in how he looks at me."

"You're safe on set and at home," I assured her. "You know I'll rip his throat out if he tries anything." I took a long chew of my kale salad before adding, "I can't tell if he's the violent type, but he's definitely desperate."

"Based on what my mom says about my dad before he disappeared into oblivion, desperate addicts can become violent ones too."

I couldn't debate that.

WALKING onto set the next afternoon, guilt chewed my heart. My baby boy had severe hearing loss. It had me fighting back tears in the doctor's office that morning.

Daniel held my hand while the doctor offered encouraging options. Duke using the hand signals I taught him was positive, and we scheduled for Duke to get a cochlear implant at age one. It would help restore some of his hearing, but that afternoon, nothing could restore my conscience.

On paper, facts told me the attempt on my life, the

premature birth—I wasn't to blame. But facts don't mean shit to parents. Fault does. And it was mine.

That shooting? That outcome? It was a down payment on a bigger price I'd have to pay one day.

No one could convince me otherwise.

Wade stood dead on his feet beside Riley's trailer. I offered him a hug of thanks for covering my shift. He tapped out to crash while I was on watch and would cover that night.

Knocking on Riley's trailer door, the utility sound tech showed up beside me, ready to mic Riley. I watched the tech hand Riley the mic pack to secure in the sports bra she wore under her dress.

An idea smoked through my mind. The hearing tests with Duke that morning buzzed in my brain while I watched the mundane ritual of the tech running a sound check with Riley.

General operation on set for sound was the actor's mic pack was turned down to nothing when they weren't shooting. When they start a scene, the Sound Mixer turns the mic up, then everyone on the Sound Team and many crew members can hear the actor's every word.

Once the tech left the trailer, I didn't trust the mic was low enough for a private conversation. Riley always took her mic off for lunch, sometimes for breaks, but not between setups.

I touched Riley's arm. I wrote a note for Riley to read in the Field Book I always kept in my vest.

"When your mic is up, talk with me about plans for coffee tomorrow. After our morning run.
At that place near Oglethorpe with iced coffee.
Do it a few times. Copy?"

Riley nodded her head with a smile, knowing what I was up to—luring a snake out of his hole.

Hours later though, our smiles had disappeared. It was a long shoot in front of The Marshall House and Redix Dean's screaming fans were driving the production crazy.

I had to help security push the perimeter back another block to keep them to where their shouts didn't disrupt filming. Most in the crowd were harmless fans horny for Redix.

One though...

He caught my eye, sending shivers down my arms. The adult man seemed out of place, his glare searing a hole in my flesh, nerves crackling in his presence. His face burned into my memory. The moment enticed me to stay, to question him, but the job insisted I turn back to protect Riley.

The crowd embarrassed Redix. He apologized several times in the hair and make-up trailer.

"I'm sorry, y'all," he said. "This shit gets fucking ridiculous sometimes." The make-up artist sponged his chin with ghostly hues. "Sometimes, I wish I could just escape it all."

"Hollywood or the Lowcountry?" I asked.

"Both," he answered with a smile that could quell a hurricane. "I'm 'bout crazy to be buying a house down here again."

I sat on a stool behind Redix and Riley in their make-up chairs. Riley's tresses were being re-curled while Redix's arousing face could make the dead appear like a GQ cover model.

"Why are you coming back home then?" My questions continued.

I felt connected to Redix. Four years his senior, I'd never forget him from the hallways of Hilton Head High School. No one could.

"Love makes you do dangerous things," he said.

That statement caught my breath, lifting my stare to meet his in the mirror. Something swirled in the air between us, a union we couldn't explain. But it was there, quieting my lips and burdening Redix's eyes.

It made Riley mutter, "I'd be so lucky to have a love like that. One that's worth everything."

"Oh, you will," Redix said. It endeared me. He acted like Riley's big brother, not a pervy creep. "You're so beautiful, you're gonna have a tough choice to make one day."

It was two a.m. before me and Riley stumbled exhausted through the door of Riley's townhome. Four hours later, my alarm woke me, keeping my promise to call Daniel. I'd operated with less sleep and under much harsher conditions before.

Sitting in the courtyard with a cup of coffee, I placed my routine call.

"Don't forget Keats is coming this afternoon," Daniel said on our video chat, setting strawberry slices out for the twins. "I'm picking him and Nikki up from the marina at noon."

I rolled my eyes. "Like I'd forget that woman is gonna be in our house for the next two nights."

I shut up after that, determined to support Daniel's relationship with his son, no matter how volatile Nikki behaved.

"I'll be home around sixish," I said. Daniel turned away, distracted by Duke gesturing for more food. "Love you. Bye."

He didn't look back at the screen. "Love you too. Bye."

I trudged up the wooden steps for Riley. If she wanted true fight training, I'd deliver. Knocking loud on the door before I opened it, Riley rose from her slumber, surprised by the intrusion.

"Rise and shine, recruit." I smiled. "Coffee's downstairs. We run in an hour."

Riley rubbed her puffy eyes. "I'll do my best, but I didn't get much sleep waiting for Ashley Lynn to call me back."

"Did she?"

"No."

I couldn't tell if Riley was rubbing tired or crying eyes.

I aimed to cheer Riley up. Running through the famous squares of Savannah, we covered more miles in minutes than I had in months. Making jokes, I had us laughing through the grueling workout.

An hour later, we sat outside our favorite coffee shop at the only table.

God, if I could shoot iced coffee into my veins. Between loving the taste and being a mom trying to work set hours, I needed an IV of it. I went inside for another hit from Jenny, the kind owner. Riley stood just outside the glass door, in my line of sight but craving the fresh air.

When I turned back toward the door with coffee in hand, I almost dropped it.

A blonde woman stood talking with Riley, hugging her, holding her hand. My first steps charged the door, but the adoring look in Riley's eyes stopped me cold, standing my guard down at the ready.

"Charlie!" Riley blurted when I stepped outside. "This is my Ashley Lynn!"

A nuclear power plant siren fired across every square mile in my mind, not trusting Ashley Lynn upon first sight.

Yet, I had every reason to. Ashley Lynn looked like the typical, "harmless" Southern White girl. Funny how me and this woman were bestowed similar physical traits but wore them so differently.

I circled around, setting my coffee down on the outdoor

table before taking my mask off while I assessed Ashley Lynn's face. It spoke a silent language only our ilk share. Every Southern woman mastered it—a soft smile on the face while the eyes put a knife to your throat.

Riley was too in love, too surprised to recognize it, but I read it on Ashley Lynn's face like a billboard on I-95. I reached my hand out. "Nice to meet you. Heard great things."

Ashley Lynn did that dead-fish handshake back, the clamminess she added to it bothering me even more. "So nice to meet you, Ms. Roberts."

This encounter at the coffee shop was as innocent as a serial killer. It buzzed the hinge of my jaw.

How did Ashley Lynn find us here? From the guilty boom operator, Scott Harris. But how? They worked seasons apart. How would their paths have crossed?

"Wow, Ri." Ashley Lynn pulled her hand from my grasp. "It's like looking in the mirror. I see why you like her so much."

"What?" Riley's face scrunched. "Y'all don't look a thing alike."

So true, Riley. Blonde hair and blue eyes can be worn like a thin, black leather belt. Most women wear it around their torsos, accentuating feminine waistlines in fashionable apparel. A rare handful twist it around their fist, ready to wrap it around any neck that threatens them.

Zero guesses on which one described me.

"We've been running around this city for an hour," I said. "How'd you find us?"

It sounded like a polite question, but it was a fork dragging across glass to guilty ears.

"Let's get her a coffee and muffin first." Riley grabbed

Ashley Lynn's hand. "She just drove in from Atlanta, and I need to feed her."

The couple disappeared inside the shop. Riley put her mask on, but Ashley Lynn had none. Like she was oblivious to the world around her or didn't give a shit about others. Probably both. I rolled my eyes; thankful the shop was empty.

Indeed, the young woman needed a muffin. Or a dozen. I studied Ashley Lynn's silhouette through the glass door. She wore the requisite reef shorts, Southern Marsh T-shirt, and Sperry loafers. But skinny wore Ashley Lynn, her hand twitching in Riley's gentle grasp with covert agitation.

Stop being a body-shaming bitch and slow your judgmental ass down, Charlie Girl.

Watching Ashley Lynn picked at old scabs on my heart. I was healed underneath, but the mark was still there, what girls like Ashley Lynn did to me.

I grew up surrounded by them. They giggled in school hallways, talking sweet to faces then stabbing pain into backs turned. Their school sport was targeting anyone different, going for the South Carolina state championship in it.

A few tried getting points on me, mocking my mother's Spanish accent, and making fun of my spitfire demeanor. But one day I had enough of the cruel taunts and spitballs thrown in my long hair. I followed my tormentors into the girls' bathroom, slamming one against the tile wall, arm pressed against her throat, swearing revenge if they kept it up.

From that moment, they left me and anyone I decided to protect alone. It taught me to wear toughness like a leather jacket, hiding the hurt underneath.

Riley and Ashley Lynn returned, all smiles with a paper

tray of muffins in hand. I tried exhaling my bias out, keeping my mind open with instinct up at max.

I smiled at Ashley Lynn. "It's destiny you found us this morning." Knowing better than to question now, I baited with pleasantries instead.

Ashley Lynn sat beside Riley, pulling off a hunk of lemon, poppy seed muffin, munching on it in reply. "Ah my gawd. I know. *Right?* I went by the house but that Black guy said y'all were out for a run."

That reference to Wade made me seethe, yanking back all reins on my wrath and words.

Ashley Lynn continued, oblivious to her offensive language, "Riley posted this coffee shop the other day, so like, it was so easy to find ya."

Fuck. Chalk up a point for her.

Between Redix Dean on set, firing up his Instagram fan base, and Riley's polite endorsement of a local business on it too, it *was* easy to ping our location. I'd advised Riley not to do it again.

Location drops were a nuisance at best, deadly at worst.

I'd survived that reality... so far.

"She's gonna stay this week," Riley announced, tearing off the other muffin top to devour. "And hopefully longer."

Shit sandwich and turd taters.

My inner child threw a hissy fit. The last thing I wanted was to spend time around this woman.

Suck it up. Stand down and do your job.

"Sounds good to me," I lied.

I avoided Ashley Lynn the rest of the day, sitting down to read a book alongside Wade in the parlor. Riley had a night shoot again. We were in a holding pattern while Riley and Ashley Lynn lounged in the courtyard until then.

But Wade didn't seem to share my distrust of Ashley

Lynn. He was all smiles at her arrival, helping with her bags, which made me want to spit nails like a pneumatic gun. That wasn't his job, though Ashley Lynn gestured, expecting it of him.

I flipped the page on my book, admonishing myself…

This is your shit. Ashley Lynn is the brand ambassador for everything you hate. It's not fair to Riley to walk around like a brooding bitch. Grow the fuck up.

I tried so hard, even giving Ashley Lynn a hug at the end of my shift that afternoon.

Pointing the bow of my boat home, I dropped my shoulders, frustrated for yet another performance I'd have to give that evening.

Nikki Sampson would be in my home.

If I thought Ashley Lynn tried my nerves, Nikki screamed in my calm face like a drill sergeant trying to get me to flinch.

It was exhausting. I hated feeling this way.

Not a bone in my body had the patience for hating women. All I ever tried to do was defend them.

Then again, I reminded myself, malice doesn't discriminate, no matter identity. What I really hated was the people who used their privilege to hide it.

CHAPTER THIRTY-SEVEN

CHARLIE

breathin by Ariana Grande

OCTOBER. **One week before...**

Laughter greeted my arrival home. I dropped my backpack on the bench in the garage doorway, drawing a deep breath to take the stage again.

And oh, what a performance I had to give.

Glancing down the hallway into the kitchen, I saw Daniel laughing beside Keats and Nikki. Fran sat quietly on the barstool at the island, watching these parents orchestrate the evening.

It had Daniel holding Duke while Keats fed his little brother spinach puffs. Nikki held Caroline, doing the same. The laughter came from neither one of my babies liking the snacks, spitting the mush out, and twisting their bodies with a grimace on their cute faces.

The adorable sight in my scope enraged me.

Oh hell, you can't do this. Not with Nikki holding your daughter like her own flesh, standing in your kitchen like it's her home, gazing at Daniel like he would be fucking her that night.

And not with how Daniel looked elated, enjoying the whole show. Like I wasn't even missed.

Reading the room in three seconds, I wanted to scream at the shatter across my heart.

He was acting like *this* was his family, like all of this was okay.

It wasn't.

That woman had betrayed us. Nikki brought more danger into our world, exposing our children when we didn't need any more threats.

And Daniel was smiling about it? Standing next to Nikki like they were the ones who promised each other forever? Or at least a woman he fucked twice in a salacious threesome, then tried to have a family with before he lied to his first wife about it.

Pain burned up my chest, tingling my throat with tears of more betrayal begging to escape.

"Hey, babe." He looked up and saw me standing in the doorway.

Giving subdued greetings and him a cold kiss, I wanted to take Caroline from Nikki's arms, having missed my babies so much. Yet, this other mother had no compassion. She swayed with Caroline on her hip, cooing, caressing the curls that matched Daniel's.

I reached for Duke, taking him from Daniel's arms and burying my nose in his soft cheeks and smell.

The feeling overwhelmed me. I wasn't used to its power. Possessive. Threatened. Protective. It was a toxic mix crushing my soul.

It turned me away from Daniel, resenting him again, like months before when he revealed this bitter lie.

How much did he expect me to take? Where was his loyalty, his compassion for me? And now our children were being used against me too? Tears swelled in my eyes.

Fran witnessed my pain and said, "Let's take him upstairs for a fresh nappy, shall we?"

I nodded, thankful to leave the room and act behind. The tears streamed down my cheeks while I laid Duke on the changing table. Fran's hand touched my shoulder, her next words touching my heart.

"It's a lot to deal with, love. Any woman would feel the same." She rubbed my back. "You've been so forgiving. But you don't have to be so strong all the time."

That was all I needed to hear. I sobbed in relief. The validation. The compassion. My sweet boy noticed too. He reached his hand up for my face. I lowered my cheek to his comforting touch.

"Thank you," I said to him and Fran. "I don't know what's gotten into me tonight. I came in the door, and that just flew all over me, breaking my heart. I feel so betrayed with her here, and Daniel loving every minute of it."

I snatched a tissue from the shelf and dabbed my tears away.

"It's hard to watch." Fran assured, "You're not the only one. I wanted to tell her to get stuffed, but I twisted my mouth into a smile instead."

I felt bad. Our family drama wasn't fair to Fran, but when I apologized, Fran refused.

"Every family has its pain and secrets," Fran said. "And if they don't, just wait. It'll come 'round and find us all, won't it?"

I knew that to be true—from losing my parents, to losing

Kai, to now, feeling my family threatened like I could lose it to another woman. The pain didn't scare me anymore. It just exhausted me sometimes. Like I wanted to lie down and surrender.

I turned my attention to Duke and finished changing him before I picked him up, resting him on my shoulder for a quiet squeeze.

Holding my son shirked off my vulnerability. I went downstairs with Fran and sat Duke in his highchair. Then I aimed my arms for my daughter. Without a word, I gently took Caroline from Nikki's grasp and held her tight.

I sat silent during dinner. Daniel and Keats did the talking. Keats's fascination with his father was touching. So was how Daniel returned his son's questions with equal curiosity.

Then it was bath time for the twins. Keats joined us for the splashing routine. Nikki stood in the doorway watching how me and Daniel knelt by the tub, making Keats laugh beside us at the squeals our babies gave for the water toys. After the twins went down for the night, we watched one of Keats's favorite animated movies. Finally, it was bedtime for him.

I used the excuse to take my depleted heart to our bedroom. I couldn't do it anymore. For the children, I'd suffer, but the adults could go to hell with this drama.

Charlie Girl, you just left your husband alone with Nikki Sampson, a master temptress. Yeah, well, zero fucks given.

I turned on the shower and undressed, waiting for the hot water to soothe me next.

"Thank you." His deep voice startled my stretched-thin emotions.

"You're welcome." I wouldn't look at him. Stepping into

the steamy glass enclosure, I'd given enough away, first to Ashley Lynn and then to Nikki. There was no emotion left.

He joined me there, not saying a word while he washed my hair. Like he could feel how this was draining everything from me.

Silently, we went to bed. I closed my eyes and fell into horrible dreams that woke me before dawn.

When I kissed my babies goodbye, I felt so damn numb to everything but them.

Daniel texted notes of his love and apologies that day. I didn't reply.

It seemed my forgiveness would ebb and flow, after all.

Before, I'd been so generous with it. But seeing it infiltrate my home, my marriage, and my family with my children? It made me pull back every sentiment I had for Daniel.

I knew that you could love someone without feeling it all the time. Like your heartbeat. It's constant. You're only aware of it when it rushes with emotion or stress.

Yes, my love for Daniel was always there, but that day?

I felt nothing.

MY APATHETIC HEART served me when I opened the door to Riley's townhome, too tired to blow a gasket at the sight. It was trashed with empty wine bottles and food delivery containers. Not like Riley to be messy, it had Ashley Lynn littered all over it.

Without thinking, I started to clean. Wade came upstairs. He told me to stop, but I said I needed to. Cleaning calmed me. He went for a run and a day off while I was on shift, thankful Riley and Ashley Lynn slept in.

Riley's call time was one p.m. We were filming exteriors outside The Pirate's House. My subdued mood traveled to set with me, and on into the evening.

Ashley Lynn hung around the edge of the secured perimeter. She wasn't allowed on set because she wasn't COVID tested but her presence was enough to be a nuisance.

When we wrapped late that evening, an excited Riley informed me that she and Ashley Lynn had invited some cast and crew over for a Friday night party. Since co-workers were the only safe company they could keep, the lovebirds thought it was a brilliant idea.

It filled me with dread. No way would I abandon Wade. This was too much for him to cover. I stuck around, drinking coffee, and watching the crew pour into the small house.

While I covered the front door, Wade stayed with Riley who sat with guests and Ashley Lynn at the kitchen table, playing card games.

I'd texted Daniel earlier that I'd be delayed. He sent a quick "fine" in reply; nothing from him since. Maybe he fell asleep, or maybe... he was pissed at me too.

Face it. This is real life and tit for tat. He tests your love with this Nikki bullshit, and you test his with your risky job.

The gathering was in full swing. I leaned against the wall, hating it all. A knock at 11:17 woke me from misery. When I checked the peephole, a low "fuck" puffed across my lips.

Scott Harris and that camera guy were at the door. Instinct told me to open it, nothing could happen with me and Wade here. Swinging the door wide with a big smile, my hand ushered them in, lips lying, "Hey guys, welcome."

Camera guy beamed at the invitation while Scott wouldn't look me in the eye.

"What took y'all so long?" I kept them in the foyer, knowing once Riley saw Scott, the party was over. But not before I could make him squirm.

"We had to wrap up set." The camera guy lied. "Then we grabbed a bite to eat."

"Really?" I asked like a cat playing with a cockroach. "What's open this time of night in the middle of a quarantine?"

"Uh." Pause for bullshit. "Subway."

That's a foot-long tale. They went to score. It was in his deceitful smile and Scott's barely shifting feet. Both looked glazed in a stupor.

They turned to follow the noise in the kitchen. I watched over their shoulders, how once Riley saw Scott she looked terrified. Wade shot me a glance. The guests didn't notice, but we did.

I took charge.

"Hey y'all. Let's call it a night. We all need sleep and you're down to the last bottle anyway."

Not giving a shit if I ruined the party, I only cared about Riley. Taking position in the middle of the kitchen between Scott and my mark, I didn't move.

Wade ushered people out with goodbyes. Riley stayed with Ashley Lynn at the kitchen table. Scott and the camera guy didn't budge. Scott's eyes kept darting over my shoulder at the women sitting there.

The muscles across my body tensed, ready to pounce if he took one step toward them.

"Guess the party's over."

I heard Ashley Lynn say to my back, not sounding sorry, only guarded.

I put my palms up. "Time to go, guys. Next time, don't stop to score... subs... if you want in on the festivities."

Camera guy shrugged and turned but Scott held his stance, staring too long at the women behind me.

My pupils aimed up through my eyebrows at him. "I only give *one* warning."

His glance flicked to mine... and read it in my glare. *Back the fuck down.*

He did.

Once I escorted him to the front door, I went back to the kitchen while Wade stood by the front window. He wasn't leaving his post until we were sure Scott was gone.

Ashley Lynn was tossing back her last of many sips of wine while Riley nervously fidgeted with a cocktail napkin. I knew instantly—Riley hadn't told her yet. Why?

"Riley," I asked, "can we talk upstairs while I pack my gear? I need to go over the weekend detail with you."

Riley nodded yes, understanding the real request.

Once we were alone in the bedroom, I spoke softly with her. "That can't happen again. Do you agree?"

"I know. I'm sorry. Ashley Lynn thought it would be fun, but I didn't think it through, that it would mean he may come too."

I reached out for her. "It's all right," I said with my hug. "Let's keep it simple and safe. You and Ashley Lynn chill at home this weekend. Wade can cover if it's just you two. Just until we get this behind us. Okay?"

Riley agreed, giving me one more hug before I left for my midnight boat ride home and weekend off.

Chewing on pensive thoughts, I swished through familiar dark waters, knowing every turn between Savannah and Daufuskie. By the time I got home, petting Captain by the garage door, I was done being angry or whatever the hell I wasn't feeling. I just wanted to crawl in bed next to Daniel, wake up the next day, and have my family back.

The house was dark except for the light over the kitchen sink. Nightlights lined the hallways like an airport runway for late-night trips to fetch bottles. Quietly, I walked up the stairs in the silent house.

As usual, I checked the nursery first. Standing for a few minutes like mother moon shining above her sleeping world, I adored Duke's button nose and Caroline's bowed lips, sucking in her sleep. Love started beating in my heart again as I closed the door gently behind me.

But the door to our bedroom was shut. *Weird.* We never did that—too many trips back and forth to the nursery to close it.

I turned the doorknob, pushing it open. Our bedroom was dark but for the light from the moon that glowed through the windows. But it was enough to stop my heart at what I saw...

Two bodies under the covers of our bed.

It quickened my pulse while my eyes slowed, scanning the sight.

Daniel lay like normal. With a soft snore, his hard body slept on its side, turned away from the center of the bed, the usual except for the crystal tumbler with a last sip of dark liquor sitting on the nightstand beside him.

A smaller figure slept next to him, on her back, her black hair falling over the pillow. A silky black dress lay piled on the floor, a pink bra and matching panties were dropped on top. Wedge-heeled sandals were kicked off, a few feet away from the evidence.

I'd seen enough. In the darkness. With a few steps back to the door, I smacked the light switches on the wall. Light and sound exploded across the room. The bodies under the sheets stirred. I returned to the foot of the bed to witness their arousal.

"Babe?" Daniel's forearm blocked his eyes from the harsh light attacking him from above. "What are you doing?" His voice slurred from sleep and Jack Daniel's.

"I'm the one who'll get the damn answers right now," I snapped at him before turning my glare to Nikki who was propped up on her elbows, eyes blinking to the light and interrogation.

Daniel exhaled, rising with his eyes focusing only on me at first. Then he glanced to his left and jumped like a cattle prod turned up to *death shock* zapped his ribs. I never saw his big body move so fast. He was out of the bed, standing in his black boxer briefs so fast exclaiming, "Fucking hell! What are you doing, Nikki?"

"I'm so sorry, Charlie." Nikki's brow furrowed in panic. "We had too much to drink. It's not all his fault. It's mine too."

Nikki sat up, clutching the sheets over her nude body, looking modest and guilty at the same time.

"What are you talking about?" Daniel pulled at his hair like he could pull the last few hours back into his drunken memory. "Why the fuck are you in our bed?"

"Exactly. A fuck, Daniel." Nikki, naked between our sheets, condemned him. "Haven't you lied enough to her? We got drunk and fucked. Tell her the truth for once."

Daniel snapped his glance at me with a face that looked like I had my gun out... and aimed at him. Like he had two seconds before I would fire.

"It's not true, babe." His body made for sex swore in his revealing underwear. "We didn't fuck." He stepped toward me. "You're the only one I want. You know that."

I put my palm up, stopping his advance with my glare. I inhaled, scanning his face before turning to do the same to Nikki's.

Nikki returned my scrutiny with a confession. "He's lying again. I'm sorry, Charlie." She shook her head in shame. "You've been through so much. You deserve better than this... better than this betrayal."

It's like Nikki read my mind, pleading a compelling, damning case for their dual death sentence.

Daniel turned to Nikki with a sneer. "You lying bi..." He choked down the slur, sobering up to the rope being placed around his neck. "I would never cheat on my wife," he said before turning to me with desperate eyes.

I returned his stare while Nikki's saccharine voice argued. "Yes, you would, Daniel Pierce. You're talking to the two women who know exactly what you're capable of, especially when you get drunk. You started throwing back Jack and Cokes after dinner, and it wasn't two hours before you were all over me in the kitchen. Saying that we were your other family now. That you wanted to fuck my pussy for old times' sake. That you were lonely because Charlie was ignoring you, working late all the time, and that she'd never know."

Nikki shook her head, letting the sheets drop to reveal her huge, gravity-defying tits for extra measure. "Charlie, please. I got drunk too. I should've pushed him away, but I guess I've been lonely. We just fucked here and passed out. It didn't mean anything."

Daniel's massive shoulders hunched up like he was ready to jump on Nikki and give her a different kind of fucking up. But his feet didn't move. He'd never hurt a woman, I knew, but he could fuck lots of them and hurt me instead.

Nikki opened her mouth like she was going to offer more closing arguments, more details sealing their guilty doom, but I stopped her.

"Shut. The fuck. Up."

The words crawled slowly from my mouth, strangling them silent while I took my tactical vest off, carefully draping it over the bench at the end of the bed.

"Babe, I—" Daniel tried pleading his innocence one more time, but my murdering glance stopped him cold.

I turned my focus back to Nikki. It made me tongue my teeth and grin, taking in the raunchy spectacle of this voluptuous, nude beauty in *my* bed with *my* sexy husband.

"Nikki," I said, "you're a brave woman."

Nikki's face twisted, confused by the compliment. "I'm sorry?" she asked, trying to understand my generosity given what she'd taken from me.

"Oh, don't be sorry." I reached behind me, unsnapping my gun holster. "I think it's brave what you're doing."

My hand knew the habit. It found the handle unseen, pulling the gun out and resting it on the bench in front of her.

The lethal weapon widened Nikki's eyes.

"You're brave to be in my home, in my bed, naked with my husband knowing what I'm capable of doing to you both."

With a fast *crack*, I whipped the black leather strap out from my belt loops and the gun holster fell to the floor.

The lightning gesture shocked Nikki, making me chuckle as I continued, "Actually, I take that back." I wrapped the leather strap around my fist. "You're either *really* brave or *really* stupid."

"We're sorry," Nikki blurted out, her face starting to register the direction of this conversation.

I kept grinning, unfazed by her apology. "Oh, let me be crystal clear... there is no 'we' in this room."

Putting my boot up on the bench, I slid the hidden knife out next. Glancing out of the corner of my eye, Daniel's stare followed my every measured move.

The poor man didn't know what his skilled wife would do next.

"Well then, *I'm* sorry." Nikki's face went from performance to fear.

Clearly, she forgot who Daniel Pierce was married to.

Slowly, I walked to my side of the bed, the one Nikki was lying on, the knife still in my hand. My boots stepped on top of the pile of Nikki's clothes on the floor, the pile by the nightstand with my wedding photos on it.

Nikki cowered at my stance above her. Fright had her covering her tits again while Daniel murmured a concerned "Babe?" in fear of my next move.

"I won't take your apology, Nikki," I said, slicing into her brown eyes with my marine pair. "But I will take your lying ass out of my bed. And I will take you signing the visitation agreement downstairs. Then I will take you calmly leaving my home tomorrow with your beautiful son. And I will take you happily bringing him back for a visit whenever the fuck I say to. Then I will take you never being so stupid to think you can fuck with my family or fool me ever again."

I stepped off her pile of clothes, bent down, and picked them up before throwing them at her. "Or I'll take more than my words to your throat next time, and I won't be polite about it... or fucking sorry."

Nikki started grabbing for her panties to put them on while she agreed, "Okay."

"Oh, hell no. Get your ass out of my bed while I'm still

in a forgiving mood." I pointed toward our bedroom door. "Now!"

Nikki grabbed her props and scrambled off the end of the bed. Clutching the pile to her chest, she scurried for the door, running naked down the hallway.

I aimed my eyes at Daniel next. He was shaking his head in relief. "Babe, I swear on our children's souls, we did nothing. I came in here with my drink to get away from her and fell asleep. Alone."

"I know," I said. "I knew it the second I came into the room."

He walked around the bed toward me, his hands raised in part surrender and a coming embrace. I set the knife and belt down, accepting him, and resting my cheek on his chest.

"You have to know how much I love you." His lips kissed my hair. "That I will never hurt you again."

"I know. And you know I'm strong. I can take a lot," I said. "The horny things people post about you or the mean things they say about me. All the rumors and pictures—I don't care. It doesn't threaten me. But when you bring it into our home, into our family, it's different, Daniel. It hurts too much and I won't take it anymore."

"That's the last time, I promise. I have to be nice to her for Keats's sake. But if she signs those papers, I can have my visits with Keats without her. He can even spend time in Madrid with us." He squeezed me tighter. "I'm so sorry. I know this is hard on you, on our family."

"I don't like what it did. I resented you and that scared me." I pulled back to face him. "I don't want to feel that way toward my husband."

"It scares me too. That's what I feel sometimes about your work—resentful." His hands cradled my cheeks. "But that's things trying to tear us apart. That's not us. We know our love. We know who we are together. We can't forget that."

"I'm trying not to. Just don't make it any harder on us than it has to be."

"Tomorrow night, let's get back to us. We'll spend the day with the twins, building sandcastles on the beach." His lips neared. "Then I need a romantic date with my beautiful wife."

I agreed, taking his promising kiss, feeling everything again, knowing—Daniel might have fucked up in the past, but he'd never harm our future.

I'd go to my grave with that truth.

CHAPTER THIRTY-EIGHT

CHARLIE

OCTOBER. ***Days before...***

The next morning, we said goodbye to Keats and to Nikki's drama. Maybe it'd been worth it. Nikki signed the visitation agreement. Hopefully, that was the last time she'd pull a stunt like that.

I checked my phone after their departure. The text on it made me smile.

JULIETTE
Ring me today, sweetie.
Got some big dish to share!

Big dish from Juliette would only be good news and I needed more of that. I missed Juliette so much. Because of the quarantine, I hadn't seen my bestie since my wedding last year.

I tried calling her back. It rolled to voicemail. I left a

quick "call me" message. Juliette was back on set. England had started up production under strict protocols too.

Daniel loaded the twins into our beach wagon. We pulled them across the sand, stopping to pick up the toys they dropped along the way. I poured water from my bottle over them, handing them right back.

"Don't you worry they'll catch something that way?" Daniel asked after I did it the first time.

I smiled, knowing my parents did the same with me. "God made dirt, so dirt don't hurt," I quipped, making him grin at another one of my Charlie-isms.

We spread a blanket out under the overcast sky. The little ones and Daniel started playing with their buckets and blocks while I took pictures with my phone. It rang in my hand.

"There you are, stranger," I answered it, looking across the Atlantic like I could see Juliette from there.

"You have no room to talk, sweetie," Juliette said. "How are my godbabies? You're behind on your pics. The last ones you sent were weeks ago."

"Sorry. I've been a bit busy. I just took some with their hot dad. I'll send 'em after our call." I winked at Daniel. "What's the big dish?"

"Are you hanging on to your knickers?" Juliette asked.

I stood up and walked away from the blanket, feeling like a naughty story may be coming.

"Yes, bitch," I said. "I got my thumb hooked in my thong now. Dish and quit teasin'."

"Are you sure?"

"No, you're right. I can't handle it. Keep it to yourself."

We never would. Juliette practically screamed the news in my ear. "Alistair and I are getting married!"

"I knew it!" I looked back at Daniel, "They're getting

married," keeping him in the drama loop. He threw his head back in a delighted laugh. "When? How? Dish now!" I insisted.

Juliette shared the common story. How she and Alistair spent lockdown together in England. That sealed their fate. They were in love, didn't want to wait, and were planning a small ceremony by the end of the year.

"Are you pregnant?" I asked, suspicious of the timing. I should know.

"Not yet," Juliette said, "but God knows we're having fun trying. This whole crazy world now, we just want some peace and love, and to be together. We don't need a big wedding. I was hoping if we time it right, you both can come. Masks and all of course, but I'd really love it if you can be there."

We chatted about plans, travel, timing, and restrictions. No telling from month to month, but we'd certainly try.

Juliette had to get back to set but promised to call the next day with more details before ending the call.

"And just think," Daniel said, lying back on his elbow next to Duke, "we were the ones who brought them together. It won't be long until they're pregnant."

"I know. Anders and Maja are pregnant again too. There's gonna be lots of babies made after all this is said and done."

Daniel raised his eyebrow at me. "Does that include us?" He leaned over, kissing the top of Duke's head for emphasis.

I knew he wanted more kids. But what did I want?

My heart warmed to it. My mind feared it was bad timing.

"Let's wait until we get settled in Madrid. I'll stop using my patch then, and we'll see what happens."

"Really?" His face was genuinely surprised. He got up and crawled over the two we had, beckoning my lips for a kiss, saying, "It may take a while. I'll be so busy and knackered once we start shooting."

"Don't worry." I returned his kiss, thoughts inspired. "You just lie there at the end of a long day and I'll climb on top and do all the work."

"That's a deal." He rested back down in his spot with a huge smile, eyes twinkling back at me. "We can practice tonight on our date."

He quieted, playing with the twins and, I knew, thinking about having more.

I did too, staring out at the horizon, trying to see our future.

With talks about Madrid, London, and life on the other side of the Atlantic, I saw it on the water—a container ship slowly gliding along the horizon, lugging toward the Port of Savannah.

I was used to the site. Savannah was the third busiest port in the US. Massive ships crisscrossed the far horizon daily.

My dad used to tell me tales of the faraway countries they sailed from. The other day, to honor the tradition, I checked online to see which vessels were in port—container ships from Libya, Malta, Hong Kong, Portugal, and on.

I always imagined what it would be like to work on the crew of one of those ships. God knows I'd prefer crossing the Atlantic over water instead of in the air, especially in a few weeks when we were off to Madrid.

It made me exhale, considering the calming sight, thinking about our happy future while a sudden dark fin glided under the water of my thoughts, headed my way.

CHAPTER THIRTY-NINE

CHARLIE

OCTOBER. ***Days before…***

We'd enjoyed a day on the beach, and then Daniel arranged an evening for ourselves.

The twins were getting spoiled by Pop and Evelyn overnight, while Daniel had booked a luxury room for Fran at the Ballastone Inn in Savannah, paying Silas to ferry Fran there.

With all drama and guests gone, so was my resentment. And Daniel was right. Be it parenting, work, or family drama; we couldn't neglect our bond, letting things rip us apart or stress slowly erode our love. We needed the romance, knowing how it reconnects us too.

I stood in our closet trying to decide which direction to go for our at-home date. Naughty or nice?

Nice? Never. Only degrees of how naughty you're feeling.

And I was feeling. A need to indulge with the man I loved. A right to hours with him with no turmoil. An urge to escape for a night together. Amused that a woman like Nikki thought she could tempt Daniel.

That woman had no idea. She was no match for the love and lust we shared. I felt sorry for her and others who were too afraid, who weren't brave enough to explore this connection—the depths of all me and Daniel had shared, letting our vulnerable bodies open our hearts.

Now the line between where I ended and Daniel began merged. We were one. Nothing could divide us.

Daniel had disappeared downstairs wearing a pair of dark grey pants, a crisp, white button-up with no tie, with only his groomed, chiseled body underneath—my poison.

He was mixing drinks, and putting together snacks. No need for a big meal, our appetite was for each other.

A hellish smile curved across my lips at the devil red dress my fingertips landed on.

I bought this Versace mini last summer in Manhattan and never got a chance to wear it. Its demure cap sleeves and modest collar were offset by a neckline slash across my cleavage, and a hemline so sinfully short it kissed my thighs two inches below where I tingled.

Between this dress, the black stiletto heels I slipped on (only for fucking), and the surprises I had on underneath, it was going to be a delicious event with him.

The sound of my heels clicking down our stairs, across our grand foyer, it signaled my approach. The candles he lit, the drinks he poured, the strawberries he'd sliced, the lube he brought downstairs—they were all set out like a four-course sex meal on a silver serving tray sitting atop the oversized coffee table in our formal living room.

We rarely used the room. It was too nice for kids, too formal for guests. But Daniel loved it for sex. His favorite spot to fuck was on the Louis XV-style Bergère chairs by the floor-to-ceiling windows. The indigo velvet on the chairs always felt plush against my knees when I was bent over for him.

"Fuck's sake." His head shocked back by the sight of me. With rushed steps, he met me in the center of the room, pulling me into his grasp. "My God, you look fit." His fingertips brushed up my naked thigh. "Where have you been hiding this saucy dress?"

I stopped his hand before it lifted the microscopic hem. "Actually, I'm hiding several surprises for you."

"Should I be worried?" His fingertips moved, tracing over my exposed cleavage. "The surprises you hide in your uniform are usually dangerous."

"The surprises in my uniforms with *you* are only dirty."

My lips teased with words before a long kiss, one that almost broke my resolve for a marathon night, his touch starting that yummy pool between my thighs.

Make this last. You both need this.

Pulling away for control, I cooed, "Pace yourself, Sex God, and enjoy a drink with me first."

Crossing the room and sitting down in one of his favorite chairs, I didn't cross my legs.

The flash made him grin. He picked up our drinks and sat beside me, adjusting his pants straining across ripped thighs and a rising cock before he took a sip.

We did as promised—no talk about babies, work, or plans. Instead, snacking on strawberries dipped in whipped cream, he asked me about the lone painting featured on the wall opposite us.

"It's a Zilia Sánchez," I told him. "My mother loved her work. It was her one and only splurge."

"Do you think your parents would've approved of me?"

"I think they would've adored you."

"How so?"

Talking about them didn't hurt my heart. It only made it soar.

"My dad would've liked how you take care of me. My mom would've liked how you stand up to me. My father could crush a man to pieces, but never would. And my mother could end someone with her stare but was too loving for it. They were a powerful, passionate couple"—the truth turned my eyes toward him—"like me and you."

"I can see it in their photos," he said. "How in love they were. And in that painting. It's beautiful." Raising his eyebrow, "It reminds me of your pus—" he stopped, grinning through his sip and observation.

He was right. It was sensual.

"Dance with me." I set my empty tumbler down on the brass table between us.

He picked up his phone resting there. "I know just the song."

"Lady in Red" played, taking us back to our romantic first date before two more songs played after that, each track getting sexier.

"I thought our first date was the best night of my life," I said while our bodies swayed. "But since then, you've given me so many more."

His fingers floated up the back of my thighs. "You turned the best night of my life into the best life for any man." I halted his hand. It made him smile, knowing it was our game, not my protest. "I swear to you, Charlie, after last night with Nikki's games, you must know you're the only woman who tempts me. I will never cheat on you. I could have dozens swarming nude around me, and I'd only want you."

"Are you proposing to test this theory?"

"It's my turn this weekend, Mrs. Pierce." He tried again, the heat of his touch up my thigh melting my glacial plan. "I'm proposing make-up sex, practicing getting you pregnant, and fucking the hell out of you... all in one night."

I hummed, "We'll see, Mr. Ravenel," pushing him back to sit down on his favorite chair.

"I have another song I want to play for you." I tried not to smile, but couldn't help it. Once the speakers played from my phone, I took my favorite seat—his lap.

He snared my hips there. "I don't have my wallet for this dance."

I looked over my shoulder at him. "You don't need it." Arching my back, I circled as it played, starting my grind. "I belong to you tonight."

His fingertips inched up my matador red hem. "What is this song?" He sounded amused and felt greatly aroused.

I swung my legs over his and leaned back, resting against his chest while I swirled over his hefty erection under taut pants. Reaching for a handful of his dark waves, I pulled his lips toward mine saying, "It's your instruction manual."

It was a new track on our sexy playlist. He tongued my mouth to it, his hand tickling slowly up my inner thigh before his deep voice steamed over my ear. "Are you my naughty minx tonight, Charlie?" His fingers stopped before the tender skin screaming for him. "One who wants me to play with her wet ass pussy?"

"I'll always be your naughty minx." I took his hand in mine. "One who doesn't want you to play with it." Diving his fingers under my lace, I sunk them between my slick folds. "I want you to conquer it, Daniel."

That set the bull charging. He scooped me up in his arms. "Where are you taking me?" I asked.

His look alone delivered edging shocks to my clit, carrying me across the house. "Where we'll need a bucket and a mop," he answered with no smile, so serious I could wet him right there.

He set me down in front of our kitchen island. Putting my back to him, he brushed my hair over my shoulder, kissing my neck while he slowly tugged the zipper down the back of my dress. His hands caressed over the top of my shoulders, his lips following his touch while his words swore across my flesh, "God, you're so beautiful." My little dress dropped to the floor.

A moan escaped his throat before he could even ask, "Fuck's sake, what are these?" He tugged at my expensive, black lacy surprise, at the tiny satin bows holding the crotchless panties together, featuring three tempting holes he could play with.

"Yours to rip," I said turning around, shocking him again with his next gift.

Tiny pearls dangled from small, gold nipple clamps for his tease. Adorning myself had turned me on, but his gawk put me four seconds away from my first climax.

He shook his head at the sight. "Goddamn, I don't know where to start with you." But his cock soared under grey pants, drawing up a detailed plan.

I gently pulled at the little pearls tugging against my nipple. "Get your phone and we can start there."

I never saw the man cover ground so quickly, even faster than last night with Nikki's charade. *Yep, this is what that man will hustle for.*

He came back with our phones and lube in hand, thrilling me with the plan, handing me the bottle. I set it behind me while he set his phone on the countertop opposite us, propping it up against a bowl of oranges. It would record our every moan and move while he kept mine in hand for different angles.

Hell yes, leave it to Daniel Pierce to venture into amateur porn production.

"Is this the tape you really want to make, Daniel?"

"Yes." A *ping* sounded action. Towering in front of me, he said, "Is this what you want me to do to you, Charlie?" He gently tugged the chain over my right nipple, recording my answer.

It was a lurid one. I'd already been so close getting ready for him, then grinding on him. Five more of his luscious tugs at my screaming sensitive nipples with the camera filming it all, and with him telling me, "You're so naughty for me to fuck, aren't you?"

It opened my thighs, throwing my head back in a scream.

Fuck yes, we'd need a mop tonight. Because he did it to me two more times. Teasing over my nipples with his warm tongue, with his dirty words—"So... fucking... naughty"—with his fingertips pulling the pearls clamped over them, arousal trickled down my thighs.

Struggling to breathe through the thrill, I begged for his mercy. It gave me pause to unbutton his shirt, ripping the last ones away since they moved too slow to reveal his allure.

"Take your cock out," I demanded, knowing he wasn't wearing boxers. He lowered his zipper. I squatted in front of him, spreading my thighs open to the sensation and the shot he was getting from above, eyes and camera.

I almost had him like this, groaning, resisting the pleasure I was killing him with. And I wanted it, wrapping my hands over his rock-hard ass clad in fine wool, I took his length deep in my throat, glucking on his shaft all the way to the base before sliding back.

The sight of his cock, screaming hard and dripping from my wanton mouth over his proper, English trousers—it drove me mad for his taste.

But he laced his hand through my hair, pulling me off and setting the phone down.

"Get on the counter, Charlie." He commanded with a tone I wouldn't disobey. Making his point, he picked me up by the waist and plopped my ass down on the marble.

I thought he'd enjoy his meal like this, but he surprised me. "Turn around, get on your knees, bend over and rest your cheek on the countertop." He directed my body to the perfect height to conquer.

"You like being in charge of me, don't you, Daniel?" I asked. And hell yes, I bent over for him, beautifully smutty and wide open with innocent ribbons decorating everything he desired.

"I like taking turns with you." Grazing his hand over my ass cheek, "We fuck fifty-fifty too," he tickled his fingertip under the edge of my wet panties. "My wife is too fit not to fuck every way we want." He grabbed his phone with one hand, teasing his cock with the other. "Spread that pussy open and show me what's mine."

I complied, parting my cheeks for his sight. The heavy sound of his breath and the light *click* of my phone snapping photos excited me.

"God, your pussy is beautiful." He didn't mumble the praise, his fingertips tracing the outline of my sex, before dipping in for the wet he took to my clit in circles next.

His toying roll made me groan. "You want more of me, don't you?" he asked, fingers teasing through the holes between the ribbons before his tongue darted across my flesh exposed by the shameless slits. "Say it." His lips demanded against mine.

I arched my back for more. "Rip my panties, Daniel."

The grunt he gave wasn't for the effort, the thin lace and ribbons easily tearing apart at his snatching grasp. It was for all that was his now, his tongue and fingers taking me more times than I could count. They always could, over and over and relentless.

I didn't know where all my desire for him streamed from, but it had no end. Certainly not when he moved his adoration to my ass, tonguing and gently opening me there, making me moan so many curses and his name.

He had me shaking with anticipation. I knew what he planned, watching from my prone perspective. When he took his shirt off and pulled a condom from his back pocket before dropping his pants to the floor, I mentally wrote an X-rated thank you note for his assumptions.

"Make room for me," he said, waiting for me to crawl forward before he climbed onto the countertop behind me.

I wrote another thank you note to my kitchen remodel years before and this massive island. Never did I think I'd be shamelessly fucked by my husband on it... and videoing it all.

"What do you want next, Charlie?" His lips hovered over exactly what he did.

I swayed my back in a bold bow for him. "I want you to fuck me, Daniel."

He gave me another circling lick before he asked, "Where do you want my cock?"

Oh, the proper Englishman wanted me to say it aloud, dirty for him now, and the video forever. But I played back. "Where do you want to put it, Daniel?"

Pouring the lube over my crevice, his fingers slipped

into exactly what he wanted, answering, "I'm going to fuck my wife's tight ass and pussy, in that order." He plunged another finger in, adding, "And you're going to tell me how good it feels while I do it."

And I did, again and again, while he crouched over me like a mating animal possessed with its singular, strangling destination.

"You like me fucking your ass, don't you?" His hard grip controlled my hips, every slow inch of him I could feel stretching, urging in like a sweet piston.

"Yes." I panted, watching his hot body for minutes on the flipped video screen across from me. Every obscene sensation I felt for him, for this; he was a fucking gorgeous, primitive sight. Literally. "Fuck me like I fucked you, Daniel."

That ignited his hips, "Like this, Charlie?" plunging into me deep and fast with abandon, the pleasure and sight of his sure thrusts took me and the show. "Is this how we fuck each other?"

The truth of it—raw, raunchy, and real—there was nothing between us but lust, secured by love, trust, and his pure grunts making me scream out while I rubbed my clit off. The force of it had him holding onto my bucking hips, the orgasm bursting all pleasure through me and dripping onto the countertop.

He slowly pulled out and snapped the condom off, dropping it to the floor. Kneeling behind me, he said, "Come here, beautiful," pulling me up in front of him.

Hugging my back tight against his chest, he put his lips to my ear, owning my senses while he slowly thrust into my pulsing pussy next. "We stay connected, Charlie. We share everything together. Forever." Time disappeared. Rifts erased. Selves obliterated. Our sweating flesh melted into the other's, souls molten with passion—he was worth it all, our love so rare.

His hands reached around, tugging on my indecent jewelry, insisting in my ear, "We live how we want, we love how we want"—with a savage pound of his cock and a hard pull of my pearls, he growled—"and fuck how we want."

The cry came from my soul, "Yes, Daniel!" Shaking against him, pleasure streaming down my thighs, all feeling gone but him, his touch was everywhere.

I disappeared into his voice and possession with his words declaring, "I'm too in love with you, Charlie, to ever want anyone else, to ever stop having you, to ever stop fucking you."

Whatever hell we faced; this was our heaven. Days and drama couldn't take this away. The feeling of him, of more than his body invading mine—it was his love taking my entire being, now and forever.

With one quake after another, he kept mastering my clamped nipples, pulling at them, mixing pleasure and pain. His tender fingertips gently strummed my clit from behind, while he hammered his cock with force to hear me swear, "Yes, Daniel," to his pleasure, to his promise, to our love. The weight of his arms holding me to him, my heart sure... he'd never let me go.

It finally silenced me, seizing my muscles, only one pulsing around him, making my eyes roll back into bursting light, submitting all my strength while I delivered my hardest ever trembling soaking end to his praise.

I only emerged at his loud, shuddering moan, at his tight embrace, and the roar of my name at his finish. Every part of me shook at our connection, at our bond, not wanting him to ever leave me, body or life.

Tears slipped down my cheeks, "I love you," I sighed, while his trickled over my shoulder.

"Always, Charlie."

I'd never be done with him either. Nothing could tear us apart.

Fate threatened otherwise.

CHAPTER FORTY

CHARLIE

OCTOBER. **Days before…**

"*Damn*, mi prima," Rob said with a low laugh. "I don't know how I feel about eating off this countertop now."

I shared a few things with him, not all. Just the song, toys, cameras, and location part. We always divulged highlights of our sexcapades. Hell, we shared so much already—tragedy and joy—there was nothing left to hide.

Daniel was outside helping Joaquin load luggage into my Jeep for their boat ride off the island.

Rob and Joaquin were leaving in two days, flying to Madrid where Joaquin was head of cast security on *The Druid* for season three. Rob wasn't cleared to return to duty but would be any day. All would reunite in Spain soon.

"Don't worry." I wore a big grin while I plated chicken salad for their farewell lunch. "We cleaned this kitchen to hospital standards. You know I'm militant about being clean."

"Uh-huh. Apparently with a bucket and a mop." Rob gave a twerk that had me rolling.

Then a shout from the baby video monitor took our attention.

Caroline was standing in the crib, pulling back on the bars, going for a jailbreak. Her protest woke up Duke. He was rising to join her riot.

"Let me get them," Rob said.

"Careful. They're almost too big and squirmy to hold one in each arm."

Rob raised his, curling his bicep before kissing it. "Not in these pythons, they're not." Yep, he was recovered, hustling at full speed up the stairs.

I watched him on the monitor. How he scooped up Duke then Caroline. Rob was right. Those little squirm worms didn't stand a chance wrapped in his hulking embrace.

The sweet sight suddenly choked me up, remembering all Rob had sacrificed to protect us. If that bullet had been two inches to the right, the outcome would have been far more tragic.

The idea shot through my mind again—what our job can ultimately require. Our work was ninety-five percent nothing, and then you give five percent of everything you had… until your last breath.

I helped Rob belt them into their highchairs while the garage door beeped with Daniel and Joaquin's return. "Y'all done already?" I asked Daniel.

"Yep. That was easy. Just their stuff to pack." He grabbed beers out of the fridge, handing one to Joaquin. "We'll need a caravan of mules to get our supplies to Madrid."

"We don't need to pack everything and the kitchen

sink." I set two full plates on the table. "Geez, you act like Spain doesn't have diapers and baby clothes too."

Talks of supplies reminded me of the stack of delivery boxes we had. Island life in a quarantine created a steady stream to our front door. After lunch, the guys washed up while I sorted through the pile, hoping the athletic socks I ordered had finally arrived.

One box on the bottom troubled me though. I didn't recognize it.

It had a USPS ground label on it from Savannah. It wasn't from a store, wasn't one of Jeremy's special deliveries either. If Riley or Lorraine sent something, their name would be on it.

With the ominous history of boxes to my door so far, the brown, cardboard rectangle ticked back at me like a bomb.

Daniel saw it on my face when I brought it into the kitchen, like he wanted me to say something dismissive.

I couldn't.

The three guys watched me. Without a word, I reached under the sink for latex gloves and a fresh surgical mask before taking the box outside to the pool deck.

Daniel followed me. Rob picked up Duke and Joaquin took Caroline. The godfathers protected the babies from what was next.

With frustration in his exhales, Daniel stood over my shoulder. I resented this too, yet again, cutting the side of the box open to protect any prints that may be on the packing tape.

Goddamnit, I couldn't catch a fucking break.

I knew this was going to fuck with me so I steeled my jaw for the punch.

What could Mason send this time? More fake nude shots? Kierra's hairbrush we never recovered? A flash drive with a video on it? One with a wicked montage of me? Or an older one of Daniel fucking another woman?

I could only imagine the genius strokes of sick creativity the fucker could try next. I was almost numb to it. *Almost.*

Closing my eyes, I reached in...

It was pliable and soft, a bunch of fabric wadded up, not folded. I pulled it out, daring the sight.

A scream escaped my throat as the fabric dropped from my hand, branded by a searing pain I'd never known.

"Charlie?" Daniel quickly knelt beside me. "What is it?" His voice grew distant.

I was slipping, ears ringing, falling into the black, but Daniel's heavy arm wrapped around me, holding me suspended there—between now and then. My mind spinning in this space of no time, it could only see...

A light blue burqa.

It had me on my knees. No voice to speak. Unable to hear. I could only watch.

How Daniel tried to get me to look at him with my face cradled in his grasp. How my eyes glanced over his shoulder instead, seeing Rob and Joaquin shouting over theirs. Fran appeared. Rob handed Duke to her, then jumped down the stairs to the pool deck.

He knelt with Daniel beside me, talking to me. I couldn't hear them, watching their mouths move before I looked back down to the blue threads woven into one sacred cloth lying on the concrete.

My concrete. My home. From thousands of miles away and almost eight years before... to now...

We were reunited.

Paksima.

It jolted my memory.

How the first time I saw the Pashtun women in

Afghanistan walking in groups, covered from scalp to toe behind their light blue burqas, it was a powerful sight.

Inside their homes and on public patrols, I also met women wearing simple black headscarves, or ones in beautiful prints, or they wore longer chadors. I never judged it. It just took a while to get used to.

The first time I met Paksima, we were inside her compound where burqas weren't traditionally worn. There, Paksima's small head was covered with a light grey headscarf while she carried an even smaller girl on her hip.

Paksima had stood behind her mother-in-law. Quiet. Respectful. But her eyes caught mine. They were curious, kind... and crying for help with no tears.

If I could have scooped Paksima and her daughter Esin up in my arms then, and never stop running to keep them safe, I would have.

Instead, I stood my deadly ground and prayed it freed them both.

Daniel's hands were on my cheeks, pulling my mask down and lifting my stare away from the pile of blue fabric to his terrified aqua eyes.

His lips were moving. Finally, I heard his voice. "Charlie." It was far away. I read his lips. "Please, babe. Come back to me." He was closer. He could always bring me back. "What is it?" That question was clear.

My mouth moved, answering, "Paksima's burqa."

"What?" Rob asked. Now all sound returned. Rob looked down at it. "That's impossible."

Is it? My instinct stood behind me.

No. It whispered dead serious in my ear. *It isn't impossible.*

I staggered up, confronting it, shoving the words and

truth out. "Nikki dropped our location months ago. It was only a matter of time. It's here for me."

This wasn't the moon threatening in the day sky. This was a solar eclipse—a complete shadow darkening my world.

"Charlie, lots of Pashtun women wear blue burqas like this." Rob pointed to it. "I remember seeing them in Kabul too. It's like some American women wear blue jeans. They all look alike, and you can buy them anywhere." He tugged my hand to look at him, to ask, "Did you ever see Paksima in a blue burqa?"

"I never saw her out of the compound, so I don't know. Most women where I was wore brown ones or just black chadors, but some wore blue burqas. I can't be sure."

"Let me see one of those gloves." Rob's big fingers gestured "gimme" while I snapped one off and handed it to him.

"What are you doing?"

"I'm going to smell it." He put the glove on.

"Are you crazy? You don't know what's on it. It could be laced with something."

"*Please.* I could get a deadly airborne virus at the grocery store. I'm not worried about this burqa from a box."

Rob lifted it to his nose, taking a big inhale with it pressed to his nostrils.

I watched in horror while he said, "It doesn't even smell like there, like Afghanistan. It's too stale. Like it's store-bought or something."

"Or like it's been stuck in a cardboard box for months." I debated him but knew what he meant.

Every place had a smell, especially a place foreign to your own. You weren't nose-blind to it like you were your home. When you were in a place where your senses were heightened for survival, the smell of it imprints on you.

So yes, if it were Paksima's, maybe there'd be a distinct odor to it. The aromatic spices the women cooked with. The earthy dirt floors under their feet. The smoke from their cooking stoves.

But still, if you stuff anything in a cardboard box, its odor can escape the fibers over time, leaving an eerie stale nothing behind.

Daniel knelt quietly the whole time while we debated the possibility. Then he stood up. When I looked over at him, I was shocked by what I saw—cold rage like I'd never seen on him before.

Only his mouth moved, asking, "Could Mason have sent it?"

"Yeah," Rob said. "Watch. I'll search for 'Afghan women, twenty thirteen.'"

That was the year. The year I was shot. Given my public work history with HGR Security, anyone with time and inclination could do the research and figure out the timeline.

Rob tapped his phone, then held up the screen to show Daniel. "See what I mean." Images of women in a variety of headscarves, dark chadors, and blue burqas appeared. "So yes, if that asshole really wanted to mindfuck Charlie, he could've done this."

"It was mailed from Savannah," I said, not disagreeing, just reasoning it through.

Daniel was right. Mason could've done this.

"No shit, mi prima." Rob rolled his eyes. "You're on goddamn Instagram with Riley Chase and Redix Dean on set with location pins there. Hell, I've seen shots with you in the background. You've got your own hashtag. We all know how Mason could get someone to send this for him even though he's under house arrest in California."

We spent the next two hours sitting in the living room debating theories and probabilities. Joaquin suggested they postpone their trip, that they should stay and protect them again.

I flatly refused. I grew impatient with the conversation running in loops, the reality didn't fucking matter, so I ended it.

"There's nothing we can do," I said. "We have no answers, just questions threatening our sanity with paranoid fear. That's a prison I escaped after last year's shooting, and I refuse to return to it."

I called Agent Cooper and arranged for a pick-up of more evidence. I'd take it to Savannah with me tomorrow and meet an agent there.

Giving Rob and Joaquin hugs, we made plans to reunite in Madrid.

Next, I started working with Fran, deciding what to send to Madrid versus what would travel with us on the charter flight. I organized our lives and future like the box never arrived.

All while Daniel went for a long walk and didn't return until that evening.

With the twins down for the night, I called Wade, checking on his weekend detail. Standing in the bedroom closet, I thumbed through clothes to take to Spain and ones to leave here while Wade updated me.

"They stayed in. Ashley Lynn ran out a few times for groceries. Then she came back with bags, put stuff in the pantry, but didn't touch it. It's like she needed an excuse to go out."

"Really? How long was she gone?"

"An hour or so," Wade said. "She came back with Kroger bags but still... I'm going with my gut."

Hell, yes. I trusted gut instinct over deductive logic any day.

On the one hand, it was innocent. Riley couldn't go to the store. She'd be recognized. So yes, it made sense that Ashley Lynn went out for them.

But I trusted Wade. Something was off with Ashley Lynn. What was it? Another woman? An itch to get out of the house, ignoring the secluded life Riley had to lead?

Either way, I didn't like it. I was glad to be covering tomorrow night, giving Wade a break and me a chance to observe. Maybe I could talk with Riley and get her to smell the trouble Ashley Lynn reeked into her life.

"All right." I wrapped up our call, "I'll see you tomorrow morning," putting my phone in my back pocket.

When I turned around with a stack of clothes over my arms, I startled at the sight.

Daniel stood right there, glaring like he caught me talking to a secret lover and not a colleague.

"So, you're going to work tomorrow?" His tone was cold. "After everything today, you're going to work tomorrow?"

Oh shit. Keep this calm, convince him and squirm your way out of this... yet again.

"Yes, Daniel. I'm going to work tomorrow." I spoke softly, setting down the pile of clothes on the bedroom bench. "And every day from now until we leave, or we wrap this up, whichever comes first."

"I see." His timbre was so quiet, so brutal, so distant.

I suddenly felt us slipping into something dangerous.

He walked over to the nightstand and picked up his phone. "I'm sleeping in the guest room." He spoke with his back to me.

"Daniel, please, that's not fair."

"Not fair?" He turned around slowly. "What's not fair is that I have a wife who values her job more than her husband and family. That's what's not fair."

"We're not having this fight again."

"No, we're not," he said, "because I'm not angry—I'm heartbroken. There will be no happy ending here, Charlie. Not if you won't change and quit being so bloody stubborn about helping others instead of helping yourself for once. To stay safe. To stay alive. I'm not fighting anymore with you, because I can't change you."

"It could be a stupid prank from one of your sick fans." I tried reasoning with him. "Or it could be Mason getting his rocks off. God knows what it is. But it's not worth me leaving Riley at risk right now. You know that."

"Charlie, I like Riley. And I love how you are. How you want to protect her. But what can be so bloody more important that she's being blackmailed about over you deciding to step down because more grave threats are coming into our life?"

"I can't tell you," I said. "It's not my right."

"Well, I'm your husband and I have a right to know what my wife thinks is worth risking her life for. When other girls were being hurt, violently, I get that. But what is it? An ex-girlfriend? A crazy relative? Whatever it is, why don't you trust me to tell me? After everything we've been through, tell me so I'll understand."

"I trust you with everything, Daniel, but this isn't about trust. If I tell you, I'll betray my integrity. Don't ask me to betray Riley and my job."

"Well,"— his beautiful face twisted into ugly apathy —"sleep with your integrity from now on since it's more important to you."

"Daniel, please." I stepped toward him, touching his arm, fearing where this was going, where he was going. It had never felt like this before, like he was pulling away. "Please don't do this to us."

His eyes rocketed from stone cold to hot rage at my blame.

"No! I'm not doing this! You are!" His voice thundered through the air, not caring that the whole house could hear. "You're doing this to us! To me! Again!"

He jerked his arm away from my touch. "I fucked up, yes, and I lied to you. And I'm willing to make up for it till my dying day by valuing our marriage, by putting you and our family first, and by never hurting you again. I've changed for you.

"But no, not you. You're addicted. You keep doing it, hurting me by stepping into the line of fire and expecting me to just watch you die. I watched my brother die before my eyes. I watched you and the twins, our children, bleeding across a bloody red carpet. I thought I lost you all, everyone I loved killed before me."

"But we were okay. We'll be okay." Pieces of my heart were breaking off, making it hard to breathe, dizzying my brain at the pending destruction in our words. "I can do this. I'm strong enough to survive this."

His stare pressed down on me. Something I'd never seen in his eyes before—fury morphing into spite right in front of me.

"*You're* strong enough?" Seethe dripped from his words. "Don't insult me. Because you sacrificed and I sinned, right? Because you were a proud Marine, and I'm a sheltered fucking celebrity?"

His steps, the distance between us grew.

"Do you know how hard it is? How I have to fight with

myself? As a man? How I can beat another man to death, choke the life from twats like Mason, fire bullets ending threats to the ones I love. I have more strength than most men, but none of it can stop my own wife from her lethal addiction. So know this"—his stare pierced my heart—"I'm strong too, and I *will* stop what I can…"

It was pounding my chest, the pain appearing across his face with his next words. "Maybe"—a swallow choked his voice—"if I stop loving you so much now, it won't hurt so bad when you die."

Tears threatened behind his lashes, matching the ones streaming down my face.

"Maybe," he said, "if we're over, if I leave you now, only half of me will die with you instead of all of me." It choked his throat. "Because it will, Charlie. It will kill me to keep loving you, to be married to you, and to bury you. To see your beaten, lifeless body in a casket. Or gone with no trace, only my imagination haunting me about your end. Missing you while my soul dies with you." A tear fell down his furious cheek. "One of us has to barely carry on living for our children. I guess it'll be me." He clenched his jaw. "So go to work, Charlie." It snarled through his teeth. "Chose your drug over me because I'm fucking done with you."

He charged out of our bedroom. Seconds later, a door slamming exploded through the house.

Tears blurred my vision. There wasn't enough air to fill my gasping lungs. I glanced at the baby monitor on the nightstand. His fury didn't wake the twins. But it woke my greatest fear, my greatest pain.

My world, my husband, he just left me. Our family; it just died before me.

I sat defeated on the edge of our bed, sobbing.

Alone. Again.

CHAPTER FORTY-ONE

DANIEL

OCTOBER. ***Now...***

I hated this, not wanting to return to the present moment, wanting to stay forever in memories of her.

"Hello?"

I listened to the painful gravel, the low rumble of Rob's voice answering his phone downstairs while the wedding photo stared back at me, taunting me.

"You were a fool to take her and tomorrow for granted."

It dropped me to my knees, praying before our pictures, begging by the edge of our bed, cursing the last words I said to her.

Talk of death, of burying her, of leaving her instead. Of being done.

What was I thinking? I'd never be done loving her, of living for her until my last day.

If only my words had been on paper, I could burn them. Instead, they'd landed on Charlie's ears, crushing her beautiful, big heart.

Had my fury turned into fate?

Please God, no. I prayed—to what I didn't know but I did to whom.

To my twin. To Flynn, my brother who only knew ten years of life. How blessed he would have been to have a love like I shared with Charlie, a love so great that it changed my every fiber, my every next breath, making my life so brilliant and cherished.

To Charlie's parents. The shame for hurting their daughter—I was so sorry. Somewhere. Somehow. They had to know how great my love was for her. How great my regret. I promised never to abandon her again.

Please, give me another chance.

To Kai. The humility made me sick, vomit threatening up my throat. Kai had never hurt Charlie like I did. No, Kai had fought until his dying day to get back to her, to be by her side.

Please, bring her back safe to me, and I promise you, in your honour, I will draw my last fighting breath for her.

"The cops are already there?" Rob's voice thundered up the stairs, through the empty, ringing air.

That statement dropped the first nail in my coffin, my slow death starting at that moment.

CHAPTER FORTY-TWO

CHARLIE

YESTERDAY

Five a.m. found me feeding the twins. My eyes hurt, swollen from crying myself to sleep. My head was pounding, dehydrated from the tears I shed.

A new terror, a new pain woke me that morning.

I'd buried love before, had known the crushing grief of a love ended by death.

But last night?

Our love was dying to something else—a demise quickened to its end by resentment. And I knew... resentment was cancer to love—a slow but sure killer.

The contrast was bitter, filling me with shame. My parents' death? And Kai's? I had no choice but to suffer that hell.

But this? This was my decision.

When I first met Daniel, when we fell in love and decided to make this work, I swore we could be together.

But I warned him that I wouldn't lose my life to him, that I wouldn't change who I was.

That was naive. That was a Charlie who forgot what real love does.

How it weaves through your heart. How it creates a new you. Like the love I have now. For our children. For him.

Of course, I'd give my life for them. They *had* changed me.

But I had to keep my commitment to Riley. I cared for her so much, I had to protect her too. At least, I had to try. Or I'd be haunted forever, worried if Riley was safe and feeling my soul slowly eroding if I abandoned her.

Just like with Paksima and Esin; I'd never know if they were okay. I couldn't bear the thought of suffering that again. That would kill me too.

How could I abandon anyone who needed me?

I cried tears over my daughter's face, holding the bottle while Caroline looked up at me.

Caroline was her father's child in looks, but mine in spirit. Right on cue, she stuck her little finger up my nose. It made me pull back with an adoring smile. Caroline giggled and did it again. The adorable gesture made me laugh... and cry.

When I fed Duke, he rested his hand on my cheek, gazing at me. I put his palm over my lips and said, "I love you." It made him smile. He could feel the vibrations, the love in my sound.

If only I could hold Daniel this morning too.

I packed my overnight bag, got dressed in my usual gear, and made our bed, properly placing the indigo pillows in a neat row. A blank piece of paper from the notepad on Daniel's nightstand beckoned me. It sat next to a photo he had printed—a selfie he took of the four of us cuddled in bed together.

How to put on one piece of paper all the love I felt—I didn't know—but I tried.

The door to the guest bedroom where he slept was closed, but not locked. Quietly pushing it open, I saw the heartbreaking sight.

How he didn't unmake the bed. How he had fallen asleep with a throw blanket pulled over his feet, a pillow nestled in front of him.

His phone sat on the nightstand. I set the note beside it. Gazing at his wide back, at his curls, I noted his muscles sadly hugging something that wasn't me. I wanted to crawl in behind him, to hold him. He loved it when I did that. When I'd kiss his bare back, pulling him into me.

But not this morning. He didn't even purr with a snore. He was dead quiet... and probably still... dead mad at me.

Tears streamed down my face as I left the bedroom and closed the door behind me.

Daniel

YESTERDAY...

I wasn't asleep.

I tossed and turned all night, had heard her get up to feed the twins. When the doorknob unlatched, I shut my eyes, pretending to be asleep.

I heard her walk in behind me, setting something down. Then she stood there. I felt her watching me. I heard her crying. But she didn't crawl in to hug me like I loved.

Instead, she left for her work. Like I knew she would,

and I hated. So I just lay there, anger and hurt coursing through my body.

The sound of her Jeep filled the quiet morning air. That was my cue. I rolled over to see what she had left.

A little white sheet of paper was folded in half. I reached, picking it up to read...

To my D, 24.7.365 and Forever,

Because you laughed at my mouse voices. Because you picked me up and carried me into love. Because you gave me your sweatshirt and soul. Because you kissed my scars and woke my heart. Because you waited for me, cherishing every beautiful "yes" we shared. Because I couldn't push you away. Because you fought for me. Because my name is not 'Pierce' but my whole life is. Because your voice brings me back. Your body is my home. Your desire is my gift. Your breath is my peace, your heart is my treasure, and our children, my soul. And because our marriage, YOU and our love together, is the most important thing to me... I will honor our vows till the end. This is the last job.
Yours always,
C

Oh God, Pierce, go get her! I jumped up to the window.
But it was too late.
She was gone.

CHAPTER FORTY-THREE

CHARLIE

Not Going Down by ADONA

TWENTY-ONE HOURS BEFORE...

Wade met me at the front door with an exhausted grin. I greeted him with a hug. His fast friendship was a salve for my heavy heart.

"Rough weekend?" He could sense it.

"I hope yours was better than mine."

I scanned the front parlor. Ashley Lynn's chaos was strewn about.

Wade caught my look. "This is *after* I tried to keep straightening up."

"Like that's our job. Anything happen since we talked last night?"

"Yeah." Wade zipped his book into his overnight bag. "How about the one a.m. walk Ashley Lynn took?"

"What? What the hell for?"

"When she came back an hour later, I asked her. She

scared the hell out of me going out like that. Riley was asleep, so I waited by the front door. When she came back in, she said she went out to look at the stars, making no sense."

"Was she drunk?"

"Worse," he said. "She was high."

That stopped my heart. *Now the pieces made sense.* Ashley Lynn's inability to land more roles. Her beyond-thin appearance. Her impulsive behavior. Her supposed random trips to the grocery store.

"Have you seen track marks on her?"

"Not on her arms," he said. "But notice how she always wears those loafers? Not sandals or flip-flops like most of us? She could be shooting up between her toes and hiding it."

"Fuck." I added it up fast. "She's an addict. Scott's an addict. Scott worked *Death March* with his uncle, and Ashley Lynn was on the show too, on a different season, but still. They could've met that way, and had mutual user friends. Addicts have a way of finding each other."

And I silently knew, without being able to tell Wade, that Ashley Lynn was one of the five. One of the few who knew about Riley.

"Makes sense," Wade said. "What do we do next?"

"I'll talk with Riley today. She's so in love with Ashley Lynn, it's gonna devastate her," I said. "In the meantime, call HGR to pull everything on her. Let's see if we can get more than connecting dots. I want evidence."

"Do you want me to stay?"

He looked drained. I needed him to rest up for this.

"We'll circle the wagons tomorrow," I said. "Give me a night to tell Riley and to get some evidence on Ashley Lynn."

Riley had a noon call time. Maybe I could talk with her on set when Ashley Lynn wasn't around.

"Why don't I come by this time tomorrow morning," Wade said, "instead of my usual five o'clock?"

It was a good idea. We needed to do this together, so I agreed.

A doorknob clicked upstairs, opening Riley's bedroom. One of them was awake. That ended this conversation. Wade left and I headed into the kitchen for a cup of coffee.

The sound of the phone in my backpack by the door caught my ear with Daniel's tone along with footsteps lumbering down the wooden stairs. It was Ashley Lynn in her loafers. Riley was more graceful with her steps.

It looks like you're gonna hit the ground running today. You'll have to face Daniel later.

DEALING with a strung-out Ashley Lynn over breakfast was a special hell. The moods she served up were as varied as the Lucky Charms cereal she shoveled into her mouth.

I heard the ping, the text message from Daniel after his missed call. I took a quick second to check it.

DANIEL
I love you and I didn't
mean it. Please ring
when you can

Love lifted my heart. Yes, I'd give up this job if it tore our family apart. He'd do the same, so this was only fair.

I typed a reply…

> I'll call tonight. I love you
> too. And I did mean it.
> This is the last job

...but the doorbell rang. It was the FBI agent here to pick up the box and burqa. I closed my screen before I sent it.

Getting Riley safely to set, I didn't have a chance to check my silenced phone again. It was a rough day. One with Riley frazzled, struggling with the script.

I knew why. Ashley Lynn was draining Riley. Though Riley may not know about the drugs, the reality was taking a toll on her.

We wrapped that night at nine o'clock. On the car ride home, I asked if she was okay.

"Yeah, I guess." Riley stared out the window. "I kinda had a fight with Ashley Lynn this morning. She said she was going home to Atlanta today to give us space, and honestly, I'm glad."

"Wanna talk about it?"

"Yeah." Riley turned to me. "Let's get home and cleaned up, and I'll pour us some Shiraz."

"I'm on duty, so I'll take the date with coffee instead."

I locked the doors, latching the front one too. Then I pressed in the alarm code for STAY.

Usually, I wouldn't take a shower. But the sweat salting my skin was foul, and I feared, offending Riley. I waited for Riley to finish her shower, before jumping in for a fast rinse.

While the water heated, I checked the time. Daniel would be ending his night too. I'd call him before my long talk with Riley. Yes, me and Daniel hurt each other. We had a lot to resolve, but I believed in our love. We'd figure this out.

The quick shower refreshed me for the unpleasant chat with Riley. At least she was disillusioned with Ashley Lynn. Breaking the drug news would be easier now. Turning the water off, a sudden *click* of the bathroom doorknob surged my pulse.

I yanked the shower curtain back.

Aggressive eyes met my stare along with the silver barrel of a Ruger .357 pointed my way.

He smiled at my dripping, nude body.

Anger rushed through my veins while the logic fired—I could charge him... but his twitching finger was on the trigger. And I had to secure Riley first.

How the fuck did he get in?

I put my hands up. "Everything's all right, Scott."

Maybe Riley gave Ashley Lynn keys, against my instructions. No, Ashley Lynn snuck out and had some made.

The courtyard. They must have jumped inside it. And the ground-level door to the house from there? Ashley Lynn could have noted the alarm code when Riley pressed it in.

I stepped over the edge of the tub, scanning for a weapon. All my gear was in the bedroom on the other side of that gun.

His left hand rose with a roll of Duct Tape in it. "Shut up and don't try anything," he said, backing out the doorway, keeping the barrel aimed at me.

I heard a muffled whimper. Riley was in the bedroom behind him.

"No one's getting hurt tonight, Scott," I said. "It's gonna be all right."

"Come tape her!" He barked at his accomplice. Aiming the gun to his left, "Don't try anything, or she's dead," he indicated to where Riley stood.

Ashley Lynn appeared in the doorway—high, nervous, gloating, scared, jovial. Fuck, she was a powder keg of emotions in three seconds.

Yep, she'd gotten ahold of Riley's keys. She probably took cash from Riley's wallet too, lying about going to Atlanta.

These assholes scored and waited for us to come back from set. Shit, eleven hours too soon by your plan.

I surrendered my arms for the tape. Lacing my fingers together, I kept my wrists wide apart. Ashley Lynn wouldn't know... but I did. It'd give me enough slack later to break the tape.

But first, I had to secure Riley.

Ashley Lynn taped my wet wrists, smiling but not saying a word. I didn't know how high she was but knew how she'd be in a few hours coming down from it, like she was that morning. She'd be easier to subdue then. Both of them would be.

When Ashley Lynn left the bathroom, I followed and saw it. How Riley stood in the bedroom doorway by the hallway, naked with her wrists taped too, crying with tape over her mouth.

Ripping a piece to put over my mouth, Ashley Lynn kept grinning.

I jerked my head back, resisting. "We're not going to yell," I said. "We're not stupid. You have a gun pointed at us." I locked on Ashley Lynn's eyes. "Riley has asthma. She can't breathe like that. Help her."

The fuck if I was going to let these two yahoos run the entire show. I'd bob and weave through their drugged minds until I could make my next move.

Ashley Lynn went from smiling to concerned in a fractured second. She turned and looked at Riley crying. Her face was red from fear and suffocated breath.

Did Riley have asthma? I didn't know, but it worked. Ashley Lynn warned her not to scream before yanking the tape off her mouth.

"Both of you, shut the fuck up and go downstairs," Scott said, waving the gun like airport ground traffic control. Damn, he was a hair trigger, redefining "nervous" for me.

Ride this out. Keep them calm and ride this out.

Quietly, I followed Riley, passing her on the stairwell landing and leading the way down.

Scott followed Riley, warning, "Don't do anything stupid," while they walked behind me.

Stupid? No. I saw the chain latched over the front door. Bad for us now because... no easy escape. But good for later.

Always, me or Wade unlatched it for the other. When Wade tried to unlock it later that morning and found the chain bolted, he'd know something was up.

For now, I did the next smart thing. I led the way, calmly walking across the parlor toward the kitchen where more covert weapons were.

Slowly, I sat at the kitchen table with my bound hands, resting them on the glass top in front of me. Riley dutifully sat beside me, trembling and biting her lip to stifle her tears.

"You want the money?" I asked them. This was business, not personal... for now.

"One million," Scott said, "in cash."

"I know you have it," Ashley Lynn snarled at Riley.

"She does," I said. "We'll sit here tonight. Calmly. Get dressed in the morning when the bank opens at ten and get it for you. Done. You have the money, and she doesn't get hurt."

"It's just like that?" Scott asked. Like he was surprised. Like this was the first time it occurred to him.

God, they're so fucking high, Charlie Girl. They don't know banks open at nine. Just be a calm parrot, repeat the scheme so they'll follow it.

"Yes. Just like that. You'll have one million in cash tomorrow at ten a.m.," I said. "For now, have the leftovers in the fridge." Keeping them preoccupied and happy. "There's pizza and Chinese in there."

I saw the clock on the microwave. 10:23 PM glowed back.

Banks opened at nine a.m. and that's when Wade arrived too. Until then, I didn't know what drugs they were on, or how long they would be high until they would crash, or worse.

This would be a minute-by-minute vigil.

Scott and Ashley Lynn started rifling through the fridge. I touched my foot to Riley's under the table. Riley glanced over. "It's okay," I mouthed at her.

A muffled ring tone, "Adore You", sounded from my phone upstairs in the bedroom. It was Daniel again. How long until he'd know something was wrong?

He knew our twenty-four-hour deal. I told him the police wouldn't do anything for a missing adult until then. But this wasn't part of it. Would he worry enough to break it? Maybe by the early morning, he would. He'd start making calls.

Scott paced in and out of the kitchen, hour after hour, repeating my scheme. He sent Ashley Lynn through the house, telling her to find bags to carry the money.

I could hear her opening closet doors, dumping my things out of my night bag to use it too. All the while I knew what hid under my pillow—my .380.

I just needed to get to it.

We sat quiet and made it until 2:36 AM gleamed like a beacon on the microwave.

My naked ass was numb on the hard wooden chair while Riley squirmed like she needed to pee. We had just over six hours to go. We weren't going to make it. Riley's brow furrowed in pain because she was holding it in.

Scott and Ashley Lynn disappeared into the parlor. I sat by the open edge of the table, protecting Riley who sat closer to the wall. Slowly, I leaned over to see what they were doing.

Ashley Lynn was sitting on the sofa with Scott, kissing him. He pulled back from her mouth and said, "You go first." She took off her loafers and started prepping the needle.

I didn't trust what was next, the rush of delusion through the drugged mind. I wouldn't risk asking for a nude bathroom break for either of them.

"Just pee here," I whispered to Riley.

Riley looked reluctant, so I went first. Relaxing my belly with an exhale, a warm puddle filled the chair, trickling down to the floor, but damn, I felt better. I gave Riley a "go ahead" nod, and she did the same.

That bought us another two calm hours while I watched our captors in the parlor.

How Ashley Lynn went first. Whatever she shot up made her look euphoric while Scott tweaked restless beside her, gun in hand. When she seemed to come down from that soar, Scott handed it to her.

Who did I fear more? Ashley Lynn with that loaded gun or a manic Scott about to shoot up.

Coaching my body to hold still, Riley followed my lead.

We sat so quietly, almost forgotten while those two rode whatever fucking wave they were on.

Though my body was frozen, the logic kept firing across my brain.

If I got up, they'd see me. The kitchen knives were five steps from me on the countertop, eight steps from them. That's too close.

If I ran past them to get my gun upstairs, I'd leave Riley unprotected. I'd never do that. It was Riley they wanted.

In the meantime, I carefully took first the pepper, and then the salt shaker on the table between my taped hands. Quietly with my palms, I twisted the lids off of each.

I pushed the pepper to Riley, silently showing her to cup her hands over it, hiding the shaker between them.

"If you need to... throw it in their eyes," I softly told her. I took the less powerful salt for myself.

Light through the windows started to change. Riley fell asleep with her head on the table, her taped hands clasped in front of her.

I sat wide awake, watching Ashley Lynn and Scott in the parlor, listening to them obsess over which bags to carry and where they would score first. Then, they fought about where to go next. Myrtle Beach was a top contender.

Thoughts of my babies and Daniel flashed across my mind, terrorizing my heart that I'd never see them again.

Softly I shook my skull, pushing them out. That logic would panic me, making me weak with fear. The numb focus I cultivated in war served me now.

I stayed on mission, on guard until 6:16 AM dawned on the microwave. If we could hold out until Wade got here, or until Daniel figured it out, that something was up and would send help, we would make...

"We need more fucking bags!" Scott snapped, stuffing

small ones into the biggest one. "How are we just going to walk out of a bank with that much cash?"

Oh fuck. His high is diluting to logic.

He jumped up and charged into the kitchen. "Wake her up!" he yelled at me.

Too late. His booming voice startled Riley's head up in shock. It took her a few tragic seconds to catch up to the hell we were in. Thankfully, she kept hold of the pepper hiding in her hands, getting her bearings quickly.

"She's awake," I said calmly.

Scott pointed the gun at Riley. "How is she gonna get all that money out of the bank?"

As sunlight started pouring in, he was getting more and more agitated. Like common sense was dawning across his mind too.

"It'll be in one hundreds," I answered. "It'll only weigh about twenty pounds. Ashley Lynn goes in with her. They'll say it's for their Vegas wedding and honeymoon, gambling and all. They'll carry it out in bags while you and I wait outside. You keep the gun on me, making sure Riley goes through with it. Simple."

Not really. No bank would do that. The bank staff would know something was wrong. But these two were too high, too desperate to think that through.

I just needed to buy the time. Time until Wade showed up, or time until we made it to the bank, and Riley made it inside. Once that happened, I'd turn my fury on Scott. But not until Riley was safe.

"They're not getting married," Scott said, leering with the barrel of the gun aimed at Riley. "Ashley and *I* are getting married."

I didn't give a holy fucking hell about his dumbass plan. All I cared about was that gun pointed at Riley.

Coating my voice with assurance, I said, "We *will* get the money for you. Then you two can go wherever you like and get whatever you want."

Scott's eyes narrowed. "Damn right I'll get what I want."

The sneer across his face warned. It was a look I'd seen before, too many times—violence with rape as the weapon.

"Stand up, Riley." He gestured with the gun for her to rise.

Hell no! It's not going down like this!

"Leave her alone." I pressed my foot down on Riley's, silently telling her not to obey. "You put a single mark on her, or get her upset, and the bank will know shit is sideways, and no one gets the cash."

Scott didn't seem to like that answer. "Oh yeah?" He was twitching for a toy to torture. "Then you stand up."

The black barrel of the gun was aimed at me now—a vision I'd confronted before. Slowly, I stood up to it with no fear, only focused rage.

"*Damn*, woman." Scott jeered at the sight, soberness introducing evil into his veins. He stepped toward my nude body. "Fuck, you're smokin' hot. Everyone on set says it. They talk about you. How badass you are. How that lucky *Zeus* actor husband of yours gets to fuck your fine ass."

Five steps away now.

"Not so badass now, are you?" he said. "And I'm gonna get lucky too." The gun waved in front of me. "Turn around. Let me see that ass."

I glanced over his shoulder and clocked Ashley Lynn in the doorway of the kitchen. She twitched, agitated and jealous, unsure where this was going.

I knew where Scott *thought* this was going. His violent

threat made Ashley Lynn shrink back, collapsing on the sofa in the parlor.

Eyes back on Scott, I smiled. "Why do you want me to turn around?" Calmly, I moved closer.

Four steps away now.

"'Cuz' I can see your fine tits." He got closer. *Three steps away now.* "I wanna see your banging ass too, to see where all those sexy scars go." The gun was down at his waist, pointing between my thighs. "And cuz' I'm gonna fuck with you."

Taking another, *two steps away now,* I asked, "You wanna fuck with me?"

"Hell, yes."

"You sure?"

One more step...

"Yes."

With a leap, I was on him, knocking us back hard onto the floor. The sudden impact made the gun fall from his grasp, two feet from his hands.

"Riley, run!" I yelled while raising my hands high above my head, ripping the tape in a fast snap to pull my wrists apart and dumping the salt in his eyes.

"Agggh, you bitch!" He screamed, grabbing his eyes with both hands while Riley stood up.

I reached for the gun over his head, but he punched at me blind, landing a blow across my brow. I didn't care. Anything to keep his hands from that gun while Riley ran past us on the floor, through the parlor, and past Ashley Lynn rocking in horror on the sofa.

He was swinging, landing punches, and moving too fast for me to get a chokehold on him through his jabs. So I punched him back, loving the bruising pain in my knuckles when my left hook crunched against his temple before my right hook crashed into his jaw.

He jabbed my mouth, three times, the familiar taste of blood filling it. Damn, the wiry fuck was raging strong on something in his veins.

But I was doing it, taking his violence and giving it back to distract him. Any pain I'd endure to keep Riley safe.

Glancing up, ignoring his punches, I saw that Riley had cleared the parlor and was running for the stairs.

Rolling off him, I tried following her, but Scott grabbed my ankle. The heel of my other foot kicked back, crushing his nose. He let go.

I scrambled up from the floor. Scott grabbed the gun. I ran to shield Riley, through the parlor, past Ashley Lynn crying on the sofa, pulling at her hair.

Running to the stairwell, I looked up. Riley was almost at the top. I was right behind her.

My fast feet took five steps up...

Then, yank!

My right ankle was in his grasp, pulled out from under me. The force crashed me to my kneecaps, my ribs smacking against the hardwood steps, his grip dragging me down the stairs.

Fuck. He's not shooting you. He's seeking the assault, the rape.

Grabbing the wooden stair post, I held on.

He mounted two steps over me, his hand unzipping his fly, his lips sneering, "Told you I'm gonna fuck with—"

Bam! My heel rear-kicked his mouth, sprawling him to the floor at the bottom of the stairs.

Get up!

My feet found the rest of the stairs, sprinting up them. Landing at the top, I saw him scrambling behind. I ran down the hallway, slamming the bedroom door shut and locking it. That bought me extra seconds.

Riley was on the balcony like I told her. But she stood frozen.

"Go, Riley! Go!" I yelled, reaching for my gun under the pillow.

Flipping the safety off. A shot rang out. Riley screamed with her hands to her mouth, dropping the pepper with her wrists still taped together.

He shot through the door but missed the lock.

I took the stance with my .380, my body blocking the balcony door, blocking his access to my mark. The corner of my eye watched Riley swing her leg over the balcony railing outside.

Another loud shot fired. *Exhale.* Wood shards exploded from the door. *Aim.* With a hard crack, he kicked it open. *Align the site.* Entering the room. *Pull the trigger. Two center mass. One to the head.*

He dropped dead, blood splattering behind him, his gun falling from his grasp.

I glanced over my shoulder. Riley, perched over the railing, struggled to trust her descent with her hands bound, shaking in shock.

"I got you." I ran out, one hand pulling her back up onto the balcony with me, the other with the gun still raised toward the door, my instinct still protecting her.

We heard a commotion below and looked down.

Ashley Lynn was on the sidewalk below with Riley's purse in her hands, running down Bull Street, and not looking back.

CHAPTER FORTY-FOUR

DANIEL

Sextape by Deftones

NOW...

"The cops are already there?" Rob's voice thundered up the stairs, through the empty, ringing air.

That statement dropped the first nail in my coffin, my slow death starting at that moment.

I rose to my feet to confront it, my mind not remembering how I got downstairs.

"Wade just arrived." Rob held his phone to his ear, updating me as I trudged into the kitchen. "The cops are there already. I'm holding while he finds out what's going on."

I picked up my phone from the counter.

6:42am

My bloody damn phone. Like it could change fate

for me.

Charlie/Wife lit up in my hand along with her ringtone song, "Adore You."

"Charlie?" I prayed for a thousand years in one second it would be her voice.

"It's me." Her honey sound sang like angels.

"Oh God, babe." I could barely heave the words. "Are you okay?"

"Yeah, I'm okay. Riley's okay. We're at her place. The police just got here. Wade just walked in. Medic is here too, checking on us, but we're fine."

"Medic?"

"I'm just a little banged up. I can't talk long. They're waiting to take my statement and all the evidence. I just wanted to call to tell you that I'm okay. As soon as I'm free to leave, I'll call back. Okay?"

"I'm coming to get you."

"No. Please stay with the twins. I'll be home. I promise. In just a few hours."

I wouldn't argue with her. "All right. Call me back as soon as you can." I grabbed a breath. "I love you."

"I will." The pause held so much between us. "I love you too, Daniel Pierce."

STANDING in the front driveway by myself, I gazed up at the Spanish moss blowing in the blustering breeze, warning of a storm.

I told everyone I needed this moment alone with her. They understood.

Rob and Joaquin went home. They delayed their departure until tomorrow and would come by later. Fran stayed inside with the twins. Scarlett took Captain for a walk.

The sound of Charlie's Jeep in the distance was a symphony to my ears. It slowly drove up the one-lane road with the soft cover zipped closed for the coming rain.

Once she pulled into the driveway and parked, I rushed her car door, pulling it open and pulling her down into my arms.

We didn't say anything.

My tears wet her hair. Hers wet my shirt. My heart pounded out of my chest for her with every prayer answered in my arms. Her hands gripped my back like she was hanging on for life, like she'd never leave again.

"God, I love you," I said. "I'm so sorry."

"No, I'm sorry," she said. "I love you too. You're all that matters. That's the last time, I swear. I can't do this anymore."

When I squeezed her tighter, she flinched with an "ouch" at my strong touch.

"Sorry." I pulled back to look into her eyes but gasped at her face instead.

I'd hugged her so fast I didn't notice her disheveled hair, how her brow was cut and swollen as was her bottom lip. Purple bruises were emerging on her left cheekbone and jaw while her left eye was blackening too.

"What happened?" I asked. "Who did this to you?"

Tears fell from her eyes, but her face held sober saying, "I had to kill a man today." Her shoulders dropped, not from pain or weakness. It was grief. And fatigue. We both were... exhausted by it all.

"You know what I want to do right now."

"You know I'll let you," she replied. "I'm too tired to fight anymore."

I scooped her up in my arms and carried her up the stairs to our front door.

"I don't want our babies to see me like this," she said. "Take me to our room, please."

I did, setting her on the bed before bending down to unlace her boots.

"You don't have to do that."

"Shhh," I replied. "Get undressed. I'll draw you a bath." I finished with her boot laces so she could kick them off.

I filled our tub with Epsom salts and almost hot water. When she walked into the bathroom naked, shock hit my face. It grimaced at the bruises on her kneecaps darkening along with ones down her ribcage. I noticed them on her knuckles too, another one emerging on her right upper arm.

God, I couldn't stand the sight of the pain written across her. For the first time ever, I turned his eyes away from her naked body.

She came up behind me and touched my shoulder. "It doesn't hurt as bad as it looks."

"That's a bloody lie," I said, turning back to her.

"Maybe." She half grinned. "Will you get in with me?"

"Yes." I'd do anything for her.

In the tub, she nestled between my legs. Resting her head back on my chest, she told me what happened.

When she got to the part about being naked and taped up, I was glad she couldn't see my face. It was a storm of rage. When she finished the whole story, pride and relief flooded me. But I knew that's not what she needed to hear then.

This wouldn't be easy on her. Even though it was justified, she'd struggle with it, having to kill that man.

"What happened to Riley's girlfriend?" I asked, holding her hand under the water.

"She disappeared with Riley's purse which had about four hundred in cash in it." She dripped water over my kneecap with her other hand. "Savannah police are looking for her now."

"So is Riley finally safe?"

I knew Charlie needed that. Needed to be sure Riley was safe, especially since she had to kill a man to do it.

She sighed. "I think so. Wade's there now. HGR will send him backup if he needs it. Riley's mom came into town. Lorraine is with her too. They'll decide next steps and I'll go see Riley in a few days."

My body tensed at her plan. She felt it, twisting under my touch, turning to face me. "Don't worry," she said. "I'm going to say 'goodbye' to her. I meant my promise."

I smoothed her hair back. "I don't want you to keep that promise to me. It's not fair to you. I'm always so proud of you. I don't want you to change," I said. "I was scared for you, for us, and that made me angry. I meant some of what I said, but I'll never stop loving you. I'll never leave you.

"Yes, your job frightens me but you're right. We're strong. You're strong. You love what you do, and you will suffer if you have to stop." I traced my finger down her perfect button nose. "Besides, you couldn't stop even if you wanted to."

"No... I can." She wasn't smiling. "I've changed. I'm done."

Turning back, she lay in my arms, pensive and quiet. Later, she kissed the twins while they napped, taking her own, then waking to join Rob and Joaquin for dinner. Rob made beef empanadas, one of her favorites.

Even though the guys knew she was tough, that she'd been through worse, I could see it in their eyes. It was hard for them to see her like that too, after all they'd been through together.

I figured maybe everyone reaches a point when they can give no more. They're proud of their work and love it, but it's time to walk away.

And for Charlie, so much had been taken from her. There was a new look in her eyes that day. I saw it. How she had to stop before she had nothing left to give.

Fran had little restraint. She pulled Charlie in for a hug and a deluge of relieved tears.

The little ones seemed to notice too. They didn't know better, patting her face, and making her wince. But she wouldn't put them down. All night she cuddled them, wanting to give them their bottles and put them to sleep.

I waited for her in bed, watching her beautiful nude body, noting every bruised inch on it before she turned out the bathroom light and crawled in beside me.

She turned to face me, lying on her side too. "Can you promise me something?"

I tried a toying smile. "Without knowing what it is?"

She didn't reply, just waited for me to change my answer to "yes" which I did.

"Promise me we'll always work it out and go to bed together. That we won't threaten leaving or being over. After everyone I've lost, those words kill me."

Fuck, I ached over that sin too. All the times I cocked up, she still slept by my side and didn't give up on me. She was right. I would've felt abandoned too.

"Yes, I promise. I'm sorry I said those things, that I hurt you." I played with a lock of her golden hair. "I belong beside you, day and night. I'm not going anywhere without you."

She got quiet. By the tremor in her lips, I knew she was trying not to cry.

"What is it?"

"There were moments I didn't think I'd ever see our children or you again. And it crushed me to have our last words be in anger."

She rose from her pillow to kiss me. I took her lips carefully. I had to, even knowing it hurt her because I desperately needed her too. But I stopped at her growing passion.

"Babe, we can't." I held her face gently in my hands. "You're too hurt right now."

"Please don't push me away again tonight, Daniel."

She never sounded so fragile to me. It shattered my resolve. I reached my lips up for hers, taking her top one, the one that drives her crazy, that makes her moan. God, I knew every secret to her magnificent body.

"Just be gentle with me," she said through our kisses.

I carefully rolled her back, holding one hand above her head, tracing my fingertips over every part of her that could bring pleasure and no pain. Her body started to arch for my touch, wanting more.

I gave her my mouth next. Soft kisses, light breath, and tickling skates across her flesh. Every delicate move I worshiped across her body fragile with ache until she was writhing, begging for me.

When her hand gripped my heavy length, I groaned at her touch. I started thrusting into her firm grasp while my tongue traced her nipple before giving the sucks we craved, pleasure surging through our bodies.

She knew my secrets too—only her. So many other women and they never had me. They never knew me. Not my heart. Not my soul. Not the depths of ecstasy she introduced to my body. Nothing existed before her.

"How do you want to do this?" I worried any weight would hurt her.

She turned us to lie on our sides, facing each other, wrapping her leg over me and spreading herself open.

"Are you sure?" I asked, careful not to push my knee into her bruised one.

"Nothing is more sure than us." She guided me in. "Please, Daniel. I need you so much."

Oh God, my body shuddered at the power of it, to be inside her, after fearing I never would again. I didn't want to move, concerned I'd harm her. But her hips rocked over mine, taking me in tight, making me slowly thrust back. I gave her gentle kisses with sighs of praise over her lips, to be with her again, desire began to own me until I tasted saline and stopped.

I searched her crying eyes. "Where am I hurting you?"

"You're not," she said. "I just thought about…"

She stopped and kissed me and didn't need to say it.

I confessed, "I thought I lost you too. I thought I'd never see you or have our love again."

Fuck, it gave me tears too, tears through pleasure, through regret, through love. I didn't know what to do with the onslaught of emotion, but it was powerful, gazing at her.

Holding her thigh higher, I buried myself in her, going slow, so slow to cherish this, to cherish her.

"Go even slower."

I stopped. "Does it hurt?"

She curved into me, grabbing my back. "No, you're making me come like this."

I'd be sure of it. Moving my hand from her thigh, I circled my thumb firm over her wet clit, taking her warm, moaning kiss, her grateful tears over my heart, her tight sex wrapping around my cock.

We'd been here before. But those were lone moments of love. Or overwhelming showers of lust. Or tragic storms of loss. But to have it all in one time with her now, together in a wave moving me into her.

Oh fuck, it was an ocean of us, and we kept slowly diving in, hanging on to each other, emerging together, and diving in again, never letting the other go. It was so intense, so deep, her swells wetting for me more and more, making me groan back my release.

I watched her marine eyes. How her tears didn't stop but her face changed, to the next slowest plunge I could deliver without halting, my thumb pressing, circling her clit harder.

She clung to me, yearning for me as much as I needed her, neither afraid to admit it. It was our truth.

"God, I love you, Charlie. Please." I treasured my lips against hers. It had been my beg, my wish, my prayer to have her back. "Please." It was in her eyes too. "Please."

She tightened around me, "I love you," silently trembling, everything pouring from her—her love, her fear, her tears, my name. With two hard-smacking thrusts into her, I cried out, mixing my pleasure with hers.

Pulling me on top of her, she wrapped her body around me. I knew my weight had to hurt in brushes across her bruised flesh, but she wouldn't let go of me.

I wouldn't her either.

Ever again.

CHAPTER FORTY-FIVE

CHARLIE

NOW...

"Y'all ever have that talk?" Pop asked, gesturing to my bruised knees.

Wearing blue jean cut-off shorts and a T-shirt, I looked like someone took a baseball bat and scored the World Series across my body. Four days in and my flesh had swirls of colors that would make anyone wince.

But Pop wouldn't relent, retired military through and through. "The one about a plan?"

I cast my line. "He doesn't want to. I've tried. I told him to wait twenty-four hours, but my stubborn husband doesn't want to talk about more than that."

Daniel glanced at me from under his baseball cap. "*Who's* the stubborn one?"

Pop chuckled. "Yes, my Minnow is stubborn as the June day is long. But not talkin' about it ain't gonna stop it from happenin'."

The top of Pop's rod bent in a sharp bow, and he was off

to the angling races. "You gotta plan for anything to strike." The timing was perfect, poignant.

After a struggle that made Pop smile through the sweat pouring down his weathered face, the tarpon lost, and he won. We all sat back, toasting with cold beers at his victory.

"It's not that I don't want to talk about it," Daniel said once the excitement died down. "It's just that I don't want to dwell on it. We've had to bloody fight so much as it is with a terrifying reality. Dare we talk about things imagined that may never happen?"

"Yeah, but look at what happened the other day," I said. "We gotta be on the same page. Even for your job. Where do we go? Who gets the kids? Who do we call? Who covers what?"

I went down the list before relishing a long sip of beer. It tasted so good. It was mid-October and still hot like fall forgot to visit our shores.

"Me and Evelyn," Pop said, "we got a plan. For hurricanes. For break-ins. Hell, looks like we could've used plans for quarantines too." Pop finished his beer in two, throat-gulping swallows.

He wiped his mouth dry with his forearm before asking me, "You remember the whippoorwill whistle plan?"

Pop turned to Daniel, filling him in. "Charlie and the other kids would be playing deep in the woods, up to all kinds of adventures. Then I'd whistle them in, loud above all other noise on the island, and they knew—it was time to come home."

"Oh, I remember," I said. "Me and Quincy had you terrified one night when you whistled us in. Twenty minutes later and nothing. Till you whistled again and threatened a whoopin' if we didn't come out. We were hiding behind a grove of fan palms. We'd found some scissors that day and took to giving each other haircuts."

I chuckled remembering, "I never heard so much Spanish cussing in my life when my mama saw my long hair cut off like I was a little boy."

Daniel wrapped his arm around me, laughing at my story.

But Pop's face stilled too soon. "Y'all are parents now," he said. "You got to think beyond yourselves. Hope for the best and plan for the worst... for the kids' sake."

I sucked my teeth, repeating that last part. "Hope for the best and plan for the worst."

If me and Daniel were a perfect match in many ways, that would be our glaring, painful difference. Because he relished the former, and I obsessed over the latter.

Later that night, we shared a cigar on the bedroom deck. We talked it all through, every contingency we could think of. What we'd do here at home. In Madrid. In Cornwall.

Then he had to stop. We both did. We'd talked ourselves into so many worsts that we needed to hold each other, falling asleep in each other's arms—still hoping for the best.

THE NEXT DAY, bittersweet news did offer hope.

I got a call from the detective in Savannah working Scott's case. Yes, he told me, they still had my gun in evidence and would for a couple of weeks. But he was calling to let me know they had news on Ashley Lynn.

It broke my heart but poured an ironic ray of sunshine across Riley's future.

Ashley Lynn had been found dead. She used the money

stolen from Riley's purse to score enough to overdose in Forsyth Park. A jogger had found her body on a bench that morning.

I raced my boat to Savannah to be with Riley. I could only imagine the torrent of feelings hitting her. Profound grief. Painful betrayal. All made worse by the ironic relief that her past had died with Ashley Lynn it seemed.

"Maybe I'll just share my story," Riley said. "Get it out there so this can't happen again."

We sat around the cafe table in her courtyard—Riley, me, Lorraine, and Riley's mom—all sipping bittersweet lemonade in honor of the passed.

I swirled the paper straw in my glass. "Think on it first. It's not wise making decisions in such grief." I knew all too well. "Besides, that's the problem with this world, isn't it? It thinks it owns our bodies and stories. This world profits off the pain of women."

I looked at Riley with dead serious resolution. "You don't owe anyone a damn thing."

"I know. Still, I wonder," Riley said, "maybe I can help others by sharing it."

Riley's long hair fell like the ghostly moss in the trees around us, but on her, I never saw a woman make such an apparition appear so beautiful.

There was so much to Riley. She had a deep soul and a generous heart she was only beginning to know. I was going to miss her, feeling like I was looking at my twenty-four-year-old self.

"Just make sure you find the balance," I said to her. "The balance between helping others and protecting yourself." I picked up a lavender macaron to devour it, not before confessing, "That lesson I'm still trying to learn myself."

Munching on the treat, I tapped my phone for the time. Not willing to spend another evening away from putting the twins down for bed, I needed to get to the marina and home before dark.

Lorraine stood up, hugging me goodbye, and whispering in my ear, "Rest up but remember—this world needs more women like you. Come back to us one day."

Riley's mom was full of gratitude. I had only just met her but liked her. Badass moms always respected each other.

Riley walked with me down the front stairs of her townhome. We stood on the sidewalk of Bull Street, under the historic oaks and iron lamp posts.

"I hope you're not retiring because of me." Riley wiped a tear away with the back of her hand. "I'm so sorry this turned out so bad."

"It didn't turn out bad. It turned out as it was supposed to."

Reaching up, I offered her a hug, adding an extra squeeze because I knew—somewhere down the road—I'd see her again.

After our embrace, I added, "I don't think 'retired' is the right word. I'll be thirty-five next month. 'On hiatus' is a better way to describe it."

We said goodbyes and I strolled up Bull Street, enjoying the walk back to Oglethorpe Square, where I'd find my favorite iced coffee before the boat ride home.

The church clocks chimed five times. I ducked in for one last cup of my liquid addiction before the owner locked up.

Standing on the street corner, I waited for the car service to take me to the marina. The app said it would be ten minutes, so I enjoyed them.

Taking my mask off to sip the coffee, I quietly stared at the cemetery across the street.

A cute couple was doing a shoot with a photographer. I guessed engagement photos. The two women looked ravishing in matching black dresses. Their photographer was snapping striking shots in front of the old, rounded brick mausoleums.

I was enjoying the show, thinking my family should do a photoshoot too before we left for Madrid but then an old, white rental van rumbled slowly in front of me, stopping the spectacle.

And my heart.

I couldn't see the driver as it turned right, but something turned in me.

What was that, Charlie Girl? My instinct sipped iced coffee beside me. *Nothing.* My hope shook it off. *Uh-huh. Well, your car is pulling up. Better escape it now.*

CHAPTER FORTY-SIX

CHARLIE

NOW...

One week later and we had almost everything prepared —either shipped ahead or washed, ready to be packed in the luggage.

Fran had been a godsend helping me get everything organized. And she was getting excited. Fran's wife was joining us in Madrid.

Daniel kept busy too.

He'd steal hours away in the gym, pushing himself to beef up even more for his return to *The Druid*, then he'd reward himself with a night on the water flounder gigging with Pop.

He geeked out with the night vision goggles they used, buying his own fancy pair. I joked with him that he just liked the toys. He joked back, reminding me I was the one with all the toys—adult toys—and he wasn't complaining.

This past week though he spent hours locked in the

office, putting the final touches on a screenplay. It was a series he planned to pitch to Lorraine.

Or at least... that's what I thought he was doing.

But the last few days he acted odd, emerging from the office distracted, quiet with guilt dripping from his pores.

It conjured painful memories of months before. Of the lie he kept from me for so long.

What was he doing in there? Whispering to some woman on the phone? Tapping away lewd, direct messages? Texting salacious secrets to a tempting fan? Snapping dick pics to an anonymous account?

Fuck, insecurity was not in my wheelhouse of emotions. Not until Daniel had exploded our trust. But we'd rebuilt from that. We'd shared so much, been through too much. I thought I could trust him.

Could he really deceive me again?

The mindfuck had to stop. "What have you been doing in there?" I finally confronted him when he sauntered into the kitchen with a shit-eating grin on his face.

"Nothing," he said, hiding his face in the fridge.

"That's the most damn guilty word in the English language, Pierce."

I almost thought he was playing with me, but I had one paranoid string on my neck, and he plucked it.

He was hiding something. I was certain.

He pulled out leftover barbeque chicken and brown rice, popping them into the microwave without saying a word. He wouldn't even look at me.

"You want to turn around and tell me the truth?" I asked, shocked by the hurt in my voice. He unnerved me acting this way.

With a big grin on his face, he turned around, shaking

his head. "Bloody hell, can't a husband surprise his wife, or do you always have to be searching for intel?"

Sudden switch in emotions. *Cool your jets, Charlie Girl.* "What's the surprise?"

"That defeats the purpose, doesn't it?"

My hands flew up in surrender. "Ok. I'll stop." I turned around to unload the dishwasher.

His lips landed on my cheek, saying, "Tonight," before he took his plate and disappeared into the office, locking the door behind him.

Bouncing Caroline to sleep in my arms, I pushed the twins' schedule to get them down early, asking Fran to cover the night for us.

I had a hunch about his surprise and wanted to be more than available for it.

Daniel had been denying me for almost two weeks given how my bruises went from dark to horrific.

And the truth was, I was hurting for days, grieving too. Peace only partially found me over the outcome of Riley's detail.

Yes, Riley was safe, but it was not the way I wanted to end it.

Even when death was justified, it still burdens your soul. Too many focus on the fictional drama of taking life. Only a tragic few know the haunting reality of it.

I thought about it every day. Meditated upon it.

Was I really done with my career? Maybe. Answers weren't required anymore. My life was a want-to now. And all I wanted was my family, my husband, and my serenity.

Grief faded along with my bruises. The pain was gone. Closing our home down for months, and sending things to our new one in Madrid helped, putting my heart toward a bright future. It was all I focused upon.

My steps found me smiling, closing our bedroom door behind me. The tease of whatever he planned buzzed in my happy body.

The gas fire in our bedroom glowed. The shower in our bathroom steamed. I met him there. Smelling the new shampoo he washed my hair with it, I asked him, "Is that my surprise? New haircare products from your stylist?"

He pressed against me, hard, answering with a deep whisper over my ear, "Can you ever stop your mind and mouth and just enjoy?"

"Not until you put something else in them." I pushed my ass back against him, knowing he loved it when I was feisty.

He laughed, finishing with my hair, and turning the water off. We made quick work of drying off.

"Stay here," he said, leaving me on the bathmat wrapped in a towel.

I watched, surprised when he reached in his vanity drawer and pulled out his claret tie.

Hell yes, the sneaky hot fucker planned this. Your turn tonight.

Placing it over my eyes, his knot was gentle, making my pulse race. He'd always been the one blindfolded. Not me. It was a leap of trust I'd been nervous to do with him. Not anymore.

Focusing on his sound, his heat, his touch, he guided me into our bedroom. He left me standing there while I heard him shuffle about. The standing and waiting blind... it heightened my other senses, particularly the one between my thighs.

I heard something. Music. And then, oh yes, he stood behind me with no towel on, pressing into my cheeks again.

"Listen and tell me what you hear, Charlie," he

demanded before his kisses trailed down my neck, his hands dropping my towel to the floor.

It was a song from our sexy playlist. Then I heard my voice. "Is this the tape you really want to make, Daniel?"

"Yes." I heard his voice in reply. "Is this what you want me to do to you, Charlie?"

Then I heard my moans with his sighs and dirty praise. Oh God, it was audio from the video we made.

The sound stopped. His lips were back to my ear. "Tell me what it is."

"It's when you fucked me on the kitchen island," I answered with my pussy fast-forwarding, excited about where this show was going.

His fingers lightly pinched my nipple while his lips kept tickling my ear. "I did much more than fuck you that night." He pinched even harder, scorching my clit up. "Do you want to see what I did to you?" He pinched again.

"Yes, Daniel."

His tie fell to the floor in our dark bedroom. The only light was from the flatscreen on the wall opposite our bed, over the fireplace.

He had moved the furniture. The wide upholstered bench from the foot of our bed was in the middle, between the bed and the screen. Like an adult theatre in our bedroom featuring only us.

"Lean back against me and watch." He lifted the remote in one hand, pressing play before dropping it on the floor while his other glided down between my thighs. "Put your arms around my neck and spread your legs," he demanded with even more pussy-wetting instructions.

I obeyed and watched. How on the screen he pulled the gold nipple jewelry on me, making me come. And playing with me again now? Watching us on the screen with his hard cock urging between my cheeks? It was going to happen fast for me again.

"You've been jerking off to this all week, haven't you?" I asked, writhing against him while he fingered me closer. I could imagine him doing it, adding to my soaring delight.

"Yes." His voice and fingers traveled deep inside me. "I've been stroking my cock off twice a day watching myself fuck the hell out of my sexy, naughty wife."

Oh fuck, that's what I needed to hear. And what I could see now. How he was taking his cock out of his pants, and I was going down on him. How his thick cock fucked my throat with a look on his face of obsessed desire, while his thick fingers claimed my pussy now to the sight of us, pleasure flooding my core ready to burst.

"See how beautiful you look with your lips around my hard cock. How you love sucking it, don't you, Charlie?" His thumb rattled over my clit. "Your pussy's so wet watching my cock in your throat."

"Oh shit, Daniel." My knees buckled but I hung onto his neck. His hand took me even harder while his other arm wrapped around my waist, keeping me standing. I forced my eyes to watch the screen while I shattered a storm across his hand and the floor.

"Do you want me to fuck the hell out of you again?" He walked us up to the bench. Hell yes, he knew the answer.

I climbed on all fours on top of it, arching my back, knowing exactly what he wanted to see. "As hard as you can, Daniel."

His hands gripped my hips. Rubbing the tip of his cock back and forth through my dripping folds, he commanded, "Watch, Charlie. Watch how I love eating your sweet pussy and making you come over my face."

With a slow stroke, he stretched me, pushing himself

inside. Then he pulled out, leaving me open, aching and desperate for more. He relished it, taking me from behind, and so did I, moaning with his every deep plunge while I watched him on the screen in front of me.

How he had edited the angles. From the perspective of the two of us with his sexy, glazed face buried between my legs, to a close-up of his glistening fingers fucking me, to an upshot of the tip of his tongue flicking my clit.

Just like his fingers were now, his cock pushing slick inside me, along with his voice. "Do you see how wet I get your beautiful pussy? How pink you get? How you open for me? How your clit swells, begging me to suck it and play with it? How I can make you come so hard that you pour into my mouth, screaming my name?"

"Yes." The sight, the sensation, the fucking naughty questions from him were making my thighs shake with every sense I had immersed in him, in our pleasure.

"Watch the screen"—his thrusts hammered harder—"and tell me what I'm doing to you."

"Fucking me. Fingering me. Eating me." It was a lush onslaught. The words from my mouth, the confession taking me. "Making me come for you."

"Do it now. Come for me, Charlie. All over my cock."

He didn't need to insist. I was there, then and now, convulsing, soaking us so hard I couldn't catch my breath.

But he didn't stop. Fucking me now, he tugged my damp hair back, keeping my eyes to the screen, telling me to watch how he was tonguing my ass, getting me ready for him.

"Tell me what I did to you," he demanded.

It was so fucking hot, making me answer him. "You fucked my ass, Daniel."

"You love it, don't you?" His fingertip circled it now.

"You love it when I fuck your naughty, tight ass." He plunged two fingers inside.

"Yes," I gasped before stifling my scream, coming so hard the strength in my thighs quivered away.

I couldn't stop. He wouldn't either. Watching how he took me with no shame, crouched over me, hot and hard for our fuck. The sound of his primal groans and brutal grunts from us played on the speakers while I begged, "Oh God, Daniel, don't stop fucking me. You feel so good."

The same fell from his lips now, his cock pounding my pussy from behind. "That's it. Keep coming for me." I was, with one wave after another, at the sight of him in front of me, fucking me like a feral animal. At the blinding strokes of him behind me, his hips slapping brutally against my cheeks, making shameless rivers stream down my thighs.

I knew by his clutching touch, by the stammer of his gasps, he was going to come. I had other plans.

"Daniel, stop." I pulled forward from his grasp. "Breathe," I said, doing the same myself while dropping my foot to floor. I looked over my shoulder.

He struggled to hold it back. "Breathe," I said again, turning around to sit on the bench in front of him.

His cock was screaming hard and dripping wet with my cum while his hulking chest heaved for me now. "Charlie, please," he said.

"I know," I said. "Just breathe it back. Breathe it back and let me give you a special thank you for your hard work this week."

He took a few deep breaths before I said, "Watch the screen, Daniel, and tell me what you did to me. What you always do to me."

My tongue tasted my cum, licking, then sucking it off his cock. Gazing up at him, I watched how his lips parted, his mouth agape, in awe of the display. Dipping my fingers into my dripping pussy, I used the slick of my arousal on my digits to take him from behind.

He roared at the pleasure, lacing his hands through my hair so he could fuck my throat. My fingers kept moving inside of his ass, making him spread his thighs and squat lower, groaning, opening for more.

"I'm fucking you from behind, Charlie." His words panted, describing what was on the screen. "I'm pounding your tight pussy with my hand choking your moaning throat, feeling your cum drip down my balls and thighs while your nipples tremble in my grasp."

My lips felt him swelling even thicker while his thighs shook. I craved this, lavishing him with as much pleasure as he always did to me. He was there and I took him even harder to the end with deep sucks while pounding my fingers into him.

"Babe, oh God," he bellowed, his salty taste exploding in my mouth. "Oh, God," he groaned, staggering into me even more, gasping while I swallowed his last drops, making him shudder when I left him with kisses to his soft end.

I gazed up at him. "I'm sorry I doubted you."

He knelt in front of me, resting his head on my thighs, letting me comb his wet waves back. He sighed. "Never will either of us doubt the other again."

CHAPTER FORTY-SEVEN

CHARLIE

NOW...

A *ping* sounded when I stepped out of the shower the next morning. An ominous feeling took my hesitant steps to my phone on the nightstand to see what call I missed. I tapped the screen.

Agent Beverly Cooper

I knew... the law doesn't call without a reason. Daniel should hear this too.

"Fran, can you give us a few minutes please?" I asked once I got the twins situated for breakfast.

"Sure, love," Fran chirped while she picked Duke's sippy cup off the floor.

I motioned for Daniel to join me in the office. I didn't need to insist. This was our normal, part of our daily soap opera with lethal stakes.

He closed the office door behind us. "What is it?"

"Agent Cooper left a voicemail. She has updates."

I called her back, putting her on speaker.

With no exchange of pleasantries, Agent Cooper dove right in. "We had a big week. We found the PC the shooter used and matched the prints from the packages sent to you."

My eyes flicked to Daniel's. There was no emotion on his face. I felt none on mine either. We were so numb to this.

The agent continued, "The package with the printed copies of the photos sent from Richmond, Virginia, and the burqa sent from Savannah, Georgia, match. David Smith. We just scooped him up from a Comfort Suites in Bluffton, South Carolina."

"Who is David Smith?" I asked.

"I sent you an email with his mug shot. He has a few priors: assault; inciting riot; drunk and disorderly."

I clicked the email on my laptop while the agent spoke. The attachment opened and my lungs filled with sharp recognition at the shot.

David Smith was the man from Savannah, the one who stood out in the crowd of Redix Dean's screaming fans at the fence around our location shoot. He was the one who had glared at me like he wanted me dead.

He did.

That asshole had been chasing us all this time? From New York City at our hotel to Richmond, Virginia, where he sent the pictures, to finding me on set in Savannah, Georgia?

I shared that intel before asking, "What did you find on him?"

"We found a *White Flag* shrine to you in his hotel room," the agent said. "He had a boat rental scheduled for this weekend. Seems he was headed your way."

The sour to my stomach was instant.

"Did he have on combat boots?" Daniel asked.

The footprints. The ones we found in the sand weeks back. Could those have been David Smith's?

The agent paused before she answered, "From what I can see from his intake records at the jail. We brought him in with... it says... 'black, engineer boots, Durango, size eleven'."

I banged out the search online, checking the pictures of the soles. Nope. Not a match.

"We also found your shooter's PC," the agent continued. "Brad Jenkins gave it to a gaming friend of his before he flew to New York for the premiere. Seems the threat of impeding a federal investigation finally got his friend to bring it in last week."

"Was he *White Flag* too?" I asked.

Maybe the shooter, Brad Jenkins, was working with this David Smith guy the whole time. Maybe both were members of Mason Hunt's evil *White Flag* cult.

"Not that we can tell, no," the agent replied. "We found his games and that he used Tor, the dark web software. We're trying to get through the encryptions, but it looks like he reached outside the US, mainly Libya from what we can tell so far."

Fear shivered across my shoulder blades, tingling down my thighs, icing to my toes.

Libya has past connections to the Taliban. The agent knew it too, answering my silent question.

"We're digging. But so far it seems Jenkins may have been a sympathizer. We can't confirm it yet that he was recruited, but we found that he tried to access your military personnel record, using the Freedom of Information Act, but was denied. He did have every article though, every photo of you on that PC. Everything on Mr. Pierce too."

"So I was chum in the water for him?" I started following the logic. "I was a target for his political statement?"

"It's looking that way. We still can't confirm that he was acting alone, but that's all we have for now."

Agent Cooper's tone was wrapping this up with nothing else to report. We thanked her; no need to ask her to keep us informed. She would.

"Let me get this straight," Daniel said after we ended the call. "David Smith was *White Flag*, one of Mason's zealots. He was in New York last December. Took the pictures of us at the hotel twenty-four hours before *The Druid* premiere and mailed them to HGR in London the next morning from Virginia, like a taunt. Then he tracked us here, thanks to Nikki, and found you on set in Savannah, and mailed the burqa here last month. And he rented a boat and was coming this way. But he had nothing to do with Jenkins shooting at you?"

"There's nothing connecting the two of them," I said, "except their hatred of me."

"And Brad Jenkins was a Taliban sympathizer?" His fingertips strummed the oak desk. "Who has been stalking you since we were made public. He missed his shot at the *Swipe Right* premiere, so he returned to *The Druid* premiere that same night as David Smith?"

His voice dropped as low as our stomachs sank to the truth. "Bloody hell, babe... you had two targets on your back."

"It sure has felt like it."

I wasn't looking at him. My gaze was on the wall, up to

the Springfield rifle hanging there. It was only natural with talk of targets, shots, and threats.

"And now"—Daniel spoke slowly—"Brad Jenkins, the shooter, is dead. And David Smith, the *White Flag* stalker, is in jail."

We paused, thinking it through. But he couldn't hide the relief in his voice. "Are we finally free of this? Is this finally done?"

"It still doesn't explain those footprints in the sand." My logic wouldn't let it go.

"No, it doesn't. But David Smith could have another pair of boots somewhere. Bloody hell, he knew our address and was renting boats to get here. Or it really could've been a curious tourist, a fan gawking outside. That's going to keep happening to us, you know."

I sucked my teeth and couldn't debate him. Two threats down in one day. Could it be true? We were finally safe? All that was left to fear were crazed fans and annoying paparazzi? The usual?

A loud cry reverberated down the hallway. Then another.

"I've got it." Daniel left to help Fran, both of us knowing she'd have her hands full with two wailing infants.

But I sat behind my dad's desk unable to move. A minute later and I heard nothing.

Staring out of the windows at the dunes, at navy water kissing Carolina blue sky, the news today should've lifted the weight of the world off my soul.

All this time... I knew someone was coming for me.

Fate twisted it into two threats—one from my past war, and one from my present hell.

And now they were gone?

But it wasn't there...

I found no relief in my shoulders tensed to my ears. No peace radiating through my firing synapses. No relaxing exhale freeing the grip on my heart.

My instinct reclined in the lounger on the back porch, looking back at me through the window with one eyebrow raised.

You know better.

CHAPTER FORTY-EIGHT

DANIEL

NOW...

The next morning, we received another call. Charlie's .380 had cleared evidence. It was ready for her to pick up from the Savannah Police Department. The case of Scott Harris was closed.

We were free to go.

I took it as a sign—time to close this dark chapter.

While the twins napped and Charlie stored the patio furniture in the garage, I schemed romantic plans. One last hoorah here before we said goodbye for months, if not a year.

Our flight to Madrid left Monday night. I overheard Charlie make plans to pick up the gun tomorrow, Saturday afternoon.

I phoned my assistant, asking Elaine to make reservations at The Hamilton-Turner Inn in Savannah for that night. Pop and Evelyn jumped at the chance to have one last time to spoil their grandbabies. Fran would enjoy the night off.

"Come on, my lady." I plopped our overnight bags on the floor of the kitchen. "Your chariot awaits," I said just as the front doorbell rang.

Charlie turned around, folding the dishtowel in her hands. "What did you do?"

I spun on my heels, answering the door while calling over my shoulder, "You have fifteen minutes to put on something sexy."

She followed behind me, greeting Pop and Evelyn, then darting upstairs. Quickly, she returned, giving pecks goodbye to the doting grandparents.

"Guess there's no flounder gigging for Pop-Pop tonight," she said.

"I timed it this way," Pop quipped back. "It's cloudy tonight. Tomorrow night is clear, and it's got the full Hunter's Moon with my name written all over it."

"Want some company?" I was eager for one more night on the water with Pop before saying farewell.

"I'll come 'round for ya at seven," Pop said.

"Y'all have fun," Evelyn chimed in. "Savannah on Halloween weekend is all sorts of spooky fun."

Minutes later, Silas waved us off from his dock with a "sure, y'all don't want to make it three tonight?" joke.

"In your dreams, Silas!" Charlie shouted back.

He smiled. "Yes!" His yell thundered over our boat engine pulling away. "It is!"

I could only laugh as if I'd ever share Charlie with anyone. Pointing the bow west toward Savannah, she didn't even interrogate me about the plans. She just nuzzled against me behind the console while I followed the GPS to the Bull River Marina.

Our private car service was waiting for us there. I traveled now as Charlie liked, in an understated luxury sedan, no big, black 4x4s that scream "target".

It whisked us to the front door of the historic mansion turned lavish suite hotel. We were thankful for the mask protocol. Behind them with our distinct faces covered, we weren't recognizable.

The concierge snapped his fingers. The bellman discreetly delivered us to the James Oglethorpe Suite where Charlie promptly flopped down on the antique bed, beckoning me to join her once I tipped the bellman and closed the door.

"So, what's the plan now?" She rolled over, crawling on top of me flopped beside her while hitching her mini sundress up.

"I've arranged for private dining at The Olde Pink House tonight, your favorite. Followed by a private Ghost Tour with just you, me, and a guide."

"A Ghost Tour?"

"Yep. All this going on about Savannah, ghosts, and *The Tour*, and I want one."

"It's the perfect night for it"—a smile wouldn't leave her face—"the night before Halloween in one of America's spookiest cities." Her gaze down at me was full of fun. "Mwahahaha!"

"And it's the perfect timing." I snuck my hands under her dress, caressing her hips. "Everyone is hiding behind masks. No one will spot us. We have a rare night out together, like a proper couple."

Her fingertip traced over the bow in my lips. "You're spoiling me, Daniel Pierce."

It tickled, making me grin. "Did I ever stop?"

"No." She beamed down at me. "Just like I won't stop

loving you."

"That I shall require daily proof of." Lingering my hands up to her tiny waist, something was missing. "Where's your patch?" It wasn't her time to go without it. That was two weeks ago.

"I figured we could start tonight. I'm not putting our life off anymore." She pulled her dress overhead before tossing it to the floor. "If that's okay with you."

"It's more than okay with me."

God, I was so ready for this. I couldn't wait to return to set, only to come home to her and the twins.

And the thought of having more? Of a pile of kids running around our home, curling up on the sofa with them watching kid movies, filling a minivan for me to drive to school, or crowded around the dinner table—I was jumping far ahead, but I could see it. All I could dare hope for.

"Dinner reservations are in three hours." My fingertips traced down her belly, loving the soft carve of her abs showing through. "The revised plan is at least twice tonight to try to get you pregnant. And by my calculations, it's probably the right time to do it."

"Are you going to start counting everything again?" The buttons on my shirt were slowly being liberated from their strangle over my chest by her deft fingers. "Yes, it is the right time," she said. "But don't put that kind of pressure on us."

"It's no pressure." I loved her hands floating over my pecs before thrilling down my trail to unbutton my trousers. "It's only fun." I nudged her bra strap off her shoulder.

"This feels different." She took my sexy hint, unhooking her bra before flinging it to the floor, giving me a glorious show. "The first time we got pregnant was a surprise."

The sunlight streaming through the massive windows with wrought iron balconies made her blue eyes glow while the air across her naked breasts made her pert nipples demand my touch. The way she looked down at me, we were fused. "It feels special to be trying now."

Fuck's sake, how this woman owned me. "It's always special making love to my wife." I marveled at the sight, at her blonde mane spilling over her shoulders, at my fingertips teasing her breasts until she was grinding on top of me.

"Come here, beautiful." I pulled her thighs to crawl up over my mouth. "I want to get you very ready to try."

Pulling her pearl lace panties aside, I buried my tongue in her, craving her taste, her smell, the sounds of her pleasure. I devoured her until she was more than ready, until she was yanking my trousers and boxers down to my ankles with no patience.

Climbing back on top of me and sinking her wet pussy down my shaft, she indulged me. I always loved the sound of it—the smacking of our lust while she rode me hard. All I could do was lie back and moan at her pursuit, our pursuit.

Watching our sex on a screen was a mind-blowing, salacious indulgence. Watching her above me, fucking me, making love to me, hoping to make our baby... it was transcendent.

It inspired me. "Come here." I pulled her off, urging her thighs back up to my chin. "I want to taste you again."

I'd never done this before, exploring the flavor of our arousal combined. It only turned us on more, making her grind over my face, making me wild for her, that animal demand to mate coursing through my veins.

As soon as she cried out, I yanked her back down, and she delivered. The hard, pumping ride over my cock had her trickling over my thighs and me finally letting go, throwing my head back with a guttural moan and hard thrusts inside her, finding my satisfying ending too.

Recovering my breath, I pulled her lips down to mine, swearing, "Now that's how you make a baby, Mrs. Pierce."

Our kiss was deep, then rolling into laughter, rolling our bodies across the bed, knowing… we would sure keep trying.

CHAPTER FORTY-NINE

CHARLIE

NOW...

The next day found me light on my feet, light in my heart with joy.

Last night's romantic dinner with Daniel, and then our fun ghost tour—it had us holding hands, walking public sidewalks. He kept making me scream when he'd jump out from behind something, amusing our tour guide too. We explored the dark, cobblestoned squares of historic Savannah until two a.m.

Sex with Daniel felt different last night and that morning too. The twins were a surprise from our first marathon week of fucking like rabbits.

Now we were trying to get pregnant. It made me feel like we were even more tethered together, both vulnerable to the whims of fate with one shared hope.

After devouring a late breakfast delivered on silver trays to our room, we got dressed and ventured outside for another afternoon of freedom.

CHASE HER

The Police Department was a ten-block walk from the Inn. With masks on our faces and baseball hats pulled low, we felt safe. No one would spot us.

We could go to the station, stop by a couple of shops, get my favorite iced coffee, and then have our car pick us up at the Inn for our trip home.

It was the oddest sensation to me—able to hold his hand in broad daylight, chatting about nothing, strolling down public sidewalks like a normal couple without worrying about a crowd or worse. I wasn't walking in my sneakers over cobblestones; I was walking on air.

The gorgeous afternoon added to my bliss. The Halloween day promised a full Hunter's Moon that night, making the holiday buzz with ghoulish anticipation. There were gatherings in almost every park with costumes and candy all around.

I loved it, soaking up every liberating moment of hiding behind a mask.

Once we were at the police station, it took a while to fill out the paperwork for my gun. Word traveled through the station we were there. A line of officers asked Daniel for photos.

He was too polite to turn them down, granting their wish, asking them to please wait to post it until tomorrow.

For half an hour he offered mask-covered selfies with the cops while I loaded my .380 and put the safety on before snapping it in its holster. I brought my backpack, tucking the weapon into the bottom of it. Then, I patiently waited for this celebrity spectacle to end.

"Do you have a preference?" I held his hand, strolling up Oglethorpe Avenue toward my favorite coffee shop. "Do you want another son or a daughter?"

"I'm hoping for another pair of twins."

"Oh, *hell* no. I'll be running all over hell's half acre with four kids under four."

That stopped us. Standing under the tree canopy in the street median, he threw his head back, laughing. "Bloody hell, you and your Charlie-isms."

He pulled his mask down. So did I. He dished out that sexiest gesture, the one where he smiles, cocks his head, and bows down for my lips. It gets me every time, crosswalk be damned.

"My only preference is you for the rest of my life," he said after his lips left mine.

"Careful what you wish for. That's a lot of me to put up with."

"Sounds hunky-dory to me." He stopped time and traffic with his gaze and grin shining down at me. "Keep putting it all over me, Mrs. Pierce."

"Oh, come on. You'll never get tired of me?"

The look in his eyes changed from flirting to fact. "Never." His hand held my cheek. "All my life is for you, Charlie."

"Deal." I sealed it with another kiss.

The brush of people passing by stopped our romance, snapping us back to reality. We masked back up. I pulled his arm along, looking right before crossing to walk up Abercorn Street.

I pointed to a quaint storefront. "Let's stop in here and get some gifts for your family." We ducked into the shop full of locally made soaps, candles, candies, and more.

The young woman behind the counter greeted us nonchalantly at first. We were the only ones in the shoebox-sized store with Daniel's brawn filling a quarter of it. But once he started loading the cashier's countertop up with boxes of pralines, there was no missing him.

"Excuse me." The young woman sang a familiar refrain. "Aren't you Daniel Pierce?"

And... here we go, Charlie Girl. Hope you enjoyed a half day of anonymity. It's gone.

But he had to do this. He was always good to his fans. A chat started about how she loved *The Druid* and *Zeus*, how she can get him anything he wanted, and would he please pose for a selfie to post on social media too?

The usual.

I rolled my eyes. This was going to take a while. I checked my phone. We had about an hour before our car was picking us up at the Inn.

Then I clicked my notifications.

Oh. Fuck. No.

Someone at the police station already posted Daniel's picture, dropping a location pin on us—forty minutes ago. #danielpierce #captaincharlotteroberts #historicsavannah stalking our next move.

The clock ticked down.

I gently touched his back. "We should get going."

He turned around, helpless eyebrows raised, politely waiting for the woman to wrap and ring it all up. She was the only one working.

"I'm gonna go to the corner for our iced coffees and be right back." I pulled out my cardholder before giving him the backpack to store the gifts. "I'll meet you back here."

Stepping onto the sidewalk, I looked left and clocked them. A group of fans stood at the corner with their phones out, obvious because the sound of chittering fanatics was burned into my brain.

They were searching, playing celebrity scavenger hunt. Shit. We didn't have much time.

I ducked fast into the coffee shop. "Hey, Jenny." The little bell above the door also announced my arrival.

"Well hey, Charlie. Haven't seen you in a couple weeks." Jenny looked up from behind the counter, dusting coffee grounds off her hands onto her red apron. "You want the usual?"

"You know it. One more time before I'm out of town for a while." I peeped out the store window and saw the scavenger hunters headed this way. The group was getting bigger. "Can you make it two, please? To go?"

"Sure thing," she said.

"Do you mind if I use your restroom real quick?"

"Right back there." Jenny pointed to the small corridor that led to the back door of the shop and the alleyway behind it.

I went in and set my cardholder on the white porcelain wall sink in the bathroom before I took the time to squat and think.

You've got a snowball's chance in hell of making it back to the Inn with that swarm of fans hot on your heels, looking for Daniel.

We should call for the car to pick us up from the shop. I heard the bell above the door ding again and prayed it wasn't one of the fans sticking their nose through every door in the five-block radius.

I could probably go unspotted, but Daniel couldn't. Even covered by a mask and baseball hat, his tall, wide tapered silhouette would give him away in seconds to eyes roaming for his distinct form.

So much for a relaxed afternoon with your husband.

Cool water and anti-bacterial soap washed that wish away. Two yanks for paper towels felt good against my frustration. I flipped my twisted bra strap under my "Feminist AF" T-shirt and half tucked it into my jeans.

Snatching my cardholder off the sink, I opened the door with trepidation, fearing fans would be in there looking for me and Daniel.

Wait...

No one was in the shop.

"Jenny?" I called out.

I stepped to look behind the counter. Sprawled feet in New Balance sneakers, jeans, and a red apron met my eyes. "Jenny, you okay?"

I knelt to help her, setting my cardholder on the ground before checking her pulse. She had one but was out cold.

The hardline phone on the counter; I remembered seeing it. I got up and turned around to call 911.

And the sight standing there...?

It shot right through me.

He was the full moon in my day sky.

A needle punched my arm while the shock of it stunned through my senses.

On instinct, I pushed him. He stumbled, then lunged, grabbing me, and knocking us to the floor. Twisting fast, I got my legs around his throat, my glare staring straight into his brown eyes.

Almost eight years since I saw them last.

My legs squeezed his neck, choking him—to death I would.

But I couldn't feel my muscles tightening. My body didn't respond. His bulging face relaxed. His gasping breath stopped. His face smeared before my eyes.

The hardwood floor softened beneath me. It was a warm, water blanket wrapping around me. All sound ceased. Light pixelated my vision. My arms were liquid lead. My top lashes met the bottom ones in a black web.

A black web.

Black...

CHAPTER FIFTY

DANIEL

NOW...

Checking my phone, I worried. *Where the bloody hell is Charlie?* It'd been over fifteen minutes. All our gifts were beautifully wrapped and loaded into her rucksack.

I slung it over my shoulder and looked out the shop window. A giggling group walked by with their noses down and phones out like they were tracking something.

I knew instantly—me.

Fuck's sake, that's what Charlie was trying to tell me.

My pulse shot up. I wasn't doing this again—waiting. No. Last time something was wrong. And now?

Yes, Pierce. It's wrong. Go get her. Fuck the fans.

I pulled the bill of my cap low, shading my eyes, pinching my mask tight over my nose; anything to conceal me.

Darting right out of the store, walking behind the searching crowd, I saw the coffee shop a half-block away. Taking fast steps toward it, I barely stopped as an old, white rental van barreled in front of me, shooting out of the alleyway without a care for pedestrians. *Fucking prat.* It turned right in front of me.

With eleven fast strides, I was in the coffee shop, avoiding the gaggle searching farther up the street.

The small shop was empty.

"Hello?" I called out. Peering down the hallway, I saw sunlight beaming in through the back door cracked open.

"Charlie?" I jiggled the doorknob to the lone lavatory. It opened. It was empty.

I turned back around to the counter, leaning left to look behind it. A woman in a red apron was passed out on the floor.

A rush torched through my every muscle, blazing to the tips of my ears, slamming my heart. "Charlie!" I yelled, pushing the curtain aside to the back storeroom. Empty. Running down the hallway to the back door, I slammed it wide open.

An empty alleyway stared back at me—nothing but garbage cans, paper on the ground, and a fresh glistening grease puddle on the pavement. Beside it? A smashed security camera, wires hanging from its former spot by the back door.

I ran back inside. The poor woman on the floor, I knelt to check her. She had a pulse. Then I saw it—Charlie's teal cardholder—it lay right beside her.

Charlie was here. And now…

She was gone.

Breathe, Pierce. Breathe.

My pulse pounded in my eardrums. My hand shook with her cardholder in my palm.

I knew what this was. We talked about it the other week

—the "what if." But there had never been an "if" in her tone. It was always a "when".

Like she always knew.

"Don't call the police." She had told me.

I knew why.

There was only one way out of this for good. She had said… no, she had made me promise that I'd give her twenty-four hours to free us forever.

But there was an innocent victim at my feet. *Think fast, Pierce. The phone on the counter.*

"Nine one one. What's your emergency?"

"I need an ambulance." I gave the coffee shop name, told them there was a woman passed out on the floor, that she had a pulse, and then I hung up.

I didn't want to leave this woman vulnerable. But I couldn't get caught here. I had to get our babies.

Our babies…

I tried calling Pop. It went straight to voicemail. He was out on the water. Who else had a boat?

"Silas." My breath panted into my phone.

"Hey dude, y'all having a good time?"

"Get in your truck. Go to our house and get the twins, Fran, and Evelyn. Get them to Quincy's. Now. Right now."

"What's wrong?"

"You know what this is, Silas. They got her. Move fast."

"On it." He ended the call.

This was OUR PLAN—get the babies first, any family too, and get them safe… above all else.

Wherever the threat found us, take everyone to the next location, one no one else knew about. Here? That was her friend's house in Bluffton, on the mainland. No threat we knew could connect her to Quincy's house.

Sirens wailed up the street. The woman would be okay.

Throwing the rucksack over my shoulder, shoving Charlie's cardholder in my pocket, I ran out the back door.

The security camera at the front door had tracked my entrance. I saw it and didn't care. By the time the police caught up to question me, my whole world would be upside down.

I turned left in the alleyway, away from the crowd and approaching ambulance.

And ran.

Thank God, Savannah was built on a grid system. And I always counted. The blocks. I was sprinting them. With the rucksack strapped over my shoulders and my phone in hand, I called the hotel concierge.

"I need my car. Any car. Now!" I insisted. This was the one time I used my celebrity power unapologetically.

By the time I ran the ten blocks down and two, no, three blocks to the right, I was there and so was the waiting black BMW.

I jumped in the backseat. "Bull River Marina, as fast as you can."

What's next? What's next? Oh God, where is she?

Watching Savannah whiz by, fuck, I wanted to call the police or the FBI. But they would be as helpless as me right now. She just fucking vanished.

No, not vanished.

She was targeted.

All along.

What could I do? Get our kids safe. Our family too. Done.

I'd meet Silas at Quincy's. Thankful now for that young man's devotion to Charlie, romantic or lustful, I didn't care. Silas wouldn't fail us. I trusted that.

What about our house? Fuck's sake, Captain was gone.

We already sent the guard dog with the pet relocation service flying him to Spain.

And Scarlett and Curtis? Our security guards? What time was it? I tapped my phone screen. 4:04pm glowed back. Scarlett was on shift. Curtis would be there in an hour.

I texted them the simple code, the one Charlie told all to use for an active threat.

RED

They'd secure the house once Silas had everyone out of there. Charlie had trusted both HGR guards, told me they were trained and knew what to do.

The historic buildings of Savannah disappeared as the car turned right onto the open highway, racing toward the marina, the driver heeding my demand for a fast exit.

Bloody hell. Exits? Charlie had always said they were the softest targets, the highest risk. When everyone was relaxed and distracted, even tired, they wait... and then... they strike.

I called Evelyn. She was at our house, dropping the twins off after their night with the grandparents.

"Silas is on his way," I said. "Only take what we'll need and clear out. Fast."

"Ok." She paused, relaying that to Fran. Evelyn was smart. She'd know what's up. "Is she with you?"

"No. It's just me." I glanced up at the driver who kept looking back at me. Between my famous face, accent, odd behavior, and this fucking cryptic conversation, I had to be careful. "I'll call you from the boat."

Evelyn and Pop? God, I was thankful for their forced talks about plans. And bloody hell, I wished Rob and

Joaquin were still here. But wishes meant fucking bollocks right now.

I took the moment to text Nikki too, worried—on the long chance—that they could be targeted too. Tragically, ironically, it would be partially Nikki's fault.

> Get Keats. Get your family.
> Stay inside, stay safe and
> do not leave until I text. And
> don't ask. Just trust me

Could I trust Nikki not to blab? Not to freak out? I didn't know, but I wouldn't risk my other son's safety. Hopefully, she wouldn't either.

I glanced up. We were crossing the bridge. The marina was minutes away.

Slinging the rucksack back over my shoulder, I remembered...

Charlie's phone is in it. Fuck, it could have tracked her. And her gun. *It's in the bottom of the bag.*

Why did she leave it with me? She could use it right now.

Or could she? She had told me, if your gun gets into the wrong hands, it's the most lethal weapon against you.

Depending on what went down, if Charlie was out cold... no, she had to be knocked out, or she'd be fighting back. So, if she had that gun on her, it would be used against her now.

Thoughts, flashes of what could be happening to her, what they could do to her—they clenched my jaw, twisting my stomach with a fear that threatened to spew from my throat.

No, Pierce! Keep your fucking shit together. You're no fucking good to anyone losing it now.

But like hell if I wasn't going to use her gun. I'd do anything to protect our kids, our family.

And her.

Once I find her.

CHAPTER FIFTY-ONE

CHARLIE

NOW...

In the blackness, I found my mom and a memory.

We were on our daily jog—a sprint really because my mother was fast.

Running down the sandy roads of the island, our feet crunched over pine needles. Ankles dodged divots and ruts. Cheeks welcomed any breeze. Scalps sought the cover of shade. Our usual track was three miles up and three miles back.

That day though, my sixteen-year-old quads strained to keep up with my mom who was on a mission. It was her birthday. She was forty-five years old, and we were running the full length of the island to celebrate.

Ten miles total.

"God bless." My mom spoke in Spanish. "I'm halfway. Halfway through this life. Just get me to ninety, and I'll lie down for the rest."

My calves were throbbing balls of fire. My lungs were

climbing up for more air and not finding it. Sweat mapped the same trail down my cheeks, and into my mouth.

We had two more miles until home, and I couldn't take anymore.

"Mama, slow down," I pleaded. "I'm gonna die."

A hand landed on my damp shoulder. "You can do this, Charlotte. Moving doesn't kill you; keeping still does." But she backed off our pace a bit out of compassion. "Besides, I gave you something stronger than pain."

"Oh yeah?" I asked. We turned right, down the road for the homestretch. "What?" The cadence of our sneakers struck the ground in perfect tempo together.

"You're stubborn, just like me."

Her comment turned my chin. We grinned at each other.

My mom's tawny eyes with matching ponytail swished behind her. Her shapely, tan legs and body near sprinted down the road. Some would mistake my mother for very cute at least, smoking hot at most.

They'd be fucking idiots.

Sophia Ravenel was a bull shark—a blend of light to dark shades, gracefully able to survive in any environment. Unlike others in its species, bull sharks can live in salt and fresh water. That's what makes them most dangerous to humans. They're swimming right under you, and if provoked, will strike.

Yeah, I inherited that from my mom too.

"When I was ten—" My mom started a story. I knew why. To distract me from the pain until we were home. One more mile to go. "—my brother dared me to jump off the roof."

The metal roof of my mom's childhood home populated my mind. I saw it several times on our trips to visit my mom's family in the Dominican Republic. My mom grew up in a humble one-story home with corrugated metal siding painted bright green with neat, white trim around the wooden shuttered windows.

"At first, I refused." My mom's breath barely huffed with her story. "I told my brother he was stupid. Why jump off a perfectly good roof? Then he said I was afraid and dared me to." She grinned at the memory. "So, I jumped, and when I did, my feet hit the ground, making my kneecap come up and hit my chin so hard it knocked me out."

My calves weren't burning anymore. My lungs were fine too. It was because my heart was full of joy, listening to my mom's story.

"The next thing I remember, I woke to someone slapping my face, not hard, but enough to wake me." She stopped and bent over, slapping her hands over her kneecaps, laughing. "It was your grandfather. I asked, barely focusing, 'Papa, why are you slapping me?' And he said, 'Because you're so damn stupid.'"

My mom stood up, chuckling. The smile on her face lit up my world.

"Stupid or not," my mom said, "I was stubborn enough to fight my fear." The knuckles of her index and middle finger pinched my nose. "So is my strong daughter. No matter if you think you'll die, no matter how bad it hurts, don't you dare stop fighting, Charlotte, all the way till your last breath."

Her swat met my butt, and we were back running. Fast. And almost home.

Daniel

NOW...

Afternoon smeared into early evening as I raced across the water. Following the GPS, I never navigated this route before, from Savannah to Bluffton. But bloody hell if my smart wife didn't have all our coordinates pre-programmed. I found Quincy's name with his longitude and latitude and pressed a button.

It guided me along with my desperate race to get there. I wanted to call Rob and Joaquin. They'd help, advising me on next steps. But that would have to wait. The roar of me pushing the engine as hard as it would go drowned out any sound from a phone.

All I could do was think. I couldn't afford melancholy musings. Any memories would collapse me.

I needed reason... now.

Who took her, Pierce? Where would they go?

Could it be another *White Flag* fanatic? Another one of Mason's sick fiendish followers picking up where that David Smith psycho left off with his stalk and packages?

Or what about what she and the agent were talking about the other day? Could it be another lethal sympathizer? To the Taliban or some other anti-American radical group?

Either way. How did they find her? How did they track her down to the one place she'd be?

The fast logic fired through me until that last thought. It slammed into my mental wall at Mach ten, making my vital insides turn to fatal chunks inside me.

You, Pierce.

Hashtag Daniel Pierce has stalked her from the day you carried her into your world, the celebrity one she's always feared.

This is why.

Someone had dropped a pin on us at the police station in Savannah. Those officers didn't know better. Even though I asked them to wait a day, they were excited. And forty-five minutes later... Charlie was gone from the coffee shop.

But how?

Riley. More specifically... Riley's deadly ex-girlfriend, Ashley Lynn.

Charlie had complained about her. Tragic addict, she was at worse. But social media addict she was at least. Ashley Lynn wanted all the followers, hearts, and views. She was the worst kind of girlfriend, riding the coattails of Riley's celebrity.

Ashley Lynn had posted by the set of *The Tour*, at all the locations, snapping pics of Riley from afar, of Riley sitting under the pop-up on location, drinking iced coffee next to Charlie. Ashley Lynn dropped multiple hashtags, #danielpierce and #captaincharlotteroberts in particular.

Then, there was Riley's shout-out to the generous coffee store owner who kept them caffeinated. Charlie had worried when Riley did that, telling me those fucking location pins were the bane of her existence. How between those and Redix Dean's screaming fans, they were a constant threat to the production.

Indeed, they were. Swishing through the marsh grass, the certainty of it made me sweat.

Social media had dropped the net on Charlie.

It made evil sense. If you sharked by the location shoots for *The Tour*, or that coffee store often enough and waited long enough... Charlie would come by.

We'd walked the three blocks, from the police station, right into the trap.

So where next? Where would they take her? My vision was locked on the vast horizon. *Anywhere, Pierce.*

The thought burned bile up my throat. They could go up the interstate nearby; down a dark, country highway; across the water to the ocean.

No. Oh God, Charlie. No.

Don't fucking do it, Pierce! You let that in, and you won't function. You need to act. Now.

Pulling the throttle back, I slowed to a sight that offered a sliver of relief—Quincy's dock, my safe harbor, straight ahead.

CHAPTER FIFTY-TWO

CHARLIE

One Space Left [Ty Unwin Remix] by Lost Colours

NOW...

Razor blades sliced my brain. My breath? It was suffocating. My body? It lay curled in a ball, all muscles liquid with something. They wouldn't move. Few senses served me, my mind reeling to find logic, to find now.

All I found was sound. Water splashing. A boat engine buzzing. A small trolling one. And feeling? We were riding low in the water. Drops were sloshing over the edges. I could feel them wetting my shoes, splashing over my scalp.

I yanked at my hands and found hard restraints. Metal handcuffs bound my wrists behind me. My eyes wouldn't open. I was blindfolded. My mouth, it was stuck, closed, lips pursed and taped over with what smelled like Duct Tape.

Controlling my breath to keep from panicking—in, two, three, four; out, two, three, four—the smell hit me.

It was welded to my memory. Rotten eggs. Sulfur mixed with salt. Pluff mud. Sweet marsh grass. Brackish water.

The Lowcountry.

Follow the inertia, Charlie Girl. The turns. Where are you?

Swish right. Count. One, two, three, four... to... forty-eight. Swish right again. Count. One, two, three, four... to... two hundred and three. Swish left. And more turns, matching the map in my mind, the path I'd know blind.

Oh, God. You know where he's taking you. Home. To Daufuskie Island.

Daniel

NOW...

"If someone wanted her dead, they would've done it there in the coffeeshop," Rob said on the phone. "One bullet and done."

I held Duke in my arms. Fran stood beside me, kissing Caroline's curls while all four stood on Quincy's screened-in back porch, watching the night begin to own the dark river swirled with marsh grass.

"So now what?" I asked Rob. "She told me not to ring the police. Just like before. To give her twenty-four hours. But we're almost three hours in, and this doesn't feel right."

Duke rested his cheek on my chest. Like my son knew I was in distress and needed comfort.

"Fuck. I don't know, man," Rob said, no doubt scared shitless thousands of miles away in Madrid, helpless to do anything but counsel me.

"Where's her phone?" Joaquin asked on the speaker. Both were listening, doing what they could to help.

"I've got it," I answered. "She left it in her rucksack along with her gun." I started bouncing, unconsciously, to soothe myself and Duke.

"If they don't want her dead, they want something," Joaquin said. "And her phone is the only way to get it. To get you. To get money. Whatever it is." His Castilian accent made it worse. Its vibrato pulsed with drama. He couldn't help it. "Keep it charged and keep it by you."

"We're going out to go find her," I replied. "Me and Silas. Quincy too. And we're trying to find Pop."

Silas stood off to the side, helpless and frantic. The poor bloke was fighting back tears when he pulled up to Quincy's dock, safely delivering the twins, Fran, and Evelyn to me.

All were here except Pop. He was out on the water. Silas kept running to his boat to radio him every fifteen minutes. No reply so far.

Quincy and his wife were freaked out. Standing downwind in the backyard, trying to smoke their anxiety away.

"What time is it there?" Rob asked. "Almost seven o'clock? You've lost daylight. Where are you going to look for her in the dark? She could be anywhere."

I closed my eyes, my lips grazing our son's dark blond hair, grown out now into thin wisps. Fuck, I couldn't hold back the tsunami of fear much longer. The truth sucked all the air from me, drawing back into one wave threatening to eviscerate me.

"I have to do something," I answered Rob. "To look somewhere. I won't just bloody sit here until the next ruining call."

I could hear the commotion on the phone. Like Rob had

walked away from it, away from the terrifying reality. Rob loved Charlie too, brother or best friend couldn't describe how much. He couldn't take this either.

There was an ocean between us, but too much bonded us, too much tragedy, too much love not to know the meaning behind every sound.

"Just wait for now." Joaquin soothed his voice into a slow strum of hope. "They're going to call someone. Her phone. Or yours."

"I'm calling Jeremy, our boss." Rob sounded from the background. "That guy who worked with Charlie in Savannah. Wade? And your guards? Scarlett and Curtis, right? They're HGR. They're loyal. They'll keep it covert, whatever happens."

The idea, the team assembling like a covert ops party, it gave me one hope to latch onto. It was like grabbing the yellow bar above your head on the London tube while your ears bled to the sudden screeching, jarring, terrifying emergency stop in a deep, blind tunnel.

Hang on, Pierce.

CHAPTER FIFTY-THREE

CHARLIE

NOW...

A wave knocked the boat up, slamming my head back down, but the surface I was lying on wasn't fiberglass. It yielded to the splash, softening.

You're in an inflatable boat, Charlie Girl. Of course. Affordable enough to buy, no records or license needed. Small enough to maneuver into small channels and inlets. And hide.

The boat was rushing to Daufuskie. I could hear the deep rumble of a colossal container ship nearby, of vessel traffic from the Port of Savannah.

The port.

That's how Jansher got here. Not by airline where security would catch him. No, he arrived on a container ship, sailing in from waters around the globe, some far less inclined to screen the identities of their crew and their contents than others... like Libya.

How he found me, I knew—a bitter reality I could not

escape.

#danielpierce

Nikki's guilty post. Riley's innocent one. The digital breadcrumbs led right to me.

And I fucked up. I got comfortable. Distracted by taking care of others, I committed a rookie mistake. Frequenting the same known location—that coffee shop—I should've known better.

But how did he get me here? Whatever the fuck he stuck in my arm took me down fast. Like a date rape drug on steroids. Butter knives were still digging into my brain tissue, the chemicals soaking my muscles. But I had my mind now and needed to use it.

He must've carried me; not hard to do if I was passed out. Just like Daniel's fetish for scooping me up all the time. I'm strong, trained, and fast... but light.

Any average man could throw my limp body over his shoulder or pull me in a Firefighter's drag with ease. Out the back door. To the alley. Into what?

A waiting car.

No. My instinct lay beside me, rubbing my wrists under the metal handcuffs. *The white rental van. Remember? You saw it. You felt it.*

So now what?

Death was certain. He'd kill me. But if not yet, he had something planned first.

Think. He's taking you back home. It's a taunt. A master play. You were in his home, so now he's in yours. It's the ultimate statement to make.

Thoughts of home made me pray to every divine soul, to every ghost—my parents, Kai, Daniel's brother—*please protect our babies.* Daniel. Fran. Pop. Evelyn. Silas. Quincy. *Get everyone I love... and protect them.*

Daniel would know what to do, right? He'd remember our talk, our plan. He'd get them safely to Quincy's. No one could trace us there. There was no familial connection, no dumbass social media location pins.

Would Daniel call the police? Would he panic and start dialing? Half of me wished he would. The other half, the instinct lying beside me who kept me company all these years, it hoped not.

There's only one way out of this.

The police can't get involved. That will get the media's attention and then you're trapped. Your family will be targets. Forever.

Daniel

NOW…

Pop phoned at 7:16pm.

"Son, what's going on?" Pop asked. "I got here to the house to take you giggin', and your guards have it locked down. Said there's an active threat."

My feet hadn't left the spot from looking over the horizon. The unnatural demand I was making of my body, of my heart to wait—it was maddening.

"They took her, Pop. This afternoon from a coffee shop in Savannah. Like she was targeted. Like they knew she'd show up there one day.

"This is our plan. No police yet. I've got the twins safe at Quincy's. Me, Evelyn, Fran, and Silas. He's been trying to radio you. He got everyone else here. We're all safe"—I swallowed hard—"except for Charlie."

Silence.

I didn't know whether to feel guilty for breaking this old man's heart, that his almost-daughter was abducted. Or to feel relief, that one of the strongest, smartest men I knew, in mind and spirit, was my ally, was my family.

"What time?" Pop asked.

"About three thirty. There was a white van nearby. I know it took her. There was a fresh grease puddle on the pavement. They killed the alleyway security camera, knocked out the shop owner, and she was gone."

"Tell Silas to double back, to roam the river, follow the path from Savannah to Daufuskie, but don't intervene if he finds anything. I'll turn my radio up. I'll hear it now."

"You think she's on the island? That they're taking her home?"

"You saw footprints in the sand outside. Combat boots. Weeks ago, right?"

"Yes."

"I'm going back around the water to watch the house. I have a hunch."

Night-vision goggles; I knew. Pop had a pair on the boat for flounder gigging. He could scope the shore all night and watch.

"You think they'd take her back to our house?" I asked.

That could be the best... and worst thing.

Her rifle hung on the wall there.

"I think a hunter leaves a trail around his perimeter," Pop answered, "watching where the prey roam, where they're most vulnerable." The sound of the engine roar fought against the treble of his voice. "Give me a couple hours. Protect my grandbabies and family, and I'll call you back."

CHAPTER FIFTY-FOUR

CHARLIE

NOW...

The engine throttled, slowing. The low bow of the boat tilted down. A small splash of the wake sloshed over the front of it, wetting my shoulder.

We'd stopped.

He said nothing. The only sound? Water lapping the sides of the boat.

I played still, slacking my jaw, telling all my muscles to flop. It's like they remembered how. All the times I really did drop into unconsciousness from a PTSD blackout, my body didn't let me down, lying like it was unconscious.

A distant aircraft. A large one. I could hear it rumbling higher. The airport. The one closest with large aircraft? Hilton Head Island. We had to be on the Calibogue Sound, on the east of Daufuskie to hear the engines above.

Why were we stopped? Was he waiting for a larger boat?

Oh, please God, no. A larger watercraft could carry me out to the ocean, and I'd be gone forever.

What else could he be waiting for?

Night. My instinct rubbed against my ankles bound by tape. *He's waiting for the cover of darkness.*

What time was it? Only with a dart thrown blind could I guess. Hours? Could be a day or more where he kept me knocked out in the van or in the boat.

But no. I would have urinated by now. I would've felt its dampness in my jeans. And water? I'd need it eventually. If he wanted to keep me alive for whatever's next, he'd have to un-tape my mouth, to do something to keep me hydrated.

If it's the same day, it's Halloween, remember? It's a Saturday night too. Even my little island buzzes with weekend activity until all quiet at late hours. That's what he's waiting on—for my world to go to sleep.

The sloshing. The silence. For minutes upon minutes. I waited forever.

Then I heard it—a sound that choked a terrified sob in my throat.

Another pair of boots shuffled near my feet.

Oh, fuck. There are two of them. He's got an accomplice. Or more.

Hope dropped to the ocean floor, drowning all my prayers.

One man I could take. Jansher was a smart one, but not a big one, not a strong one, not like what I'd fought before. Between my spars with Scarlett and my fights with Joaquin, I was in top form. Once I had my strength, if I could break from these restraints, I could take him.

But two men? And they have me bound and defenseless?

It strangled my neck, thoughts colliding in my mind.

Caroline's curls. Duke's nose. Daniel's eyes. I'd never see them again. My family? My friends? They'll bury me... if they ever find my body.

Memories threatened to press play in my mind. Fears held a knife of all I was going to lose to my throat.

I didn't care what pain I'd endure. I only cared about theirs, their grief of what they'd suffer over my death.

My babies would grow up without a mom, never remembering me. And Daniel would be devastated, grief-stricken and alone to raise—

Don't you fucking dare!

My instinct pressed its lips to my forehead, hissing the command into my brain. *Don't go there. Breathe and stay here. You know how. Control your mind.*

Everyone you have to live for now; you're going to fight like fucking hell, with all you got to see them again.

Daniel

NOW...

Fran sat puffy-eyed on Quincy's sofa. The twins slept in their car seats between her and Evelyn on the other side. The look on Evelyn's face was one I'd seen on Charlie's so many times. Stoic. Focused.

It reflected mine, but I could feel the exhaustion behind my eyes and in my muscles. Hours of an avalanche of stress had stormed my system, but I'd never rest.

Me, Quincy, and Silas sat on the back porch, watching the horizon. Silas had doubled back and found nothing, no trace of them on the water between Savannah and Daufuskie.

It had my knee bouncing, minutes away from jumping in Silas's boat and doing something careless, crazy.

In the darkness, my phone lit up. **Pop** appeared on the screen.

"Yes?" I answered.

"I found her."

I could hear the relief in Pop's voice. "Where is she?" It matched the flood across my heart.

Quincy and Silas sat up in their wooden rocking chairs to my question.

"I watched the house for an hour. Nothing there. So I went up the shore and spotted an inflatable boat. It's out on the water by the old Melrose Inn. It's her. Got to be her."

I stood up. "We'll meet you there."

"No, son." Pop's breath sounded hushed. "Listen to me good. There's two of them. Two men have her."

That was too much, threatening to take me.

Two men? Two men had my wife, knocked out, hurt, and bound? God knows what they did to her. What they'll do to her.

"We don't know how many more we're dealing with." Pop kept me focused, his retired Navy tactics deploying the logic. "No one's going in there guns-blazing until we know for damn sure what we got."

"All right." I inhaled all strength I could pull into my lungs. "Wade, Charlie's backup from HGR, he's driving up from Savannah. He's fifteen minutes out. Once he's here, we'll go to Silas's dock and wait for your call."

"No, son." Pop stopped my impulse again. "Y'all come up with another plan. Silas's location is burned. Your boat is always docked there. We don't know how many have been chasing you. How much they observed and if they followed her, you, or the babies. You gotta protect them now. Let me watch and see what happens. Don't anybody dock anywhere or go ashore till I tell ya."

He ended the call.

"Where else can we dock near the old Melrose Inn?" I turned to Silas. "The closest we can get to it?"

"Haig Point," Silas said. "No, wait. It'd be faster comin' into the landing and cross the island. My buddy keeps a truck there. The keys are always on the driver's tire."

I wanted to go now, grab the gun from Charlie's backpack, and we could be there in thirty fast minutes.

I looked over my shoulder, through the window into the living room. Fran and Evelyn sat by the twins. I turned and looked back at the dark water in front of us.

What if Pop was right? What if there were more than two chasing us? Had someone been hunting long enough to know about Quincy's place? From months back when Charlie was making the supply runs over here?

Once she started working, Silas brought stuff over for her. Could someone be headed this way? Or waiting now out there on the water, waiting to ambush us?

I promised Charlie I'd protect the twins and our family, no matter what.

Yes, but you promised yourself, Pierce, and you promised her too, that you'd never abandon her again. You made that promise to every soul buried between you two. I rubbed the wedding band on my finger. *You swore... you'd always fight for her.*

CHAPTER FIFTY-FIVE

CHARLIE

NOW...

Minutes ticked into hours, of me trying in vain to count them. Time abandoned me. All I had was sloshing water, random sounds of faraway watercraft, a few distant jets above, and not a word from either of them.

They must be watching me and planning something. What?

I couldn't go down the rabbit hole of why. Why me? Why this? Not now. I needed to stay focused.

What's next?

My bladder tightened with a tingling pressure of the need to release.

Do it. They'll think you're still unconscious. It'll scare them that they overdosed you. That they underestimated your small body metabolizing whatever the fuck he injected you with, and hopefully, not hit you with another shot of it.

Maybe it would gross them out too, making my body as repulsive for whatever they planned to do to it.

I released the warm stream through my jeans, feeling it trickle between my thighs, soaking my crotch. Were they watching? Did they see? No, it had to be too dark. But maybe they could smell it. I could.

A click. A rustle. The engine sputtered back to start. Water started splashing over the low bow. We were going again.

Where?

Faster and faster, I was aware of the speed, the buzz of the engine revving higher and higher.

He's banking you.

A long, hissing scratch of sand sounded under me with a sudden stop and then a splash of feet in shallow water. A movement lifted the boat up—and yank—they pulled it farther ashore.

Nylon scratched with a clank, like a gear bag with a clip. A pack snapped around a waist maybe?

Fingers were on me, digging down my side, groping my body, arms wrapping around my waist.

No tension, Charlie Girl. Sandbag your body.

I was being lifted, rising in the air. One of them had me. His smell? It was the formaldehyde of new clothes, rough cotton scratching my cheek.

Inertia took my body, flinging me up and punch—my belly landed against his shoulder blade, knocking the air from my lungs. Like a fucking sack of potatoes, I fell.

Flop your head down. Let it bob inches from his sweaty back.

Scratching sand sounded beneath his feet. More boots crunched and followed. A lapping sound of water was distinct, not over sand. It was splashing against a structure—a wall.

A sea wall. There are several on the island. Where are you?

He started huffing, carrying me, stepping and climbing, lifting me up. To where?

He can't be in great shape. I could smell it, his straining sweat mixed with what? Sweet grass. We were walking past it with footfalls following behind us.

I could still hear waves. Ninety-nine of his steps I counted before metal was scraping, like chain-link grinding across pavement. He was stepping over something. More steps, until… wait, he was stomping up them. The waves were getting distant. Glass crunched under his boots. And oh God, the smell. It exploded up my nostrils—wet decay, organic and foul, mold so thick there was no other air.

The old Melrose Inn.

I knew exactly where we were.

The luxury resort hotel was abandoned by bad investors and to the elements over thirteen years before, falling into eerie disrepair on the order of horror-movie-meets-Lowcountry nightmare.

It was three miles from my home.

I knew its every square, rotting inch—from its heyday when it opened and my parents brought me here, to sneaking in as a teen when it shut down, to surveying the final blow from Hurricane Matthew a few years ago with Pop and Evelyn.

Why did he bring me here?

The sound of broken glass under boots was overwhelmed by the odor seeping into my every pore, threatening to flood my mind with a tidal surge, losing all other senses to smell.

Upstairs. He was carrying me to the second floor, the other man following him while my logic did too.

They've been in here a while, mapping this out. This place was perfect for deadly deeds. Between the fencing, torn down in a few places, and "No Trespassing" signs warning, the location threatened to have zombies or masked sociopaths emerge. It kept all—most—away.

I pulled back from my senses, to stay sane, to not choke.

Think. There's no electricity here. No water.

They had to have a stockpile: food, water, and batteries. But they couldn't have brought in too much. Yearly residents and seasonal renters were all around, some within screaming distance.

With a sudden shift, my body was falling down with a thud over shards of glass, slicing my bare arms. I collapsed onto a thick layer of squishy fibers, slimy ones that used to be carpet.

Daniel

NOW...

"Go on, now." Evelyn stood on the dock. The 9mm in her hand still shocked me. I had no idea she carried that on her. "I got this covered," she said. "No one is getting my grandbabies. Go get my girl and bring her home."

The sight filled me with pride. I'd worried aloud about leaving the twins unprotected but wanting to go help Pop. Then Evelyn surprised us all, pulling the gun from her handbag. Quincy backed her up, pulling a shotgun out from under the sofa.

Bloody hell this country and its guns.

I understood now why Charlie had conflicted feelings,

why she hated them, but still carried them. At times like this, you had no choice. They were your only chance.

Quincy jumped down into Silas's boat. Wade too. He'd arrived minutes before and was ready to roll.

I followed, landing in the boat, and sending every prayer up for the children I was leaving behind, trusting they were in good—and armed—grandmother hands.

Hope filled me that I'd bring their mother home... and alive.

The phone in my back pocket buzzed. I whipped it out, answering Rob's call, updating him with the intel Pop had so far.

"Two men?" The skepticism in Rob's voice popped my balloon of belief. "Man, Charlie's got mad skills. She's strong as fuck and smart as hell. But this ain't Hollywood. If they have her bound at a disadvantage or have skills of their own, she could do with backup."

Impatience fired through my nerves, hearing Rob's dismal assessment while I watched Silas untie the bow of his boat.

I wanted to be there, at that old Inn, now.

"We're on our way there," I reported to Rob. "We've got four of us meeting Pop, and two guards at the house too. That's a team of seven. Surely, we can handle them."

"Remember, man, this isn't an English pub fight," Rob warned. "I know you'd win that. This is bullets flying. Muscle doesn't matter."

I winced at those words from Rob. Last December was proof of that. One bullet through Rob's lung, and his massive body was down.

I had to admit it, all the stunt fights I'd done, bench-press and deadlift max reps, they meant bollocks in the real world—this American one—full of guns.

"We'll be careful."

Rob sighed. "I think you need to call this one in. This can go sideways too fast. Call the police."

"That's the last thing she said to do." Fuck, it made me sick, fighting all my instincts to do everything to help her. "She said she didn't want the legal investigation or the press that would follow it. That if this went public, we'd never be safe, that we'd be targets for copycats."

"She's right." Joaquin's voice was clear on the speaker too. "You know where she is. You have people on the way, ones with skills. She's got a chance. And I've fought her myself. It's a fierce, fighting chance."

The volley from hope to despair and back to hope again dizzied my brain, mucking up my plan.

Silas stood waiting at the boat console, ready to fire the engine as soon as this call was done.

What are you going to do, Pierce?

"Look, man," Rob chimed in. "I'll call the Beaufort County Sheriff's office. I'll say I'm a friend of hers. That she got in a fight with her husband, and I'm worried about her. She's not answering her phone. I'll say she was last seen at the house at four p.m, then she left. Seven hours ago. That'll fire up a missing person report. It'll send help in a few hours without flashing blue lights."

Resignation dropped my shoulders. It sounded like our best odds. "Do it," I said.

My phone beeped. Pop was ringing in. "Gotta go." I ended Rob's call, taking Pop's.

"They just went ashore," Pop said. "I watched them. They carried her into the Inn. One had her, passed out like, over his shoulder. They're not big guys, but they got gear on them. I don't know what for."

I could hear the crunching of underbrush, the snapping of twigs over the phone.

Pop said, "I just anchored nearby. Had to wade ashore. I'm working my way to her, through the woods, using them as cover. Still don't see anyone else."

"We're leaving now," I updated him. "We're going to the landing. Silas can use a friend's truck there and we'll meet you soon."

"Y'all stay back." Pop's deep voice lowered to almost less than a whisper. "They'll be watching, and they'll hear you coming. The birds by the ponds beside this old Inn? They could whip up a warning ruckus if y'all come stalking in. Get to that dock and wait for my call."

Of all the people in the world who could dictate my next steps, Pop would be one.

Yes, I had his own might coursing through my veins, especially when it came to my wife and kids.

But this terrain wasn't mine. If anyone knew that island, it was Pop. He knew which way it would turn, how its nature would zig if you zagged.

And if anyone thought tactically, anywhere equal to my wife... it was Pop. No wonder—he helped to raise her.

My ego dropped along with the phone from my ear. I nodded to Silas to roar the engine, to get us the fuck to the island as fast as he could.

CHAPTER FIFTY-SIX

CHARLIE

NOW...

A jagged fingernail dug into my cheek. I stifled a yelp when a stinging fast yank of tape ripped flesh from my parched lips.

"Drink."

The word was spoken in Pashtun.

That language. That accent. That memory. It threatened to shift my world off its axis.

I sat up, shaking off the dizziness. Tepid water poured over my lips. I opened them and took two sips, only enough to wet my mouth. If it was drugged, I didn't want any more.

I jerked my head away.

"I've been waiting for you to come for me." I spoke his language.

"And I've been looking for you."

His affirmation soothed my every frayed nerve. Every nightmare I had—confirmed. Every maddening taunt in my mind—gone.

You were always right.
He's been coming for you.

More crunching glass sounded to my right. Then a light bang clattered beside me of a handle dropping. An empty bucket? It was shoved against my right arm, warm blood from the cuts on my flesh was cool against its plastic.

"This is for your filth," he said.

"I have no need now."

I didn't move.

No words. No sound I heard until a deep, hoarse cough burst through the air. Another one followed, barking in stereo through both their lungs. A plastic cap snapped opened. One of them was drinking from a water bottle before more sputtering coughs.

With no tape returned to my mouth, I could eat the mold spores in the air. They were crawling over my lips, wanting to seed in my mouth and infest my lungs.

In here, the moldy stench was its own universe.

I tried focusing on something else.

Your ankles might be bound, but your mind isn't. Get five steps ahead of him. What is he up to?

I knew to be friendly, to be cordial. By the book, you're supposed to try to get on your captor's side.

This time that was bullshit. He spent almost eight years chasing me. This was long past either one of us holding sympathy for the other or having a change of heart.

But I was still alive. For now.

"What do you want?"

The foreign language came back to me with shocking ease. It's not like I could negotiate with him. Light that textbook lesson up with a blowtorch.

I was just curious. All this time? Fuck it. What game would we play before they tried to kill me?

His huff sounded amused, satisfied. "For America to watch their sweetheart soldier die."

A sudden punch, a force crunching against my cheekbone exploded pain across my skull. It stunned me, but I wouldn't flinch.

It was delivered from my right, from the other guy doing the dirty work. I could smell him. He was the sweaty one who carried me in.

With no tape on my mouth, I smiled, turning blind toward his presence. "If you were a real man"—instinct told me Jansher's accomplice was American, speaking English—"if you wanted a real fight, you'd take these cuffs off."

"Fuck you, Marine bitch." Another blow landed on my grinning face, knocking me over.

Yep, American.

I sat back up, laughing. "Oh, your fuck would be a *very tiny* punishment."

"Enough!" Jansher speaking in English sounded odd. "Don't mark her face."

Jansher was in front of me. That's where his eerie presence and voice came from. A breeze tingled my bleeding left arm. It must be coming in from broken windows. We had to be in one of the abandoned hotel rooms upstairs.

The logic clicked through my brain. How a lot of effort went into this, to find me, to get to the US, and to my island. Jansher must be pretty damn proud of himself, even though it required help. And like most men, I waited for him to boast about it, giving me more intel.

It took seven minutes by my roughest guess. He must have been contemplating me, his prize, all along.

"You Americans and your egos." He spoke in his native tongue. "You made yourself the perfect target. I always wanted you dead—the occupiers who invaded my home.

But it wasn't worth my resources. Then I saw the picture. One of my sons had it on his phone. I knew that was you in Madrid. That scar on your cheek. And the one through your shoulder. The ones my brother gave you. You were hanging from your western god's arms. I found some sympathizers to look for you, to follow and make sure it was you."

Menorca. They followed you there. When you were on location for The Druid, *protecting Kierra. Remember it? That first shiver down your spine? That was Jansher's doing. He locked in on you then and didn't stop scoping.*

"The hunt was too easy," he said. "You with your media. With every pathetic ego needing to be loved, to be liked, posting to a screen like it affirms your soul. The trail to your god led straight to you, straight to those big film parties in New York. The first shot; he couldn't get a clear one. The second shot was closer, spectacular. Too bad he missed. Good that he knew to be a martyr. Good that I had another soldier waiting until you emerged again."

Coughs burst through his words. His rasping chest was sucking in the air he wasted on his soliloquy, sucking in mold spores with every word.

All while I started slowly tugging on my left hand, subtly dragging my flesh against the hard metal handcuffs, inching my bound hands below my buttocks.

I knew I could do it. My body was small enough, limber enough to get my hands under me and in front. I just needed a chance...

"Then I was blessed again," he continued, his voice getting hoarse from coughing. "More media. More idolatry for you—the heroine. You were everywhere. Online. Interviews. Magazine covers. Their golden soldier became their goddess—married now to their global hero, their god. And now you're a mother with two children with him? It made it worth it. I had to do it myself. My soldier found your house and waited here for me." He paused. "It's terrifying, isn't it? When an occupier takes your home and your family?"

I refused the fear from his message because I already knew—he wanted me, then Daniel and our family, dead. My soul wanted to plead for their safety, to scream out that I was the guilty one, that I'd sacrifice for them.

It wouldn't stop him, and I wouldn't give him the satisfaction of my beg.

Instead, I listened to his breath, not his threats. With each utterance from his mouth, that rasp, his lungs were filling with more toxic spores.

And I could hear it on my right. The asshole wheezing beside me, sniffling, glass crunching under his steps. He was standing up. His breath sounded like he was breathing through Jello. The heavy crunch of his boots? Combat weight. It had to have been him outside my home in the dunes. His trudging steps left the space, growing distant and shuffling down the hall, leaving us behind.

Where was he going?

Down the grand stairwell, I could barely hear him. My other ear was dominated by Jansher's coughing in front of me.

Maybe this was it—my saving grace.

For me, and most who grew up where everything was in a constant state of wet rot, mold, and mildew were your daily lotion. It seeped into your pores. Yes, it was toxic to all, but for some, like me and others born in the Lowcountry, we had a higher tolerance for it.

I struggled in Afghanistan—his arid home. My sinuses had cracked, bleeding dry. The skin over every inch of my body flaked, forming crusty patches that could be picked off in small chunks from my elbows and heels. My gums, tongue, and lips never stopped pleading for moisture.

But now, he was swimming in my humid, moldy world.

And it was drowning him.

The rick-rack of birds filled the air, coming from the sanctuary by the pond next to this dilapidated hotel. I knew its every curve. How egrets and cranes filled the trees with their calls while alligators meandered underneath.

Their sound was odd at night. Something had disturbed them.

The other guy. He must have gone outside. For what? More gear? To check their boat? To get a gun? Maybe. For fresh air? Definitely.

There was no way these two camped out in this hotel for weeks. Not in the time since I found those footprints. This place smothers you in hours, days if you're lucky.

But they'd been in here enough to scope it out, sucking it into their lungs. It was starting to weaken their resistance with each new exposure, making it worse.

That's if you could avoid the hunks of the roof falling in, the infestation creeping along the floors, and the occasional people on golf carts whizzing right by it in broad daylight, watching this haunting structure fall into the ocean.

No, they had camped out somewhere else, probably a secluded empty inland lot, using the tree canopy and low palms for cover.

But how much time had they spent on the island? What did they see? Me come and go from my house with my family to Silas's dock, going across the river to work? Probably. What if they knew about Pop and Evelyn too? Where they lived?

Fuck, there were too many people I loved, too many he could hurt, no, kill.

His coughing ebbed. A plastic bottle crinkled, crunching like he was taking its last sip. When his cacophony stopped, I heard it…

A whippoorwill whistled in the distance.

Daniel

NOW…

The running lights on Silas's boat shone in front of us. The dark water glistened under the beam of the full Hunter's Moon above.

If this day had not become a nightmare, it would have been a beautiful memory to cherish.

The twins' first Halloween. Charlie had their costumes lying on our bed. One was to be a pea, the other a carrot. I was supposed to decide who.

Silas raced his boat so fast we were a knife slicing across the liquid surface. No words were exchanged, the engine was too loud, leaving us to their thoughts.

I let mine wander. For just a second, indulging in a memory of her…

"You know, you can change your mind, and I'd still love you forever," I'd said, lying next to her in bed, my fingers twirling the four blue pearls dangling from her throat. "We don't have to get married tomorrow."

Her cheek had rested on the pillow, her marine eyes beaming back at me. "Are you getting cold feet, Pierce?"

I rubbed my warm soles over hers under the sheets. "Not at all. I wanted to marry you the day I put these pearls around your neck. Before then, actually. I just don't want you to feel trapped in my world."

"You're in my world as much as I'm in yours." She had gestured to her bedroom, to her home around us. "I *want* to marry you, Daniel Pierce. And no one is trapping me anywhere."

"You're a paradox, Charlie Ravenel. Since when does the stubborn, tomboy from Daufuskie Island want to follow the rules and get married because I got you pregnant?"

"Why does the cute, nervous boy from Walney Island want to do the same?"

"I'm English. We made the rules." My legs intertwined with hers. "You're American, the ones who rebelled from them."

She laughed. "Rebel? Yes, I am, so I'm not marrying you because of any damn rules."

"Then why are you?"

"Because for so long, I was so lonely. I had no one, so I became my own best friend in that solitude. And then you came along, and you loved me more than I loved myself. And after everything I've lost, I know to cherish that love, to cherish you, because you're such a gift."

I twirled a lock of her hair around my finger like a golden ribbon. "I'm always afraid you're a gift that will be taken from me. Just like my brother was."

"No one is taking me from you. Tomorrow, I'll promise it in front of everyone. Tonight, I'll promise you"—her small palm had cupped my cheek, holding every piece of me in her touch—"I will love you forever."

"Forever ends. You know that more than anyone."

"No, I know that life ends." Her eyes smiled back at me. "Forever doesn't... and neither do we."

The roar of the engine quieted.

"Dude, get the fenders." Silas brought me back to the

moment, back to the damned reality while Quincy scoped the shore with his binoculars.

I peered into the darkness, flipping the fenders over the side of the boat.

Wade started tying us up. I liked him already. I knew how he had backed Charlie up, helping with Riley, and I'd forever be grateful if he could help me do the same tonight.

We had a strong team. The question was, what's next?

CHAPTER FIFTY-SEVEN

CHARLIE

NOW...

The whistle. A whippoorwill.

Pop is calling you home.

I bit my lip to keep from crying out in relief.

Pop had found me. He was waiting outside. I knew it—with the pistol he always had on him, the one with a silencer on it. He was always careful not to let a shot ring out across the water, or across our small island if he had to use it, usually only to scare off gators in the yard.

That other man? That whistle meant Pop got him. The threat outside might be eliminated.

But that didn't help me in here.

Was Jansher alone now? I hadn't heard any other voices, any other movement than two pairs of boots. It was just his pair now, crunching over glass, his cough sounding like he was breathing through toxic foam.

The mold is getting to him. That was his one mistake.

No, he made two actually.

His bias against me, against all women—it was his other.

It made him underestimate me. He saw a small woman's body and dismissed it as no threat. I'd erect a shrine to his sexism once this was over.

Yes, I had a small body, but it was fast and strong... and one with no fear of pain. And my mind, like many women's, it was a pit bull. Once I sunk my teeth into something, or someone threatened my children? Hell no, I wouldn't let go.

It had me tugging now at my left hand, my weaker one, not my trigger hand. I'd rip half my flesh off to yank free from these cuffs. It was a running joke—how small my hands were. My body too, able to circle my arms under and in front of me.

And the glass around me? It'd make the perfect knife to cut the tape around my ankles. I could feel for a big enough piece, slicing his jugular with it too.

But I was running out of time.

He wanted to kill me.

"America's sweetheart" he'd said of me being a soldier.

That amused me. I was anything but. I was the rebel. The loner. The smart-ass. I was as sweet as a shot of vinegar. Yes, I had a big heart, but like a trained soldier, I guarded it with perfect aim.

What's he waiting for? And tuck your thumb in tighter, exhale with each tug of bleeding, wet skin against metal.

What did he always want? My public ruin. A symbolic, deadly gesture. It was no good if others didn't see my death.

A zipper sounded in the background. He was rummaging through a bag. A clink. A sliding sound. Another one. It sounded like the smooth glide of a metal tube. And click. Another glide. It was three. A tripod. For a camera.

He was setting up a studio. I remembered the tech in his

compound years ago. Even by standards back then, Jansher impressed me with his technology.

That's how he communicated with "his sympathizers." That's how he was going to reward them. He was going to record my death for the world to witness. But he had to wait for daylight to do it. And he didn't want my face marked up for the show.

I had no idea how many minutes I didn't have to waste. *Get the fuck out of here, Charlie Girl. Now.*

Daniel

NOW...

The four of us sat quietly in the truck Silas borrowed. The engine and lights were off while we waited for Pop's call.

The waiting sizzled every fiber in my body. My mind tried resisting the seductive train of horrific thoughts about Charlie that followed.

The phone vibrated in my hand. I answered it. "We're here, waiting for Pop's next call. They have her in the Inn."

"I called the police," Rob said. "Dispatch said it's Halloween night, that they're swamped with calls, but she'd put it out. She said it would be answered in the morning."

"That gives us five hours until dawn."

"They'll be calling her then. I gave them your number too. Someone is headed your way. Charlie better show up at the door or the dock, or the whole world is gonna find out what's going on. But by then, you'll have more backup... because you'll need it."

Imagining Charlie doing just that, standing on the dock,

telling the cops she's okay, that it was just a misunderstanding... it was all I could hope for, our best outcome now.

I ended that call, the thud of my heart not wanting to wait for Pop's. But finally, it came.

"I took one out," Pop said.

The simple sentence disturbed me—murder described in four words. But that's what Pop would do, any of us would, to protect each other.

Pop said, "I want y'all combing this island to be sure he's working alone now."

"Can you see who he is?" Because I was going to kill him.

"I can see him step outside on the porch above. But there's a magnolia tree blocking him. He's got a hat on too. I got no idea who it is. But so far, it's just him, coughing like he's dying from the mold in there."

Every cultivated muscle on my body hung helpless on my frame. Power was useless without control. Now, the only one in control was the man holding Charlie hostage.

What was he doing to her? How was he hurting her? The torment was hell.

It's like Pop read my mind. "Son, we gotta think this through. If we storm in there with all that glass and debris everywhere, he'll hear us coming, and it's over for her."

"But he hasn't done it yet, so that gives us a chance," I said. "He's waiting for something." I tapped Silas's shoulder. "In the meantime, let's clear this island and make sure he's working alone."

Pop would call if anything changed.

And we'd make sure only one more body would be dead that night.

And that it wouldn't be Charlie's.

CHAPTER FIFTY-EIGHT

CHARLIE

What's Up Danger by Blackway, Black Caviar

NOW...

It started to hit me, the magnitude of it. Every time his steps walked outside; I could hear him gasping asthmatic for fresh breath.

One of us would take our last one that night.

I'd fight like hell that it wouldn't be me.

Blood dripped from the fingertips on my screaming left hand hidden behind me. It was almost free, reminding me what was next.

To protect my children? To hold Daniel? To hug my family? I'd do it.

But my soul would suffer for it.

Two lives I'd already taken in my thirty-four years, both justified. This third one, I'd live every day haunted by it too.

When people die, they live on in those who remember

them, for better or for worse. I was surrounded by those ghosts, counting on three of them to protect me that night.

His crunch and clicking sounds returned. The camera gear he was setting up passed his time.

"It won't stop if you do this," I said. "My death, anyone's death, it hasn't changed anything in decades. Everyone is still fighting."

Talking to someone who knew the exact war I spoke of; we shared an eerie connection.

"That's why I'm doing this. Nothing will change. But the suffering will be more even."

He was right. There was a disproportion. Innocent civilians always suffered the most, regardless of reason or who was right.

Visions of Paksima, of her baby Esin, they filled my blindfolded mind. They were the most innocent of all, the women and children caught between warring sides.

"I had to do it," I said. "What was happening to those girls was wrong. No custom or God condones it. You know that."

I always respected someone's beliefs. But this wasn't about disrespect. Nothing justified the violence those girls suffered.

That truth started coursing anger through my pulse, the one dripping blood over my wet fingers. It focused my fury, just like that day when I killed their abuser, Jansher's brother.

Jansher had watched in horror, his brother died before him, just like Daniel had with his twin. Fuck, the irony struck me.

"Don't flatter yourself," he replied. "This isn't about revenge or about two girls. They don't matter. The message does. America needs to see real pain, real death too—yours."

I didn't care about myself. The girls—that's all I focused on. "Is she still alive?"

It was the closest I'd ever get to peace, to know if Paksima was okay. Because if Paksima was okay, so was Esin, her daughter.

"She is my wife. The mother of four now, three more sons, all mine. You didn't change a thing."

Relief exhaled from my lungs. Paksima was alive. She'd be twenty-two years old by now. Esin would be nine. Still, there was no changing fate. Paksima was just married to a different kind of monster now.

"And you must decide tonight... the last words you will say to your husband and children," he said. "It's how they will remember you, condemning your country to the camera before you die."

Like hell, you will. It's time...

Minutes later, his wheezing breath and steps walked outside to survive.

It was my chance.

To those who've never known a real fight or war, it doesn't drag out. It doesn't take slow steps. It happens in seconds, in less than a minute. All hell, all action breaks loose. The smart thing is to be the one who acts first.

Falling to my side over shards of glass, they slashed my skin open while I wrenched my arms under me to pull my hands up in front. Reaching for the blindfold, I pulled it down to see...

Where was he?

Diffused light hit my pupils, blinded for seconds until I could focus.

He stood outside, muffling his coughs with a kerchief. The Hunter's Moon shattered his silhouette through the broken window.

Clenching my molars to choke back the scream, thinking of my children, of protecting them, I yanked the last hunk of flesh off my hand, pulling it through the metal cuff—the pain of it threatening vomit.

One of the shards of glass, my shaking hand grabbed it, cutting my palm while I slashed my ankles free.

I could take him and choke him out. But when I moved my body to stand, it warned with ache. That drug was still in my veins, stealing my full strength.

This fight you must win. The risk? It was too great if I lost it in hand-to-hand combat.

The plan changed, one that seemed destined all along, like the moon in my day sky, like every beloved spirit whispering to me...

Your rifle. It's your only chance.

His steps moved, turning to come back into the room. I could see him now, his frame rushing toward mine unbound.

Surging up with my next inhale, drawing in all strength I had along with a prayer, the trusted punch I knew to throw, it saved me. It landed hard across his soft throat, stunning the vulnerable nerve in his neck, the veins and artery too.

He collapsed on the floor, giving me vital seconds to escape.

Across the broken glass, I ran through the dilapidated doorway, feet landing on the decaying wood of the porch. I saw the magnolia tree growing beside the railing. It greeted my climb down.

I was two stories up. Grabbing branches, ignoring the searing pain in my hand, my next grasp found the wooden porch post below. I wrapped around it, lowering to the ground, smearing blood behind me.

A whippoorwill whistle hit the air again. I turned left and saw his large silhouette emerge from behind the corner of the building. Running toward it, I'd never felt such relief.

"I got the other one," Pop said, holding his gun up, covering my shoulder for Jansher's sure pursuit. "How many more are in there?"

I squatted, checking the treads of the dead man feet away from Pop. I recognized them. "With this one down, it's just him, I think." They matched the ones from the sand. Odd how I didn't recognize his white face though—just another pathetic sympathizer.

"Who's the man inside?"

"It's the brother. The brother of the man I killed." I didn't need to explain more. Pop knew, his eyes lit by the moonlight, registering the threat too.

"You know what I need to do," I said.

He nodded his head. "We got minutes. The house is secure. The family is safe. The guys are back on the island, making sure it's clear."

No need for names, the plan was obvious. "Get his boat," I said. "He's not leaving this island. This ends tonight."

"Take this." He shoved his gun into my right hand, the one not seeping blood.

"No, you keep it."

I could hear him. Jansher was running over broken glass, on his way after me. I didn't want him turning on Pop.

"I got my own gun," I said, "and I'm gonna lead him right to it."

Two things I could do better than almost any man—outrun him and outshoot him.

Two facts Pop knew, not debating me. We turned in

opposite directions; Pop to block Jansher's only escape, and me to lure him to his sure end.

His form emerged from the building, standing at the top of the former grand entrance. I made sure he saw me, made sure he heard me too.

Feet pounding over pavement, I started to run like hell.

The road was as familiar to me as the breath through my lungs. With sweat releasing the poison from my body, I was sure—this was his last fight too. After all he'd sacrificed to find me, he wouldn't waste it.

He'd chase me. He'd come for me. No doubt, his hunt would find its end. And he knew where I was going...

The final place to even the score...

Home.

The full moon gave me enough light on the dark island. There was no stopping me either. The miles home, I knew them, sprinted them.

Would he follow on foot? On wheels? I didn't know. It didn't matter. I knew the unmarked crumbling roads, the sandy trails that gave me shortcuts there.

The only thing that slowed me down? The red drops I was leaving behind like deadly liquid breadcrumbs for him to follow. The flesh hanging from my left hand burned, exposing horrific wounds that looked better than they felt.

Anger and adrenaline ignored the pain. It pushed me harder than I'd ever run before. Hoping I might see car lights, lights of familiar faces.

Daniel was here somewhere. Was he waiting at home? Or was he on a dock somewhere, scoping for any remaining threats?

I trusted him. He got our family safe. He'd know what to do. And he had help too.

The minutes it took. The miles I ran. No other thoughts could slow me, fury fueling my race.

The sand under my sprinting feet turned into pavement. It was the final stretch home.

My mom ran it with me. I could feel her beside her, urging me on. *"Don't you dare stop fighting, Charlotte, all the way till your last breath."*

My dad was waiting for me, his spirit standing right by my rifle on the wall. It was his father's and then his before he taught me to use it. When the world gifted him with a daughter, it was like he knew how to protect me—he raised me to fight.

And I would.

The lineage of that sniper scope wouldn't fail me. Daniel's night vision goggles—they'd be on the bench by the garage door, guiding me too.

I'd meet Kai in the dunes. His spirit was in the sand where he had liked to camp with me, holding me tight under a sleeping bag as we fell asleep to the sound of the waves.

Death took him from me, but never his love. He'd always be with me, out there by the ocean, waiting for me.

Would I join the ghost of my parents and first husband, or would I live on to be a mom and wife myself?

You know who you were born to be. Now pull the fucking trigger and prove it.

Daniel

NOW...

We didn't find anyone skulking around the docks or

wandering down the sandy roads. We couldn't be sure of the deep brush; the woods could hide anyone. But I had a hunch. It was clear.

Silas hot-wired a boat. He took it out, watching the east shore of the island. He left his boat for Quincy who did the same, watching from the west. Wade took position at the marina. All were sure no one escaped without their notice or their pursuit.

"You know how to shoot that thing?" Scarlett did her job, on guard beside me, gesturing to the gun in my hand.

We stood in the driveway of our home, waiting in the shadow of the front porch steps for any threat. Curtis was covering the backyard.

Funny how I didn't notice Scarlett until now, until everything mattered. At that moment, I took sudden note of her.

How skilled she was. How fierce her glare was into the darkness. How stunning that contrast was with her delicate profile and wavy russet strands tamed back into a ponytail under a black baseball hat.

Kinda like Charlie, but not.

I never noticed Scarlett's beauty, her allure, or how deft she was because why? Because no offense—my wife made everyone else pale in comparison.

"Yes, I know how to shoot it." I clenched the gun, my face smiling for the first time in what felt like days at the memory. "My wife taught me how."

"They all talk about her, you know." Scarlett had her gun in hand, an impressed smile taking her face. "Whenever I visit my friends at the Sheriff's office or go into HGR Atlanta. Hell, anywhere… they all ask me about Captain Charlotte Roberts. They wanna know if she's really as badass as she seems like she's a legend almost."

That soared my cheeks high.

Was it weird, inappropriate in that moment as we stood guard over our house, ready to take out any threat coming down the road, to be smiling, thinking about how incredible my wife was?

No. I couldn't help it. My heart was full of pride, not fear… for just one moment.

"She's a helluva sparring partner," Scarlett added. "And a helluva boss—makes me wanna keep doin' this, you know? Protecting good people like y'all." Scarlett cocked a confident grin up at me. Fuck, just like Charlie. "I've already sent two of my friends her way and Charlie recruited them. It's like she's building an army. More of us women working for HGR? I'm game."

Yes. Charlie was the reason we were here. Well, half the reason.

I was the other.

That truth humbled me. How we could never stop the gravity of our worlds colliding. The pull to Charlie from the moment I met her was futile to resist.

I never did, loving every moment of it.

It was Charlie who had fought it at first, terrified we'd find ourselves right here. But it was too strong. We'd live together, no matter our end.

I knew it then. Fault wasn't at play. Fate was.

Charlie Ravenel and Daniel Pierce—we were two cosmic bodies, destined to align.

Scarlett elbowed me, startling me from my wandering mind. I could hear it too—the pad of footfalls nearing the house.

We had our large home lit inside and out like Las Vegas, shining light on anyone who approached. It had my pulse climbing higher, as if that were possible, staring into the darkness over the road.

Someone was stepping out of the shadows, feet crunching this way.

My index finger curved over the trigger, eyes and barrel rising, aiming into the black.

The sight emerged and knocked the air from my lungs.

"Charlie."

I could barely breathe, taking in the vision, like I couldn't comprehend it, like she wasn't real. My gun lowered. My steps covered ground faster than I could control, wanting to hold her.

But it was written across her face, deep love in every wrinkle twisting her huffing lips into a smile for me, before it fell, along with the words, "We don't have much time. He's coming for me."

Who? Why? How? I wouldn't ask. Faith in her was all I needed. "What do we do?"

Her steps didn't stop. I followed her, up to our front door.

"Scarlett," she ordered, "cover the front. Is Curtis here?"

"Yes, ma'am," Scarlett replied.

"He'll cover the west corner," she said.

The reach of Charlie's hand for the doorknob grabbed my attention. Her hand was seeping blood from raw, gaping flesh wounds. Oh fuck, I could see her blue veins. Then I heard it—the jangle of handcuffs hanging from her small right wrist.

Horror and rage barreled through me, but I steeled my mouth shut. We had no time for my concerns. Any pain she felt was oblivious to her actions.

"Come with me," Charlie said, leading the path through

our front door. I knew her destination—our home office and her rifle gleaming on its wall.

She called out over her shoulder, "You've got my .380 loaded, right?"

"Yes," I replied, gripping it tight in my hand.

The lights in the house illuminated the gashes down her arms, scabs, and bleeding slices across her beautiful flesh. I swallowed hard, ignoring them.

"Take it and my .22." She grabbed my night vision goggles off the back hallway bench. "Both are loaded. Kill the lights on the back of the house. You take position on the back deck, low and watching. Cover me and don't let anyone in."

Quickly, she yanked my dirty rugby shirt from the last load of laundry on the floor. Wrapping it around her bleeding left hand, she didn't stop, steps next racing for the office.

"I'm going to the beach," she said. "He's coming that way. He knows we have guards on the house." Her empty right hand landed on the polished wood stock of the rifle. "He won't approach from the secured front. He knows that path, the one through the dunes. He'll use it and then you'll hear my shot. You'll know when I'm done."

It was like watching a movie. So surreal. So unbelievable. My eyes recorded it all, the lethal drama unfolding before me at record pace. How the set was designed to replicate our home. How her moves were rehearsed. How her lines were confident; her blocking to the next spot sure.

She wasn't my wife in that moment. She wasn't the mother of my children. She wasn't a protection officer, a body guarding others. She wasn't even the most breathtaking, sexy woman I'd ever met, one whose body I knew its every lush curve, its every carved muscle, its very taste and pleasure.

No, I was watching a golden bullet, lethal power harnessed in a small form, one whose path you could not escape. The storm of her blonde mane swirled before me as she turned to pull a case hidden under a bookshelf.

I never knew that was there. She opened it and took cartridges out, loading them into the rifle and bolting it into action. Her right hand moved like lightning across the weapon, prepping it for the shot.

It stilled me, for just a moment. Marveling at the sight, my heart hammered at the spectacle, my mind terrified for the outcome. My silence stopped her.

She glanced up at me. "You okay?"

"Yes," I said, shaken out of it. My steps aimed for the .22 hiding behind the *Frankenstein* book. I tucked that gun into the waistband of my jeans.

"I know you have lots of questions." She pulled my night vision goggles over her head, resting them on her forehead. "I'll have to answer them later."

"Just promise me I have a later with you."

"I promise you everything with me." She fused her look to mine. "Just get my back."

"Always," I said, following her lead.

Our path took us to the kitchen. My palm slammed the switches on the wall. Darkness fell across the kitchen, across our backyard.

Our eyes were dominated by the only light now, the one from the full moon glimmering over the ocean beyond the large windows. It's like it beckoned her there. Like she was lured by its hunting call.

I followed her outside. The open air filled me with dread, with fear.

"Charlie"—I gently grabbed her arm, halting her steps—"just come back to me."

It was the oddest moment. Bigger than me but I trusted it. I believed in her.

"I always come for you." She smiled, dropping the most smart-arse, inappropriate joke at the gravest time.

That's your wife, Pierce. Gawd blimey, do you love her.

"Go," I said with a nod of my chin.

It was the hardest thing—letting her go. But "letting" wasn't the right word.

She was never under my control or under anyone's command.

But she was my greatest love, one I watched slip from my hands, every part of me praying for her return to them.

CHAPTER FIFTY-NINE

CHARLIE

NOW...

Despite the urge, the one to rush to him, to hold him and take him in a kiss, I turned away. If I wanted forever with Daniel, I had to do this. *Now.*

With one smart-ass joke and his faith in me, my steps took me toward the dunes, toward the dark water beyond.

The glow from the moon was enough to light the path. But it wouldn't be enough for the shot. The shadows in the mounds of sand could hide too much. The clumps of beachgrass on top of them, standing tall in the calm night, they could hide even more.

The hour was the darkest, the one before navy takes the sky into a spectacular show of golden light across the water.

My breath was calm, sure. Like I've been waiting for this. The polished wood under my right hand gripping the rifle; it was familiar. The searing pain in my left hand wasn't.

The wooden boardwalk creaked under my roam. The

sound of the tide, high up on the beach, it covered my approach and the light clank of the handcuff against my weapon.

I could feel it—Daniel covering me, loving me. I looked back once and saw his large shadow looming on our deck, and then... I disappeared behind the dunes.

Sand filled my shoes; salt air filled my lungs. With a deep inhale, I asked, *"Which way?"*

To my left, the east—Pop was out there somewhere on the ocean, sending an inflatable boat and a body down to its depths.

To my right, the west—it was the direction the footsteps had come from. Instinct poured through me, relaxing my muscles, locking my stare.

He's coming that way.

Dropping to my knees, I lowered the goggles over my eyes, pressing them to my scope. Greens and blacks filled my vision. The only source of limelight came from the moon above.

Resting my elbows in the sand, my body locked into hide site—the perfect concealed position to surveil and aim. I didn't worry about what could harm me from behind. Nothing. Not with Daniel covering me.

The blonde hairs on my arms stood up. Not rising to the cool air or to the ominous night. They recognized the presence. Of my dad to right. Of my mom over my left shoulder. Of Kai in the sand right behind me.

You got this, Charlie Girl. This is your shot.

A hard swallow choked it back. All I'd lost. Them. All I had to lose. My children. Daniel. Everyone I loved and guarded. And of those girls. Of every fated step I took to be here.

You'd do it all again.

Yes, it was my addiction, protecting them. And to have this love now, because of it?

You'd risk all for it.

My only regret—staring into the night, through the tall stalks of beachgrass gleaming green in the goggles, any movement would appear in bright flashes through them—I didn't want to have to do this.

He was a life like mine. Even though I could take it, I still valued it. I'd still mourn it.

But he threatened my world. My daughter's clever giggle. My son's comforting hand. My husband's warm embrace. All I loved, it was on the line, under the pressure of my fingertip curled over the metal trigger.

This was meant to happen. Destiny or love? Don't be a fool. They're the same thing, the same fate.

Worlds aligned above; it pierced an electric shock down my spine, along with a flash between the dunes.

That's him.

Which way would he go next?

Moving the muzzle, the sight, my right cheek tingled, the one scarred by a bullet.

That way. Scope right.

I did.

Wait for him.

I always could, not feeling my sore muscles or my hand dripping blood through the shirt wrapped around it.

I felt the cool wood of the rifle pressed against my right cheek, my breath steaming over its polish.

Patience was my second weapon.

It held my fingertip with two pounds of pressure pulling against the trigger. Waiting... wishing we hadn't found ourselves here, tumbled by waves of politics, war, and blood upon this beach that already knew such history.

But we were...

Suddenly, a bright silhouette rose from the sand like a ghost rising above the dunes. *Exhale.* It threatened. *Aim.* Protect them all. *Fire.*

One shot rang out under the Hunter's Moon.

He fell.

CHAPTER SIXTY

CHARLIE

Legend by The Score

NOW...

I felt warm with Daniel's sweatshirt soft over my flesh; it draped over my long peasant skirt. With his heavy muscles wrapped around me too, squeezing tight, I was back home in his arms. With his lips kissing my cheek before soothing over my ear with the gentle joke we needed. "You always make me wait, don't you?" I was safe.

"We have all the time in the world now." Together, we watched the sun rise over the horizon.

"You're not cross with me, are you?" he asked while I leaned back against him, into his strength. "We had to do it. Rob had to ring the police. We had to be sure we'd get you back."

We huddled together against the cool morning, standing on the dock at the Daufuskie marina, waiting for the boat from the Sheriff's office to arrive.

"I'm anything but mad at you." Even the smell of him warmed me—cedar, apple, and sexy. "I just want this to be over and then to get in our boat and on with our lives. I want you, our kids, and our future. Nothing else."

A quiet moment stirred around us before his embrace tightened.

"I keep thinking about it," he said. "How I almost lost you again. How you could've been hurt much more, in ways I can't bear to imagine. Then I have to stop myself before it consumes me."

"We have years to process it, bit by bit." I folded into him. "We control our fate now. No one else."

"Do you think they've done it?"

That troubled me too.

How we had to tie up this loose end while Pop, Silas, and Quincy wrapped up the other. Jax had come over too before dawn. I'd called him. It was his right, his need to make peace with this too.

I sent Wade, Scarlett, and Curtis home, not wanting them party to anything, even though they were willing. The trail to HGR Security had to stay clean.

The others though? They made sure all evidence disappeared. The only proof remaining was a loyal group of witnesses, the bruise I tried to conceal with makeup on my cheek, and the bandage wrapped around my left hand.

Scarlett had dressed it, cleaning it long enough for me to make it to the mainland in a couple of hours where a nurse, a friend of Scarlett's, would covertly tend to the rest.

Wade had brought a handcuff key, helping me with that too. The distinct ligature marks the cuffs left around my wrists were hidden by the long sleeves of Daniel's sweatshirt I wore over them.

"Yes," was all I could say to the finality of it, holding onto Daniel's hands wrapped around me.

"Let's just hope," he said, "that this Sergeant Bryant the Sheriff's office is sending over doesn't ask too many questions."

"I'll charm him," I said, "don't worry."

"Him? You know better. What if Sergeant Bryant is a woman?" Ah, my husband was learning, and right. "If so, I have skills in that regard too, you know."

That turned me around in his embrace, staring up at a face I treasured, at a smile that stopped my heart, that always took my whole body.

"Yes, you do. You have lots of yummy skills but save them for me."

"Is tonight too soon?" Fuck, he was so hot with that sexy grin. The love, the gleam in his eye, he was my cure. How he knew to focus on what we had together; not on what we almost lost.

"Maybe," I teased back. "We have a lot of traveling ahead of us."

"That never stopped us before. Remember? We have more babies to make."

"Keep playing your romance cards right, Pierce, and you'll win."

We let the minutes pass. My cheek rested against his navy sweater, feeling his heartbeat. His hand cradled me there, keeping me close.

I let a drop of it seep in. How much I loved him. How we almost...

Stop. Now's not the time.

A white boat on the horizon neared, raising my concern.

Were we finally free? Or would this begin another tormenting chapter? One with a police investigation that would stir up a global frenzy of ugly press. And more lethal threats.

The boat neared. Two people were on it. I let go of Daniel to pull the mask up over my face. Walking toward the edge of the dock, I stood ready to confront this.

Please, not one more shitshow, I begged fate.

As the boat approached, a figure stepped portside.

It flushed me with relief. It *was* a woman. Her dark brown hair was fashionably styled, cut short and tapered in the back with thick, long bangs to her chin, cloaking one eye, but the rest of her feminine beauty she couldn't hide.

Something about her, I recognized.

"Captain Roberts?" The woman called out over the engine, the boat slowing to the tall man steering the vessel.

"Sergeant Bryant?" I called back, admonishing my sexist assumption that an officer would be a man.

"Yep," she answered, letting the boat dock and tying the stern before she climbed up like she owned the gesture. There was a smile in her eyes though she wore a mask over her mouth. "Thanks for meeting us out here this morning," she said. "We just wanted to come out and make sure you're okay."

Her steps neared me. Other than Daniel standing a few feet back, we were the only ones on the dock.

"I'm fine, thank you," I answered. "I'm sorry to be such trouble, to make you come out on a Sunday morning."

"It's no trouble." Sergeant Bryant stopped a safe distance from me.

When she took her mask off, my breath hitched, not sure if I was responding to this woman's stunning face, or that it looked familiar.

"I heard the call come in last night on my radio," Sergeant Bryant continued. "I took it. I wanted to come out and meet you myself but had to wait until morning for my backup."

Her eyes glanced over my shoulder, clocking Daniel standing behind me.

"Can we speak privately?" Sergeant Bryant nodded her head toward the far end of the dock, the one away from Daniel's ears.

I respected why, following her. "Sergeant Bryant, I promise"—I assured her once we stopped with eyes on each other—"I'm fine." I kept my mask on. "I just needed a break last night. We've been under a lot of stress getting ready to move with two babies in tow. I just needed some air, some me time." I hoped the bullshit from my mouth didn't sound like it too.

"Is that a bruise on your cheek?" Fuck, Sergeant Bryant saw straight through my disguise.

I took off my mask; hoping the brave reveal would deceive her. "A stack of boxes fell on me." I willed my eyes to make it seem true, softly smiling at the woman.

But I caught it. How Sergeant Bryant's eyes flicked down to the bandage on my hand next. "And how did that happen?"

"I'll never cut another avocado again." The lies were getting thicker. "It was the straw that broke my back. I just needed a fucking break last night."

Silence swirled between us. It didn't unnerve me. No, it was like I was staring in a mirror, not at a similar look, but a similar soul.

"Captain Roberts, are you sure you're okay?" Her concern sounded sincere.

"Call me 'Charlie' please."

"Okay. Please call me 'Cade'."

That name? Where do you know it from?

"Charlie, I can help you if you need it. Are you sure you're all right? That you're not in any danger?"

"Cade"—it dropped from my tongue like truth serum because it was... all true... finally—"I assure you I'm very safe, very happy, and very in love with my husband. He'd never hurt me."

Cade glanced over my shoulder again, considering Daniel in the distance. I noticed it then. How Cade's eyes were so dark blue they sparkled violet and spellbinding.

God, and her face.

She didn't look like a Sergeant. Cade looked like a cover model with a pixie profile—big eyes, tiny nose, lush lips, and a delicate chin. Her beauty mesmerized your soul, but there was a hardness to her that sobered it.

I noted it too. How Cade's tall body moved with the grace for any lens. Though she concealed it under a black, puffy jacket—her slight, sexy curves couldn't hide.

"Besides"—I pushed past the sight enchanting me—"I can protect myself."

That put Cade's glance back on me. "Oh, *I know*." She smiled. "When I heard your name on the call for service, I had to come out and thank you."

"Thank me?"

"You don't remember me, do you, Charlie Ravenel?"

"I recognize you from somewhere."

And the way she just said your real name?

"We went to high school together," Cade said. "You were a senior. I was a freshman. You protected me one day on the bus. Some assholes were picking on me 'cuz my mom used to be the Sheriff. And you got up and punched one of them in the dick."

The power of that moment hit me. "That was *you*?"

"Yeah. You're like my hero. You have no idea what that

meant to me, that another girl stood up for me. It changed my life."

It changed mine too. It was the first time I stuck the needle in my arm, addicted to protecting others ever since.

"I've seen the news and stuff online too," Cade said. "It's been a helluva year for you and Mr. Pierce. That's why I got out here early. I know you've dealt with some threats. I came to back you up."

Her eyes darted back down to my hand. The breeze on my arm made me flinch, realizing my right sleeve was up, revealing the cuff marks.

Cade's stare returned to mine, our eyes speaking a secret, silent language.

Cade knew.

I let the truth travel between us along with the breeze, for just a moment before I answered, "We don't have threats anymore. I made sure of it."

Something. No. Everything told me... *Cade won't betray another woman.*

"Glad to hear it," Cade said. "And to return an old favor, I kept this off the scanners so the media doesn't know. It's the least I could do. And that shot someone reported hearing at four a.m. from Bloody Point Beach? I'll report that as a gator on someone's porch."

If I could hug Cade, I would, but social distance and professional dictates wouldn't allow it.

"Thank you." But my eyes said it. My relieved smile did too. "That means the world to me and my family."

A world I could finally see. No hunt. No chase. Me and Daniel would take our children for their first ice cream cone, to their first everything without looking over our shoulder, without fear stealing any more of our joy.

It almost rushed grateful tears over my tired lashes, my whole body registering the relief.

"Speaking of," Cade said, "I bet you wanna get back to them now."

"You have no idea."

"Just one more thing," Cade said before pulling her mask back over her captivating face. "Redix Dean says 'hi'. He says he owes you an afternoon fishing."

A meteor shower flew across my mind. My connection to Cade and Redix—it felt cosmic. More than the same high school. More than one act I took protecting Cade.

"Oh yeah?" I struggled to dismiss the intensity, to casually chat. "You know Redix?"

"You could say that."

The guilt in Cade's tone struck me as fast as the logic. It was nine o'clock on a Sunday morning. The only way Redix Dean could send his best between now and last night's call, was if he'd spent it with Cade.

"Please send him my best." That warmed my heart. "He was fun to work with, though his fans made my job tough."

"Tell me about it." The smile didn't leave Cade's eyes. "Guess we have that in common too."

Cade jumped back into the boat, her boots landing with a firm thud. She turned around. "Let me know if you ever need anything. I'm happy to help. Just a boat ride away."

"Will do."

When I said those words, a prophecy stirred within.

CHAPTER SIXTY-ONE

CHARLIE

Be Your Love by Bishop Briggs

NOW...

Standing behind the console of our boat, me and Daniel raced through the paparazzi blasts of lights off the water.

It was Zen in my veins. Our children were safe, waiting for our arrival. Our family was okay too. With Daniel's body nestled behind mine, the comfort of his touch brought me pure peace.

He wrapped his hand over mine cupping the throttle. "Stop," he said.

"What's wrong?"

"Nothing is wrong."

I slowed the boat to neutral until it sloshed still in the water. He turned me around, cradling my face in his big hands. "I just want to stop right here with you, to just be us for a minute." That minute found me diving into his aqua eyes, content to never emerge.

"I want right now and forever with you, Charlie. I don't want to change you or any moment we share. Every second we breathe and live together, I swear, after all of this... each one I will be so thankful for."

It strained his throat—the stress leaving his heart. I felt it too.

"It's okay." I reached for his hands, wrapping my fingers around his. "We're okay. Everything is okay now."

"I know. But that doesn't matter. *That's* what I know now. This whole crazy world can turn to hell around us, but if we have each other, any suffering I can survive, as long as you are my dawn and dusk."

The ocean, its depths around us couldn't contain the love we shared.

Yes, our worlds had collided. The bloody show... I survived it. We survived it.

And to have this love now, this life with him? I could fall again, get knocked to my knees in pain, but still, I'd get up, rising to my feet time and again to fight for our love...

And I wouldn't lose.

"Do you remember me telling you about the moon?" I asked. "The one in the day sky that used to haunt me?"

"Yes." His thumb lingered across my cheek's scar.

"It *was* a haunting. But it was also a promise. A sign that even with my parents and Kai gone, that I wasn't alone. I know that now. It was a promise that you were coming for me, that we would meet, and that our two worlds would be forever combined."

His kiss found mine. What force pulled us together? It was sacred, fated.

"I think after every tear I've shed, after all my pain"—I brushed my lips over his—"you are my karma, Daniel, my gift, and I'm so thankful for you."

"You've changed me so much. I don't need fans or for the world to love me. All I need now is to be *your* love." He pressed his forehead to mine. "I'm a lucky man who has a beautiful, stubborn wife with a dangerous job. And I love it because I love you. I'm proud to be that man for you."

"It takes a strong one to love me."

"You don't say?"

Our half tears sparkled in our laughing eyes. His sexy bowed lips brushed over mine, kindling the passion between us. "I wish you had more stubborn fingers."

"Oh, kinky man." I liked the direction this was going. "Yes, please." There's that grin to my smart-ass comment; his smile that lit up my world.

"Not for that, Sex Goddess." He chuckled. "Although, I love it when you do that too. I want your stubborn fingers to put more rings on them, for putting up with me, to promise I'm yours forever."

"I'm not the kind of woman who needs rings." My gentle bites found his neck, his soft groan vibrating against my lips. "I only need you." God, I could devour him. "I feel you to my soul. I feel how much you love me." His body pressed into mine; the cool morning on the water no match for the heat building between us. "And I love you, Daniel." It was taking me over, making me lift my skirt. "And after what I survived, I need you right now."

Lose almost everything in one night and you learn to seize each minute, each moment, and defend it. And now, all I wanted was to have him.

"I need you too, Charlie. Always." He helped me, trailing his hand up my thigh, his lips clinging to my neck. "And I don't care who watches me show you how much."

The tips of his fingers tickled over where lace met my flesh while he swore over my lips, "I'm strong enough to take it now." His fingertips found my sex, teasing inside of it. "Every time you leave, I'll believe in you. I know you'll come back for me. Just know that when you do, I'm going to love you so much"—he thrust them in hard, making me gasp—"and then I'm going to fuck you so much."

"Do it now," I urged.

He pulled my panties down to my ankles. I kicked them aside. The boat sloshed on the water. No hum of others around. Not like I cared. I'd just survived hell. This heaven now of fucking him? I'd have it too.

He picked me up by the hips, "Oh, I'll start now," and plopped my ass on the plush console bench, wedging my skirt above my waist. He dropped to his knees. "And I'll never finish with you."

He pulled me to the edge of the seat before his kiss landed on my exact aching spot. "God, Daniel." He *was* my beginning... and I'd always be his end.

His mouth dove into my folds, moaning and licking my taste while he unbuttoned and unzipped his jeans. "God, look at you, babe," he sighed with his gaze on me, freeing his generous cock, touching himself to the sight. "I fucking worship you." His eyes were heavy, hungry before his tongue started fucking me again, fluttering over my clit before lapping down to tease my soaking entrance.

I shuddered and could never imagine it—a time when his pleasure didn't possess me, or my lust didn't make him moan.

And the thrill of it now. How he spread my thighs more, open to him here on the water—the air, salt, and sea taking my senses. How the cool breeze excited my exposed flesh against the warmth of his hands, of his firm, hot tongue circling my clit. How he flicked across it before his thick fingers worked their magic next.

God, looking down at the sight of him, of his perfect nose, of his full lips, of his wide tongue licking across my pussy. Jeans open to his hips, his massive cock dripped hard for me. The ache he moaned with each lapping stroke from his tongue, with his fingertips curling hard inside me; he had me screaming out, my pleasure filling the open air and his mouth. But he didn't stop relishing my sex, devoted to my pleasure until my next burst and scream.

"Daniel, please." I heaved for breath after it, pulling at his massive shoulders. The need for him painful. "Now."

I motioned for him to sit on the bench. He stood up, kicking his jeans and boxers off. He took the position, demanding, "Come here." This wasn't our usual tantric indulgence. "Right now." This was a frantic need, a frenzy to seize what we have, to take the other and never let go.

I climbed on top of him, straddling him, grasping his thick cock, my eyes promising everything to him without a word. I sank down, wrapping around him—thighs, sex, body, and love—it was all for him. My fingers laced hard through his loose, dark curls, holding them like reins for my hard, desperate ride. It had me hanging from the edge he always lured me to.

The force of him surged, his grip taking my hip firm, his other hand tugging my hair. "Say it." He pulled my lips to his. "What are you doing with me?"

There was so much strength in him, all his muscle and might. I cherished its restraint and craved its release, feeling it mount beneath me.

"I'm riding my pussy over your thick cock, Daniel Pierce." I rolled my hips, sliding slick, up and down his length, my clit screaming at the friction.

"Does it feel good? Do you want more of me?"

"Yes." I quickened my pace. "Give me more."

He snatched my sweatshirt up, ripping the bra away from my breast before taking my nipple with a ferocious, wet suck that threw my head back.

Anyone could see us, and I didn't care. I'd suffered enough, endured too much. This with him, with no shame—I lived for it.

It quaked my thighs, the swell of it rising between us. He ripped his dripping lips from my breast to watch it. I knew—to witness his favorite show.

"Say it, Charlie." He thread his fingers through my hair, pulling my face, my eyes to hover over his. There was no place I could go, but with him. "Tell me what your pussy will do, what your beautiful body will do, your whole gorgeous life, what will you do with me? Always?"

I rode its swell, its edge, relishing the power, feeling the volume of it cresting to crash over us. It was in his aqua eyes. In his face I held onto. In every moment we shared. How his storm wrecked my world into the most beautiful one I'd known... and I let him.

Our love hit my shores, pouring from me, crying from my trembling lips, "I'm coming with you, Daniel." The pleasure he gave, the love I felt, the tears I'd been holding back. It surged through me, washing away every last piece of my pain.

We had our love. There was nothing to fear anymore.

"Oh God, Charlie." The depth in his eyes, the sound of his groan while he came deep inside me, of his next soft gasps, knowing what we were hoping for. It was the sweetest music to my ears along with his words through the breath we had to catch, his lips dusting over mine, swearing, "We're having two more, two more blessings together."

This morning on the water with him? Of every night

with him? And of every moment in between? It was my nirvana.

My eyes cried to his. "I used to be so alone out here, on the water all by myself. All my family. All my love. Taken."

It was simple. I wasn't afraid to hope with him, to cry for him, to love him—my only truth now. "And now I have you. And I know…"

I glanced up and only saw a bright day sky before I gazed back into the blue of his eyes, smiling, "…that we're going to have much more together."

THANK YOU

Thank you for reading **_Chase Her_**,
and for loving Charlie and Daniel.
If you please, tell your friends about our badass heroine and
her hot alpha. Your reviews, posts, and shares are such gifts.
My readers mean the world to me.
Humbly, I write with you in my heart… so stay tuned.

There's a world of badass women coming…
Who is Cade? How does she know Redix?
Where will Scarlett take her fierce skills next?
What twist of fate will bring them all back together?
Charlie's inspiration continues in *After Her*
(sneak peek next)
Releases 2022
Sign up to hear about it first at kellyfinley.com

AFTER HIM
SNEAK PEEK

Running Up That Hill by Meg Myers

Two years before...

Tonight I'll make a deal with you, God.

I'm watching three men in this ballroom.

If I promise to kill one and ruin the other, can I finally be free of the third one? The beautiful man I hate so much that I'll love him forever?

After all… you know it too.

They deserve it after what they did.

That deal tastes sweet. Sweet like the candied almond sliding over my glossed lips. The crunch—the sugary shards pulverized by my hard bite—I love it.

Candy calms me.

Sitting at this table while a magnolia centerpiece blocks the view of one of my targets across the room; *that annoys me*.

My other target stands at nine o'clock, slamming SoCo and lime shots down his throat. I can feel his glower sliding down my body.

He deserves the heel of my stiletto stabbed in his neck.

But that'd be bad manners.

I won't make the hard-working staff at this golf resort scrub blood from the cream carpet.

The third man?

Redix Dean, Hollywood's Romeo.

Of course he fucking smolders over my right shoulder, sitting beside his sexy date.

My hand shakes to the syrup of his voice. Fighting back every emotion, every pain and memory, I don't think I can do this.

Ten years is a long time to go without seeing the love of your life.

The stunning sight of him walking into the ballroom an hour ago slammed my heart into a brick wall. I didn't think it could break anymore.

I was wrong.

Redix makes calm breath and logic impossible. He destroys me all over again.

But it doesn't hurt me anymore.

That's what I tell myself so I can breathe.

"Don't you dare let him get to you." A silky hand grabs mine trembling under the table. "You hear me, Cade Bryant? Keep your chin up and your cheeks dry. You can cry about him later."

My mom can see past my stone facade. Her command fills my heart, steeling my spine.

"I know, Mama." I force a smile her way. "I won't give him the satisfaction. None of them."

"That's my girl. You can live with a broken heart. But like hell if you won't die with your pride too."

She lifts a crystal glass of sweet tea to her lips. It rattles against her teeth. Mama hides it well, what the second round of chemo's doing to her. But I see it, hiding my concern. Mama refuses pity.

"You should be drinking water," I warn, "not sugar and caffeine."

"Take my sweet tea from my grasp"—she winks—"and I'll give you a fight you won't win."

Damn, I love her.

If people think *I'm* headstrong, Mama wears hard-headed like a well-coifed hairdo hiding hairpins that can take your eyes out. No one fucks with her. Sheriff Gloria Bryant is a force.

And as her daughter, Sergeant Cade Bryant, I'd be wiser stealing a steak from a starving Rottweiler before fighting with Mama.

"I'm fine." She takes another ornery sip. "Quit fussin' over me and focus on this shindig."

"This shindig is bullshit."

No, it's hell.

A hell I won't back down from. No way I'd miss this confrontation with Redix, no matter how he left me in pieces.

"No, it's part of this island's game and you know how to win it." Mama raises her chin, considering the swanky ballroom full of Hilton Head Island's biggest players. "Smile pretty for these bow tie-wearing, golf-club swinging, rich men in God-awful madras pants and you can get away with murder... like *they* try to do."

Redix didn't wear madras tonight.

No, he's proudly freeballing in tuxedo pants, making my mouth water.

I mutter, "Madras pants shrivel my dick."

Mama cackles, patting my hand again. "Not as much as bow ties shrivel mine."

Our inside jokes. Our crass mouths. I can't live without her.

Please God, give me more time with her.

Okay, fine, I've been making lots of deals with heaven, and hell, so why break a bad habit?

But after six years on the police force, I know Mama's right. Madras pants or khakis—not all these men are as innocent as their attire.

I resisted it at first. Fighting like mad, I went in the opposite direction of my mom.

All the boys who bullied me, calling me "giraffe". All the adults who cooed, "You're so pretty you should be a model." Well, far be it from me to ever listen, but I did.

I spent a decade in that hellacious industry. What else can you do when you're thirteen and soaring to five feet ten? Because like hell if I was playing basketball.

But after what happened. To me? To Redix?

I became just like my mom—the law.

Because I want justice.

And apparently, I still want Redix Dean.

Because my pulse is racing. My cheeks are flushed. My thighs are weak. My pussy wants to put on these Christian Louboutin heels herself and walk the runway to him and jump his dumbass, sexy bones.

But my heart won't budge. It's barely holding back the tears stinging to fall.

What's even worse? I can feel Redix feet away, laughing.

Is it at me?

"Are you gonna work the room?" Mama tries scratching, unseen, at the brunette wig itching her scalp. "You got seven pairs of eyes on you; three sets I know you're watching too."

"No." Facing straight ahead, I raise an eyebrow. "I'll make them come to me."

Finally, my target steps into view from behind that damn centerpiece. That smirk on his face? It's for me. His grasp is controlling his wife's body, but his eyes are fucking mine.

That evil man deserves to choke blood on a magnolia flower.

That stain? I'd scrub it myself with my toothbrush from this carpet.

Uncrossing my long legs, I pour one back over the other. The attention it draws. The heat of his stare sliding up my bare calves. It's been a long time since I wore this dress with these heels.

So fuck Redix Dean.

If he thinks he can come back after ten years, strolling barefoot in his tux across this ballroom, smiling while every asshole on Hilton Head Island toasts to his charitable contributions... he can *suck it*.

Laugh all he wants; he's watching me.

This outfit is driving him wild with tender memories. The Hervé Léger vintage purple bandage dress wraps my curves so tight; men can vacation in my cleavage. And these black heels let me tower over most in the room.

Not Redix.

His beauty reigns supreme—I grin—but he dropped to one knee for me in this dress.

We were eighteen then, officially adults, hating the glamorous job, but loving each other always. We were supposed to get married that summer. No one could stop us—young love on a rampage. With the money from our modeling exploits, Redix wanted to buy a house for us somewhere high over an ocean cliff, together as we were destined to be.

Turns out—destiny is a motherfucker.

It ruins everything, including us.

Now marriage isn't on my mind; murder is.

It's either that or release this sob choking my throat. Pain swirling with passion and revenge, I can't stop the memory of that soul-destroying night.

The one when Redix left ten years ago and never spoke to me again.

Why's he back?

Is it to make me pay for the fault that's mine?

That pain threatens to fall over my lashes... but I won't do it. I'll take this damn salad fork on the table and stab my smoky-lined eyes out before I let him see a tear fall for his celebrity ass.

"Well, I'll be,"—Mama elbows me—"here comes one now."

I didn't need the alert. The approach of his body tingles my flesh. His aroma—vanilla and leather—it arrives next.

Goddamnit. I'm still attracted to him.

And it's on a he-better-fuck-me-now-before-I-kill-him level making a black widow blush. But the shell of my skin hides it.

"Mama G"—Redix purrs the childhood name he gave my mom—"I just had to come over and sit down next to the prettiest lady in the room."

"I'm no lady." Mama's not amused. "I'm the law."

That bad-boy grin on his face? Curling his lush lips back to his square jaw?

That's the look that drops panties and shatters hearts, including mine.

His big hand turns a small gold chair around. His strapping thighs straddle it like he's riding a horse across the ballroom, lassoing every pussy in sight. He takes the empty spot on the other side of my mom while my teeth clench, fighting it all back.

"You're looking beautiful as always, Mama G." His sky blue eyes won't meet mine. "I've missed you." The genuine concern in his voice? Fuck him. He has no right after all this time. "How you been feelin'?"

"I feel right as rain anytime a handsome man sits down beside me."

Typical. Mama's playing back. No man gets the upper hand on her, not even one she's known since he was nine years old.

Redix was a beautiful boy back then. By his teens, he left beauty behind for hot-as-fucking-hell.

Secretly, I've watched him on the flatscreen since. Sometimes it hurts too much. Remembering the kiss of his lips, his tongue teasing my mouth, how he used to dance with my heart.

But sitting this close now in the flesh at twenty-eight?

Redix Dean's allure travels across a room like a sexy slug leaving a trail of slick lust behind. A trail that everyone wants to slip in and break their necks, because his sex is worth the fall.

"My mama told me about this last diagnosis." Redix props his chin on his forearms folded in front of him, obvious he actually cares. "But if anyone can kick cancer's ass, it's you."

"I feel like kicking more than cancer's ass," Mama answers. "I feel like kickin' yours. You just up and left. You got a lot of nerve coming back now."

God, if I could reach out and hug my mom. Every furious thought I have... it's firing from her mouth.

"Ah, come on *now*. You can't stay mad at me." No matter how many years he spent in Hollywood, he still deploys his Southern drawl with a sly grin. It disarms nukes. "I'm too cute. Besides, I'm a good boy now, here for a good cause and all."

"You can sponsor all the Teen Crisis centers you want across this state, that don't excuse it." Nope, Mama's locked and loaded. "It's pretty damn rude coming home without a peep prior. Who do you think you are? A boy raised with manners, that's who. But it seems you've sold 'em and your soul to Hollywood."

"No, ma'am." Redix doesn't flinch. He's smiling at her smack down. "I could never forget you, my manners... or my home."

That butter knife on the table? It just stabbed my heart.

Redix didn't forget Mama. Or his home. But he forgot me and the manners it takes to even look at me.

It's willful.

Past ignoring me—it kills me. He's blaming me for what destroyed us.

In perfect, bullshit timing, his date approaches our table. Resting her hand on his shoulder, offering a smile to the table, "Are you going to introduce me?" *she* has the manners he forgot.

He cups his hand gently over hers. Their intimate touch backslaps my jaw. "Angie Conrad, meet Sheriff Gloria Bryant. 'Mama G' as I called her because she kicked my ass to Sunday and back with all my trouble."

"Ms. Conrad"—Mama's smile is sincere—"it's a pleasure."

My ribs heave two inches higher. Redix didn't even introduce me.

"Ms. Conrad, this is my daughter, Sergeant Cade Bryant." Mama flicks her eyes at me with a don't-lose-your-shit look. "She and Redix were quite close growing up. 'Friends' doesn't even describe it."

"Oh?" Angie barely grins my way. "Redix has never mentioned you." Was that innocent or bitchy? "Still, nice to meet you."

"Likewise." I smile, emptying the gun of my glare, firing back at her, and then aiming five shots into Redix who refuses to turn his face my way.

It's embarrassing me, hurting me... and he knows it. My God, he really hates me.

Fine. The feeling *is* mutual.

And *I'm* full of shit.

Tension takes a seat at our table. The urge to run hits me but *hell no*, I won't move.

"I'm off to the Ladies Room." Angie can't handle it.

"And then"—she's cooing into Redix's ear—"I want that sexy dance you promised."

Redix smiles, shamelessly eyeing her ass while she sashays away.

Is it possible to want to cry, kill, and fuck someone all at the same time?

Yes, right here on this table.

I want to rip Redix Dean into sex-stained shreds.

"To what do we owe the honor then?" Mama's raising questions and her iced tea. "What finally brought the King of Coligny Beach home?"

That beach? That night? That pain?

It surges through me, remembering Redix there. Along with the other man stalking me on my left and the third one looming across the ballroom.

These three men haven't stopped haunting my world like a nightmare that won't end until God makes good on her deal.

I see it; how the same memory washes over Redix too, making his asshole act waver.

He rakes his left hand through his long strands before tucking one side behind his ear.

That gesture? It's the last one Redix made before he turned his back on me and walked away.

And I never stopped loving him since.

"I came home for amends." He answers my mom… before slowly… and finally… aiming his penetrating eyes into my soul. "Ain't that right, Candy Cade?"

Murder or mad sex?

I'm gonna commit both.

ALSO BY KELLY FINLEY

Come for Me Trilogy

Protect Her, Prequel Novelette
Pierce Her, Book One
Hunt Her, Book Two
Chase Her, Book Three

All for You Duet

After Him, Book One
With Him, Book Two

And more coming very soon...

Get more from Kelly Finley on Amazon

ACKNOWLEDGMENTS

This story came to me in a flood of a dream—one that woke me up to a heroine that took two years to write and release.

That time—I'm so thankful for it. In it, I have met the most wonderful readers, reviewers, supporters and friends. Truly, I can't believe how my world and heart has grown to love all these people.

Some authors don't read reviews. I do. All of them. I respect the time you took to read my book/s, and the dedication you show to the community when you share your passion and reaction as a reader.

It's heart-warming to read how Charlie is loved by so many. How Daniel makes us crave a new kind of "alpha male." And how more readers want more badass, steamy women on their pages. Hell yes! I'll sure try for you.

Along the way, I can't do this without the support and patience of my family and loved ones. They put up with my closed office door on the daily.

To my beta readers, Sarah, Deborah and Melissa… thank you for chapter-by-chapter notes. I'm such a sucker for them. And gosh, do I need them.

Kat Wyeth and Meredith Sweet at Kat's Literary Services, I don't know how the stars aligned to have such an incredible editor and proofreader team, but I ain't complaining. Thank you for your tireless support.

For Deborah Richmond, who stumbled into my DMs

and life, your keen eye and kind heart is such a gift! Thanks for joining our team.

To Caroline Johnson who keeps creating my beautiful covers. I fall in love with them every time. Here's to many more!

And again to my readers. There is more to come. Charlie has inspired a world of women who destroy stereotypes, warm our hearts (and sheets), fire up some pages and make us proud.

Get ready. It's all for you!

ABOUT THE AUTHOR

Kelly Finley hates writing bios but appreciates that you made it this far. So here you go...

She lives in the Carolinas with her sexy husband and cherished family. A rebel with many causes, she fancies black leather, dirty jokes, big hearts and smart mouths.

Thrilled by a flipped gender script and ticked off by women portrayed as weak, she noticed how many steamy, sexy heroines were missing, particularly from romance pages.

Her friends shared the same frustration and told her to practice what she has taught for over twenty years—women who kick ass.

Dedicated to writing books featuring heroines we champion and love—ones with shameless heat, brave hearts, and whip-smart minds—she's most likely at her keyboard putting the next one on the page for you.

- amazon.com/author/kellyfinley
- patreon.com/kellyfinleyauthor
- goodreads.com/goodreads_kelly_finley
- bookbub.com/authors/kelly-finley
- instagram.com/kellyfinleyauthor
- tiktok.com/@kellyfinleybooks
- facebook.com/KellyFinleyBooks

Printed by Libri Plureos GmbH in Hamburg, Germany